MURDER AT THE
TOWER OF LONDON

By Jim Eldridge

MURDER AT THE TOWER OF LONDON

JIM ELDRIDGE

Allison & Busby Limited
11 Wardour Mews
London W1F 8AN
allisonandbusby.com

First published in Great Britain by Allison & Busby in 2023.
This paperback edition published by Allison & Busby in 2024.

A CIP catalogue record for this book is available from
the British Library.

10 9 8 7 6 5 4 3 2 1

ISBN 978-0-7490-2992-0

Typeset in 11.5/16.5 pt Sabon LT Pro by
Allison & Busby Ltd.

By choosing this product, you help take care of the world's forests.
Learn more: www.fsc.org.

MIX
Paper | Supporting
responsible forestry
FSC® C171272

Printed and bound by
CPI Group (UK) Ltd, Croydon, CR0 4YY

This one, again, is for Lynne,
without whom there'd be nothing.

CHAPTER ONE

London, August 1899

His Royal Highness Prince Albert Edward Saxe-Coburg-Gotha, the Prince of Wales and heir to the throne of Great Britain and Ireland, looked anxiously at Viscount Harold Dillon, the curator of the armouries at the Tower of London as he unburdened himself of his dreadful news.

'Murder?' the Prince repeated, shocked. 'At the Tower?'

'The body was found in the Line of Kings,' confirmed Dillon. 'Though we're not sure if he was actually killed there.'

The Line of Kings, thought the Prince. The impressive display of life-sized carved wooden horses in the White Tower, installed in the Seventeenth century, during the reign of Charles II, with the armour of each king atop a carved horse. The monarchs depicted were: William the Conqueror, Edward I, Edward III, Henry IV, Henry V, Henry VI, Edward IV, Edward V, Henry VII, Henry VIII, Edward VI, James I, Charles I, Charles II, William III, George I and George II. *And me alongside them,* thought the Prince, *but first I have to become king*, which was not looking as certain as it had a few years ago. The Prince was approaching sixty, and his mother, the Queen, seemed as mentally alert as ever at the age of eighty. Yes, she was slower and creaked more, but those who thought she would not last long after her beloved Prince Albert died had been proved wrong. Albert had died almost forty years before, but Victoria seemed determined to live and rule for ever.

'The victim?' the Prince enquired.

'The dead man was one of the Yeoman Warders of the Tower. His name was Eric James. He was found inside the suit of armour belonging to Henry VIII. He had been run through with a sword.'

'Ghastly!' groaned the Prince. 'The police have been informed?'

Dillon nodded. 'I initially received the report of this tragedy from the resident constable of the Tower, General Sir Frederick Stephenson, and the major of the Tower, Sir George Bryan Milman. They decided that it would be better for the investigation to come under my direction as curator of the armouries. Accordingly, I arranged for Scotland Yard to attend, but I've told them that nothing is to be released to the general public, and especially the press. My concern is that a situation such as this – a royal employee murdered on royal premises – might have sinister connotations. As you know, Your Highness, there have been some . . . activities of late by those people who oppose the very idea of monarchy.'

'Irish Republicans.' The Prince nodded unhappily.

'Not just Irish, I'm afraid. There are radical home-grown

elements harbouring the same disgraceful sentiments. My concern is that publicity about this tragic event might encourage those who seek to damage the person and the reputation of the monarchy.'

Prince Albert Edward fell silent for a thoughtful moment, then he turned to look at his private secretary, Michael Shanks, who stood in dutiful attendance, waiting for a command from his master.

'What do you think, Shanks?' he asked.

'Regretfully, I have to agree with the viscount, sir,' he said. 'We live in turbulent and unsettled times. We must be constantly vigilant to ensure that what happened in France does not happen here.'

The Prince nodded. 'Unhappy times indeed. But surely instructing the police not to make the public aware of this hampers their investigations.'

'That is, unfortunately, a possibility,' agreed Dillon. 'I would therefore suggest we look at an alternative.'

'Private investigators?' queried the Prince doubtfully. 'By definition they are limited. They do not have the resources of the police.'

'True, but there are some who have had great successes in such cases, especially where museums seem to be involved. And the Tower of London is the oldest museum in England.'

Prince Albert Edward looked at Dillon with concern.

'If you're suggesting the people I think you are, I must inform you that I have had difficult relations with the gentleman in question, not just in the past but as recently as this year.'

'But they did prove extremely successful when answering Her Majesty's request to undertake an enquiry. It was not only successful but it was conducted as Her Majesty had insisted, with the greatest discretion. No mention of it ever appeared in the press.'

The Prince looked unhappy at the prospect, but he deliberated on it, and eventually gave a reluctant affirmative nod.

'Very well,' he said. He turned to his private secretary. 'Shanks,' he said, 'send a letter.'

CHAPTER TWO

Daniel Wilson looked full of trepidation as he and his wife, Abigail – known to the public at large as 'the Museum Detectives' – approached Marlborough House, the London residence of the Prince of Wales and his wife, Princess Alexandra of Denmark.

'The last time I was here, the Prince had me thrown out.'

'But not literally,' Abigail pointed out.

'He would have if I'd refused to leave,' said Daniel. 'I could tell by the look on his face. His man, Shanks, would have summoned a few more servants and I'd have been sitting on the pavement with my dignity in tatters. Yet today, here we are calling at the Prince's invitation. I don't understand it. What's going on?'

'The last time you came here it was to question him on his relationship with one of his mistresses,' Abigail pointed out. 'That is not the case this time.'

'I'm still doubtful, about us being here,' said Daniel. 'He doesn't like me.'

'But he invited *both* of us,' pointed out Abigail. And she took the brass bellpull beside the black oak door in her hand and gave it a tug.

At Scotland Yard, Chief Superintendent Armstrong slammed a big beefy fist down hard on the top of his desk.

'The commissioner himself has ordered a blanket of silence over this matter!' he snarled, enraged.

Inspector John Feather looked on in what he hoped appeared like sympathy. The fact was that over the years he'd seen the chief superintendent in similar rages when he'd been barred from what he saw as his right to publicity – in this case, the murder of a Yeoman Warder at the Tower of London.

'A murder in *royal* premises!' Armstrong raged. 'The Tower of London, no less! There could be honours arising out of this case.'

'We haven't been barred from investigating the murder,' Feather pointed out.

'As good as!' snorted Armstrong indignantly. 'No involving the press. No talking to anyone. How are we supposed to catch the killer with our hands tied?' He looked sharply at Feather. 'This Dillon character. What's he like?'

'Viscount Harold Dillon, sir. The curator of the Tower of London. Quite a reserved sort of man. Very cautious in his manner and his speech. At least, that's the impression I got when I met him.'

'Has he got the ear of the royal family?'

'Definitely, sir. The curator of the Tower is a royal appointee.'

Armstrong scowled. 'We've got to get him to change his

mind. We can't solve this without talking to people. We need information.'

'Yes, sir,' agreed Feather, thinking to himself even as he said it: *no chance.*

'You've got to find a way round this, Inspector,' said Armstrong firmly. 'We need to unmask this murderer. As I say, there could be honours at stake here.'

And I have a good idea who'll be getting them if we do, thought Feather, *and it won't be me.*

'You're investigating the murder of that Salvation Army officer in Whitechapel, aren't you?' asked Armstrong thoughtfully.

'Yes, sir,' said Feather. 'Captain Merchant. He was found beaten to death not far from a pub, the Blind Beggar. By all accounts, the local publicans have no love for the Salvation Army; they accuse them of costing them money with their drive to stop people drinking.'

'So, the publicans are the chief suspects?'

'I wouldn't say *chief* suspects, sir. There are rumours concerning the immigrant communities in the area, notably the Ashkenazi Jews and the Irish.'

'No matter,' said Armstrong dismissively. 'The point is that Whitechapel is right next door to the Tower of London, so you'll be over there, on site, so to speak. You can pop in and out without upsetting the curator, this bloke Dillon. Tell him you're investigating the Salvation Army killing, and you've come to update him about the murdered Yeoman. See what he's got.'

'But if I say I'm there to update him, he'll expect some progress,' pointed out Feather doubtfully.

13

'Make something up,' said Armstrong. 'The important thing is to be seen to be doing something, so that when a lead pops up at the Tower, it'll be recalled that we – the Metropolitan Police – were the ones who were there. It was us who cracked the case.'

'Yes, sir,' said Feather.

'Good,' said Armstrong. 'We have a plan.'

Daniel and Abigail perched on the sofa in the Prince of Wales's library and listened attentively as he told them the reason for his summons. A Yeoman Warder had been murdered at the Tower of London and his body stuffed into the suit of armour that had once adorned the body of King Henry VIII, and was now on display in the White Tower as part of the famed Line of Kings.

'Viscount Harold Dillon, the curator of the armouries at the Tower, feels it could be an act of violent sedition aimed at the royal family,' said the Prince. 'The concern is that it may be the tip of the iceberg, and there could be even more dangerous acts to follow. Assaults on members of the royal family themselves.'

Including you, thought Daniel.

'I would like to commission you to conduct an investigation into this tragic affair and get to the bottom of it. Find out who is behind it. *But . . .*' And as he stressed the word, he fixed them both with a determined look. 'This must be done with no publicity of any sort. Such publicity could possibly inflame the situation, if it is republican anti-monarchists at work here, and encourage others to follow suit. It is important no word of this outrage leaks out. Not just to the press, but it must be kept from the public at all costs, by whatever means.'

'We understand, Your Highness,' said Abigail. 'We assume

the police have been informed. It is a legal requirement . . .'

'Yes, yes,' said the Prince impatiently. 'They have. Viscount Dillon has been in touch with Scotland Yard. In fact, it was he who suggested we commission you to carry out his investigation, in parallel with the police. But, and I stress again, with no information going out to the press or the general public. That is paramount.' He looked towards his secretary, Shanks, who sat at a nearby desk. 'My secretary has prepared a letter to Harold Dillon authorising your investigation. He'll give you that and you can make yourselves known to Dillon at the Tower. He'll give you everything you need to know. And you'll report to him.'

Shanks stood up and said, 'If you'll follow me to my office, Mr and Mrs Wilson, I'll give you the letter, and at the same time fill you in on the background of the organisation of the Tower, which I feel may be of help.'

As Daniel and Abigail followed the Prince's secretary along the corridor to his office, Daniel mouthed quizzically at Abigail, 'The organisation of the Tower?'

Abigail nodded and put a discreet finger to her lips, followed by a wink to let him know that she would explain to him later if there was anything he didn't understand.

Shanks's office was small and spartan: a desk, his own chair behind it and two other chairs facing the desk. There were no paintings on the walls, no photographs on the desk, the shelves were filled with imposing reference books and registers of Europe's aristocratic families.

Shanks gestured to the two empty chairs and they sat. He passed them the letter he had prepared authorising them to investigate the murder. 'I have already sent a copy to Viscount Dillon by messenger,' he told them. 'Have either of you been to the Tower?'

'Some years ago when I was a detective at Scotland Yard,' said Daniel.

'And I visited as part of my studies when I was at Cambridge,' said Abigail.

Shanks nodded. 'As I'm sure you know, the Tower is a royal palace. The building of the White Tower began shortly after the Norman invasion of 1066. I understand that you are known as the Museum Detectives. Effectively, the Tower is a museum, the oldest in Britain, but it is also a royal palace, and as such it comes under the authority of the Crown.

'The most senior person in charge of the Tower is the constable. The constable is always chosen from the most senior ranks of those members of the military who have retired from active service. You may recall that earlier this century, the famed Duke of Wellington was appointed constable of the Tower. The current constable is General Sir Frederick Stephenson, a former commander-in-chief of the British Army of occupation in Cairo. The second most senior officer at the Tower is Sir George Bryan Milman, the current major of the Tower of London, also known as the resident governor.

'However, Viscount Dillon is the person you will be dealing with. He is the curator of the armouries at the Tower, and as it was at the Line of Kings, which comes under the remit of the armouries, where this heinous crime was discovered, it was felt he will be able to give you the best information.' He looked at them firmly as he added sternly, 'There is no need for you to approach Sir Frederick or Sir George directly. Anything you wish them to be informed of will be passed to them by Viscount Dillon. Is that clear?'

'Very clear,' said Abigail.

He stood up to indicate that their interview was over.

'The important thing with this case is discretion,' he said. 'His Highness has made it clear that there must be no publicity of any sort about this situation. Certainly not any deliberate leakage to the press or any members of the public. Neither should there be any accidental leakages.'

'We understand,' said Abigail. 'You can rest assured we will keep everything secret.'

CHAPTER THREE

They waited until they were at home before discussing their meeting with the Prince and his secretary.

'Thank heavens we won't have to deal with those two knights of the realm who are in charge of the Tower,' said Daniel. 'I've met some of those retired military types and all they ever do is want to talk about the battles they were in and how many of the enemy they slaughtered. At least we won't have to endure that with this Viscount Dillon.'

'You don't know that,' said Abigail. 'For all you know he could well be an ex-soldier, especially as he's in charge of the armouries at the Tower.'

'Let's find out,' said Daniel. He went to the bookcase and took out a thick copy of *Who's Who*.

'He may not be in that,' said Abigail.

'Someone with that kind of job has got to be,' said Daniel, flicking through the pages. 'In fact, here he is. Harold Arthur Lee-Dillon, 17th Viscount Dillon. Born in Westminster, January

1844. Educated at private school and the University of Bonn in Germany.' He scanned the rest of the entry before saying, 'It looks like he did have a military career, although nothing as grand as the two top men at the Tower. He was in the Rifle Brigade and rose to lieutenant, but resigned his commission in 1874. He then joined the Oxfordshire Militia as a captain, promoted to major in 1885. Retired in 1891. Succeeded his father as 17th Viscount Dillon in 1892, the same year in which he was appointed curator of the Royal Armouries.' He replaced the book on the shelf. 'The Prince of Wales, a couple of knights and a viscount. It seems that once again we are moving in exalted company.'

'Not bad for a workhouse boy.' Abigail smiled. 'You have definitely risen in the world.'

Viscount Dillon was in his office when Daniel and Abigail arrived at the Tower. He took from Abigail the letter that the Prince of Wales had given them and studied it at some length, even though both Daniel and Abigail knew that Dillon was perfectly aware of the contents of the letter even before they had given it to him.

The viscount was a man in his mid-fifties, balding, thin-faced, with a look of permanent suspicion, not just with Daniel and Abigail but everything he encountered. Daniel and Abigail struggled to reconcile the wary-looking man in front of them with the fact that it was he, according to Prince Albert Edward, who'd recommended that the Prince commission them to investigate the murder. Dillon stroked his small Van Dyke beard thoughtfully as he handed the letter back to Abigail.

'As the Prince asks, I will do everything I can to help solve this dreadful crime, providing the Tower is not exposed to publicity of any kind.'

'Absolutely.' Daniel nodded. 'We'd be grateful if you could tell us everything you know about the Yeoman Warder who was killed, and any information you may have that might point towards a motive in this case.'

'Certainly,' said Dillon. 'But before I do, I'd like to bring Algernon Dewberry in on this. He's my deputy curator here at the Tower. If you'll excuse me for a moment, I'll go and fetch him.'

Viscount Dillon left the office and returned a few moments later with a tall, thin man in his early forties. Algernon Dewberry was as serious-looking as the viscount, sallow-faced, clean-shaven and with his hair kept short. He shook hands with Daniel and Abigail as they were introduced, and then seated himself beside Dillon's desk. The viscount slid the letter from the Prince of Wales to him. Dewberry read it, then handed it back.

'A tragic situation,' he said.

'Indeed,' said Daniel. 'What can you tell us about the victim?'

'The dead man was Eric James,' said Dillon.

'Had he been with you long?'

Dillon looked at Dewberry, who replied, 'Six years.'

'Can you think of any reason why anyone should want to kill him?'

'Absolutely not,' said Dewberry. 'All of our warders have to be of good character. They must have served in the British Army as warrant officers, with at least twenty-two years of service. They must also hold the Long Service and Good Conduct medal.'

'That's why I cannot believe his murder was a personal matter,' said Dillon. 'It can only have been because he interrupted some criminals engaged in nefarious activity, perhaps some sort of theft, or it was carried out by persons as a form of showing their contempt for all things royal.'

'Anti-monarchists?' said Abigail.

'Sadly, there have been instances recently of such anti-royal actions. You'll remember the assassination attempts on the Queen?'

Daniel and Abigail nodded. 'Eight attempts, as I recall,' said Daniel.

'And then there was the attempt on the life of the Queen's second son, Prince Alfred, while he was in Australia.'

Daniel and Abigail both frowned, as they did their best to recall this.

'It was in 1868,' said Dillon. 'He was shot in the back by an Irish republican while he was in Sydney.'

'That was before our time,' said Daniel. 'We were both just infants then.'

'Was he seriously injured?' asked Abigail. 'As Daniel says, it was before our time.'

'The bullet struck him but glanced off his ribs instead of entering his body. Fortunately, it wasn't a serious wound and he was nursed back to health. It doesn't help that certain politicians make speeches calling for the abolition of the monarchy and making Britain a republic.'

Charles Dilke, thought Daniel. The radical Liberal member of parliament who made speeches calling for the abolition of the monarchy. Although a series of scandals in which he'd been named in two divorce cases had lessened his influence on the general public.

Sensing that Dillon was about to enlarge on his theme with more examples of anti-monarchist sentiments, Daniel determined to get the conversation back to the actual murder they were being asked to investigate.

'What time was Mr James's body discovered?' he asked.

'7.30 a.m. yesterday morning. Another of the warders was starting his rounds and went to the Line of Kings, and noticed that the armour on the effigy of Henry VIII looked as if it had been disturbed. He went to put it back as it should have been, and he became aware there was something inside it. That was how he discovered poor Mr James's body.'

'Who was this warder?'

'Hector Purbright. He was a particular friend of Eric James. He was absolutely devastated by the discovery, but he acted with alacrity and efficiency, as befits a former soldier. He summoned his immediate superior, the divisional sergeant major, who then took over. The sergeant major reported it to me. After discussion with the constable and major of the Tower, it was I who ordered the police to be informed. To avoid tittle-tattle spreading, which might have occurred if we'd summoned a beat constable, I sent one of our warders to Scotland Yard to advise the detective division. He returned with an Inspector Feather and two uniformed officers.'

'Inspector Feather's a good man,' commented Daniel.

'Yes, that was my impression as well,' said Dillon.

'When was the last time anyone saw Mr James alive?'

Dillon looked at Dewberry, who said, 'We're still checking on that. Mr Purbright said he spoke to Mr James at about half past nine the previous evening. They were both on their rounds. The warders patrol the grounds while visitors are here to make sure that nothing untoward might be occurring.'

'So Mr James was killed at some time between a half past nine that evening and seven o'clock the following morning,' said Daniel.

Dillon shook his head.

'No,' he said. 'The murder must have been committed between half past nine and ten o'clock that night. The main gates are locked every night at ten o'clock without fail. Do you know the ceremony of the keys?'

Daniel shook his head, but Abigail declaimed in dramatic tones, 'Whose keys are these? Queen Victoria's keys. Pass then, all is well.'

Dillon nodded. 'Yes,' he said. 'You have witnessed the ceremony?'

'No, but it came up when I was studying history at Girton College.'

'Ah.' Dillon nodded. 'So you are one of the privileged few.'

'We had a lecture by one archaeologist who was involved in a dig here at the Tower. They were excavating for Roman remains.'

'Then you'll know that once the gates are locked, no one can leave or enter the Tower, except with authorisation, which is recorded in a book. So the only people who would have been inside the Tower would be the resident staff, and I cannot believe that any of them would have committed this outrage. It must have been an outsider who left before the gates were locked for the night.'

'How many Yeoman Warders are on duty at the Tower?' asked Daniel.

'At the present moment, thirty-six,' said Dewberry.

'And they all live at the Tower?'

'They do. Some are bachelors; some are married with families.'

'Who else lives here?'

'The constable of the Tower, Sir Frederick Stephenson and his family; the major of the Tower, Sir George Bryan Milman and his family, and myself and my family. It helps to have the deputy curator permanently on site,' added Dewberry, 'in case there is an emergency that needs immediate investigation. As the case with the Line of Kings.'

'Have there been any such emergencies that have called for your attention, Mr Dewberry?' asked Abigail.

'Thankfully no,' said Dewberry. 'This is the first time it has happened in all the time I've been here.'

'Would it be possible for us to look at the place where the body was discovered?' asked Daniel. 'The Line of Kings?'

'Certainly,' said Dewberry. 'I'll take you there myself.'

Daniel and Abigail followed Dewberry out of Dillon's office in the New Armouries block and they walked the short distance across a courtyard to the White Tower. Two Beefeaters were on duty at the entrance to the Tower. They stepped aside as they recognised the deputy curator, allowing the three to enter the White Tower. They climbed the wooden staircase to the top floor, where the Line of Kings was on display. Daniel and Abigail exchanged glances, and both knew what the other was thinking: this was a very impressive display. A line of exquisitely carved wooden horses. Astride each was a life-sized suit of armour, each representing a royal ruler.

'This is one of the oldest exhibits at the museum,' said Dewberry. 'It was created in the seventeenth century by Charles II to promote the restored monarchy.'

Daniel walked along the line, reading the name of the monarchs. 'No queens,' he observed. 'No Queen Elizabeth, no Queen Victoria.'

'Queen Victoria has never worn armour,' said Dewberry.

'But Queen Elizabeth did,' said Daniel.

Dewberry gave an apologetic smile. 'I believe that King Charles II only wanted kings featured.'

'A pity, as Elizabeth was one of our strongest and most intelligent monarchs,' commented Abigail.

Dewberry led them to the armour of Henry VIII.

'Either this isn't his real armour, or it's been made deliberately flattering,' said Daniel. 'In portraits I've seen of him, he's a very large man.'

'It was decided to depict him in his youth. This is the suit of armour he wore as a young man.'

Daniel studied it. The suit of armour was very ornate, but so was the armour that the horse wore. The horse's chest was protected by what looked like a circular metal skirt with a large boss on each side. The horse's flank was protected by a wraparound sheet of metal, and on the wooden animal's head was a metal helmet from its ears – which had their own cone-shaped metal protectors – down to the creature's mouth.

'The protection on the horse's front, around its chest, is called the peytral,' said Dewberry, noting where Daniel was looking. 'The metal protecting its rear is known as the crupper. The whole thing is called the bard.'

'It's not until you get up close you realise that every inch of the armour, the rider's and the horse's, are decorated with very fine engraving,' said Daniel.

'The decoration is the work of Paul van Vrelant of Brussels, who was Henry's harness gilder,' said Dewberry.

Abigail joined them in examining the intricate engravings on the metal.

'The work is incredible,' she said. 'Beautiful. Delicate and so clear.'

'The figures depicted are St George and St Barbara, the patron saints of Henry and his then wife, Katharine of Aragon,' said Dewberry, pointing them out.

'Is it heavy?' asked Daniel.

'Not as heavy as you might think. It's made of steel, offering enough protection without weighing the wearer down.'

'It would have taken some difficulty to put a dead body inside that particular suit of armour. How tall was Eric James, and what sort of build did he have?'

'He was quite a short man, and of narrow build, so I think he would have fitted inside the suit of armour without too much difficulty. The police have removed his body to Scotland Yard, so you'll be able to examine it there.'

'Is this area patrolled at night?' asked Daniel.

'There's no real need,' said Dewberry. 'Once the gates have been closed for the night, only the residents are on site. He looked at his watch. 'Is there anything else you need to know at this moment? I know you'll want to talk to Yeoman Purbright, who found the body, and others who might have been witnesses.'

'Indeed.' Daniel nodded. 'But we think that's enough for the moment. Thank you for your assistance.'

CHAPTER FOUR

As they walked away from the Tower, Daniel asked, 'What's your opinion of that morose-looking pair, Dillon and Dewberry?'

'As you say, morose. But then, having a dead Beefeater suddenly appear in the White Tower is hardly going to cheer them up. What do you think about what Dillon said – it must have been an outsider?'

'In my opinion he's bound to say that,' said Daniel. 'His duty is to protect the reputation of the Tower, and that includes everyone who works in it. Personally, I've got an open mind. We need to talk to John Feather.'

They decided to take the Underground because there was a direct line from the Tower to the Embankment, which made their journey faster than if they travelled by bus, and also because ever since she'd been introduced to London's underground railway system, it was Abigail's preferred choice of getting around the city.

They walked into the large reception area at Scotland Yard, both of them keeping a wary eye open for their particular nemesis, Chief Superintendent Armstrong, and made for the reception desk, which today was manned by an old friend of theirs, Sergeant Callum McDougall.

'Mr Wilson, Mrs Wilson.' McDougall beamed. 'Good to see you again. I trust you are keeping well.'

'We are indeed, thank you, Sergeant. We're here to see if Inspector Feather is available.'

'He's supposed to be. I can send a message up to his office.'

'That would be much appreciated. Before you do, is Chief Superintendent Armstrong also in?'

'He is indeed.'

'In that case, would you send this up to Inspector Feather?' Daniel took a sheet of paper and wrote on it:

John, we are in reception and going to Freddy's. We'd be grateful if you would join us there for coffee.
Daniel & Abigail.

McDougal took it and grinned as he read it.

'You're not banned again, surely,' he asked.

'Not as far as we know, but there's no sense in tempting providence,' said Daniel.

McDougall summoned a messenger and gave him the note, folded over, with instructions to take it to Inspector Feather's office. Abigail pointed to a device on the reception desk, a bulky object with a wire coming from it, and a separate piece of equipment resting in a cradle on the top, also with a length of wire trailing from it.

'I see Scotland Yard are getting modernised,' she said. 'A telephone. We came across them when we were in Manchester.'

'The plan is to have one in every office in the building,' said McDougall. 'But at the moment this is the only one here, and it's for emergency use only.' He looked at it suspiciously. 'To be honest, I'm still not sure how useful it will be.'

'The ones we saw in Manchester were very useful,' said Abigail. 'You can talk to people almost anywhere in the country.'

'Yes, but they can also talk to you,' said McDougal doubtfully. 'And maybe they're people you don't want to talk to.'

Daniel and Abigail made their way to Freddy's, the coffee bar close to Scotland Yard that served as an unofficial meeting place for police personnel. They ordered three coffees, which were being delivered to their table as the slim figure of John Feather entered the café and joined them.

'I assume some sort of intrigue is afoot if we're meeting here,' said Feather, taking his seat.

'Yes and no,' said Abigail. 'We don't consider it intrigue, but the chief superintendent might if he knew about our latest commission.'

Feather gave them a broad grin. 'Let me guess. The Tower of London.'

'You've heard?' asked Abigail, surprised.

'No, but it was a logical step in view of how you handled the last case involving the royal family. Who contacted you?'

'The Prince of Wales,' said Daniel.

'So, orders from the very top,' said Feather, impressed, as he sipped at his coffee.

'We weren't sure how Chief Superintendent Armstrong would react once he found out,' continued Abigail.

'We thought he might ban us from the Yard again,' added Daniel. 'He tends to do that when he gets upset with us. He's convinced we're trying to undermine him, but we're not.'

Feather lapsed into thoughtful mode for a few moments, then said, 'There may be a way round this, and actually persuade Armstrong to let us work together. Albeit unofficially, but with his personal approval.'

'How?' asked Daniel.

'The royal family have insisted there must be no publicity of any sort. No press, nothing to the general public.'

Abigail nodded. 'That's what we were told very firmly by the Prince himself, and by Viscount Dillon.'

'Which has infuriated the superintendent because it effectively ties our hands. We can't even talk about it to some of our uniformed officers in case word leaks out. However, if I tell Armstrong that you've been commissioned by the Prince himself, and suggest that I keep in close contact with you, finding out what you're up to in the case and following up any likely leads, we stand a good chance of getting to the bottom of things. And, as there's been a bar on word about this getting to the press, any arrest would be made by Scotland Yard, so we – or rather, he – gets the credit.'

Daniel and Abigail exchanged looks, and smiled at one another.

'Do you think he'd agree?' asked Abigail.

'I think he'd leap at the opportunity,' said Feather. 'After all, we're getting nowhere with it, and unlikely to with the restrictions placed upon us.' He smiled. 'This way, if anything did leak out, he could blame you two.'

'Not something that would please our patron,' said Daniel unhappily.

'I'm confident you two could assure him it wasn't your fault,' said Feather. 'The thing is it would mean we could work together, swap information. After all, there's no credit to be gained from this if there's not going to be any publicity. But Armstrong would claim the credit with the commissioner, and at the moment he needs every bit of credit he can get.'

Abigail nodded. 'That's agreed, then. You sell him that idea, and you and us keep each other abreast of what's going on.'

'Agreed,' said Feather.

'So, let's start by you telling us what you've got,' said Daniel.

'The biggest thing I've got is that James's twin brother, Paul, was murdered two days before Eric was murdered. Paul James was stabbed to death.'

Daniel and Abigail stared at Feather, shocked at this news.

'So the murders are connected!' said Daniel.

'That's my feeling,' said Feather. 'The problem is that the Prince, and also Viscount Dillon, aren't being very co-operative about Scotland Yard investigating the murder of Paul James. They're terrified that news will leak out about the murder and get into the papers. They're insisting that the two murders could be coincidence.'

'So the authorities at the Tower are in denial,' said Abigail.

'Which ties our hands for investigating both murders as being connected,' said Feather. 'It was the people who found Paul James's body who told us that his twin brother, Eric, was a Yeoman Warder at the Tower. So we got hold of Eric James to identify his brother's body. But Eric didn't give any indication that he might know why Paul was killed. He admitted to us that he hadn't had much to do with his brother, that Paul was a ne'er-do-well, a drunkard who went about with bad companions. Eric was a very respectable Yeoman, a teetotaller.'

'Yes, Dillon told us he was eminently respectable, a holder of the Good Conduct and Long Service medal as all Yeomen have to be,' said Abigail.

'Eric was obviously upset at what had happened to his brother, but he said considering the people he mixed with, his death in that violent way hadn't come as a surprise,' added Feather. 'One thing we didn't reveal to Eric, because we thought it would only upset him further, was that Paul's tongue had been cut out.'

'The underworld warning to others to keep their mouths shut,' said Daniel.

'Exactly.' Feather nodded. 'Which suggests he was involved in something criminal and someone had got word he was about to grass on them, or they suspected he might. Which is why I'm saying it may not be connected to the killing of Eric James. Having met Eric and learnt about his good character, I don't believe he would have been a party to any criminal activity involving his brother.'

'It still sounds like there might be something there,' said Daniel.

'If we're exchanging information, what have you got so far about Eric James's death?' asked Feather.

'Only what we learnt from Harold Dillon. Eric James was a Yeoman Warder of impeccable character. His dead body was found inside the armour of Henry VIII in the Line of Kings in the White Tower. He'd been run through with a sword. Dillon is convinced he must have been killed by an outsider and that the murder happened before ten o'clock at night, when the gates to the Tower are locked, but we have our doubts about that.'

'The doctor reckons he was killed some time between nine o'clock and eleven o'clock, give or take an hour either side,' Feather told them.

'He was last seen alive at half past nine, so that reduces the time-frame,' said Daniel. 'It still means it could be an outsider, or one of the residents. Who have you spoken to so far at the Tower?'

'Hardly anyone,' said Feather with a sigh. 'Viscount Dillon is being very protective. The only person I was allowed to question was the man who found the body, Yeoman Warder Hector Purbright, but I was only allowed to do that in the presence of Viscount Dillon, which meant that Purbright kept looking at his boss the whole time and only gave very short and not very helpful answers. My advice is for you to talk to Purbright alone. I was told he was Eric James's closest friend amongst the people at the Tower. You've got the backing of the Prince so you should be able to talk to him on his own, away from Dillon. Purbright's also the Ravenmaster at the Tower.'

'Ah, the ravens,' said Abigail with a smile. '"If the Tower of London ravens are lost or fly away, the Crown will fall and Britain with it".'

'How do you know so much about the Tower?' asked Daniel.

'The history of Britain formed part of the Classical Tripos at Cambridge. Only a small part, admittedly, but those of us who found it fascinating did our own research. The Tower is, after all, almost a thousand years old, that's a large span of this country's history.'

'You said you were investigating two murders in the area,' said Daniel. 'Whose is the other one?'

'Edward Merchant, a captain in the Salvation Army,' Feather told them. 'He was found beaten to death not far from the Blind Beggar pub on Whitechapel Road. With the Salvation Army's emphasis on abstinence from alcohol, there have been attacks on Salvation Army officers by thugs hired by pub owners, upset at their loss of revenue in places where the army's anti-booze campaign has had an effect. This could well be another such attack but one that got out of hand.' He paused, then added, 'It was outside the Blind Beggar pub that William Booth gave his first sermon against the evils of the demon drink. I wondered if it was a coincidence that this Salvation Army captain was killed at the same place where General Booth made his speech that launched the Salvation Army. Sending a message, so to speak.'

'It's feasible,' agreed Daniel. 'Any suspects?'

Feather shook his head. 'You know what Whitechapel's like, Daniel, from the time you were there on the Ripper case. No one sees or hears anything. It's just going to be a matter of painstaking questioning until we catch someone out.'

CHAPTER FIVE

As Feather walked through the main doors of Scotland Yard after leaving Freddy's, he saw Chief Superintendent Armstrong standing at the reception desk talking to Sergeant McDougall. The superintendent had obviously been asking after Feather, because Feather saw McDougall point towards him. Armstrong turned, saw him, and came striding towards him.

'Where have you been?' demanded Armstrong.

'I've been doing as you ordered,' said Feather. 'Getting inside information on the dead Beefeater at the Tower.'

'Who from?'

'The Wilsons.'

Armstrong looked at Feather, suspicion on his face. 'How come they're involved?'

'The Prince of Wales has hired them to look into the case.'

'Damn! It would be them!' Armstrong scowled, and Feather fully expected him to punch a wall or a desk. Fortunately, they were at a distance from either.

'But this could be to our advantage,' said Feather quickly.

'How?' demanded Armstrong.

'It might be better if we talked about it in your office,' said Feather. 'Away from prying ears.'

'Yes, good point,' said Armstrong.

Feather followed the chief superintendent up the wide marble staircase to the first floor, and then into Armstrong's office, where Feather told him of his conversation with Daniel and Abigail.

'In short, we work unofficially together, but at the end when we've unmasked the killer, the police get the credit because the Wilsons have promised the Prince of Wales there'll be no publicity,' Feather finished.

'So what's in it for the Wilsons?' asked Armstrong suspiciously.

'They get paid. Plus, the top nobs in society will get told about it by the Prince during social chit-chat because he won't be able to resist telling his cronies how clever he was in hiring the Wilsons to solve the crime.'

Armstrong thought it over, then asked, 'You sure they'll tell you whatever they discover?'

'They have on previous occasions,' said Feather. 'I've always found them to be honest. And, as I said, they won't be able to claim any credit for it because of their promise to the Prince.'

Armstrong nodded. 'Right. Do it. But watch your step. We don't want to upset the royal family, so no publicity leaks from us.'

'There won't be,' Feather assured him.

* * *

Daniel and Abigail returned to the Tower to seek out Yeoman Purbright, but this time Daniel stopped on Tower Green and began to look around him.

'What's the matter?' asked Abigail. 'Have you had a sudden thought about the case?'

'No,' said Daniel. 'I must admit that when we came here before to talk to Viscount Dillon, my mind was on what we would find. I was thinking about Eric James being killed and stuffed inside that suit of armour. But now, I'm noticing the Tower of London properly and taking it all in.' He gestured at the old wooden Tudor buildings on the green. 'Look at them. How long have they been here?'

'Since Tudor times at least,' said Abigail. 'Possibly before that.'

'Five hundred years,' said Daniel.

He looked at the high defensive walls that surrounded the vast area of the Tower. 'Look at the stonework. Can you imagine how long it took to do all this?'

'It was developed and expanded over hundreds of years,' said Abigail. She gestured at the huge bulk of the White Tower that dominated the centre of the whole place. 'The White Tower was started in the 1070s, soon after William had conquered England, and it was completed in 1100. So, almost forty years.

'The rest of the place was developed a few hundred years later, after Richard the Lionheart came to the throne. He wanted the whole place strengthened. However, as he headed off to the Crusades almost as soon as he became king, he left the work in making the Tower into a proper fortress in the hands of his chancellor, William de Longchamp, the Bishop of Ely. It was the Bishop who doubled the size of the Tower. Later, Henry III went even further. Those very tall defensive curtain walls you admire were his creation.'

'Making it an impregnable fortress,' said Daniel.

'Almost,' said Abigail. 'In the case of Richard, no sooner were the walls in place than his brother, John, mounted an attack on the Tower, aiming to take control. Longchamp held out as long as he could, but John laid siege and, in the end, when Longchamp's supplies ran out, he was forced to surrender.'

'And John became king.' Daniel nodded.

'Yes, but not then. When Richard returned from the Crusades, he took control of the Tower, and the country, back from John. John begged his brother's forgiveness, which Richard granted. He also named John as his successor. And that's when we have the reign of Bad King John.'

'Amazing,' said Daniel. He headed for the White Tower. 'I'm so glad you're here to tell me about all this. Not having had a proper education, it's a place that's just been here, but I don't know the details, just the most well-known bits. The Crown Jewels. The Traitor's Gate.'

'Oh, there's a lot more to this place than those,' said Abigail. 'If we're here long enough, I'll take you on a tour.'

They found Yeoman Purbright patrolling inside the White Tower on the same floor as the Line of Kings. The crowds of visitors had been allowed back in and Purbright was keeping a close watch on them. Daniel produced the letter of authority from the Prince of Wales and handed it to

Purbright, who read it then handed it back.

'As you can see, we're here at royal command,' said Daniel. 'We just need to ask you a few questions, if that's all right.'

'What about?' asked Purbright.

It suddenly struck Daniel that, instead of reassuring him, the Prince's letter seemed to make Purbright more nervous.

He's suddenly being asked to take on a responsibility that he doesn't want, realised Daniel.

'I suggest we talk outside,' said Daniel. 'It'll be more private.'

Purbright nodded and followed Daniel and Abigail outside to Tower Green.

'We understand from Inspector Feather at Scotland Yard that Eric's twin brother, Paul, was killed just two days before Eric himself was murdered, and Eric was the one who identified his brother's body,' said Daniel.

'Yes,' said Purbright.

'We're curious that you didn't mention this to Inspector Feather when he talked to you after Eric's death.'

'He already knew about it,' said Purbright. 'Eric told me that an Inspector Feather had taken him to look at Paul's body.'

'But you didn't discuss it with Inspector Feather when he was here after Eric was killed,' persisted Daniel.

Purbright hesitated, then said reluctantly, 'Viscount Dillon told me it wasn't appropriate to talk about it. He said it would have had nothing to do with Eric's murder. So that was the answer I gave when the inspector asked me about Paul James. That I'd been told by my superiors that it wasn't a matter to be discussed.'

Daniel and Abigail exchanged concerned looks; this was what Feather obviously meant when he'd told them that the people at the Tower weren't being co-operative and were tying his hands. Aloud, Daniel said, 'With respect to the viscount, this information is very appropriate. I think you need to tell us everything you know about Eric James and his brother.'

'You think it's connected with Eric's murder?'

'Two brothers are killed within two days of one another. That certainly suggests a connection of some sorts.' He looked thoughtfully at Purbright. 'Did Eric and Paul have much to do with one another?'

'No,' said Purbright. 'I never met Paul, but from what Eric told me about him, I got the impression they were two very different sorts of men. They would have had nothing in common. That's what Viscount Dillon said to me before the inspector talked to me in the viscount's office, which is why it wasn't considered appropriate to talk about with the inspector.'

Daniel studied the unhappy Yeoman, who seemed to be struggling with some sort of internal turmoil. Then Daniel said, 'I'm told that Eric was a good man. I can't believe he just ignored what was happening to his brother. There's something more, isn't there?'

The unhappy Purbright looked away from Daniel's probing gaze.

'We need to know everything if we're going to catch Eric's killer,' Daniel pressed. 'Paul was killed, then Eric. We're sure there's a connection between both murders. What were Eric and Paul involved in together?'

'Nothing!' burst out Purbright. 'Not in that way. Lately Eric had been trying to help Paul turn his life around and get on the straight and narrow.'

'How was he doing that?'

'About a week ago, Eric persuaded Paul to accompany him to a local Salvation Army Mission Hall to listen to General William Booth speak. Eric hoped that listening to General Booth would help him turn away from his life of wickedness. Eric was convinced that Paul's troubles stemmed from drink. Paul seemed as if he was prepared to take heed, but things must have gone wrong for him again, because he was killed. Stabbed to death.'

'Was Eric a member of the Salvation Army?' asked Daniel.

'No. He went to a few meetings, but he couldn't join. The Salvation Army expects its officers to work for them full-time. That was out of the question for Eric, so long as he was a Yeoman Warder in the British Army. But Eric was very sympathetic to the Salvation Army and the good work they do.'

'Before Eric took Paul to that meeting, had they had much to do with one another recently?' asked Abigail.

'No,' said Purbright. 'I don't think they'd had any sort of contact for a year.'

'So who got in touch with who? Did Eric seek out Paul, or Paul seek out Eric?'

Purbright thought about it, then said, 'It was Paul. He came here to the Tower looking for Eric.'

'When was this?'

'About a month ago. Eric told me about it afterwards. He

said Paul had turned up looking for him and asked one of the other Yeomen where he could find him. He told the Yeoman he was Eric James's brother. The Yeoman went and found Eric and brought him to the public area where Paul was. Eric told me that Paul said he'd come to ask Eric for help.'

'What sort of help? Financial?'

Purbright shook his head. 'He said he wanted to sort his life out, and he wondered if Eric could help him. Eric was surprised, but I got the impression he was pleased. Paul came back a week later and Eric told him that he was looking into getting in touch with someone he was sure could help Paul. Paul asked if Eric would mind showing him round the Tower. Eric said he could, but only the areas where the public were allowed. So Eric gave Paul his own personalised guided tour.'

'Did you meet Paul on either of those times he came to the Tower?'

'No, I thought it best to leave them alone. After all, they'd been estranged for a long time.'

'Did Paul return to the Tower after Eric had given him the guided tour?'

'About a week later. He'd left his address with Eric and Eric wrote to him saying he thought he'd found the best person to help Paul and telling him he'd introduce Paul to him. He suggested Paul come to the Tower and he gave him a date, which was a week ago.'

'And Paul turned up?'

'Yes, and that was when Eric took him to the mission to hear General Booth.'

'Which day was that?'

'Friday, at the end of last week. It was my day off.'

'And it was on Tuesday, four days later, that Paul was killed?'

Purbright nodded.

'And then Thursday morning, yesterday, Eric was found dead?'

Again, Purbright nodded. 'Yes.'

'Viscount Dillon told us you said you'd met Eric at about half past nine the previous evening.'

'Yes, that's right. We were doing our last patrols before the gates were locked for the night at ten o'clock.'

'And it was you who discovered his body at half past seven the following morning.'

'Yes, after I'd carried out my main duty as Ravenmaster. There are six ravens at the Tower and at dawn each day my job entails releasing the birds from their cages and preparing breakfast for them. After I'd done that, I made my way to the White Tower, and that was where I discovered poor Eric's body.'

It was Abigail who asked, 'Out of curiosity, how do you stop the ravens flying away? Bearing in mind the legend that if they leave the Tower, the Crown and Britain will fall.'

'By clipping their wings,' explained Purbright. He looked nervously at Abigail and Daniel and asked, 'I won't get into any trouble with Viscount Dillon for telling you this, will I?'

'No, absolutely not,' Daniel reassured him. 'On the contrary, if what you've told us helps to bring Eric's murderer to justice, I'm sure the viscount will be pleased with you.'

As they walked away, Abigail whispered, 'You're sure of

that, are you? What you told Purbright about the viscount being pleased with him. I got the impression that Dillon was keen to suppress any information about Eric's brother in case it brought the Tower into disrepute.'

'I'm sure Dillon will see it in a positive light if the killer is found, and without any publicity,' said Daniel. 'Right now, I think we need to let John Feather know what we've discovered about the James brothers. It points to a definite link between both murders.'

Feather was just leaving Scotland Yard as Daniel and Abigail arrived.

'Back again?' asked Feather.

'We've got some information that puts a new light on the murders of the James brothers,' said Daniel. He looked past Feather into the reception area of the Yard. 'Shall we go back to Freddy's?' he asked.

'No need,' said Feather. 'I've cleared us working together with the chief superintendent, so it's perfectly all right for us to be seen together.' He looked at his watch and said, 'Let's go to my office, but I've only got a few minutes. Vera's sister and her husband are coming over this evening.'

'We'll be as quick as we can,' said Daniel.

The three hurried up the stairs to Feather's office, where Jeremiah Cribbens, Feather's sergeant, was puffing on his pipe, sending out clouds of foul-smelling smoke.

He stood up as they entered with a broad smile for Daniel and Abigail. 'Mr and Mrs Wilson!' He beamed. 'This is a pleasure!' Hastily he put his pipe down. 'If I'd known you were coming, Mrs Wilson, I wouldn't have lit it,' he apologised.

'Ha!' snorted Feather at him. 'So it's all right for me and Daniel to be forced to endure this smog, but not Mrs Wilson?'

'I only meant—' began Cribbens.

'I know what you meant, Sergeant.' Abigail smiled at him. 'And I thank you for your courtesy.'

Cribbens looked reprovingly at his boss. 'I was just about to go home, anyway. I only lit up in here because it's easier than trying to light it outside in the street.'

Feather nodded and gave a sigh of apology. 'Very well, Sergeant. I'll see you in the morning.'

Cribbens doffed his hat to them, then left.

'You do give him a hard time,' said Abigail to Feather.

'I give *him* a hard time? What about me, breathing in those fumes?'

'Think of it as "live and let live",' said Daniel.

Feather settled himself down in his chair and gestured for them to sit. 'So what's this new information?' he asked.

'We've just been talking to Yeoman Purbright, and without Viscount Dillon watching over us, it appears that there are a few strands that seem to be linked,' said Daniel. He ticked them off on his fingers: 'Eric James is murdered at the Tower. His brother, Paul, is stabbed to death in an area close to the Tower. This happens shortly after Eric has taken Paul to hear a sermon preached by William Booth, founder and leader of the Salvation Army. Captain Edward Merchant of the Salvation Army is beaten to death outside the Blind Beggar pub in Whitechapel. The Blind Beggar is where William Booth gave his first open-air sermon.'

'It doesn't necessarily mean they're all connected,' said Feather.

'No, but I'm not a great believer in coincidences,' said Daniel. 'Not where murders are concerned. In this case we have three murders, all committed within a few days of one another, and each one with a Salvation Army connection.'

'You're surely not suggesting the Salvation Army are involved in this?' asked Feather incredulously.

'No, but Abigail and I have been discussing it on the way here, and we've got a theory that might link the murders of the James brothers, although at the moment the killing of Captain Merchant is still unexplained.'

'What's your theory?' asked Feather.

Daniel looked at Abigail and said, 'You tell him. Most of it's come from you.'

'It starts with Paul James,' said Abigail. 'A low-life who mixes with other low-lives who are involved in all sorts of criminality. Let's say Paul and his cronies are planning some big theft, something from the Tower of London.'

'The theft of what?' asked Feather.

'At the moment we're not sure, but it has to be something big because a gang is involved, who all want shares in whatever money they get.'

'The Crown Jewels?' asked Feather, amused.

'Possibly,' said Abigail. 'The thing is the Tower of London is not an easy place to burgle. The gates to the outside are locked at ten o'clock every night, which means the gang have to find the weak link in the Tower's defences, a way they can carry out the robbery without being caught.

'So Paul James goes to see his estranged brother, Eric, who's a Beefeater at the Tower and knows the inside workings of the place. But Paul knows that Eric will have nothing to do with aiding any crime, so he uses the pretext of asking Eric for help in getting his life sorted out. And Eric is pleased to do that. He even gives Paul a private tour of the Tower, and arranges for Paul to accompany him to a sermon being preached by General Booth.

'But somewhere along the line, the gang get suspicious of Paul. Maybe they're worried he might be starting to genuinely think of reforming his life. They're worried he might grass them up. So they kill him, and to drive the message home, they cut his tongue out as a warning to the rest to stay silent. It's possible that they're worried that Paul might have talked to Eric, especially if he was suddenly serious about reforming and turning over a new leaf. So, taking no chances, they kill Eric.'

She stopped talking and looked questioningly at Feather, who asked, 'Is that it?'

'It fits with the facts as we know them,' said Daniel.

'If you're right it raises more questions than it answers,' said Feather, concerned. 'Who are the gang? What are they planning to steal? When are they planning to steal it?'

'The key to that is Paul James,' said Abigail. 'Find out who killed him and we'll find out what their plan is.'

'I'm already working on that,' said Feather. 'We're trying to compile a list of his known associates.' He gave a rueful sigh. 'Not that it's easy. As I've said before, people in that part of London don't like talking to the police.'

'In the meantime, we thought we'd have a word with Eric James's senior officer, who, we understand, is Divisional Sergeant Major Arnold West,' said Abigail. 'He might be able to give us an idea of what Eric James was doing in the Line of Kings, and whether he was there officially. If he wasn't, what was he doing there?'

CHAPTER SIX

That evening, as they washed up the dishes after supper, Daniel said, 'I'm impressed that you know so much about the Tower of London.'

'Viscount Dillon or Mr Dewberry know far more than I do', said Abigail. 'As would Sir Frederick Stephenson and Sir George Bryan Milman. Not to mention any of the Yeoman Warders.'

'Yes, but theirs would be the official line, a kind of lecture. I'm interested in finding out the feel of the place.'

'You've been there before.'

'Only in passing if my work as a detective took me anywhere near there. As a workhouse boy I never studied history. What I know about it I picked up from stories in the newspapers, and I only paid attention to those stories that were related to any case I was working on. As I said, today was the first time I actually was able to look at the place properly.'

Abigail looked thoughtful. 'The Tower has a history stretching back almost a thousand years. That's a lot of history.'

'Give me the feeling of the place. I know it was a place of execution and many famous people were executed there.'

'Yes, the execution site was on Tower Green, the large area of grass near the oldest houses. Many of those executed were women. Two of Henry VIII's wives, Anne Boleyn and Catherine Howard. Both were accused of adultery, although neither may have been guilty. Lady Jane Grey, just sixteen years old, who had been queen for just nine days, was also executed.'

'Why?'

'Because her father-in-law, the Duke of Northumberland, held a military coup to put her on the throne and thus gain control of the Crown for himself.'

'Then there was Sir Walter Raleigh,' said Daniel. 'I do remember reading of his execution.'

'Except he wasn't executed at the Tower,' said Abigail. 'He was imprisoned there for some years by Queen Elizabeth on charges of treason, but eventually she released him. However, after she died, her successor, King James I, had him arrested, once more on charges of treason. He was executed at Old Palace Yard in Westminster.' She smiled and said, 'Bringing things nearer to our own time, I've always thought the menagerie was interesting.'

'The menagerie?' said Daniel, puzzled.

'From early days, since the early thirteenth century, exotic animals were kept at the Tower.'

'How exotic?'

'Lions. Elephants. A polar bear. A group of monkeys. An alligator. Wolves.'

'Not roaming free, surely,' said Daniel.

'No, they were kept in cages for the amusement of the royal resident of the time. Sadly, that entertainment also included things such as bear-baiting, setting dogs on a bear, and also lions fighting bears.

'That all changed with the appointment of the Duke of Wellington as constable of the Tower in 1826. One of his first acts was to cause the removal of the wild animals from the Tower and send them to the recently created London Zoo at Regent's Park. Wellington was first and foremost a military man and he saw the Tower as a vital fortress should there be outbursts of public disorder. There was no place there for wild animals to be gawped at.' She looked at him. 'Is that enough of a history lesson for today?'

'More than enough,' he said with a smile. He took her in his arms, hugged her close and kissed her gently on the lips. 'I thought we could move on to another subject.'

She pressed herself against him and moved her hand down to stroke his thigh. 'Biology?' she whispered.

'My thought exactly,' he said. And he lifted her up in his arms and carried her towards the stairs.

CHAPTER SEVEN

Feather and Sergeant Cribbens knocked at the door of the lodging house in Muscovy Court, a short road not far from Fenchurch Street railway station, where Paul James had lived, and where he'd been discovered stabbed to death, lying on the pavement outside the front door. This was their third visit to the house, and to the elderly sisters, Ettie and Gladys Woodward, both in their sixties, who shared a room in the tall narrow terraced house. They lived on the ground floor, their window looking out onto the street. Paul James had lived in an attic on the third floor, the top storey. It was Ettie, the younger sister, who opened the door to the two police officers.

'Back again?' she asked. 'This is the third time.'

'I'm afraid so,' said Feather.

The two policemen followed Ettie the few paces down the narrow, gloomy passageway to the door of the Woodward sisters' room. Gladys was sitting in a rickety armchair by the empty fireplace, just as she had been on their previous visits.

Their first visit had been in response to a beat constable's request for Scotland Yard to investigate the dead body of a man found stabbed in the street. It had been their first introduction to the Woodward sisters.

'We heard this shout right outside our window, a really horrible yell, and then a thump of someone falling,' Ettie had told them on their first visit. 'We went out and there was poor Mr James lying on the pavement in a pool of blood. Gladys knew he was dead at once. She used to work at an undertaker's, getting the bodies ready for funerals.'

'Palmers,' Gladys had put in. 'Over in Fenchurch Street.'

'Did you see anyone running away?' Feather had asked.

Both women had shaken their heads. They'd told Feather and Cribbens the man was called Paul James and that he lived in the attic on the top floor. While the beat constable had stood guard over the dead man as they waited for the police doctor to arrive, Feather and Cribbens had found a keyring with two keys on it in one of the dead man's pockets and gone up to the man's room.

The small room had stunk of stale tobacco, sweat and unwashed clothes. Four empty gin bottles lay discarded by the grimy single bed. There was little else in the room. Two unwashed glass tumblers that smelt of gin. A screw of newspaper that contained tobacco. There was no sign of food of any sort, or plates and cutlery. The only book was a bible with the symbol of the Salvation Army on the cover.

'Maybe he was looking for salvation,' Cribbens had suggested, picking up the bible and flicking through the pages. 'Someone's marked some bits in it.'

They'd gone back downstairs to discover the police van had arrived and the body of Paul James was being loaded into it.

'Scotland Yard or a hospital, Inspector?' the driver had asked Feather.

'Scotland Yard,' Feather had replied. 'I'll be along as soon as I've finished talking to the witnesses.'

As Feather and Cribbens had discovered, there were no witnesses. Ettie and Gladys hadn't seen anything, just heard the commotion outside their window. They'd said that by the time they got out to the street, Paul James was lying on the pavement, dead. It had been the large amount of blood around his mouth that had prompted Feather to look into his mouth and notice his tongue was missing.

'It must have taken a bit of time to cut that out,' Feather had said. 'But the old women said they didn't see anyone.'

'They don't look like they move very fast,' Cribbens had pointed out. 'And, in this sort of area, no one's going to rush out until they're sure the people who did it have gone.'

'Yes, that's true,' Feather had admitted.

They'd then gone through the routine of knocking on doors inside the lodging house, but getting no responses at all, then knocking on doors of the houses in the short street. Those people who did open their doors said they had seen and heard nothing.

Feather and Cribbens had then made their way to the local police station in Fenchurch Street, where they spoke to the uniformed constable, PC Bernard Moss, who had been first on the scene of the murder, and the duty station sergeant, Wesley Sims. Neither could offer any insights into the murder, or why it may have happened.

'I expect he got into a fight with someone,' PC Moss had suggested.

Feather had wondered whether to mention about Paul James's tongue being cut out, then decided against it. A sixth sense gave him a suspicious feeling about this pair and the business of the tongue would keep till later.

'Did you have much to do with Paul James?' Feather had asked the two uniformed policemen.

Both men had shaken their heads.

'We'd find him sometimes lying drunk in the street,' Moss had told them. 'He was a drinker.'

'The two old ladies who found him told us he's got a brother, Eric James, who's a Yeoman Warder at the Tower of London. Do you know if Paul saw much of his brother?'

Moss and Sims had looked at one another enquiringly, before both shook their heads.

'I didn't even know he had a brother,' Moss had told them.

After, as Feather and his sergeant had left the police station and made for their waiting carriage, Feather had asked, 'What did you make of that pair?'

'Lying through their teeth,' said Cribbens.

'Yes, that same thought struck me,' said Feather.

Later, after Eric James was killed, Feather and Cribbens had made their second visit to Muscovy Court and the Fenchurch Street police station, again to see if anyone had any information of any sort about the murder of Paul James. As before, the answer was negative. No one had seen or heard anything on the day of Paul James's murder. No one had come in with any stories about him.

'Do you know who he went around with?' Feather had asked Sergeant Sims.

'No,' Sims had replied. 'Like we told you before, we didn't have many dealings with him, except to pick him out of the gutter when he was drunk.'

On this, their third visit to the area, they again called at the lodging house in Muscovy Court to talk to the Woodward sisters. As before, the elderly women had nothing new to tell them.

It was as they left the lodging house that Feather became aware of a short, thin, badly dressed woman watching them from the other side of the road. The two detectives walked a few steps further on, then Feather stopped, and they noticed the woman did the same.

'Either she's following us, or she wants to talk to us,' said Feather. 'Let's make it easier for her. You stay here and I'll see what she wants.'

He set off to cross the road, while his sergeant stood and watched. The woman suddenly looked panicky, casting nervous glances about her as Feather approached.

'Good day,' said Feather politely. 'I get the impression you've got something to tell us.'

The woman hesitated. Feather reckoned she was in her thirties or forties; it was difficult to tell. Her skin, hair and clothes were grimy. Of one thing he was certain, she was frightened.

'I won't hurt you,' he promised her. 'But if you've got any information about Paul James—'

'Not here,' she interrupted him, still casting apprehensive

look about her. 'Do you know St Martin's Church?'

'Yes,' said Feather.

'I'll meet you there in ten minutes,' she said. 'Just you. Your pal over the road looks too much like a copper.'

'What's your name?' asked Feather.

'Later,' she said. 'At the church.'

With that, she hurried off, moving fast like a startled deer and casting anxious looks about her the whole time.

Daniel and Abigail walked across the Tower Green with Divisional Sergeant Major Arnold West as they asked him about Eric James. Here, in the open, both Daniel and Abigail felt it would be easier to get honest answers from the sergeant major when there was less chance of them being overheard by anyone, or of being interrupted without warning.

'Eric James's body was found at half past seven in the morning in the Line of Kings in the White Tower,' said Daniel. 'Was there any official reason why he should have been there? Would he have been carrying out any duties?'

'Not during the night,' said West. 'Nor at that time of the morning. All the men carry out a tour of duty, for which they have a scheduled walk.'

'Can you think of any reason why Eric James should have been there?'

'Often, our men take a walk around the grounds after the gates have been shut. Sometimes it's to make sure no one has managed to stay behind. There have been occasions when someone has stayed behind and hidden themselves somewhere in the grounds. Usually it's young men doing it for a dare, but those are rare occasions. When it has happened, they are usually apprehended very swiftly.'

'Could that have been what happened here?' asked Abigail. 'Mr James saw someone entering the White Tower and followed them, and they went up to where the Line of Kings is?'

'In theory it's possible, but a responsible and experienced soldier like Yeoman James would not attempt to intercede on his own. He would summon assistance. After all, although most intruders do it simply for a dare, one might have serious malicious intent, and could be armed. It's more likely that he entered the White Tower to check on the exhibits and make sure that everything was secure. Our men take the responsibility of keeping security here at the Tower very heavily indeed.'

'Or perhaps he had arranged to meet someone by the Line of Kings?'

'That's possible,' said West. 'But if that was the case, it would be to meet someone attached to the Tower, either as staff or family of staff. Many of the resident staff have families living here with them on site.'

'Do the families have much to do with one another?' asked Abigail.

West smiled. 'The Tower of London is a small, enclosed community, less than a hundred people. Think of it as a small village where everyone knows everyone, so they know who to go to if they need assistance of any sort. Waterloo barracks is here, of course, but that's a separate community.'

'Did Yeoman James have any particular close acquaintances amongst the other people here?' asked Daniel.

'I believe he was particularly close to the Ravenmaster,

Yeoman Purbright,' said West. 'Two old bachelors, veterans of the long wars.'

'Did they serve together?' asked Daniel.

'Not as far as I know. I believe that Yeoman Purbright spent much of his army career in Afghanistan and India. Yeoman James was an old campaigner from Africa. He was at Rorke's Drift, you know. The Zulu Wars, 1879. Eleven members of the garrison there were awarded the Victoria Cross. Outstanding bravery.'

St Martin's Church was a small and very old building. Ninth century, thought Feather, before the Norman conquest. There were still a few of these old pre-Norman churches dotted around the older parts of London. Most of them, just like this one dedicated to St Martin, looked neglected. The walls seemed decidedly rickety, some of the old stones loose and threatening to fall out. Feather pushed open the ancient wooden door and stepped in. The interior had no pews, just old wooden chairs set out in rows. Feather spotted the woman at the end of the back row. He looked around to check that no one was around, just in case it was a trap of some sort. Reassured, he moved to take the chair next to the woman.

'Here I am,' he said.

The woman looked at him, nodded, then turned her face away from him.

'Do you mind telling me your name?' asked Feather.

'Ellie Mercer,' said the woman. She shook her head, obviously angry. 'They shouldn't have killed him. He wouldn't have said anything.'

'You're talking about Paul James?'

Ellie nodded.

'Who did it?' asked Feather.

'Not so fast,' she said. 'If they know I've talked to you, it'll be me who's next to go. They're ruthless.'

'Who are they?' asked Feather.

She shook her head. 'I need protection if I'm going to say anything.'

'We can protect you.'

'Not round here you can't. I need money to get away. Get a new name, a new life, far away from here. Somewhere where nobody knows me.'

'That can be arranged,' said Feather.

Although he said it with an air of quiet confidence, he knew that his chief superintendent might be difficult. He could almost hear Armstrong saying, *It's a con, Inspector. A scam to get money out of us. Once she's got the money, she'll vanish, leaving us with a load of hot air. We want the information first, and then if it works out she'll get the money. And she'll get what we decide to give her. We can't have these people calling the tune.*

'You knew Paul?' he asked.

She nodded. 'We were together. Me and him. Had been for four months. He wanted to get out of it and go straight. We was gonna get married.'

'What was he into?' asked Feather. 'Who was he working with?'

'No,' she said firmly. 'Not till I've got the money in my hand and I'm at a railway station about to catch a train to where I'll be safe.'

'Was it a robbery of some sort?' pressed Feather.

She looked at him, her expression hard. 'I've told you, you get nothing till you see me safe. These people are dangerous. Killers.' She looked around the church. 'I've already been here too long. They've got eyes and ears everywhere.'

She stood up.

'How will I get hold of you?' asked Feather.

'You don't. I'll get hold of you,' said Ellie. 'How soon will you know if you can arrange the money?'

'Tomorrow,' said Feather. 'How much will you want?'

'Seventy pounds,' she said.

Seventy pounds, thought Feather, his heart sinking. *Armstrong will tell me to get lost.* He looked at the woman and thought, *She's telling the truth, I'm sure she is. Seventy pounds will crack the whole case wide open, the murders of both Eric and Paul James. If the Chief Superintendent says no, I'll ask Daniel and Abigail. They're getting paid by the royal family, and if anyone can afford seventy pounds, it's the Prince of Wales. He must spend that on food and drink in a couple of days.*

'All right,' said Feather. 'I'll have the money the day after tomorrow. How will you get in touch with me?'

'I'll come to Scotland Yard and hand a note in at the desk. The two old dears at the house said you was called Inspector Feather.'

'That's right,' said Feather. 'Ask for Inspector Feather and I'll send my sergeant to come down to reception to bring you up to my office.'

'Is that the fat bloke you were with?'

'That's him,' said Feather.

'You promise to keep me safe?' she asked.

'I promise,' said Feather.

'I'll see you tomorrow.'

'What time?' asked Feather.

'I'll be there at eleven o'clock.' With that, she was gone.

CHAPTER EIGHT

As Daniel and Abigail made their way towards Viscount Dillon's office, they discussed the conclusion they'd reached from talking to Yeoman Purbright and Sergeant Major West.

'Eric James wasn't there at the Line of Kings in any official capacity,' summed up Abigail. 'So, either he'd elected to take a walk up there for some reason, or he'd arranged to meet someone there.'

'I feel it was an arranged meeting,' said Daniel. 'If he'd just walked up the stairs to make a casual inspection, he'd have heard the noise from any intruders before he got there. As Sergeant Major West has said, as an experienced soldier he'd have gone for assistance before confronting them.'

'Not necessarily,' said Abigail. 'If he didn't realise they were there until he'd walked into the room and they grabbed him before he could get away.'

'But what were they doing there?' asked Daniel. 'Nothing has been taken from that part of the exhibition.'

'True,' said Abigail thoughtfully. 'In that case, we're back to an arranged meeting. But why did it end in murder?'

'I feel there's a connection between the murder of Eric James and that of his brother,' said Daniel. 'Paul James was a known thief with suspect contacts. I think he was part of whatever criminal activity was being planned. Paul James is killed, but it's possible that his contacts wanted to meet with Eric for some reason.'

'About the planned robbery,' said Abigail. 'At the Tower.'

'Yes,' said Daniel. 'They wanted his help in carrying one out. For some reason they'd been led to believe by Paul that his brother would help them. When they discussed it with him, he refused and threatened to tell the authorities, so they killed him.'

'Who are *they*? Someone from inside the Tower? A couple of Yeomen?'

'I don't know,' Daniel admitted.

'But we've been told that all the Yeomen here have to have the Good Conduct medal,' pointed out Abigail. 'And twenty-two years of loyal service. It's hard to think that after all that, suddenly some of them have turned rotten.'

'Every organisation has its share of rotten apples,' said Daniel.

'Viscount Dillon won't like to hear that,' said Abigail.

'For that reason, I suggest that at this stage we don't mention to him we think it could be an inside job. We'll only get another lecture from him about how that's impossible and he'll get defensive, and at the moment we need him on our side.'

'So we just give him the broad strokes of our theory about a possible robbery being planned?'

'Yes,' said Daniel. 'And we'll see what he has to say about it.'

The chief superintendent listened, stunned, as Inspector Feather told him about the offer Ellie Mercer had made.

'Seventy pounds!' exploded Armstrong. 'That's more than most people earn in a year! I can't ask the commissioner for seventy pounds!'

'She needs to start a new life, somewhere far away.'

'With that much money she could go to America!' snorted the chief superintendent.

'Perhaps that's what she's planning,' said Feather.

'It could be a con,' said Armstrong. 'Once she gets the money, she feeds you a load of piffle and vanishes.'

'I think she knows who killed Paul and Eric James, and what's behind it,' said Feather.

Armstrong fell silent, thinking. Then he asked, 'When's she coming in?'

'The day after tomorrow.'

'Right,' said Armstrong. 'When she comes in, we take her into custody and force her to tell us what she knows. She'll tell us or she'll rot in jail. Tell her that.'

Daniel and Abigail sat in Viscount Dillon's office, the curator watching them warily.

'We have reason to believe the attack on Eric James was not carried out as a symbolic attack on the Crown, but to silence him and stop him passing on any information he may have gathered from his brother, Paul,' Daniel told him.

Dillon frowned. 'The brother who was murdered?'

'Indeed,' said Abigail. 'We have reason to suspect that a gang of thieves, of which Paul James was a part, had been planning a robbery at the Tower. We believe both Paul James and Eric were killed by the gang to stop them passing on any information about the proposed robbery.'

Dillon looked at them, doubtful. 'How sure are you of this?'

'It fits the facts that we've managed to assemble,' said Daniel. 'The question is, of course, are the gang still planning to carry out this robbery? If it was them who killed both James brothers, it suggests they are.'

'And what do you believe to be the target of this robbery?' asked Dillon.

'This is where we need your specialist knowledge of the Tower and its treasures. Eric James was found in the Line of Kings, but we feel that the treasures in the Line of Kings are too large and bulky to be able to be removed easily. And the question remains: how valuable are smaller items such as the weapons on display in the Line of Kings? The thieves will be after items that are smaller, but whose value cannot be questioned.'

'Diamonds,' added Abigail. 'Gold.'

Dillon hesitated, then said, 'You are suggesting the Crown Jewels?'

'There was a previous robbery here when the Crown Jewels were stolen,' said Abigail.

'The infamous Thomas Blood in 1671.' Dillon nodded grimly. 'Fortunately, he and his accomplices were caught in the act and arrested.'

'There was also another attempt to snatch the royal crown in this century,' said Daniel. 'A woman who tried to break bits off it.'

'In 1815,' said Dillon. 'She was found to be insane.' He looked at them with a serious and concerned expression on his face. 'You really think these people have designs on the Crown Jewels?'

'At the moment it's just speculation,' admitted Daniel. 'Can you think of anything else that has similar value here in the Tower, and small enough to be carried out easily?'

Dillon rose to his feet. 'If what you tell me is in the realms of possibility, then we should look at the Crown Jewels together and examine the security arrangements. They are kept in the Wakefield Tower.'

'Not in the White Tower?' asked Daniel as he and Abigail followed the viscount out of his office.

'They've never been kept in the White Tower,' said Dillon. 'At least, not the replacement jewels.'

'Replacement jewels?' asked Daniel.

'Following the restoration of the monarchy with Charles II in 1660,' said Abigail.

'Exactly,' said Dillon. 'You know your history, Mrs Wilson. But then, that's only to be expected of a historian and archaeologist of your reputation.'

They followed Dillon out of his accommodation, making for the Wakefield Tower.

'During the time of the Interregnum, the so-called Commonwealth, when that blackguard Oliver Cromwell and his murderous ruffians were in control of the country,'

Dillon explained as they walked across the Green. 'They took the diamonds from the Crown Jewels, then melted down the crowns and other objects to get the gold from them. They claimed it was to prevent any encouragement for the monarchy to be restored and a new king to be installed, which has been traditionally done by the use of the Crown Jewels, hence they are known as the Coronation Regalia. They include swords of state and ceremonial maces, which are carried in procession before the sovereign at the coronation, along with orbs and sceptres and trumpets and tunics. However, if you ask me, it was done purely to turn the jewels into money so that those villains could support their infamous enterprise.

'When Charles was restored to the throne in 1660, he had a new set of Crown Jewels made for his coronation in 1661. Those are the ones on display there today.' His face darkened with anger as he muttered, 'Just think all of those precious coronation relics assembled over hundreds of years, destroyed for plunder. Unthinkable!'

CHAPTER NINE

Daniel and Abigail climbed the stairs of the Wakefield Tower, following Viscount Dillon as he made his way to the top floor. A Yeoman Warder was on guard outside a pair of double doors, and he stood sharply to attention when he saw Viscount Dillon emerge from the stairwell. Dillon opened the double doors and Daniel and Abigail followed him into the room, which had a high ceiling formed of stone arches supporting the roof.

Immediately beneath the vaulted ceiling, a large cage filled the centre of the room. The cage had four sides, each composed of upright iron bars about fourteen feet in height. These bars were fixed together at the top by cross-piece iron bars, atop which were sharp spikes sticking upwards.

Inside the cage was a pyramid structure, on which the various items of the Coronation Regalia were displayed, with a large diamond-encrusted crown at the top, and then other crowns, orbs, sceptres and items of rich gold and diamond adornment on show on the descending shelves.

'This cage was constructed here in the Wakefield Tower when the Jewel House building, which is where the Crown Jewels were displayed before, was judged to be a fire hazard,' Dillon told them. He pointed at the locks on some of the bars. 'Small barred doors set into the cage, kept locked and only opened for cleaning, or rearrangement if it's needed. It's impenetrable, as I hope you'll see. Since the unfortunate incidents with Thomas Blood and the madwoman, no further attempts have been made on the jewels.'

'It certainly looks secure,' agreed Daniel. 'Although experience has taught me that however secure a place may be, there will always be someone planning ways to open it.'

'Not this Jewel Room,' said Dillon firmly. Then, for the first time since they'd met him, his face relaxed into a smile. 'As you are here, I hope you'll allow me to elucidate you on the items you see before you.'

Oh no, thought Daniel. *He's an enthusiast. We're about to get the whole history of every piece on display.*

He was on the point of making an apologetic excuse that, having seen the security up close, they needed to get on with their investigation, but Abigail, aware of what he was about to say, trod warningly on his foot.

'That would be wonderful.' She smiled at Dillon.

The viscount pointed at the large crown at the top of the display, the centrepiece.

'The crown at the top is St Edward's Crown, named after Edward the Confessor. Along with most of the other items on display, it was completed in 1661. It's made of gold and is embellished with four hundred and forty-four precious

72

stones, including amethysts, garnets, rubies, sapphires, topazes, tourmalines, peridots and zircons. As you can imagine, it's very heavy, which is possibly why it was absent from the coronation of our present queen's investiture in 1838.'

Daniel could feel his eyes glazing over as Dillon continued, pointing at each piece and giving a full description of the item, its value, its weight, the craftsman who'd made it. In spite of himself, his curiosity was aroused when Dillon said:

'Take note of the long-handled silver-gilt spoon. When I said earlier that Cromwell and his ruffians had everything made of gold from the pre-Interregnum Crown Jewels melted down, there was one piece that escaped. That coronation spoon. In 1640, the Yeoman of the Removing Wardrobe, a man called Clement Kynnersley, bought it for sixteen shillings. When the monarchy was restored, Kynnersley returned the spoon to Charles II. It is the oldest piece here, dating from the twelfth century, although the four pearls set into the handle weren't added until the seventeenth century. At the coronation, the holy oil with which the monarch is to be anointed is poured into the bowl of the spoon, which, as you can see, is divided into two halves by a ridge. The Archbishop of Canterbury dips two fingers into the bowl, one in each half, in order to anoint the sovereign.'

The monologue by the curator continued for a further half hour, when it was interrupted by one of the Yeoman Warders entering and, after apologising for his arrival, informed the viscount that his presence was required by the arrival of a member of parliament who wished to discuss something with the curator.

'I'm so sorry,' Dillon said to Abigail and Daniel. 'I'm afraid this happens all the time, and as the government are our paymasters . . .'

'Of course you must go,' said Abigail sympathetically. 'But thank you so much for your time today showing us the collection; it has been so instructive.'

'Perhaps we can do the rest another time?' suggested Dillon.

'Absolutely.' Abigail nodded.

They left the Wakefield Tower together, then Dillon made for his office, while Daniel and Abigail headed for the exit.

'Well, that was an hour of my life I'm never going to get back,' complained Daniel.

Abigail looked at him disapprovingly. 'I don't know why you're complaining,' she said. 'You seem happy enough to ask *me* about the history of the Tower.'

'Yes, but you make the history of the place interesting. I'm sure as a history lesson, it was instructive, but he tells it in such a boring style.'

'Instructive, but not quite accurate,' said Abigail. 'The viscount blamed Cromwell for turning the crown jewels into money, but in fact Charles I had done the same thing. Soon after he came to the throne, one of the first things he did was to take forty-one precious items from the Jewel House and send them to Amsterdam – the centre of Europe's jewel trade – to sell them. When he tried to do the same thing again some time later, parliament tried to stop him by declaring the Coronation Regalia as "Jewels of the Crown", stating that their ownership was vested in the monarch only because of his public role as king, and he did not have personal ownership of them. Charles got his wife, Henrietta, to smuggle some of the Crown Jewels abroad and try to sell them on the Dutch jewellery market. She was able to dispose of a few items before parliament discovered what was going on and put a stop to the scheme.'

'How do you know all this stuff?' asked Daniel, impressed.

'Because I went to Girton College to study history and archaeology. While your official education, my dear husband, ended on the day you left the workhouse, and that limited education, from what I can gather, was basic reading and writing and picking oakum.'

CHAPTER TEN

I suppose that reaction was what I'd been expecting, thought Feather gloomily as he sat in the small horse-drawn carriage heading for Primrose Hill, and the house where Daniel and Abigail lived. Ordinarily, Feather might have come to the same decision as Armstrong, but the difference was he'd met Ellie Mercer and he believed her. She knew who had killed Paul James, and therefore who'd killed Eric James and why. If there was a major robbery planned at the Tower, as Daniel and Abigail believed, then Ellie Mercer's evidence was vital to stop it happening. Yes, seventy pounds was a lot of money, but it was worth it if the cases were solved and the robbery prevented. If the robbery went ahead, then Feather was sure that property worth a lot more than seventy pounds would be at risk.

Daniel and Abigail were just arriving home as Feather's carriage pulled up outside their house.

'Good, you're here,' said Feather, getting down from the carriage.

'We've just arrived back from the Tower,' said Abigail.

'Anything new?' asked Feather.

'Just telling the viscount our theory that the murders may be connected with a planned robbery at the Tower,' said Daniel.

'How did he take it?'

'He doesn't like to think it's possible,' said Daniel. 'What brings you here? What's happened?'

'I'll tell you when we're indoors,' said Feather.

Once inside, they put the kettle on and Feather told them about his meeting with Ellie Mercer, and her offer of information. For a price.

'Seventy pounds!' said Daniel, shocked.

'Yes, I know,' groaned Feather. 'It's as much as most ordinary people earn in a year. Chief Superintendent Armstrong has made me fully aware of that fact.'

Daniel and Abigail studied the inspector, then Abigail asked, 'Do you think she's genuine?'

'Yes, I do,' said Feather. 'I get the impression this is her revenge for what these people – whoever they are – did to Paul James. But she knows she won't be safe once they're arrested; they'll guess it was her who grassed them up. That's why she feels she has to disappear.'

'Seventy pounds is a lot of money,' said Daniel.

'I know,' said Feather ruefully. 'In some parts of England you can buy a house for seventy pounds. I'm very aware of that.'

'Will she take less?' asked Daniel.

'I could try,' said Feather. 'But I strongly doubt if the chief superintendent will go for fifty, or even thirty. He thinks it's throwing away good money on a bad cause.' He looked hopefully at Daniel and Abigail. 'I was wondering if it was worth approaching the Prince of Wales. After all, he's hired you to solve the murder of Eric James, and if it's the same person who murdered both men . . . ?'

Daniel and Abigail again exchanged looks, then Abigail said, 'It's worth a try, if you feel she really knows who's behind all this?'

'I do,' said Feather.

Viscount Dillon looked at his deputy, Algernon Dewberry, and Sergeant Major West, who stood before his desk, grim expressions on both their faces. As befitted his military background, the sergeant major stood rigidly to attention as he listened to the curator, while Dewberry seemed to need the support of the back of the chair nearest to him.

'A robbery?' he croaked, aghast. 'Here?'

'I find it hard to believe, but we have to be on our guard,' said Dillon. 'I suggest we increase our security on every part of the Tower where valuables are kept.'

'That's nearly every part of it, Your Grace,' said West. 'As well as the obvious valuables like the Crown Jewels, the armour and weapons would fetch a pretty price on the open market. And there are ancient relics that may not look as impressive as the Crown Jewels, but certain people will always be interested in acquiring them.'

'Do the Wilsons believe such a robbery will happen at night, or during the day?' asked Dewberry.

'They didn't say, but if it has been planned, it must surely be intended during the daytime. At night the gates are locked and we only have our own people on the premises. I cannot imagine any of them would be involved in such an outrage.'

Daniel and Abigail's visit to Marlborough House in their quest to get seventy pounds from the Prince of Wales seemed to hit a problem immediately when they asked if the Prince was in, and Michael Shanks told them, 'Their Highnesses are away for a few days.'

'Are they contactable?' asked Abigail.

'By letter,' said Shanks. 'They are in Scotland. They are expected back in London next week.'

'Too long,' groaned Daniel. 'A letter won't reach them before tomorrow at the earliest.'

'What exactly is it you wish to ask His Highness?' asked Shanks. 'As he made you aware, I am in his complete confidence, and I also manage his affairs.'

'It concerns the murder at the Tower of London,' said Daniel. 'The Yeoman Warder. An informant has claimed to know who killed him, and why. However, she fears for her life if she informs the police, so she has offered to sell the information for the sum of seventy pounds. She is due to call at Scotland Yard tomorrow to collect the money and give Inspector Feather the information. Unfortunately, the chief superintendent is disinclined to authorise the money be paid to her, which is why we have come to you. Or, rather, the Prince.'

'Seventy pounds is a lot of money,' said Shanks doubtfully.

'It is, but we hope that, as the Prince has hired us, he would consider it as part of our fee.'

Shanks looked thoughtful. 'He might consider that, but it

would be his decision. I'm afraid that I could not authorise such a large sum without his approval. I am prepared to write to him, but I doubt if his reply will be here for some days.'

'How much do we have in the bank?' Abigail asked as they left Marlborough House.

'Thirty-five pounds,' said Daniel. 'We should have asked the Prince for an advance as a retainer when he first gave us the commission. As it is, I suppose we'll have to wait until we solve the murder before we get paid.' He sighed. 'That's the trouble with the apparently wealthy: getting money out of them.'

'I suppose that's why they're wealthy,' said Abigail. 'They hang on to it.'

'At least when we're hired by a museum, or some organisation, the money's available,' said Daniel. 'If you remember, it took a while for us to get paid by the Queen on that recent escapade.'

'I rather think that was her private secretary who was the cautious one,' said Abigail. 'We could always try the bank.'

'You think they'd loan us the money?'

'I can't see why not,' said Abigail. 'We've got a good name with them. Our bills are always paid on time.'

'We don't have a large amount deposited with them,' said Daniel. 'Thirty-five pounds at this moment, and some months we just about scrape by while we wait for our bill to be paid by our client.'

'I'm sure the Prince will pay us back,' said Abigail. 'Especially once we tell him this could reveal who was behind the murder.'

'John said this Ellie Mercer is calling him at eleven o'clock tomorrow morning,' said Daniel. 'The bank opens at ten. That would just give us time to get the money and get to Scotland Yard.'

'If the bank lend us the money,' pointed out Abigail, her voice full of doubt.

Early the next morning they made their way to their local branch of the bank, where they were lucky enough to find the bank manager, Gerald Benson, was free. After the usual pleasantries with Benson enquiring after their health, and they asking after his family, they told him the reason for their visit. His initial reaction was not welcoming.

'Let me make sure I've got this straight,' said Benson. 'You wish to borrow seventy pounds to pay an informant for information you believe will close a case that you have been hired by His Majesty the Prince of Wales to investigate.'

'That is correct,' said Abigail. 'The Prince's private secretary, Mr Michael Shanks, is writing a letter to the Prince, who is currently in Scotland, to ask him to approve the money. However, the money is needed to pay this informant *today*, but the reply from the Prince with his instructions to release the money will not arrive in time.'

'And if the Prince refuses to grant you the money?' asked Benson.

'Then we would make arrangements to repay it back in instalments over three years,' said Abigail. 'Twenty-five pounds a year for two years and the final twenty in the third year. Plus interest, of course. Either way, the bank gets its money back, either from the Prince of Wales in a few days, or from us over three years.' She fixed the bank manager with a friendly but determined look as she added, 'Of course, we will inform the Prince that none of this could have been achieved without your assistance. We're sure the Prince will be very grateful to you and this bank.'

As they left the bank, with an envelope containing fourteen large white five-pound notes in Abigail's bag, Daniel said, 'That was a very clever move, invoking the Prince's name like that.'

'The end justifies the means,' said Abigail. She patted her bag. 'Hopefully, we'll be able to have this case solved very, very shortly.'

CHAPTER ELEVEN

Ellie Mercer looked across the River Thames towards Big Ben. The big clock face showed ten minutes before eleven.

Please, God, let them have got the money for me, she prayed silently. She remembered when she'd heard the awful news about Paul. That he'd been stabbed to death outside his lodging house and the bastards had cut his tongue out. She'd gone to the house to talk to the two old ladies who'd found him, but they hadn't been able to tell her anything except that they'd found him dead on the pavement. They knew Ellie by sight from the time she used to stay overnight with Paul in his attic room. The two used to talk and dream of a new life for both of them, once Paul had made enough money.

'There's a big one coming,' he told her. 'We'll have the money to get away once this one's done.'

Instead, they'd killed him. The nasty business with the tongue meant they thought he was going to talk. It was a warning to others. They shouldn't have done that. Paul would never have talked. For one thing, being part of this big job meant he'd have good money at last, something he'd dreamt about. Something they'd both dreamt about. Well, she wasn't going to let them get away with that. She'd make sure they swung for it. And then she'd be on her way, with everything she needed to make a fresh start. A new name.

She was just turning in to the alley that led to Scotland Yard when two men stepped out from a doorway and barred her way. A feeling of panic hit her, and she turned abruptly to head back the way she'd come, but stopped. Three men were there. She guessed they'd followed her, but she hadn't seen them, even though she was sure she'd been careful. They'd obviously taken turns to follow her separately, one at a time, changing places.

The two men who'd barred her way came strolling towards her. The taller of the two had a genial smile on his face; the other – a short, thin, wiry man – scowled at her.

'Going to visit someone, Ellie?' asked the tall man.

'No.'

The tall man shook his head.

'Ellie,' he said sorrowfully, 'you should know by now we've got eyes and ears everywhere.' He leant forwards and whispered. 'Even inside St Martin's Church. Seventy pounds, you told that inspector, and you'd tell him everything. That wasn't nice, Ellie. We can't have that.'

'I was never going to tell him anything. I just saw it as a way of getting hold of some proper money.'

'Very commendable.' The man nodded. 'Enterprising.' He gave her a sad smile. 'We need to talk.'

* * *

84

Daniel, Abigail and Sergeant Cribbens sat in John Feather's office and watched the inspector as he paced nervously backwards and forwards. On Abigail's lap lay her bag with the seventy pounds inside it. Feather looked at the clock on the wall.

'Twenty past eleven,' he said. 'She's not coming.'

'Give her time,' said Abigail. 'From the description you gave us of her, she sounds like she may not be the best organised of people.'

'I think she would be for seventy pounds,' said Daniel.

They jumped as there was a knock at the door, which opened and a uniformed constable stepped in. He was holding a grubby scrap of paper, which he held out to the inspector.

'From Sergeant McDougall at the front desk, sir,' he said.

Feather looked at it. 'To Inspector Feather, Scotland Yard,' he read.

'It was pinned to the clothes of a dead woman who was found in a nearby alley,' said the constable. 'Her throat had been cut.'

'Where is she?' asked Feather.

'In the mortuary, sir.'

The medical orderly looked up from his desk as the door of the mortuary opened and Feather and Cribbens walked in, his expression changing to one of annoyance as he saw Daniel and Abigail.

'No civilians allowed,' he said curtly.

'They're not civilians; they're acting temporary police officers,' snapped Feather.

The orderly pointed at Abigail, outraged. 'But she's a woman,' he protested.

'Congratulations on your observational powers,' said Abigail.

Before the orderly could launch any further protests, Feather snapped at him, 'Where's the woman who was brought in a few moments ago?'

The orderly pointed to where a sheet had been draped over a body lying on a table.

'I haven't had time to deal with her yet,' he complained. He gestured at the mess of papers on his desk. 'All this paperwork.'

'I want to see her,' said Feather.

Reluctantly, the orderly rose to his feet and walked to the sheeted body. He pulled the sheet back, revealing the woman's head and shoulders, and they could see the gash in the front of her throat where a sharp blade had cut through her windpipe. She was still fully clothed.

Feather stood beside the table, looking down at her. Gently, he opened her mouth and looked inside. He closed her mouth and turned to the others. 'They cut her tongue out,' he said, and they could see the despair and anger in his face. 'I promised her she'd be safe.'

He pulled the sheet up to cover her.

'It wasn't your fault,' said Daniel. 'They were obviously watching her.'

'I should have taken her in, put her in protective custody.'

'I doubt if she'd have let you,' said Abigail.

* * *

86

They left the mortuary and Sergeant Cribbens excused himself to go outside and light his pipe. 'It always makes me feel like a smoke when I've been in there,' he said. 'It's the smell.' He pulled his pipe from his pocket. 'I need this to fumigate myself.'

'We're not going to get anything from the locals,' said Feather bitterly as he, Daniel and Abigail walked up the stairs to his office. 'Whoever's behind this has the local community terrified. Lots of people must know, but no one's going to talk after what happened to Paul James and now Ellie Mercer.'

'The local police must have an idea,' said Daniel. 'Especially the beat constables.'

'Sergeant Cribbens and I talked to the men at Fenchurch Street, which is the local police station, but they claim they don't know anything,' said Feather.

Daniel caught the note of scepticism in his voice and asked warily, 'You're suspicious of them?'

Feather nodded unhappily. 'It struck me they're either in the pay of whoever is behind it, or they're just frightened.'

'We ought to talk to Stanley Wherstone at Whitechapel,' said Daniel. 'It's the adjacent patch to Fenchurch Street, and Stanley's pretty good at what's going on in that part of East London.'

Feather nodded. 'Yes,' he said. 'I should have done it before, but I didn't want to put Stanley in a spot where he might be grassing on colleagues, but Ellie Mercer being murdered has just changed all that.'

Abigail tapped her bag. 'We need to get this back to the bank,' she said. 'Then we have to let Mr Shanks know we won't be needing the Prince's money after all, so he'll have to write to him again. And we should let Viscount Dillon know about this latest development.'

'You're right,' said Daniel. He turned to Feather. 'We'll do that and see you back here, then we'll head off to see Stanley Whetstone at Whitechapel. Is that all right with you?'

'Fine,' said Feather. 'It'll give me time to make a few notes about the pertinent things I want to ask Stanley.'

Daniel and Abigail said goodbye to Feather, then made for their bank, where they returned the seventy pounds in cash to Mr Benson and all three signed the forms certifying the loan had been repaid. They then returned to Marlborough House, where they told Michael Shanks that the money was no longer required.

'Why?' asked Shanks. 'What happened to change things?'

'The lady in question was murdered,' said Daniel. 'They cut her throat to stop her talking.'

'We're dealing with very dangerous people,' said Shanks. 'I trust you are taking steps to ensure your safety.'

'That's a very good point,' said Daniel as they left Marlborough House. 'What steps are we taking to ensure our safety?'

'Very long, fast ones at the first sign of danger,' said Abigail.

Their final port of call was on Viscount Dillon at the White Tower, where they brought him up to date.

'Another murder?' he said, shocked.

'I'm afraid so,' said Daniel.

'So that makes three,' said Dillon. 'Eric James. His brother, Paul. And now this woman.'

'The police are also investigating the murder of a Salvation Army captain in Whitechapel, although we don't feel that's related to these,' said Daniel.

'I should hope not!' said Dillon. 'It's bad enough as it is!' He looked anxiously at Daniel and Abigail. 'And you've still been able to keep all his private? No chance of it leaking to the general public, or the press? The Prince is desperate to ensure the reputation of the Tower is not tainted in any way.'

'So far it's been contained,' said Abigail. 'The deaths of Paul James and this woman, Ellie Mercer, didn't happen here, so there's no reason why anyone should associate them with the Tower.'

'Thank you,' said Dillon, obviously relieved. As he saw that Daniel and Abigail were rising, about to leave, he said awkwardly, 'Please, before you go, I have something else to ask you.' They sat down again and looked at him, curious. 'It's actually of you I need to ask a favour, Mrs Wilson.'

'Oh?' said Abigail.

'At this time we have a team of archaeologists carrying out an excavation on the northern boundary. You'll know that there is a section of the original Roman wall that surrounded London adjacent to Tower Hill Underground station. From calculations that have been done, it is conjectured that same wall may have extended into the Tower, and been built over when William the Conqueror began building the White Tower.'

'Yes, that's often been raised as a possibility,' said Abigail.

'The archaeologists are looking for signs of Roman relics. We've been fortunate that the Duke of Cranbrook has agreed to financially sponsor part of the dig to ensure it goes forward.'

Abigail frowned. 'I don't know him. Has he sponsored other archaeological digs before? I ask because, in discussions with other archaeologists, his name has never come up, and one of the things that is quite a feature of discussions between archaeologists is where the funding would be coming from.'

'Actually, the Duke is quite new to the world of archaeology,' said Dillon. 'He's a very wealthy man with many and varied interests. It seems that when he heard about this proposed dig here, he expressed an interest in providing a certain amount of financial backing for it.'

'That's very commendable,' said Abigail.

'The thing is, Mrs Wilson, I was approached by two of the archaeologists, female students who are involved in this work as part of their studies, and they came to say they had seen you walking around the Tower and they wondered if you were here in a professional capacity.' He grimaced as he said, 'I told them that you were but I didn't say what you were actually doing here, as you recall we'd agreed to keep things as secret if we could. Unfortunately, the two young ladies misinterpreted my remark to believe that you were here as an archaeologist. It turns out that both are great admirers of your work and have read many of the articles you have written about your time in Egypt and in Rome, as well as reading other articles about you.' He looked embarrassed as he asked, 'In short, Mrs Wilson, I wonder if you would do me – and them – the kindness of talking to them. They really are so enormously keen to meet you and talk to you.'

'Of course,' said Abigail. 'Anything I can do to encourage young women to follow in my path would be a great pleasure. Who's in charge of the dig?'

'Professor Stanford Clement from University College London. Although he's not here very often. He comes to inspect the work that's being done and to make notes of any finds that require his expertise.'

'I know Professor Clement. He's the ideal person to lead a dig on a Roman site. I worked with him a few years ago on a site on Hadrian's Wall.' She frowned and asked, 'Should we ask him out of courtesy if he has any objection to my being involved? After all, this is his dig.'

'Rest assured, that was the first thing I did when the students approached me. I wrote to Professor Clement and he replied almost immediately, saying that he would be delighted for you to talk to the students, and he looks forward to meeting you again if you are still here when he makes his next visit. I haven't told him why you are here, just that we have asked you to help us with some ancient records we need deciphered.'

Abigail laughed. 'As my particular area of expertise is ancient Egypt, I'm sure he'll be puzzled how ancient Egyptian hieroglyphics came to be discovered at the Tower of London.'

'We didn't specify the actual records we had asked you to look at.' said Dillon. He stood up. 'Perhaps you'd allow me to take you to the site by the north wall and introduce you.'

'In that case, while you involve yourself here, I suggest I accompany Inspector Feather to Whitechapel,' Daniel said.

'Are you sure you don't mind?' asked Abigail.

'It would be good for you to reacquaint yourself with your profession, and talk with aspiring young archaeologists,' said Daniel. 'I'll let you know how John and I get on at Whitechapel.'

CHAPTER TWELVE

Inspector Feather left Sergeant Cribbens with the task of finding out everything about Ellie Mercer – where she lived, who her friends were, every last detail – while he and Daniel made their way in a single-horse police carriage to Whitechapel and the main police station there.

'So Abigail's got herself involved with some archaeology students,' commented Feather.

'I'm pleased for her,' said Daniel. 'I know she likes the work we do, but her first love always has been archaeology. Luckily, this excavation is at the Tower, so she doesn't have to go gallivanting off to Egypt or somewhere equally far-flung.'

They parked outside Whitechapel police station and, leaving the driver with the horse and carriage, went inside. Sergeant Stanley Whetstone gave them a beam of welcome as he saw them.

'Well, this is an honour,' he said. 'Scotland Yard's very own Inspector Feather, and one of the famous Museum

Detectives. What brings you to these parts?'

'Local information,' said Feather. 'What do you know about Muscovy Court?'

Whetstone seemed to hesitate before answering, and when he did it was with some diffidence. 'I know where it is, but not much more than that. It's not on our patch. It comes under Fenchurch Street.'

'You might have heard about the dead body found there. Paul James, stabbed to death.'

Whetstone shrugged. 'Yes, I heard about it, but it's one for Fenchurch Street to sort out.'

'And do you think Fenchurch Street will?' asked Daniel.

Whetstone suddenly seemed uncomfortable. He looked at them and said awkwardly, 'It's not something I want to talk about.'

'Why not?' asked Feather. When Whetstone didn't reply, Feather said, 'Stanley, you, me and Daniel have known one another for years. We know you do the right thing here in Whitechapel, in what is a difficult place, and I've always admired you for that. The same *could* be said for Fenchurch Street, which has got a similar population, but lately things appear to be going wrong there.' He stopped and waited. Still Whetstone said nothing, just watched them warily.

'We've had Paul James killed in Muscovy Court, along with his brother, Eric, at the Tower of London two days afterwards,' said Feather.

Whetstone frowned. 'I knew Eric James. He was one of the Beefeaters. A good bloke. There's been nothing about him being killed in the paper.'

'There won't be,' said Feather. 'Orders from on high. Nothing to be put into the press, or even local talk. So, officially, you don't know about it.'

Whetstone looked at them, puzzled. 'What's going on? What's all this about?' He looked at Daniel. 'It's more than just police business if you're involved, Daniel.'

'Abigail and I have been hired by a private individual to investigate Eric James's murder. It seems to us to be connected to the murder of his brother, Paul, who, as John has just said, was stabbed to death outside the lodging house where he lived in Muscovy Court. His tongue was cut out.'

'A warning to others not to talk,' said Whetstone.

'Exactly,' said Feather. 'I was approached by Paul James's girlfriend, a woman called Ellie Mercer, who said she'd tell me who was behind it. But, before she could talk to me, someone killed her and also cut her tongue out. So what we're trying to find out is: who's got everyone in the Fenchurch Street patch so scared? What's going on there, Stanley? What's happened at Fenchurch Street nick that's made things this way?'

'It's not the nick,' said Whetstone. He hesitated, then added awkwardly, 'Although it hasn't helped.' He hesitated again, then nodded as he said reluctantly, 'Yes, the nick's part of it.'

'Part of what?' asked Daniel.

Whetstone came from behind his counter and walked to the door that led to the street. He looked out, then returned to them.

'If anyone comes in, I'm shutting up and we'll talk later,' he said.

'Fair enough,' said Feather, and Daniel nodded in agreement.

'About six months ago a new bloke appeared in the Fenchurch Street area. Harry Pickwick. I didn't know anything about him till recently. Apparently he moved here from Islington. He wasn't on our patch here so we had no need to look at him. We only really do that when someone causes trouble and it spills over into our area. It was after three months that we began to pick up gossip about what was happening over there. The station sergeant at Fenchurch Street, Charley Brown, and his deputy, Ernie Maddox, quit.'

'Did you know them?'

'Yes, on a casual basis, just to say hello to and swap information on the few occasions when we met.'

'Why did they quit?'

'Well, that's the thing. The word on the street was that their lives were being made hell by some of the locals. Locals who were on the payroll of this Harry Pickwick.'

'Payroll for what? Did Pickwick have a business?'

'Yes. He bought a rag-and-bone business. So he had these types collecting all manner of old junk, which he kept in his yard and sold. Though, by all accounts, he didn't seem to sell much. At the same time there seemed to be a lot of petty crime going on there. I mean, there's always been petty crime, but this started getting worse, and violent.'

'Couldn't you and your boys do anything about it?' asked Daniel.

'Come on, Daniel,' reprimanded Whetstone. 'You know how it works. Our demarcation line is Tower Hill. We look after the patch east of it; west of it comes under Fenchurch Street. So we just kept an eye on things and our eyes and ears open, but because Pickwick was careful to keep his operations out of Whitechapel, there wasn't much we could do. I warned our blokes to watch their step, which included staying away from the Fenchurch Street lot. Not getting involved with them. I didn't want the rot spreading here.'

'Are you saying the coppers at Fenchurch Street are on the take?' asked Feather.

'Not all of them,' said Whetstone. 'But the good ones gradually left, and the ones who replaced them were part of the whole business with Harry Pickwick.'

'What about the superintendent at Fenchurch Street?' asked Feather.

'Barney Potts. He took early retirement. Ill health. He hasn't been replaced.'

'Why?'

'Because, until this murder of Paul James, Fenchurch Street's patch has become very law-abiding. As far as the top brass are concerned, finding a new superintendent for it hasn't become a priority; it seems to run itself well enough.'

'Or, rather, Harry Pickwick does,' muttered Feather.

'Exactly,' said Whetstone. 'He runs it like his own little kingdom, with his thugs acting as his police force. Crime happens, but not on Fenchurch Street's patch. People know what will happen if they step out of line.'

'People like Paul James.'

'I made enquiries about that. After all, it's close to our patch. They're saying it was a domestic dispute that got out of hand. So, nothing to alarm the powers that be.'

'Where have you been getting your information from?' asked Feather.

'From a bloke called Bob Grillis. He was a sergeant at Fenchurch Street, one of the old-timers, and he hated what was going on. He came to me and told me, asked me if there wasn't something I could do.'

'Did he tell you what sort of thing were going on involving the local police?'

'Thefts, mainly. Bank raids. Burglaries. Mostly off Fenchurch Street's patch, though they made sure they stayed away from Whitechapel. I told Bob there wasn't a lot I could do. Fenchurch Street wasn't my patch, so if I attempted to report it I'd be shouted down for acting outside my authority. I said to Bob the only thing he could do was take it to a senior officer, but he said the senior officers at Fenchurch Street were in the pockets of Pickwick. So he decided to take it to the police commissioner himself.'

'And did he?'

Whetstone shook his head. 'He didn't get the chance. A week later he was dead. Accidental death, they said. He fell and struck his head on a kerb.'

'Was it ever investigated?'

'No need. A uniformed copper he was with at the time saw it happen. He said that Bob tripped and fell, banging his head on the ground.'

'Did you believe that?'

'No, and nor did anyone else. Especially Bob's daughter, Dorothy. She came to see me here because she knew her dad and I were good mates. She wanted his death investigated.' He gave them a rueful look as he added, 'I told her there was little I could do. For one thing it had happened off our patch. For another, a police officer had given a statement on what had happened.'

'What was the officer's name?'

'Josiah Grundy.'

'Is he still at Fenchurch Street?'

'No, it seems he came into some money – an inheritance, he said – and he opened a tobacconist's shop somewhere in the city.'

'I'm beginning to smell a rat already,' said Daniel.

'What about your own superintendent here at Whitechapel?' asked Feather. 'Bob Downey. What's he say about it?'

'The same as me,' said Whetstone. 'Nothing. If he says anything to the people at the top, it's just as likely it'll bounce back on him. We haven't got any evidence against Harry Pickwick, and we're not likely to; he's got everyone on his patch scared. And not just on his patch.'

'But surely, if you here in Whitechapel know what's going on, it'll be the same for the other forces adjacent to Fenchurch Street. Their patches must be being targeted by Pickwick's lot.'

'They are, but no one will give evidence against him. Too scared. And most of the victims are keeping quiet for the same reason.'

Daniel looked at Feather. 'We need to talk to Dorothy Grillis.' He turned to Whetstone. 'Where does she live?'

'14 Pepys Street, just down from Muscovy Court. It's the same house where her dad lived. He was a widower and Dorothy was his only child.' Whetstone gave them both a warning look. 'She might talk to you, Daniel, because you're not on the force any more.' To Feather, he said, 'But it could well be different with you, John. You're a serving officer. Dorothy blames the police for what happened to her dad. She said they covered up the truth. She's angry. She knows in her heart her dad was killed to stop him talking and the police were involved. As a result, she doesn't trust anyone in the police. Even me.'

As Daniel and Feather returned to their carriage, Daniel said, 'This puts a different aspect on everything. This bloke Harry Pickwick seems to have created the perfect little crime empire. Taking over the police station and putting his people in place gives him power over everyone. It means he can bump people off at will with no fear of being touched. Bob Grillis. Paul James. Ellie Mercer. And Lord knows how many other people.'

'I can do something straight away,' said Feather, his expression grim. 'I can take the murder of Paul James into the jurisdiction of Scotland Yard detective division. The same with the killing of Ellie Mercer. And I've already got the murder of Eric James on my list, which you and I are working together on. That ought to be enough to start to unravel Harry Pickwick's nasty scheme.'

'What are you going to do about Pickwick?' asked Daniel.

'I'm going to pass a message to him through the little

weasel he's got acting as duty sergeant at Fenchurch Street.' He gave a grim smile. 'I'm hoping that will kick the hornets' nest and make him do something silly.'

Daniel nodded. 'In the meantime, I'll go and collect Abigail and we'll go and see Dorothy Grillis. She might talk easier if there's a woman there.'

'Do you want a lift to the Tower?' asked Feather.

Daniel shook his head. 'It's just a short walk. Shall we meet back at the Yard after we've seen Miss Grillis and you've been to Fenchurch Street?'

'Yes,' said Feather. 'I'm heading back to the Yard first before I go and see slimy Sergeant Sims, mainly because I want to assign something to Sergeant Cribbens. You remember Stanley said that Pickwick had come to this area from Islington?'

'Yes.'

'Well, Sergeant Cribbens has got a cousin who's a sergeant at Islington nick. I'm going to send him there to see what he can find out about what Pickwick was up to before he moved to this area.'

'You're going to nail Pickwick, aren't you?' Daniel grinned.

'You bet your boots I am,' said Feather determinedly.

Daniel found Abigail at the north wall that surrounded the Tower, across the road from Tower Hill Underground station. She was standing in a partly dug trench talking with two young women, both of whom held small trowels in their hands. Beside them were buckets, some containing soil, others with small objects in them.

'Am I interrupting anything?' called Daniel.

'Nothing serious,' said Abigail. 'Come and join us.'

Daniel descended the wooden ladder and joined them in the trench, where Abigail did the introductions. 'Daniel, meet Sophie Connor and Alice Potts-Weedon. Sophie and Alice, this is my husband, Daniel Wilson.'

The two young women smiled in greeting and held out their hands to shake his.

'This is so exciting for us, to actually meet the great Abigail Fenton—' began Sophie, before Alice interrupted her.

'She's Abigail Wilson now.'

Sophie's hand flew to her mouth in embarrassment. 'Of course. I'm so sorry.'

'No need to be,' said Daniel. 'She was famous with her own name long before we married.'

'The girls are conducting a dig to see how far the original Roman London wall intruded into what became the Tower of London.'

'We're looking at the foundations of the north wall to see if any parts of it are made of ragstone,' explained Alice. 'The Roman wall was built of ragstone and the Normans were great ones for using stones that were near to hand when building anything. It meant they could build faster, and speed was vital in the early days of the Roman occupation, especially when building military fortifications.'

'Although the rebellion by the British had virtually ended with the destruction of Boudicca and her rebel army, the Romans were still prone to attacks by marauding bands of Britons,' added Sophie.

'Have you found any ragstone here?' asked Daniel.

'Some,' said Alice. 'But we're still not sure if it's an extension of the surviving section of the wall that's at Tower Hill, or if it's separate.'

'What we have found are some interesting objects that seem to be Norman. Coins, decorative brooches, that sort of thing.'

'Fascinating,' said Daniel. Then, in an apologetic tone, he said, 'Actually, I hate to do this but my reason for coming is because Mrs Wilson and I have to go and see someone.'

'To do with the dig?' asked Alice.

'No,' said Daniel. 'But it is important we go.'

'Of course,' said Abigail. 'But I shall return,' she told the two young women.

As they walked away from the trench, she asked, 'Who are we going to see?'

'A young woman called Dorothy Grillis. She's the daughter of a police sergeant who was killed in the Fenchurch Street area a few months ago.'

'How was he killed?'

'According to the police constable who was with him, he fell and hit his head on a kerb. But there is some doubt as to what happened. His daughter certainly doesn't believe that. She believes the constable killed her father.'

She looked at him, shocked. 'Why would he have done that?'

Daniel told her what he and Feather had learnt from Stanley Whetstone about Harry Pickwick and the corruption of the police at Fenchurch Street police station.

'The thing is, as a result, Miss Grillis has no faith in the police. Not even officers like John Feather or Stanley Whetstone. So we've been detailed to talk to her and find out what she can tell us about what's going on at Fenchurch Street. It looks as if it may hold part of the answer to the murders of Eric and Paul James, and Ellie Mercer.'

'That's horrible, if it's true,' said Abigail.

'There's always been suggestions of corruption and bribery among some officers, but it's usually beat coppers turning a blind eye in exchange for a few shillings. This sounds like it's at a whole different level.'

'What does John Feather say?'

'He's conducting his own investigation. He's going to confront the alleged corrupt sergeant at the police station and put the fear of God into him and see if it flushes him out. The problem is that everyone's so scared, no one will talk, so it's hard to get concrete evidence against them. Hence our visit to Miss Grillis.' His tone changed to a more genial one as he said, 'By the way, it was good to see you in that trench today with your two young fans.'

'Yes, they're both good girls,' said Abigail. 'Bright and keen. Not afraid to get down and messy.'

'Where are they from? They didn't sound particularly local.'

'They're both studying in Cambridge.'

'Your old university? Girton?'

'No, Newnham College.'

'So, universities for women are increasing?'

'Alas, no. The number of colleges may be, but most

women are still not accepted by the universities. Women who study at both Oxford and Cambridge are still not granted degrees, even though we sit exams of the same level of academic rigour. London is ahead on that. In 1880, four women were actually granted Bachelor of Arts degrees by the University of London, but nearly twenty years later, neither Oxford nor Cambridge will consider it. Instead, we sit an exam and, if we pass, we receive a certificate. We sit what is claimed to be the equivalent of a Tripos. There are two different sorts of Tripos, the Classical and the Mathematical. I did the Classical. Do you know that in 1890, a woman student at Newnham scored higher in the Mathematical Tripos than the Senior Wrangler, the top male student at Cambridge in the same subject. He got a degree; she didn't.'

'You sound angry.'

'Well, wouldn't you be? Yes, we have come some way from the days when women weren't even allowed to attend lectures, but the establishment still refuses to recognise that women are capable of being the equal of men when it comes to study, whatever the topic.'

'But you've achieved an international reputation and fame.'

'But I still don't have a degree.' She gave a groan. 'I'm sorry, Daniel. Usually I can ignore it, but talking to those two today, to Alice and Sophie, I felt enraged on their behalf. Yes, some men in the different professions, the ones with real brains and intellect, recognise the work that women do in those professions as their equal, and in many cases superior to men's. But unfortunately that doesn't extend to the men in charge of the establishments.'

'Except the University of London,' pointed out Daniel. 'It has to start somewhere. Perhaps the others will be forced to catch up.'

CHAPTER THIRTEEN

Sergeant Cribbens was in the office when Feather got back to Scotland Yard, and Feather was pleased to see his sergeant had carried out his enquiries into Ellie Mercer with sterling results.

'I've got the address of where she was living, which was a lodging house in Cooper's Row, not far from Muscovy Court. I spoke to some of the others who lived there, but they said they didn't have much to do with her. I thought I'd go back there and ask around some more, find out if she had any family. The people I spoke to suggested she worked as a prostitute, operating from Fenchurch Street railway station, so I thought I'd talk to some of the station staff and the beat officers who patrol that area.'

Feather shook his head.

'Forget the police officers in that area,' he said. He then told him what he'd learnt about Harry Pickwick and the Fenchurch Street police force as Cribbens looked at him in horror.

'They're crooked?' he said, uncomprehending. 'The whole lot of them are crooked?'

'Maybe not all of them, but enough, especially the key figures at the top.'

'We can't let this happen!' said the shocked sergeant. 'What are we going to do about it?'

'I'm going back to Fenchurch Street to put the fear of God into their crooked station sergeant. What I want you to do is go to Islington.'

'Islington?' Cribbens frowned, puzzled.

'You've got a cousin who works out of Islington, haven't you?'

Cribbens nodded. 'Derek. He's a uniformed sergeant. Good bloke'

'Islington is where Harry Pickwick was before he came to Fenchurch Street. I'd like nothing better than to bring this Pickwick character in and grill him. The problem is we've got nothing concrete to pin him with anything criminal, just rumours from Whitechapel. Whitechapel can't move on him because Pickwick's place comes under Fenchurch Street, and they've been protecting him. What we need is evidence so we can pick Pickwick up. What sort of things is Pickwick up to? We'll get a good idea if we find out what he was up to when he was in Islington. And did it involve killing people? So, I'd like you to go to Islington and see what your cousin Derek knows about Pickwick and his activities when he was there. But don't tell Derek about the dead Beefeater at the Tower. That's still officially to be kept secret.'

* * *

Daniel and Abigail knocked at the door of the small, neat terraced house in Pepys Street. It was opened by a short, plump blonde woman in her early twenties who looked at them suspiciously.

'Good day,' said Abigail. 'Are we addressing Miss Dorothy Grillis?'

'You might be,' said the young woman warily.

'I'm Abigail Wilson and this is my husband, Daniel Wilson. We're calling as part of an investigation we've been asked to undertake.'

'An investigation?' repeated Dorothy, puzzled. She studied the pair, then her face cleared. 'I know who you are,' she said. 'I've read about you in the papers. They call you the Museum Detectives.'

'They do,' said Abigail with a rueful smile.

'So why are you here?' she asked suspiciously. 'There's no big famous museums around here.'

'There is,' said Abigail. 'The Tower of London is the oldest museum in England.'

Dorothy frowned, puzzled. 'The Tower? What's gone on there, then?'

'I'm afraid we're not allowed to say,' said Abigail. 'At the moment, because the Tower is Crown property, it's what you might call an official secret. The thing is, so far our enquiries have raised questions about policing locally, in particular about Fenchurch Street station.'

'Ha!' She gave a snort of angry derision. 'Don't talk to me about that bunch of bastards! They murdered my dad!'

'Yes, that's one of the things we want to look into.'

She looked at them suspiciously. 'You're not with the police?' she asked.

'No,' lied Daniel. He gave a rueful chuckle. 'In truth, Scotland Yard don't approve of us. They've tried to get us kicked off nearly every case we've been on.'

'In that case, you'd better come in.'

They followed her into the small front room, in which the dark wood furniture gleamed with polish and the cloths that covered the armchairs smelt of being recently laundered. She offered them tea, but they politely declined.

'We don't want to take up any more of your time than we have to,' explained Daniel. 'We've come to see you because we understand that your father, who was a sergeant at Fenchurch Street, died recently, and there's a suggestion that another police officer might have been involved. Is that what you meant when you said they'd murdered your dad?'

'It was,' she said, her face grim and angry. 'But what's that got to do with whatever's happened at the Tower of London?'

'Information we've received has linked what's going on there to concerns about Fenchurch Street.'

'Concerns!' she exploded. 'No one's shown any *concern* about what's going on at Fenchurch Street, even though everyone on the streets knows what's happening.'

'And what is happening?' asked Abigail.

'The bloke behind it is a villain called Harry Pickwick,' said Dorothy. 'He lives in the area and the local police are in his pay. To keep everything sweet, Pickwick's gang do most of their stuff outside Fenchurch Street station's patch.'

'What sort of stuff?'

'Robberies, mostly. Then they come back here where they can't be touched.'

'The stations in those other areas must know what's going on,' said Daniel. 'It was Stanley Whetstone at Whitechapel who gave us the nod about getting in touch with you.'

She nodded. 'I used to think Stanley was straight until I went to see him.'

'He is,' said Daniel. 'I've known him for years.'

Dorothy looked at him warily. 'I remember now. It was in the paper. Daniel Wilson. You were on the force with Abberline doing the Ripper inquiry in Whitechapel.'

'That was when I was on the force,' said Daniel. 'I left eight years ago. But I know that Stanley Whetstone's straight. The problem is there's an unwritten law in the police. They don't grass one another up.'

'That's what my dad said, but he'd decided to do just that because he was so sick of what was going on. That's why they killed him.'

'Josiah Grundy?' asked Daniel.

'So you've heard?'

Daniel nodded. 'Stanley Whetstone told me. He also told me Grundy had left the police and taken a tobacconist shop. Do you know where his shop is?'

'It's in Poultry, at the Mansion House end, near to the Bank of England.'

'You've been there?'

She nodded. 'I wanted him to see me and know that I was keeping an eye on him. I thought it might rattle him.'

'Did it?'

She shook her head sadly. 'No. At least, it didn't seem to.'

'Why didn't they kill you?' asked Abigail. 'Daniel got the impression from Stanley Whetstone that you wanted Grundy brought to justice. Your going to see him at his shop must have been part of that.'

'It was, and I still do want justice for what he did.'

'But they've left you alone. Even though you're still living on their patch.'

Dorothy gave a laugh of derision. 'That's deliberate. They let me live because I'm an example of what happens to anyone in this area who causes trouble for them. People around here see me and they say, "That's the woman whose dad was a copper who tried to sort them out, and he was killed. And no one did anything. If they can do that to a copper, they can do whatever they like."'

John Feather walked into Fenchurch Street police station and found Sergeant Wesley Sims on duty, just as he had been on Feather's previous visit.

'Back again?' Sims greeted him with a smile. 'What can we do for the gentleman from Scotland Yard?'

'We're still looking into the murder of Paul James,' said Feather.

'Ah well, we've got a bit of information that might help to put that one to bed,' said Sims. 'It seems that Mr James was very friendly with a woman called Ellie Mercer. Not a very nice woman, by all accounts. A prostitute and a drinker, she was said to have a fierce temper on her. The word is that James upset her in some way and it was she who killed him in a fit of rage, possibly after she'd drunk too much.'

'Where did you hear that?' asked Feather.

'From asking around,' said Sims. 'We take our job here very seriously, you know. One of our blokes spoke to a friend of Mercer's and she told him that Ellie Mercer spilt it all to her one night while she was drunk, about how him and her had a fight in the street outside the house where he lived, and she pulled out a knife and stabbed him. Then we heard that Mercer was found dead not far from your place, Scotland Yard, with her throat cut. So, the way we see it, Mercer kills Paul James and gets guilty about it and decides to hand herself in to your lot. But on the way everything gets on top of her. She can't stand it any more, so she tops herself. Cuts her own throat.' He shrugged. 'Tragic, but that's the way things are with some people.'

Feather looked at him quizzically. 'Why did she cut her own tongue out before she slit her throat?' he asked.

Sims frowned, puzzled. 'Cut her tongue out?'

'Yes,' said Feather. 'When I saw her body, her tongue had been cut out.'

'That would be the medical people,' said Sims. 'They do that sort of thing when's someone's murdered; they cut 'em open to see what happened to them.'

Feather shook his head. 'I saw her before the medical people had had a chance to start work on her. Her tongue had been cut out. I can't imagine she'd have done it herself. My sergeant and I also examined the place where her body was found. There was no trace of her tongue.'

Sims let this sink in, then he offered: 'Some dog must have run off with it.'

'A dog?'

'Or a rat. Lots of scavenging animals roam around London. We get them here.'

Feather studied him, then asked, 'Did Ellie say to her friend why she'd cut Paul James's tongue out after she stabbed him?'

Sims frowned warily, then said, 'Who knows why people do that sort of thing?'

'A bit of a coincidence, don't you think?' asked Feather. 'Paul James is stabbed to death and his tongue is cut out. Which is a well-known message among the underworld warning people to keep quiet. Then Ellie Mercer's throat is cut and her tongue is cut out, too, just as she's about to make a visit to Scotland Yard.'

'You don't know she was going to Scotland Yard,' said Sims.

'Yes, I do,' said Feather. 'She had arranged to meet me there. It sounds to me like someone had found out about it and wanted to stop her talking to me. And then cut her tongue out as a warning to others what would happen if they said anything.' He gave the sergeant a hard look as he asked, 'Do you have the name of this friend of Ellie Mercer's, and where we can get hold them?'

Sims looked uncomfortable. 'No,' he said. 'We never got that information.'

'In that case it's lucky that Scotland Yard are in charge of investigating her murder, and that of Paul James, and not you,' said Feather.

'The murder of Paul James is ours,' said Sims defiantly. 'It happened on our patch. Fenchurch Street have got the investigation.'

'Not any more,' said Feather. 'Scotland Yard are taking over.'

'On what grounds?' demanded Sims.

'On the grounds that it's connected to at least two other murders. So you can expect a number of outside constables and other officers coming into your patch and doing some nosing around.' He looked enquiringly at Sims. 'One thing – during our initial enquiries, the name of Harry Pickwick came up. Do you know him?'

Sims hesitated, then said, 'Yes. Why did his name come up? Mr Pickwick's a respected local businessman.'

'Who runs a rag-and-bone business.' Feather nodded. 'Yes, we know. There's a suggestion he was upset because Sergeant Bob Grillis, who used to be based here, thought he was guilty of criminal activities and ought to be investigated. But Grillis died before he could lodge a formal complaint.'

'Bob Grillis died when he fell and banged his head on a kerb,' said Sims. 'We had a reliable witness who saw it happen.'

'Former constable Josiah Grundy,' said Feather. 'Currently running a tobacconist's, bought after he came into money following the unfortunate death of Bob Grillis.'

Sims scowled at the Scotland Yard detective. 'I won't have this sort of allegation against our people,' he said angrily. 'This is all coming from that mad daughter of Grillis's, Dorothy. I don't care what she's told you . . .'

'She hasn't told us anything,' said Feather calmly. 'We haven't even talked to her. But we will. Thanks for the tip, Sergeant.' He doffed his hat. 'I'll be back with some more officers to continue our enquiries.'

CHAPTER FOURTEEN

Sergeant Cribbens sat with his cousin Derek in the canteen at Islington police station, both men puffing on their pipes as they sipped at mugs of strong sweet tea.

'Harry Pickwick,' said Derek thoughtfully.

'That's the one,' said Cribbens. 'My boss wants to know what he was like when he was here in Islington.'

'A nasty piece of work,' said Derek. 'In the end he had to leave the area because he crossed some very dangerous people. You know the Pullman brothers?'

'Everyone knows the Pullman brothers,' said Cribbens.

'Well, he robbed a place he didn't know they owned. They gave him a choice. To get out of the area with a finger missing, or stay and have both his arms cut off.'

'A finger missing?'

'They said it was the price he had to pay, and that way every time he looked at his hand it would remind him of what would happen to him if he stepped out of line again. They reminded him that they had fingers in lots of pies in different parts of London, and this would be one more finger. It was like a joke on their part.'

'Which finger did they take?'

'The little finger of his left hand. The pinkie.'

'What sort of things did Pickwick get up to while he was here, before he left?'

'Thefts. Robberies.'

'Did he ever serve jail time for them?'

'No. He paid a couple of thugs to take care of his interests. If there was ever a witness who was prepared to give evidence against him, he sent his thugs round to give them a warning.'

'What happened to these thugs?'

'They disappeared along with Pickwick. The word was they went to wherever he did.'

'Do you know where he went?'

Derek shook his head. 'No. And we didn't ask around. As far as we were concerned, it was good riddance to bad rubbish.'

'He moved to the Tower of London area. These thugs of his, did they ever kill anyone while he was here?'

'No. Leastways, not as far as I know. Leaning on people was about as far as it went. But they were a nasty pair. Josh Kent and Nipper Sedgewick.'

'What about Pickwick? Did he kill anyone?'

Again, Derek shook his head. 'Not that I know of. If he did, it never came to our ears. But I don't think so. If you ask me, he was too scared of being hanged.'

* * *

Daniel and Abigail had come to Scotland Yard to tell Inspector Feather what they'd learnt from Dorothy Grillis, and at the same time to find out how he'd got on with his enquiries. Feather told them about his meeting with Sergeant Sims. 'I think I left him rattled at the idea of flooding his patch with coppers from outside who'd be digging into everything. I'm hoping it will push him into doing something that will give us a chance to kick him and his nest of vipers out so we can replace them with good officers.' He gave a rueful sigh as he added, 'The trouble is, as you know well, Daniel, it's not easy to root out that kind of corruption when it's so deep-rooted. But we'll do it.'

'What about Josiah Grundy?' asked Abigail. 'Are you going to bring him in for questioning?'

Feather shook his head. 'It's going to be difficult to do that before we get the rot at Fenchurch Street station sorted out. At the moment, the serving station sergeant says it was an accident. Before we can go for Grundy, we need to get Sergeant Sims. I'm pretty sure he'll do a deal when he's aware of the spot he's in and spill the beans, and then we can round up Grundy and Pickwick. I've also sent Sergeant Cribbens to Islington police station to dig out as much as he can about what Pickwick was up to when he was there, and why he decided to up sticks and move to the Fenchurch Street patch.'

'Would you mind if we had a word with Grundy?' asked Daniel.

Feather looked at them, puzzled. 'How does he fit in with your case? The murdered Beefeater?'

'We're not sure,' said Daniel. 'It's just that there are so many points where these cases seem to interconnect. Eric and

Paul James. Ellie Mercer. The rot at Fenchurch Street. Harry Pickwick. Bob Grillis. Even your dead Salvation Army captain.'

'I suppose we're looking for the weak link that might open all the others up,' added Abigail. 'We haven't had much luck at the Tower so far, so we thought we'd put Grundy under pressure. He was a policeman in the local area, and one who was prepared to kill another more senior police officer if Dorothy's story is true. Is he part of the gang that killed both Eric and Paul James because of something that they're planning at the Tower, maybe in the pay of this Harry Pickwick?'

'It all sounds a bit tenuous,' pointed out Feather doubtfully.

'I agree it's clutching at straws, but we need to find an opening somewhere,' said Daniel.

Feather nodded. 'Be my guest,' he said. 'Go and talk to Grundy. And if you do find anything that might help us to build a case against him, let me know.'

'We will,' said Abigail as she and Daniel got to their feet. 'And you'll keep us informed with anything you find?'

'Of course,' said Feather. 'I think the main thing now is to find out who our potentially helpful witnesses are, and keep them alive.'

Harry Pickwick sat at his desk in the office of his rag-and-bone yard and stared in a mixture of astonishment and outrage at Wesley Sims, who stood apprehensively on the other side of the large desk, having just delivered the news about his encounter with Inspector Feather.

'Scotland Yard are moving in?' Pickwick echoed.

Sims nodded. 'They're looking into the murders of Paul

James and Ellie Mercer, and also the death of Bob Grillis.'

'Bob Grillis was an accident,' said Pickwick.

'Well, I got the impression they didn't believe it. The way the inspector was talking, I think they're going to talk to Josiah Grundy.'

Pickwick sat, stunned, taking this all in. Then he stood up suddenly and leant across the desk, his face suffused with anger, and he shouted at Sims, 'What do I pay you for? You're supposed to keep me safe from the law poking around.'

'It's not my fault,' protested Sims. 'This is all because your blokes did Paul James and Ellie Mercer.'

'My blokes never touched them!' snarled Pickwick.

Sims looked at him, bewildered. 'But you were the one who said to tell anyone who was nosing around that Ellie killed James and then topped herself.'

'That was to stop anyone digging into it, because if they did they might find out what *we've* been up to,' raged Pickwick, 'Trust me, my blokes never killed anyone. *I've* never killed anyone. I know where to draw the line. No one's putting my head into a noose.'

CHAPTER FIFTEEN

Feather listened as Sergeant Cribbens related what he'd learnt about Harry Pickwick from his cousin at Islington.

'But not a killer?' he asked, surprised.

'Not according to Derek. But that doesn't mean these two thugs of his, Josh Kent and Nipper Sedgewick, would be averse to it.'

'We need to find out who Pickwick's working with,' said Feather thoughtfully. 'If he's taking a share of the loot from burglaries and robberies and suchlike and we can find out who are doing the jobs, we can lean on them. One of them's bound to give up information about Pickwick's involvement.' He looked at Cribbens and announced, 'I'm going to get some of our plain-clothes men and get them to watch Pickwick's yard. See who goes to see him. We'll draft in a couple of men from Whitechapel to accompany them; they're more likely to recognise which ones are known villains.'

'Fenchurch Street won't like that,' observed Cribbens. 'Whitechapel men on their patch.'

'Temporarily attached to the Scotland Yard detective division.' Feather smiled. 'What are they going to do, complain about it? Who to? Scotland Yard?' He chuckled.

'They'll warn Pickwick he's being watched,' said Cribbens.

'Good,' said Feather. 'That'll unnerve Pickwick, put him on edge. And a man on edge usually makes mistakes. And it'll please Stanley Whetstone to know that something's being done. I was thinking of having another word with Stanley anyway, because it struck me that with all this stuff about Paul and Eric James, and Ellie Mercer, we've lost track of the first murder we were supposed to be looking into: Captain Edward Merchant, the Salvation Army man.'

'I was wondering if it wasn't connected to the others,' said Cribbens thoughtfully. 'Remember, we found that Salvation Army bible in Paul James's room. It was Eric who took Paul to that Salvation Army meeting. The Salvation Army keeps popping up every time we start digging.'

Feather nodded. 'Yes, Daniel and Abigail expressed the same thought about all the cases being connected. We need to talk to someone in the Salvation Army, see if there is any connection between Merchant and the Jameses. Merchant was killed outside the Blind Beggar pub. What was he doing there?'

'Selling *The War Cry*, I expect. That's what these Salvation Army types are usually doing outside a pub.'

'If that was the case, you'd have expected to find copies of the magazine lying around, but there were none when we got there.'

123

'The local beat copper was there before us. Maybe he picked them up.'

Feather shook his head. 'Leave the crime scene exactly as you find it – that's one of the first things they're taught. Especially if it's a suspected murder. Maybe he wasn't selling *The War Cry*. Maybe he was doing a bit of open-air preaching. After all, the Blind Beggar is where the Salvation Army started, with General Booth preaching there on the pavement.'

'But there were no reports of him doing any preaching,' countered Cribbens. 'In fact, there were no reports of anyone seeing him there outside the Blind Beggar before he was found dead. We asked around everyone in the area, the people inside the pub, the nearby shops, and no one said they saw him there.'

'It *is* Whitechapel,' Feather reminded him. 'No one sees anything; no one hears anything. That's nearly always the case right after anything happens.'

'But it's been a few days now since it happened,' pointed out Cribbens. 'People sometimes talk a bit easier after a while. Usually by then they've found out what's gone on, and they realise they might be safe.'

'Yes, that's good thinking,' said Feather. 'I think now is a good time to go and see Stanley Whetstone about it, get his thoughts. Get him to put some of his men asking questions. After all, they're local; they know who to lean on and the best way to do it.' He got up. 'Come on, Sergeant, let's get ourselves to Whitechapel.'

Daniel and Abigail caught the Underground train to Bank station. The train was too noisy for them to be able to have a conversation, and anyway what they wanted to talk about was hardly fit to talk about where other members of the public would be listening, so they waited until they were mounting the stairs to the street.

'How are we going to tackle this?' asked Abigail. 'A direct confrontation and accusation and see how he reacts?'

'I doubt if that will work,' said Daniel. 'It doesn't seem to have had when Dorothy Grillis tried it. I thought we'd tell him we were acting on behalf of an insurance company who'd had a death claim against his insurance. They wanted to know the exact details of his death and needed a sworn written statement from the witness to the alleged accident.'

'Alleged?' asked Abigail.

'That's what the insurance company said, as there are discrepancies in the nature of his injuries that are not consistent with an accident.'

Abigail looked doubtful. 'I have my doubts that Bob Grillis had any death insurance.'

'But Josiah Grundy doesn't know that. If he raises that, we tell him that he took out the insurance as protection for his only daughter.'

'Yes.' Abigail nodded. 'That should work.'

They walked into Poultry and saw the shop with a sign saying *J. Grundy, Tobacconist* above it. However, as they neared it they saw the shop window was empty of any display, and when they reached the shop they saw that the premises were completely empty. A sign had been fixed to the door which said, *Shop to Let*. The name of the letting agents, Fishcock and Purse, was underneath, with an address in Cheapside.

'Well, at least they're not far away,' said Daniel.

They carried on walking along Poultry, then continued along the road when it changed its name to Cheapside, and came to the office of Fishcock and Purse, which was in a narrow building that housed companies of different sorts, mostly insurance companies. Fishcock and Purse were on the top floor.

The office was small and crowded with papers, some tied in scrolls, others on desks. A young man in his twenties, wearing a dark suit, that had worn and frayed cuffs and patches at the elbows, looked up at them from his paper-strewn desk as they entered.

'Yes?' he asked. 'Can I help you?'

'We're calling about the tobacconist shop in Poultry, vacated by Josiah Grundy,' said Daniel.

The young man gestured for them to take the two chairs opposite his desk.

'A very valuable property,' he said. 'In a wonderful position close to the Bank of England. Lots of passing trade. Are you intending to use it as a tobacconist?'

'No,' said Daniel. 'We are private inquiry agents and we are keen to track down Mr Grundy.'

The young man gave a short a derisive laugh. 'You and half of London.'

'Other people are looking for him?'

'All sorts,' said the young man. 'Respectable types. Rough types.' He looked at Daniel and Abigail warily and asked, 'What's your interest in him?'

'Our client wishes to talk to him,' said Abigail.

'What about?'

126

'That is a private matter between our client and Mr Grundy.'

The young man shrugged. 'Suit yourself. I'll tell you the same as I told all the others. I don't know where he is. He left no forwarding address. He came in a few days ago and handed the keys in, and said he'd decided to move on. He owed for another week on the lease, so he paid that. And that was that.'

'Can we look inside the shop?' asked Daniel. 'There may be clues as to where he's gone.'

The young man shook his head. 'Sorry,' he said, 'the owner won't allow unaccompanied people in. He's had stuff go missing before.'

'We'd be very happy for you to accompany us if that would allay the owner's fears.'

Again, the young man shook his head. 'I can't do it today.' He gestured at the papers that covered his desk. 'I've got to get this lot cleared. I might be able to do it tomorrow. Mr Purkiss will be in tomorrow and I could do it while he looks after things here at the office.' He looked at them slyly as he added, 'Of course, there'll be a fee.'

'How much?' asked Daniel.

'Five shillings,' said the young man.

'For taking us to look at an empty shop? Do you charge that to prospective tenants who want to inspect it?'

'No, but that's because they're thinking of taking it on. You ain't.'

'Very well,' said Daniel. 'We'll return tomorrow.'

'With the five shillings!' called the young man as they made for the door.

'Five shillings,' grumbled Daniel in outrage as they made

127

their way down the stairs. 'It's criminal.'

'I think you'll find it's business,' said Abigail sagely.

'Well, I've got another thought about it,' said Daniel. 'We mention to John Feather that it needs inspection, and suggest he turns up with a warrant. That way the shop gets opened to us for free.'

'Us?' queried Abigail.

'When John turns up to inspect the shop, he'll find us waiting there, and he'll invite us in.'

'That won't endear us to that young man.'

'I'm not aiming to endear him to us,' said Daniel. 'Anyway, he won't be there.'

'Yes, he will.'

'Not if we can get John to do it today. After all, he's told us he can't leave the office today. And John has the power to demand the keys from him.'

'You can be quite petty and mean,' said Abigail. 'All to save five shillings.'

'No, to gain a day. The sooner we can get in there, the better. Today is better than tomorrow.'

'How did you get on at Fenchurch Street?' was the first question Whetstone asked as Inspector Feather and Sergeant Cribbens appeared in the reception area at Whitechapel station.

'I told Sergeant Sims that we at Scotland Yard are taking over the investigations into the murders of Paul James and Ellie Mercer, and we'd also be looking into the death of Sergeant Grillis.'

'How did he react to that?' asked Whetstone.

'He wasn't happy. He got even unhappier when I started asking questions about Harry Pickwick.'

'Good,' said Whetstone. 'Maybe things will change. If things do and they need some good people in there, there's a lad in our lot who I think is ready for promotion. Barney Brick. He'd make a good sergeant. And he lives local, just this side of Tower Hill.'

'I'll mention it,' said Feather. 'To a great extent it depends on what we uncover about Bob Grillis, Paul James and Ellie Mercer. I've told Sims we're putting in officers from outside his patch to carry out investigations, so maybe that'll be a good opportunity for this lad of yours.'

'I'll have a word with him,' said Whetstone. Hastily, he added, 'Not about any talk of promotion, but investigating Fenchurch Street. I know he'll be up for it. None of us here like what's been going on over there. It taints us all.'

'It does,' agreed Feather, 'and with a bit of luck we'll put an end to it.' He outlined his idea to put plain-clothes men watching Harry Pickwick's yard. 'If we can use some of your men to go with them, they'll be able to identify any known villains, and we can haul them in for questioning. Get some evidence again Pickwick.'

Whetstone nodded. 'Barney Brick, for one, will be perfect. And there's another couple of lads who'd like to get involved.'

'Good,' said Feather. 'The other reason we've come is about Edward Merchant.'

'The Sally Ann captain?'

'We were thinking – well, my sergeant was thinking, so the credit goes to him – that time enough has elapsed that we could start digging. Asking questions. Who had Captain Merchant upset recently? What was he doing at the Blind Beggar? Did anyone see him with anyone before he died? What do we know about him? Was he married? Did he have family?'

'The Sally Ann will be the best people to tell you about him,' said Whetstone.

'Yes, I was thinking the same,' said Feather. 'If me and my sergeant talk to the Salvation Army, can you get your blokes asking questions of people who might have been near the Blind Beggar when Merchant was killed? Or anyone who knew Merchant?'

'Leave it to me,' said Whetstone.

CHAPTER SIXTEEN

Harry Pickwick stood in his yard looking at the heaps of old bones, rags and scrap metal piled up around it. Everything here was the perfect cover for what he'd had planned. People brought the stuff in, for which they were paid pennies. All cash trade, so there was no paperwork to bother about. The bones, Harry sold to a company that ground them up for fertiliser; the rags went to another company that employed women working at home to take them apart and turn the waste back into balls of wool from which new clothes were made. The metal went to a foundry, where it was melted down and turned into ingots of differing grades. It was all proof for any nosy parkers that everything Harry got from this trade was all open and honest, and that's where his money came from.

The truth, of course, was different. When his departure from Islington was forced on him by the Pullman brothers – a traumatic memory that was brought back to Harry every time he looked at his left hand and the tiny stump where his little finger should have been – Harry had come to this godforsaken spot, along with his two trusted henchmen, Josh Kent and Nipper Sedgewick. Luckily, he still had enough cash from his time in Islington to be able to rent the yard and the office building, and also to invest in finding new people. Burglars, mostly, and break-in specialists. His master stroke had been finding out that some of the coppers at Fenchurch Street nick were on the take, ready to turn a blind eye to what went on in exchange for some ready cash. Some of them were painfully honest and, as the blind eyes to localised crime became more and more obvious, those honest ones talked about putting in a complaint to the police commissioner. A series of visits by Josh and Nipper to the houses of those coppers who expressed such thoughts brought home to them the danger of making such a complaint. Where words didn't have the required effect, the threats to the copper's family usually did the trick, especially if accompanied by a bit of a beating. Who could the coppers complain to? The other coppers at the station, more and more of whom were either involved or had decided it was too risky to take sides.

Harry had felt very satisfied. It was like having his own private army. Everything was safe and secure. Until Sergeant Sims had turned up with his disastrous news. Scotland Yard poking their noses in! Something had gone wrong, and Harry wanted to know what, whose fault it was and how to recover the situation.

He saw Josh Kent and Nipper Sedgewick come through the gate into his yard and gestured for them to join him, then walked into his office.

'Here we are, H,' said Kent. 'We got your note. What's up?'

'We got trouble,' said Pickwick. 'What do you know about this woman who had her throat cut near Scotland Yard?'

Kent and Sedgewick looked at him, bewildered. 'Who?'

'Ellie Mercer. She lived in this patch.'

'I don't know what you're talking about,' said Kent.

'Nor me,' said Sedgewick.

Pickwick studied them. 'So you didn't do it?'

'Of course we didn't do it!' exploded Kent angrily. 'What do you think we are?'

'You're my muscle,' said Pickwick pointedly.

'Yeah, your *muscle*,' said Kent, thumping the top of the desk to emphasise the word. 'We warn people off. Maybe we might give 'em a bit of a punch now and then, if we think they need it. But that's as far as it goes.'

'So, you didn't have anything to do with this woman getting killed?'

'No, we just told you.'

'And what about the bloke who was stabbed at Muscovy Court?'

'What bloke?'

'Paul James.'

Again, Kent and Sedgewick looked at one another, uncomprehending, then they turned back to Pickwick.

'Nothing to do with us,' said Kent.

'Where are you getting this stuff from?' demanded Sedgewick angrily. 'Accusing us of topping people?'

'Because I've been told the police think I was behind both of 'em. They've got something from someone, and they think it was my blokes who done 'em. And, since you're my blokes—'

'We're your muscle,' Kent interrupted sharply. 'That's all we are. We never killed nobody.'

'Well, someone's putting me in the frame for it. You're my muscle, so find out who it is who's doing it to me.'

Daniel and Abigail left Scotland Yard, Daniel with a feeling of frustration. Neither John Feather nor Jeremiah Cribbens had been in the building.

'We could always ask Chief Superintendent Armstrong,' suggested Abigail.

'No,' said Daniel. 'There'd be all manner of hoops he'd want us to jump through for it, and in the end he won't give one to us. No, I've got another idea. I'm going back to that money-grabbing young man at Fishcock and Purse and I'll tell him that I'm arranging for a detective inspector from Scotland Yard to get a search warrant to inspect the tobacconist's shop tomorrow. However, if he can let us have the keys, or get someone to accompany us today, I'll give him a shilling. It'll be up to him.'

'This all sounds rather unpleasant,' said Abigail.

'It's the only way to deal with people like that,' said Daniel. 'I'm giving him something. It may not be the five shillings he tried to extort from us, but it's proper coin.'

'It could turn into a nasty argument,' said Abigail. 'And there's no guarantee that John will provide the search warrant. I really think this is all unnecessary and you could be in for an unpleasant confrontation.'

'I can deal with him,' said Daniel. He stopped and looked at her. 'There's no need for you to be involved; I can do this.'

134

Abigail thought it over, then said, 'We are partners. I should be with you.'

'Not if you don't think it's right,' said Daniel. 'The young man will spot that and definitely cause a row.'

'Perhaps you're right,' said Abigail. 'Actually, I promised the girls at the dig I'd come back and see how they were doing. Would you mind?'

'No,' said Daniel. 'That's a good idea.' He took her hand and smiled at her. 'I know I'm being petty. It's not about the money; that young man annoyed me with the way he tried to take advantage of us.'

'But it's also the money,' said Abigail.

Daniel was about to deny it, then he stopped and burst out, outraged, 'Five shillings! For some people that's a week's wages!'

Abigail squeezed his hand, then kissed him. 'Go on,' she said. 'Go and put him in his place, and watch he doesn't put you in yours.'

The Duke of Cranbrook sat in his favourite armchair in the study of his elegant Georgian house in Belgravia, studying the profit and loss accounts of his holding company, Mercantile Manufacturers. The truth was it neither made anything nor did any merchant trading, but the Duke liked the title because it sounded respectable. Just as his title of Duke was neither earned nor inherited, but acquired from a penniless aristocrat just before he died. As a result, the Duke's very astute lawyer was able to recover the money the Duke had paid to the aristocrat, who fortunately had no surviving relatives to lodge a complaint.

The tall, bulky figure of his manservant, valet and bodyguard,

Perkins, appeared in the study doorway.

'Pardon, Your Grace, but two persons have arrived.'

'Male or female?' enquired the Duke.

'Both male, sir.'

'So, gentlemen, then?'

'No, sir,' said Perkins firmly.

'Do I know these persons?'

'Mr Kent and Mr Sedgewick. They said they had news.'

Josh and Nipper, thought the Duke. He gave his valet a smile. 'Perkins, you are a snob,' he said.

'Yes, sir, Your Grace,' said Perkins firmly. 'And proud to be one.'

'Where are these persons?'

'At the rear entrance, sir. As usual.'

'Please show them to the office. Tell them I shall be with them shortly.'

'Very good, Your Grace.'

Perkins left the study, and the Duke rose and checked himself in the mirror. Yes, he told himself reassuringly, every inch a gentleman. From his smart expensive clothes, including the cravat held in place by the jewelled tie-pin, to his dark and luxuriantly coiffured hair, and his long, slightly reddish moustache with its elegantly waxed ends.

He left the study and walked down the passage to his office at the rear of the house. Unlike his study, and the living rooms of his house, which were extensively – and expensively – decorated, the office was a bare room with the minimum of furniture: a desk, behind which was a leather-covered armchair, and facing the desk four sturdy, plain wooden chairs.

Two men stood by these chairs, watched over by Perkins.

'Thank you, Perkins,' said the Duke.

As his valet left the office, the Duke gestured for the two men to each take a seat, then settled himself in the leather armchair behind the desk.

The Duke looked at the two men: Josh Kent, the taller of the two, who made a respectful bow of his head to the Duke as they took their seats, and Nipper Sedgewick, small and wiry and with a look of perpetual suspicion on his face.

'Perkins informs me you have news,' said the Duke.

'About Harry,' said Kent.

'And how is Mr Pickwick?' enquired the Duke.

'He's worried.'

'Crackers with worry,' put in Sedgewick.

'The police are investigating him,' said Kent.

'How interesting,' said the Duke. 'What are they investigating him for?'

'The dead bodies,' said Sedgewick.

'The two James brothers and Ellie Mercer,' Kent elaborated. 'And also that sergeant from Fenchurch Street who died. Grillis.'

'Ah yes, Bob Grillis,' said the Duke. 'Such a tragedy.'

'The law are also digging around as to what's going on at Fenchurch Street nick,' said Kent. 'It's all got Harry rattled.'

'Poor Harry,' said the Duke. 'What's he going to do about it?'

'He ain't saying,' said Kent. 'Not so far, anyway. But he's planning something.'

'Well, when you discover what it is he's planning, do let me know,' said the Duke. He reached out for a small brass bell on his desk, picked it up and rang it, and Perkins appeared. 'Show these gentlemen out, if you would, Perkins. And then return to me. I have something to discuss with you.'

'Yes, Your Grace,' said Perkins.

He escorted the two men out of the office, returning shortly after, and looked enquiringly at the Duke.

'Do you know a man called Josiah Grundy?'

'No, Your Grace.'

'He was formerly a constable at Fenchurch Street police station. He left the force and took on a tobacconist shop in Poultry near the Bank of England, but latterly he seems to have disappeared. I wish you to find him.'

'Yes, Your Grace. And then what?'

'I'll tell you when you have located him.'

'Very good, Your Grace.'

When Abigail returned to the trench, Sophie and Alice were kneeling on pieces of rolled-up sacking and very carefully scraping away at something protruding from the base of the trench by the remains of the ragstone wall.

'You look like you've found something,' said Abigail.

The two young women turned towards her and there was no disguising the delight on both their faces.

'It looks like a bone!' said Alice.

'A bone?' Abigail climbed down the ladder and joined them in the trench. The two young women stood up to let Abigail get a view of their discovery. Something white and curved, and very discoloured, was poking up through the earth. Abigail bent down and felt it gently.

'I might be wrong, but it looks like the top of a skull,' she said.

'Yes, that's what we thought,' said Sophie excitedly.

'Someone should get a message to Professor Clement,' said Abigail. 'And Viscount Dillon will need to be told.' She looked again at the fragment of discoloured bone. 'If it is a skull, then either someone's been beheaded, or the rest of the skeleton will be there, which will take some doing to uncover. Do you mind if I go to see Professor Clement on your behalf and report this to him? Or would one of you rather do it?'

'No, please,' said Alice, and Sophie nodded energetically in agreement, adding, 'We'd rather stay here and uncover the skull, or whatever it is.'

'Good,' said Abigail. 'If my husband turns up looking for me, tell him what's happened and that I've gone to UCL to see Professor Clement.'

CHAPTER SEVENTEEN

Daniel stood in the small flat above the tobacconist's shop. It had cost him a shilling, but the Prince of Wales could afford that. The young man hadn't been a problem, especially once Daniel had used the magic words 'police search warrant'. He'd tried to bargain Daniel up to three shillings, but the expression of grim stubbornness on Daniel's face ended up with him pocketing the shilling and handing over the keys.

'But I want the keys back today,' he'd said.

'You'll get them,' Daniel had told him.

Daniel had searched every nook and cranny in the flat, and the only thing he'd found of interest was a screwed-up scrap of paper which had *H. Pickwick. Five shillings* scrawled on it. Was it a receipt from Harry Pickwick, or was it a note to pay Pickwick? Whatever, it was an indication that there was a tie-up between Josiah Grundy and Harry Pickwick.

Sooner or later we're going to have to talk to Harry Pickwick, he decided.

He locked up the flat and returned the keys to the young man at Fishcock and Purse, then made his way to the Tower to see Abigail.

Barney Brick and Detective Constable Bert Reeves from Scotland Yard sat in the storeroom above William Oakes's locksmith shop and looked out of the window at Harry Pickwick's rag-and-bone yard. Reeves had a notebook open on his lap to keep a note of everyone who came in to the office building where Harry Pickwick was holding court. Brick had chosen this as their observation point because he knew William Oakes disliked what was going on in Fenchurch Street nick as much as he did.

'Take my upstairs store room, Barney,' he'd told Brick when the young police constable had approached him.

Brick and Reeves had been watching the rag-and-bone yard for three hours. So far most of the visitors had been people bringing bundles of rags, a cart laden with metal, and two children pushing a pram loaded with newspapers and bits of carboard. Two men had called for a brief visit. Brick identified them as Pickwick's muscle, Josh Kent and Nipper Sedgewick. 'They're the pair who went round to the houses of the decent coppers who worked at Fenchurch Street and leant on them to quit.'

'Worth picking them up?' asked Reeves.

Brick shook his head. 'No evidence. They made threats against the coppers' families, told them what would happen if they talked. The coppers live in the area; they couldn't take the chance.' Suddenly Brick was alert. 'Here's someone we know.'

They looked at a small, thin man in a shabby suit who walked through the gates of the yard and made for the office.

'Slim Jim Adams,' said Brick. 'Burglar.'

'Maybe we ought to pick him up,' suggested Reeves.

Again, Brick shook his head. 'He's not got a bag or anything with him. The time to pick him up is when he walks in there carrying a bag with the loot. The trick will be catching him and the swag with Harry Pickwick. But now we know he's involved, we can keep an eye on him.'

'What's he doing here if he isn't getting rid of the goodies?'

'Come to make a deal,' said Brick. 'He'll tell Pickwick what job he's got in mind and how much it's worth, so Pickwick will okay it and grease the palms of the local police to turn a blind eye to wherever it is he's going to burgle. That's how they've got everything sewn up.'

'Bastards!' Reeves scowled. 'I hate crooked coppers.'

Caleb Perkins sat in the lean-to shed of the small run-down farm in Essex and looked unsmilingly as Josiah Grundy was pushed into the shed by two burly men.

'Mr Grundy,' said Perkins. He gestured at a wooden crate near to him and said, 'Sit.'

Grundy looked around, nervous desperation in his eyes.

'Who are you?' he asked. 'What do you want with me?'

'Sit,' said Perkins again, his tone of voice firmer, and this time his words were reinforced by the two men grabbing hold of Grundy and forcing him down onto the wooden crate.

Perkins's enquiries into the whereabouts of Josiah Grundy

had begun in a pub in Fenchurch Street where he'd been told that Wesley Sims usually drank. He'd found Sims in there on his own, looking miserable, and the pair had got into conversation, with Perkins buying a pint of strong ale for the unhappy police sergeant.

'I'm being persecuted,' Sims had complained.

'Who by?' Perkins had asked.

'Everyone!' Sims had exclaimed.

Perkins had gestured to the landlord and soon another pint of strong ale was in front of Sims.

'The police are after me,' Sims had groaned.

'The police?'

'Among others.'

'But didn't you say you were the police?' Perkins had asked.

Sims had looked at him, suspiciously. 'When?' he'd asked.

'A few minutes ago. When I sat down with you. I'm sure you said you were with the police?'

Sims had nodded. 'I may have done,' he'd agreed. 'I'm a station sergeant at Fenchurch Street.'

'Fenchurch Street,' Perkins had repeated, intrigued. 'I knew someone who was a constable there. A bloke called Josiah Grundy.'

'Josiah Grundy!' Sims had groaned. 'There's another one who's persecuting me!'

'What's he persecuting you about?'

'It's not actually him, it's others.' He'd given another groan. 'He's left the force now, but he left things behind that are still causing me trouble.'

'Left the force?'

Sims had nodded.

'Where did he go?'

'He took over a tobacconist's ship in the City.'

'Where in the City?'

'Poultry. Why?'

'Well, I last saw him about a year ago. I was having a bit of a hard time and he lent me ten bob to help me. I'd like to see him to pay him back. I've got the money now, and when someone does you a good turn like that it's only right to pay him back. Poultry in the City, you say.'

'Yeah, but I've heard he ain't there any more. He's moved on.'

'Where?'

Sims had shaken his head. 'No idea.'

Perkins had gestured to the landlord, and another pint of ale appeared in front of Sims.

'Didn't he have family?' Perkins had asked.

'Not a far as I know,' Sims had said. 'He was a bachelor. He used to say he couldn't afford to get married on a copper's wages.'

'I meant relatives,' Perkins had said.

Sims had thought for a moment, then said, 'He had a sister. She's married to some farmer type out in Essex.'

'Essex.' Perkins had nodded. 'I'm sure he mentioned it.' He'd frowned thoughtfully. 'What was her name? He did tell me.'

'Barbara,' Sims had said. 'Barbara Grundy, as was. Barbara Hickworth she is now. The bloke she married is called Hickworth.'

'That's right.' Perkins had nodded. 'And they're in . . .' He'd hesitated and frowned. 'You know, it's gone right out of my head.'

'Loughton,' Sims had said.

'Of course,' Perkins had said. 'Loughton.'

And so he and two companions had come to Loughton in Essex and found the smallholding where Barbara and Fred Hickworth lived. They'd discovered that Fred was out and Barbara was in a bad mood because she was having to look after her ne'er-do-well brother who'd landed himself on them.

'And he's eating us out of house and home,' she'd complained. 'And has he put his hand in his pocket since he's been here? No!' She'd looked at Perkins suspiciously. 'Who did you say you were again?'

'Private enquiry agents, madam,' Perkins had said. 'Acting on behalf of a firm of debt collectors.'

'Ha!' she'd said derisively. 'I might have known!'

'Perhaps if you could tell us where he is at this moment, we might be able to persuade him to return to London with us, solving both our problems,' Perkins had said.

'He's upstairs in the spare room,' Barbara had said.

'Is there any place that we can talk to him in private?' Perkins had asked.

'There's a lean-to shed at the side of the house.'

Perkins had given her a grateful smile. 'That would be perfect,' he'd said.

And now they were in the lean-to, Perkins sitting on a wooden chair, Grundy on a crate, the two muscular men standing immediately behind Grundy.

'Who are you?' asked Grundy anxiously again.

'I'm the man who decides whether you live or die,' said Perkins.

Grundy leapt to his feet in alarm, and was immediately pushed back down onto the crate.

'Your disappearance from your shop has caused major upset for some *very* important people,' continued Perkins. 'Why did you leave so suddenly?'

'Well, I heard some talk about the police not being satisfied about Bob Grillis's accident.'

'So you did a runner.'

'I thought it best to drop out of sight for a bit.'

'Not a good idea,' said Perkins. 'It looks suspicious.'

'It was an accident!' said Grundy. 'Grillis fell and banged his head on the kerb. That was what happened. I told my sergeant at Fenchurch Street. He believed me.'

'And now Scotland Yard are looking into it, which causes a lot of upset among some people who'd prefer it if it wasn't looked into.'

'Who?' asked Grundy.

Perkins shook his head. 'No names,' he said. 'But they have asked me to give you a message. They want you to go to Scotland Yard and tell them it was an accident.'

'It was!' protested Grundy.

'But you disappearing the way you did sort of suggests that maybe it wasn't. Which means they open an investigation that no one wants. So, you put a stop to that by going to Scotland Yard and telling them you'd heard they're looking for you to ask you about what happened to Bob Grillis. You've only just heard this because you've been staying with relatives in the country and you've come in to tell them exactly what happened. How Bob fell and banged his head.'

'That's what happened. I've already told the police.'

'At Fenchurch Street, not Scotland Yard, who are the ones who want to know now. So, like I say, this is nice and simple: you go and see a detective called Inspector Feather and tell him about the accident. And how what happened was nothing to do with you, or anyone else. You saw Grillis fall. You reported it. But there was nothing anyone could do to save him.'

'That's what happened.' Grundy nodded. He looked suspiciously at Perkins. 'But why have I got to tell this Inspector Feather?'

'Because these very important people want you to,' said Perkins.

'Say I choose not to?' asked Grundy. 'After all, if this Inspector Feather is looking for me, he must have his suspicions. For all I know he's going to fit me up for Bob's death.'

'He won't,' said Perkins.

Grundy shook his head. 'That's all very well for you to say; you're not walking in there and putting your neck on the line. Give me one good reason why I should do it.'

'Because if you don't, my friends here will kill you,' said Perkins calmly. 'They'll break your neck and dump you in a river. When you're fished out, there'll be a note in your pocket that says, *I didn't kill Bob Grillis. It was an accident.*

He fell and banged his head on the kerb. But no one believes me. I can't take any more.' Perkins produced a sheet of paper with writing on it. 'This is that note, already written out. However, if you do as asked, there'll be a fiver in it for you, and you keep your life. So, that's the choice. It's up to you.'

CHAPTER EIGHTEEN

Sir Henry Pomeroy, the commissioner of police, looked up from the report he was reading at the tap on his door, and his secretary, Jason Ormerod, looked in.

'Excuse me, Sir Henry, Bramwell Booth is here and he wonders if he might have a moment of your time on a very urgent matter.'

'How urgent?' queried Pomeroy, his heart sinking. Any meeting with Bramwell Booth, or his father, invariably meant a lecture on the evils of drink and the need for laws to protect the public at large from these failings.

'It concerns the murder of a Salvation Army captain in the East End of London,' said Ormerod.

Pomeroy gave a small groan. The murder of a Salvation Army captain was not something he could dismiss or ignore, not with the power the Salvation Army seemed to have built up among the ruling figures in the establishment.

'Very well. Send him in.'

Ormerod bowed and left the room, and a moment later the tall figure of Bramwell Booth, resplendent in his Salvation Army uniform, entered.

'Thank you for seeing me, Commissioner,' he said, taking a seat.

This is going to be a long one, thought Pomeroy with an inward groan, *or he'd have remained standing.* 'You are here about a murder, I understand.'

'I am,' said Booth. 'I'm sure you're aware of the number of serious attacks that have taken place on our Salvation Army members.'

I am, thought the Commissioner, *but I'm sure you're going to tell me again.* Aloud, he said, 'I have heard of such attacks a while ago, but not any recent ones.'

'Ever since the Salvation Army began, the sellers of alcohol have launched attacks upon our members,' said Booth. 'In 1882 alone, six hundred and twenty-two Salvation Army soldiers—'

'Were seriously assaulted,' Pomeroy finished for him. 'Yes, Mr Booth, I have heard about these attacks from your father on many occasions, but I thought they had subsided.'

'They have never subsided,' said Booth. 'The most recent, on our Captain Edward Merchant, resulted in his death. A most violent death. Although we know the police are investigating his murder, our concern is that it does not merit the priority it should. We do understand that the police are under a great deal of pressure, with many investigations to carry out, but unless the people who committed this heinous act are brought to justice swiftly, the attacks on our people will only increase.

150

More murders will take place. Commissioner, we urge you, we implore you, to put pressure on the police in order to prevent these malevolent and murderous assaults.'

'You may rest assured, Mr Booth, that I will take this up with Scotland Yard immediately. I can only apologise on their behalf that they have not lived up to their excellent reputation in this matter. We cannot allow these thugs to decimate such an important organisation as the Salvation Army.' He stood up and held out his hand towards Booth. 'Thank you for coming to report this to me.'

Booth looked at the outstretched hand with reluctance – he had obviously been hoping to enlarge on his message – but then he stood and took the commissioner's hand and shook it. 'Thank you, Commissioner,' he said. 'I trust you will keep me informed of developments.'

Pomeroy sat down and watched Bramwell Booth leave and the door close behind him. *A lucky escape*, he thought, *to get away without a long lecture.* But he wouldn't get away with it so easily next time. Booth was right. Pressure needed to be brought to bear on Scotland Yard. He picked up the small brass bell on his desk and rang it. His door opened and Jason Ormerod looked in.

'You rang, sir Henry?'

'Yes. Send a message to Chief Superintendent Armstrong at Scotland Yard and tell him I need to see him as soon as possible. Use that new machine you have on your desk.'

'The telephone, sir?'

'Yes, it will be faster than sending a letter.'

* * *

151

Daniel arrived back at the Tower and found Algernon Dewberry standing by the trench, watching as Sophie and Alice scraped away the earth to reveal what was definitely a human skull.

'Mrs Wilson has gone to University College London to inform Professor Clement of the find,' Dewberry told him. 'This is really unexpected and most exciting.'

The words were right, thought Daniel, but he could see little of excitement in Dewberry. He looked the same as before, burdened down with worries and responsibilities. Daniel climbed down the ladder into the trench and joined the two young women, both hard at work, but working very carefully with small trowels and fingers to uncover the find fully.

'It's a skull,' he said.

'It is,' said Sophie.

'But a small one,' said Alice.

'A child's,' said Daniel. 'But not a young child. I'd say it belonged to a ten-year-old.'

Alice shot a look filled with hope at Sophie. 'You don't think—?' she began.

'The princes?' finished Sophie, her voice echoing that feeling of hope.

Surely not, thought Daniel. The two princes held in the Tower and murdered on the instruction of their uncle, the Duke of Gloucester, later King Richard III, but whose bodies had never been found.

No, that's not true, he told himself. They *had* been found, or – rather – their skeletons had been found by labourers doing some repair work at the White Tower, and they'd been buried somewhere. Not at the Tower, but somewhere Royal. But say they had not been the skeletons of the two missing princes, but from some other time?

He heard the sound of horses' hooves and the wheels of a coach pulling up near him, and he turned to see Abigail and a large red-bearded man climb down.

'Daniel!' Abigail smiled. 'This is Professor Stanford Clement, who's in charge of the dig. Professor, this is my husband, Daniel Wilson.'

Clement extended a huge hand to Daniel, and the two men shook hands.

'A pleasure, Mr Wilson. This sounds an exciting find.' He turned to Algernon Dewberry. 'I trust you and Viscount Dillon are pleased by this discovery, Mr Dewberry.'

'Indeed,' said Dewberry. 'Although we have yet to ascertain how relevant this find is to the history of the Tower.'

'Whatever or whoever it is, it will be relevant,' boomed Clement jovially. 'After all, this is Tower property.'

He went to the ladder, lowered his bulky body into the trench, and walked to where Alice and Sophie were working. The two young women stopped and stood aside to let him see the skull. Clement pointed to where Alice had just uncovered another piece of discoloured bone. 'That looks like the tip of a shoulder blade. There could be a whole skeleton there.' He smiled at the two women. 'This is a major find. We need to get a bigger team here. Bigger, and experienced at this sort of thing. I'll head back to the university and organise a team of students and volunteers. Tomorrow, we'll throw everything at it and find out what we've got.' He beamed fondly at the two young women. 'In the meantime, Alice and Sophie, carry on. I am so proud of you. This is your dig just as much as mine, and I'll make sure you both get full credit.'

He pulled himself up the ladder and addressed Abigail. 'Would you mind if I left you to oversee the girls while I get back to UCL and arrange things? Not that they need it, but if they do discover anything else that needs to be identified, I know no one better than you.'

'Thank you, Professor, that's very flattering,' said Abigail.

Clement turned and bellowed down into the trench to the two young women. 'I'll be back here tomorrow morning with a gang. Make sure everything's left protected before you go.'

The two young women promised him they would, then the professor clambered back aboard the carriage and headed off.

'You don't mind if I stay here and work with the girls, do you?' Abigail asked Daniel.

'Not at all,' said Daniel. 'In fact, I need to talk to Yeoman Purbright again, so I'll leave you here while I go and find him. I'll see you later.'

Daniel left Abigail with Sophie and Alice and made his way towards the White Tower. He became aware that Algernon Dewberry had joined him and was walking alongside him.

'I hope you don't mind my accompanying you, Mr Wilson,' he said. 'But I did tell the curator that I'd report back to him about this recent find at the dig.'

'Not at all,' said Daniel. 'Have you been at the Tower long?'

'I was appointed deputy curator two years ago, in 1897.'

'You must work very closely with the curator,' said Daniel.

'We do.' Dewberry nodded. 'The estate is large and the

organisation of it is quite complex. It needs the two of us.'

'I recall you said you lived at the Tower?'

'I do. We – that is, my family and I – live in one of the houses on Tower Green.'

'How do your family find living here inside the Tower of London?'

'Generally, they enjoy it, although the business of the gates being closed overnight restricts any social contacts my wife and our daughter may like to enjoy. But there are many positives to living here.'

'Yes, I can imagine,' said Daniel. 'At least, as a family, you can feel secure here. Safe. I'm sure your wife appreciates that aspect.'

'She does,' said Dewberry. For a moment his gaunt features softened as he confided, 'We were childhood sweethearts, Petunia and I. Our families were next-door neighbours. Even when we were children, I always felt there was something extra special about what we had, our relationship.' He gave a wan smile as he said, 'I was overjoyed when one day she told me she felt the same. I knew then this was someone I was meant to be with for ever.' He looked at Daniel, an almost earnest fierceness in his voice as he said, 'I would do anything to keep her safe. Anything.'

A strange choice of words, thought Daniel. Before he could ask what he meant by that, and what in particular worried him about his wife's safety, Dewberry asked, 'How are your enquiries going, Mr Wilson? Into the death of Eric James?'

'Slowly, I'm sad to say,' admitted Daniel ruefully. 'But we are gradually making inroads.'

'What sort of inroads? Do you have any idea of who may have committed this atrocity?'

'We have theories and loose ends, but at the moment we lack the evidence to support them. But that evidence is out there, and I'm confident we shall be able to tie the loose ends together.'

By now they had reached the White Tower, and Daniel spotted the figure of Yeoman Purbright striding along towards the Tower, resplendent in his uniform, his pike over one shoulder.

'And there's the person I want to talk to,' said Daniel. 'Excuse me, Mr Dewberry.'

'Certainly,' said Dewberry. 'And if there's anything I can do to help, don't hesitate to let me know.'

Daniel thanked him, then hurried to intercept Yeoman Purbright before he reached the steps to the White Tower.

'Yeoman Purbright!' he called.

Purbright stopped and turned. 'Mr Wilson,' he said.

'I'm sorry to trouble you, Mr Purbright,' said Daniel, 'but I just want to double-check a few things. Viscount Dillon told me you met Eric James at about half past nine on the evening when it is assumed he was killed.'

'Yes, sir,' said Purbright.

'I'd like to walk through with you your movements when you met him that evening,' said Daniel.

'Of course, sir. He was crossing Tower Green in the direction of the White Tower, and I was making my way to the Chapel Royal. If you follow me, I'll show you where we met.'

Daniel walked with the Yeoman to Tower Green, which

fronted the ancient Tudor residences.

'We met here,' said Purbright. 'And Eric was making for the White Tower.'

'Who else was around?' asked Daniel.

'Just some members of the public, each group accompanied by Yeomen, taking a tour. We get a lot of people coming when it gets late. They're hoping to catch a glimpse of one of the ghosts.'

'The ghosts?' asked Daniel, unable to prevent a smile appearing on his face.

'Yes, sir,' said Purbright.

'I'm afraid I don't believe in ghosts,' said Daniel.

'You would if you lived here, sir,' said Purbright.

'Have you ever seen one?'

'No, but I've heard them. They whisper. You can hear the pain in their voices.'

'Oh? Who?' asked Daniel, intrigued in spite of himself.

'Well, there's Anne Boleyn, who's possibly the most famous. Had her head chopped off.'

'Yes, I recall,' said Daniel.

'Then there's Lady Jane Grey. Sixteen, she was. Queen for nine days after Henry VIII died. Bloody Mary had her executed for treason because her father-in-law, the Duke of Northumberland, launched a military coup to take the Crown. They all paid for it with their heads. Lady Jane. Her husband, Lord Dudley. The Duke. And then there's Margaret Pole, the Countess of Salisbury. She's the one I've heard moaning. I'm sure you know about her execution?'

'No,' admitted Daniel.

'It was a disaster. She refused to kneel at the block. Then she tried to run away. The executioner chased after her with his axe and started to hack at her. He chopped her up and all the time she was trying to run.' He shook his head. 'It's no wonder she haunts this place.'

Daniel let this image sink in. It was a far cry from the image of strictly choreographed executions, with the victim compliant.

'The groups of people you saw, were they headed for the White Tower, or walking away from it?'

'They would have been walking away from it. At that time of day we encourage visitors to start to think about leaving because there are always some stragglers.'

'If someone was a visitor, could they slip away and find somewhere to hide?' Daniel gestured around them at the vast site. 'After all, the Tower occupies a huge area with lot of nooks and crannies.'

Purbright looked unhappy. 'I suppose it would be possible,' he admitted. Then he brightened as he added, 'But they'd be sure to be found. Those of us who live at the Tower often walk around the grounds at night.'

'But if someone deliberately sought out a place that wouldn't necessarily be looked into?' persisted Daniel.

Purbright looked uncomfortable. 'I suppose it's possible,' he said.

'Has anyone ever done it, to your knowledge?' asked Daniel.

Reluctantly, Purbright said, 'It has happened a couple of times, usually young men doing it for a dare. But on both occasions they were found and escorted from the Tower with a warning that if they tried it again they'd be arrested for trespass.'

'And those are the ones you know of,' said Daniel.

'Yes,' said Purbright shortly.

'But if they hadn't been found, if they'd been able to avoid discovery during the night, they would have been able to walk out the next day along with other visitors as they left.'

'I suppose it's possible,' admitted Purbright.

'Thank you,' said Daniel. 'Is a record kept of the names of visitors?'

'Only of those who arrive after the gates have been closed for the night,' said Purbright.

'It was you who found the body of Eric James at half past seven the next morning,' said Daniel.

'It was.'

'This was after you had released the ravens from their cages and given them breakfast.'

'Yes, sir.' He smiled. 'Best steak, they have. Fresh from Smithfield Market. As protectors of the Tower, they're also Beefeaters, so they're treated the same.'

'What took you to the Line of Kings at that hour?'

'It was on my regular duty rota,' said Purbright. 'Every morning, after I've given the ravens their breakfast, my walk starts with the White Tower. I begin at the bottom and work my way to the top.'

'What about Eric James? Where did he begin his regular routine?'

'At the hospital block. From there he proceeded to the armouries.'

'So he shouldn't have been at the White Tower at seven o'clock in the morning on the day you found his body.'

'No, sir. Definitely not.'

Chief Superintendent Armstrong entered the office of the police commissioner and strode to the large desk, behind which sat the commissioner, Sir Henry Pomeroy. The commissioner's attention was devoted to some documents he was poring over, which Armstrong knew from experience was a bad sign. Not looking up to acknowledge him. No handshake of welcome. Armstrong waited for a full minute before giving a discreet cough. The commissioner looked up at him.

'Ah, Chief Superintendent. Thank you for coming.' He gestured at the empty chair opposite him, and Armstrong sat. 'I have asked you to come in because I had a visit from Bramwell Booth. He is the son of General William Booth of the Salvation Army and also acts as his chief of staff.'

'Yes, sir. I'm aware of who Mr Booth is.'

'He came to see me because he's concerned about the attacks on the Salvation Army's members, in particular the recent attack on a Captain Edward Merchant, which resulted in the captain's death.'

'Yes, sir. Inspector Feather is investigating it.'

'But is he doing it with enough rigour?' asked the commissioner. 'Mr Booth seems to think that not enough is being done to bring the murderers to justice.'

'With respect, sir, the case is complicated by the intervention of the Prince of Wales.'

The commissioner frowned. 'The Prince has expressed an interest in this case?'

'Not in this particular case, but Inspector Feather believes that the recent spate of murders in the East End – of which the murder of Captain Merchant is one – may be connected to the murder of Yeoman Eric James in the Tower of London.'

'On what does he base that?'

'One of the victims was the twin brother of the murdered Yeoman at the Tower. His name was Paul James. He was stabbed to death just two days before the Yeoman Warder was killed. The woman who was killed was the mistress of Paul James. These deaths followed soon after Eric James took his brother to a Salvation Army meeting. It was soon after that the Salvation Army captain, Edward Merchant, was murdered in Whitechapel, close to the Tower of London.

'As the Prince of Wales has issued a demand that the press not be informed about the murder of Eric James, it presents a difficulty over telling them about the murder of Paul James or the Salvation Army captain, because they would soon discover about the murder of Eric James.'

The commissioner nodded in understanding, his face grave. 'I'm sure there must be a way out of this impasse. The murder of the Salvation Army captain has to take priority. You must be aware of the influence that General Booth and his son have in parliament, and among the most important people in the establishment. Find the people who committed this heinous crime and bring them to justice. And soon. That is your job, Chief Superintendent, to resolve this situation without breaking the orders from the Prince. I'm sure you can do it.'

'Yes, sir,' said Armstrong. Inside, he seethed. He wanted to say, *How? How do you square a circle such as this?* Instead, he got to his feet and said, 'Thank you, sir,' then departed, leaving the commissioner to return to the documents he was studying.

Chief Superintendent Armstrong's first action on returning to Scotland Yard was to barge into the office of Inspector Feather, where he found the inspector and Sergeant Cribbens.

'Inspector, I've just come from seeing the Commissioner,' he announced.

'Yes, sir,' said Feather.

'He is not happy with the slow rate of progress in your investigations.'

'Which particular investigations, sir? We have four murders at the moment. And one of them, the murder of the Yeoman Warder at the Tower, is of interest to the Prince of Wales.'

'Yes, well, that one is vital, obviously. If we can tell the commissioner that it was us, Scotland Yard, who solved the Tower of London murder rather than the so-called Museum Detectives, and the commissioner passes that on to the Prince of Wales, this will be a major feather in our cap. The other important one is the murder of this Salvation Army captain. And at this moment, the Salvation Army captain is to be your top priority.'

'What about the other two cases I'm working on? The murder of Eric James's brother, Paul James, and that of Ellie Mercer. Do I put them on the shelf for the moment?'

'I'll allocate them to another inspector.'

'Who?'

'Inspector Jarrett.'

'Jarrett?' echoed Feather in a tone that couldn't hide his disapproval.

'He's a good officer,' snapped Armstrong. 'He does everything by the book. He doesn't go off on flights of fancy or weird theories.'

'Nor do I, sir,' protested Feather.

'I'm not referring to you, Inspector. I'm talking about the Wilsons.'

'With respect, sir, they do have a very high level of success.'

'Luck, Inspector. And half the time their success is built on the work Scotland Yard has done. Or, more exactly, on what you've done. I've said it before: you're too close to them. They take advantage of you and grab the credit for themselves.'

'Perhaps you'd prefer it if Inspector Jarrett took over the investigation into the murder of the Beefeater at the Tower of London, sir.'

'No,' grunted Armstrong. 'Despite what I said, you're still the best detective on this squad. It's just that sometimes you seem to forget whose side you're on, the Yard's or the Wilsons'.'

'With respect, sir, I've always been loyal to the force and Scotland Yard.'

Armstrong nodded grudgingly. 'Yes, I'll give you that. Just don't forget it.' He tapped the thin brown manila file on Feather's desk. 'I've been thinking about the Tower of London case. What about this bloke Purbright?'

'What about him, sir?'

'He was the one discovered the body?'

'Yes, sir.'

'At half past seven in the morning?'

'He was doing his regular rounds. He always checks the White Tower at that time.'

'From experience, never trust the person who finds a body. Half the time they're the one who did it. He could have killed this Eric James at half past seven that morning.'

'The doctors put the time of death at between 9 p.m. and 10 p.m. the previous night.'

Armstrong gave a dismissive shrug. 'Half the time these doctors make it up.'

'Not Dr Wardle, sir. We've always found him to be as accurate as possible when it comes to time of death.'

'Accurate *as possible*,' barked Armstrong, thumping the desk. 'It's still speculation. And I've been reading your interview with Viscount Dillon. He claims that the murderer must have come from outside, but we don't know that for sure. The killer could have been someone resident at the Tower.'

'It could have, sir, that's true.'

'This Purbright character and the dead Beefeater were friends, right?'

'Yes, sir. Very good friends.'

'So it's quite possible they could have met up at some time during the night in the White Tower at the Line of Kings. And, for some reason, an argument breaks out, and Purbright kills James, then stuffs his body in the suit of armour.'

'It's possible, sir, but I've interviewed Yeoman Purbright and I didn't get the impression he was the one.'

'Because he's covering up. Admit it, Inspector, at the very least he's a suspect.'

'Not one that's high on the list. I still favour the idea that James met with someone who came in from outside, and this person killed him. Or, more likely, *persons*, because it would have taken two people to force the body into the armour and put it on the wooden horse.'

'Not necessarily. These old soldiers know what they're doing. I think you ought to bring him in. Sweat him. Put him in a cell overnight; that usually does the trick. That'll make him cough up.'

'That won't be easy to do, sir,' said Feather uncomfortably. 'Yeoman Purbright is the Ravenmaster at the Tower.'

'So?'

'He's the one responsible for letting the ravens out of their cages at dawn and feeding them breakfast.'

The chief superintendent stared at the inspector in bewilderment. 'Feeding them their breakfast?'

'Yes, sir.'

'Well, the Tower can arrange for someone else to do it. This is a murder inquiry we're talking about!'

'Yes, sir, but I doubt if Viscount Dillon will agree with that proposal. He's very firm on regulations and procedures as far as the Tower is concerned. The Ravenmaster needs an intimate knowledge of the ravens and how to handle them. A Ravenmaster is specially trained.'

The chief superintendent stared incredulously at Feather, then gave a grimace and said sourly, 'All right, forget having him in the cell overnight, but bring him in for questioning during the day. Sweat him.'

With that, he stumped out of the office. Feather looked at

Cribbens and gave a sigh. 'Well, we have our orders, Sergeant.'

'At least we'll have less on our hands with Inspector Jarrett taking on the other two murders,' said Cribbens.

'Jarrett,' groaned Feather.

'Yes, sir,' said Cribbens politely, discreetly avoiding giving an opinion on the other inspector. 'His sergeant's a good man, sir. Thomas Pick. Quite bright, in my opinion. He's got a good brain.'

'Let's hope Jarrett allows him to use it,' said Feather.

CHAPTER NINETEEN

That evening at home, as they prepared their evening meal together with Abigail in charge of marinading and cooking the breast of lamb, and Daniel in charge of the vegetables, Daniel told Abigail about his talk with Yeoman Purbright.

'This business of the gates being locked at night to keep out intruders is a red herring. There have been examples of people finding somewhere to hide once they're in, and then simply walking out again the next day when the gates open.'

'So the killing of Eric James could have happened at any time during the night.'

'It *could* have, but I somehow doubt it,' said Daniel. 'We're told that Eric James was an honest and respectable person. I can't imagine him being in the White Tower, and on the top floor, without a very good reason. And not in the middle of the night. Unless he had an arrangement to meet someone there.'

'What are you thinking?' asked Abigail.

'He makes an arrangement to meet someone from outside at the Line of Kings. He heads towards the White Tower at half past nine. But whoever he's meeting only just manages to get in before the gates close. They meet and something happens. The visitor, or visitors – there could be more than one in order to pack his dead body in the suit of armour – kill him, running him through with a sword. They put his body in the armour, then hide somewhere in the Tower, and walk out when the gates are open the next morning.'

'They're taking a chance,' pointed out Abigail. 'I've been talking to people here, and many of them go for a stroll around the inside of the Tower once the gates are closed. They enjoy being able to walk around without members of the public being here.'

'So it's someone from outside who's very familiar with the Tower. Knows the nooks and crannies, the best places to hide.'

'But why would Eric James be meeting with them at that time of night? They're outsiders. He knows that's not allowed.'

'I don't know,' admitted Daniel. 'Maybe he was under pressure from them.'

'What about, if he was so honest and respectable?' asked Abigail.

'Maybe it wasn't anything about him, but someone else. His dead brother, for example. Maybe someone had information about who'd killed him, and why.'

'Perhaps it was the people who killed his brother,' said Abigail. 'They might have told Eric they had information, but in reality they wanted to find out how much Eric knew. And then they killed him.'

'But why?' asked Daniel. 'Eric didn't know who killed Paul. He told John Feather that.'

'Maybe he lied,' said Abigail.

'An honest man like him lying?'

'Why not? We've all lied at some time or other, if it's about something important that we're protecting.'

'By the way,' said Daniel, 'I got the impression that Sophie and Alice think the skeleton they've uncovered might be that of one of the two Princes in the Tower.'

'Either King Edward V of England, aged twelve at the time he disappeared from the Tower, assumed murdered in 1483, or his nine-year-old brother, Richard, Duke of York.' Abigail nodded. 'The only sons of Edward IV.'

'But I thought the remains of the two princes had already been found,' said Daniel. 'I remember being told that some men working at the Tower found their skeletons.'

'*Assumed* to be their skeletons,' said Abigail. 'It was in 1674. Some men working at the White Tower dug up a wooden box from beneath a staircase containing the skeletons of two boys. King Charles II had the bones buried in Westminster Abbey.

'If you go to Westminster Abbey, on the wall of the Henry VII Lady Chapel you'll see a decorated stone with an inscription in Latin, which says in translation: "Here lie interred the remains of Edward V, King of England, and Richard, Duke of York, whose long desired and much sought-after bones, after over a hundred and ninety years, were found interred deep beneath the rubble of the stairs that led up to the Chapel of the White Tower on 17th July in the Year of Our Lord 1674."'

'So Sophie and Alice are in for a big disappointment.'

'Not necessarily,' said Abigail. 'As students doing the Classical Tripos, they'd know about that discovery, but they'd also be aware of the academic question mark hanging over those remains. The skeletons dug up in 1674 were *assumed* to be of the princes, but there are some doubts. For one thing, the staircase beneath which the bones were found had not been built at the time of Richard III, suggesting they may have already been in situ there before 1483. Also, there is nothing in the accounts of the discovery of the skeletons to show they were male. Their gender was never considered. No proper medical examinations were carried out. As far as I can recall, the only investigation was to find out if the bodies had been suffocated, as the rumour was that the two princes had been smothered on the orders of their uncle.'

'Their wicked uncle.' Daniel chuckled. 'Richard the hunchbacked child killer.'

'Even that is debatable,' said Abigail.

'What is?' asked Daniel, puzzled.

'The princes may not have been murdered by their so-called wicked uncle Richard.'

'Not in person, perhaps, but he caused their deaths. I read somewhere that he got his servants to bump them off. Smothered them in their beds. And it's got to be true because one of his servants admitted to the crime and was executed.'

'Not strictly accurate,' said Abigail. 'That story alleges that they were murdered in 1483 by Miles Forrest and John Dighton, on the orders of Sir James Tyrrell, who was indeed a faithful servant of Richard III, and that Tyrrell confessed. But

Tyrrell only confessed to the murders after Henry VII became king. I've read other accounts that say that the two princes were still alive when Henry Tudor came to the throne, and it was he who had them murdered because they posed a threat to his kingship.'

'But you've just said Tyrrell confessed to killing them.'

'In 1502,' said Abigail. 'Seventeen years after Henry Tudor took the throne from Richard.'

'Why did he confess if he didn't do it?'

'I would imagine torture was the answer. That usually produced a confession. And even if it didn't, the unfortunate man would be in no position to deny he'd confessed if he'd been executed.'

'But Shakespeare wrote a play about it!' protested Daniel. 'It's all there. The villainy. The murders.'

'Shakespeare was a propagandist for the Tudors,' said Abigail. 'He wrote what they wanted him to write. According to other accounts I've read, Richard was a good and kind person who looked after his nephews.'

'Tosh!' snorted Daniel. 'He put them in the Tower!'

'At that time the Tower was not thought of as a prison. It was a royal residence and comfortable.'

Daniel shook his head. 'No,' he said. 'If that was true this would have come out before.'

'Not while the Tudors were in power, and their reign lasted a long time, and merged into the Stuarts'. They'd hardly want an alternative story to be made public, one in which they weren't the true monarchs of this country. It wouldn't go down well.'

Daniel fell silent, then he said, 'So there is a possibility that the skeleton Sophie and Alice have been uncovering could be one of the princes?'

'It's possible,' said Abigail carefully. 'To be honest, I feel it's unlikely, but one never knows.'

CHAPTER TWENTY

Daniel and Abigail were just putting away the breakfast things the following morning, prior to heading off to the Tower of London, when there was a knock at their door. The caller was Sergeant Cribbens, who handed them a note from Inspector Feather.

'Josiah Grundy turned up first thing this morning,' he told them. 'He arrived at the Yard to see Inspector Feather. He wanted to talk about what happened to Bob Grillis at Fenchurch Street.' He indicated the note and added, 'Inspector Feather wondered if you wanted to join in talking to him.'

Daniel and Abigail exchanged looks, then Abigail said, 'I think we do. Thank you, Sergeant.'

'I thought you wanted to get to the dig and take a look at the skeleton?' said Daniel.

'That skeleton has been there for a few hundred years,' said Abigail. 'The elusive Mr Grundy is alive and available now. This is too good an opportunity to miss.'

'In that case, I've got a police van outside.' Cribbens beamed. 'Mr Grundy's waiting at Scotland Yard for your pleasure.'

On their arrival at Scotland Yard, they were greeted by Inspector Feather.

'This is a turn-up for the books,' said Daniel, as they made for the stairs that led to the interview rooms in the basement. 'Have you talked to him yet?'

'Briefly,' said Feather. 'He's told me a little, but I feel sure there's more to come. I decided to wait until you joined us.'

'What's your impression of him?' asked Abigail.

'Shifty, and somewhat frightened,' said Feather.

'Of what?' asked Daniel.

'That's why I'd be interested to hear your thoughts after you've talked to him,' said Feather.

Josiah Grundy was sitting on a chair at a bare wooden table in the interview room, two burly constables standing watchfully by the door. Feather, Cribbens, Daniel and Abigail walked into the room and took the empty seats at the table. Grundy looked at Daniel and Abigail suspiciously.

'Good morning,' said Feather. 'These are Mr and Mrs Daniel Wilson.'

'What do they want?' demanded Grundy.

'They want to ask you some questions concerning Sergeant Bob Grillis.'

'I've already told you all I know about that. Why do they want to know about it? What's their interest?'

'You might know them better as the Museum Detectives,' put in Feather.

Grundy stared at Daniel and Abigail, suspicion writ large on his face.

'All right, so I've heard of you,' he said. 'But how does what happened to Bob Grillis have anything to do with a museum?'

'Because our client is interested in finding out,' said Daniel. 'What prompted you to hand yourself in?'

'I've already told him,' said Grundy, gesturing at Feather.

'We'd like to hear it from yourself,' said Daniel.

'Why?' asked Grundy.

'Because it may have a bearing on another case we're working on.'

Grundy hesitated, then said in very defensive tones, 'I've already told Inspector Feather here what happened. And before that, when it happened and poor Bob fell over, I told my sergeant at Fenchurch Street station. It was an accident. It was an accident then and it still is an accident.'

'But what prompted you to come to Scotland Yard and hand yourself in?' Abigail repeated Daniel's question.

'I met an old pal of mine who told me the police were looking into Bob's death.'

'Where did you meet him?' asked Daniel.

'Out in Essex. I've been staying with my sister and her husband at their place at Loughton. He turned up and told me.'

'What's his name?'

Grundy looked at them warily. 'Why?' he asked.

'We need to talk to everyone who's involved, just to verify things.'

'What's the need to verify? I told you what happened.'

'We'd like to hear it from him.'

175

Grundy looked at them, torn by indecision. 'He ain't around any more. He popped in to tell me he was going north. Newcastle, somewhere like that.'

'To do what?'

'I don't know,' said Grundy. 'I didn't ask.'

'His name?' Daniel asked again.

Grundy hesitated, then said, 'Charlie Smith.'

'Where did you know him from?'

'He used to come into the tobacconist's now and then.'

'Why did you decide to leave London and go to Loughton?'

Grundy patted his chest. 'The smog and everything was getting to my chest. I decided to give myself a break out in the country. Fresh air. Healthy living.'

'So you went to stay with your sister.'

'Yes.'

'A bit short notice, wasn't it? You didn't even leave a forwarding address with the agents who were handling the shop.'

'Well, at that time I didn't know where I was going. It was only later I thought of my sister.'

'But this old customer of yours knew where you were. You told him.'

'I didn't exactly *tell* him,' said Grundy defensively. 'I must have mentioned about my sister in Loughton to him, and when he found I'd moved from the shop he must have taken a chance I'd gone to her.'

'That's quite a haul out to Loughton on a chance,' said Daniel. 'He must have been very keen to find you.'

'Well, we was good mates,' said Grundy.

Daniel pushed a sheet of paper and a pencil across the desk to Grundy. 'Can you write down the address of your sister in Loughton, along with her name.'

'Why?'

'As I said, so we can verify what you've told us.'

'You don't need to see her. She's a busy woman. Her husband's busy as well.'

'Just write their names and address down,' said Daniel. 'Are you planning to return to Loughton?'

'I don't know,' said Grundy.

'In that case, can you write down the address where you'll be staying tonight.'

'Why?' demanded Grundy.

'In case we need to talk to you again.'

Grundy scowled. 'I came in here of my own accord, to do the right thing. I help the law. And you're treating me like a criminal.'

'You were a policeman,' said Daniel. 'You know how things work. Rules and regulations.'

'But I haven't done anything except come in and give you information to help you!' burst out Grundy.

'For which we're sure Inspector Feather is very grateful.'

'I am,' said Feather. He pointed at the sheet of paper in front of Grundy. 'But I'd still like the address of where you'll be staying tonight. Just in case we need to contact you.'

'I haven't got anywhere booked,' said Grundy. 'This all came a bit sudden. Too sudden to get myself a lodging. So that's what I'm going to do as soon as you let me out of here.' He smirked as he added, 'And you can't keep me here because

I've done nothing wrong. I'm innocent of everything.'

Feather looked at Daniel and Abigail, who nodded in agreement.

'Sergeant,' said Feather to Cribbens, 'you can take Mr Grundy to reception and let him go. Mr Grundy, we'd appreciate it, once you have arranged lodgings for this evening, if you'd come back and give us the address. You can leave it with the duty sergeant at the reception desk.'

Feather waited until Cribbens had escorted Grundy out before asking, 'What did you think?'

'He's a wrong 'un,' said Daniel. 'All that business of that old pal of his popping in to Loughton to see him. Loughton's not a place you pass by and pop in to see someone, unless you know them very well. And I didn't get the feeling that was the case here. Notice how vague he was about this old pal of his.' He chuckled as he added with a note of scorn, 'Charlie Smith.'

'But why come all this way to see us to tell us he was innocent and that Bob Grillis died in an accident?' asked Feather. 'That was already on record at the local police station.'

'Because he was forced to. Someone went to Loughton to lean on him and get him to come in and say that.'

'Who?' asked Feather.

'Someone's who's been keeping close tabs on the investigation,' said Daniel. 'Grundy didn't just come to Scotland Yard; he came to see *you*. Inspector Feather. Someone told him who to ask for.'

'But why? It wasn't as if he was at risk of being arrested. Bob Grillis's death is still logged as accidental.'

'Someone wants to put an end to any investigation

happening. Which suggests to me this is part of that same someone wanting to cover up whatever's going on in the Fenchurch Street area.'

'Harry Pickwick?' asked Feather.

'Maybe.'

'But how is it connected with your case? The murder of the Beefeater at the Tower?'

'I don't know yet, but I feel it is.' Daniel began to tick things off on his fingers. 'Eric James killed. Paul James killed. Ellie Mercer killed. Your Salvation Army Captain, Edward Merchant, killed. Bob Grillis dies in what I believe are suspicious circumstances involving Josiah Grundy, who turns up at the Yard to profess his innocence, because he's pressurised by someone to do it. Harry Pickwick and the corrupt police crew at Fenchurch Street nick. And, at the heart of it, I believe there's something planned for a big robbery at the Tower of London, and all the other things and people I mentioned are part of that.

'So far we've been hitting a wall of silence. So what we need to do is we start picking at the things we've got until one of them starts to crack. Once one gives up, we use what we get from that to go on to another. At this moment, it looks to me Josiah Grundy is a weak link. We start to ask questions of the people around him, like this sister of his, and we get under his skin.'

'I have an idea that Sergeant Sims at Fenchurch Street is another possible one who'll crack,' said Feather. 'I also think a visit to Harry Pickwick could be productive.'

'I agree,' said Daniel. 'Any news on your other investigation?

Salvation Army captain Edward Merchant?'

'As of yesterday, that's what we're concentrating on,' said Feather.

'Oh?'

'Orders from the chief superintendent. He's told us the murder of the Salvation Army captain has to be our top priority, along with the killing of Eric James. Sergeant Cribbens and I have got a meeting with General Booth. As the Salvation Army seems to feature in almost every part of this case, we thought it might work for us on everything else.' He looked enquiringly at Abigail and Daniel. 'Do you want to come with us to meet the general? After all, there is a link between your case and the Salvation Army, with Eric James's involvement. Bramwell Booth, the general's son, is going to be there. The general has appointed him the Salvation Army's chief of staff. The general himself is seventy and recently his eyesight has begun to fail, though it hasn't stopped him preaching. But Bramwell Booth may be more up to date on recent events at the army.'

'I believe Abigail has another meeting today, digging up some remains at the Tower,' said Daniel.

Abigail shook her head. 'Professor Clement has a small army at his disposal. The bones will wait. The murders won't. We'll both come with you to see General Booth.'

CHAPTER TWENTY-ONE

Their meeting had been arranged for the Salvation Army's HQ, Congress Hall in Clapton. The police van pulled up at the end of a cul-de-sac and Daniel, Abigail, Feather and Sergeant Cribbens walked the short distance to the huge building that dominated the end of the street. It looked like a Roman temple, with its two towering Doric columns either side of the entrance. Above the entrance were the giant words, *SALVATION. CONGRESS HALL.*

'This is some impressive building,' murmured Abigail. 'It must have cost a fortune.'

'It was formerly an orphanage,' said Feather. 'But yes, it did cost quite a bit. It has the space to hold four and a half thousand people.'

'The Salvation Army has come a long way from William Booth preaching on the street,' commented Daniel.

They entered the large building and found a woman in Salvation Army uniform waiting for them inside.

'You must be the police,' she said. 'General Booth and his

chief of staff are waiting for you in the anteroom.'

They followed her to a sparsely furnished room where an elderly man sat to attention on a tall carved chair that had the appearance of a throne, and a younger man stood rigidly behind him. Daniel and Abigail both had the impression that these stances had been posed for their benefit.

Inspector Feather introduced Daniel and Abigail to the two men, and they sat on the chairs that had been set out for them.

General William Booth was an imposing figure with his long white beard cascading down to his chest. His eyes were milky white and he looked past them, and they realised that he was blind, but it in no way inhibited him.

'As you suggested, I have asked my son, who is also my chief of staff, to join us as he is my eyes, if not my ears, in everything affecting the army.'

Bramwell Booth was a man in his early forties, dressed as was his father in the traditional red and gold uniform of the Salvation Army. Where his father favoured a full-length beard, Bramwell obviously preferred being clean-shaven, although he sported a magnificent pair of mutton-chop side-whiskers.

'We're here to get some information on two things, General,' said Feather. 'As you know, we're investigating the brutal death of your Captain Edward Merchant, and we're trying to find out who may have wanted to kill him, and why?'

'The sellers of alcohol,' said the general. 'Ever since we began in 1878, anyone in a Salvation Army uniform has been a target for attacks. In the 1880s there was even a group of thugs who called themselves the Skeleton Army who disrupted our marches and meetings calling for the abolition of alcohol, with violence. In 1882 alone, six hundred and twenty-two Salvation Army soldiers were seriously assaulted. Two hundred and fifty-one of them were women and twenty-three of them were under the age of fifteen. Some of them died. Sadly, the death of Edward Merchant is not uncommon.'

'Another possibility we've heard is that his death might have been the responsibility of the Ashkenazi Jews or the Irish in the area.'

'No,' said William and Bramwell in union, their answer emphatic.

'Immigrants are an easy target,' said the general. 'They have no political voice, no one to defend them, so they are accused of everything bad that happens in the area. Neither the Jews nor the Irish have anything to fear from us. There have been attacks on our people, but not by the Jews or the Irish. Why would they?'

'There have been reports of violence between the two groups,' said Feather.

'Very rare, and blown out of all proportion,' said the general.

'When things like that do occur, it can usually be traced back to drink,' put in Bramwell. 'The Irish getting drunk and attacking the Jews.'

'Why?' asked Daniel. 'What have the Irish got against the Jews?'

'Are you a religious man?' asked Bramwell, rather stiffly.

'I would hesitate to describe myself as such in present company,' said Daniel carefully.

'The Catholics are taught that our Lord, Jesus, was killed by the Jews. Sometimes, when things become inflamed, usually by drink, the Catholics decide to take their revenge.'

'But Jesus was Jewish,' pointed out Abigail.

'And it happened two thousand years ago. And it was the Romans who judged him and crucified him,' added Daniel. 'Do they also attack Italians?'

'When drink enters the body, intelligent thought is driven out,' said the general.

'Actually, General, I've had another thought,' said Feather. 'In order to find the people who committed this outrage, it would help us if you could provide the names and addresses of your members who have been attacked. My thinking is that it might well be the same people who attacked them as those who murdered Captain Merchant. What we need are as many descriptions of those attackers as possible, so we can compare and find out if the same descriptions keep occurring.'

William Booth nodded and said, 'If you would take care of that, Bramwell.'

'Certainly, General,' said Bramwell. To Feather, he said, 'We already know who most of the victims were. I'll have the list sent to you at Scotland Yard.'

'Thank you. And keep it to those attacks that took place in the Whitechapel area for the moment.'

Bramwell nodded.

'There is another matter we wish to ask for your help over,' said Feather. 'And this is the main reason Mr and Mrs Wilson are here today.' Feather looked at Abigail, who took up the thread.

'General, recently you preached a sermon at which one of the attendees was a Yeoman Warder from the Tower of London, an Eric James.'

The general nodded. 'A good man. He brought his brother,

Paul, along. A troubled man, by all accounts.' His face showed his disgust as he added, 'He had the smell of strong drink on him. Unlike his brother, Eric, who is firmly tee-total. I believe it was to set his poor brother on the right path that Eric brought him to the meeting.'

'Yes, that's what we were told,' said Abigail. She hesitated, then said warily, 'Sirs, what I am about to tell you, I do so in spite of being ordered by a certain party not to relate this incident to anyone else.'

'You are intending to betray a promise,' said the general, his tone heavy with disapproval.

'No, sir, I did not give my promise, but I am aware that this person – a very important person – wishes the matter be kept secret for the moment. But at the same time, this person has commissioned my husband and I to investigate a murder, and the only way we can do this is to try and gather the facts of the case together, and that entails asking questions. However, we are only asking questions of those we feel will not pass the information on. Inspector Feather has already been made aware of the tragic events, and has been sworn to the same secrecy. It is our opinion that you two gentlemen, being entirely honourable, would keep the facts such as they are to yourselves until you can be relieved of such secrecy.'

Bramwell Booth looked at her with suspicion. 'On what grounds do you ask us for this imposition?' he demanded.

'At the request of His Highness Prince Albert Edward, the Prince of Wales.'

Both Bramwell's and his father's faces showed their stunned surprise.

'We have to tell you that it involves someone you are familiar with,' added Abigail.

'Very well.' The general nodded. 'We are loyal servants of our royal family, enthroned by Holy God.'

His son nodded as well. 'We shall keep the facts between ourselves. No one else will be told.'

'Thank you,' said Abigail. 'The victim was Eric James. He was found run through by a sword in the White Tower at the Tower of London. His brother, Paul, had been stabbed to death just two days previously. As Eric was killed on royal premises, the royal family have asked for this information to be kept secret.'

'Poor Eric!' exclaimed the general.

'Did he ever express to you fears for his life?' asked Abigail.

'No,' said the general. 'But then, we only met when he came to a meeting. I would not say we knew one another intimately. The only time he expressed concern was when he asked me if he could bring his brother to a meeting where I would be preaching. He explained the problems Paul had, and that most of them came from his drinking with bad companions. I said I hoped my words might encourage his reformation.'

As they left the mission hall, Abigail said to Feather, 'That's a good idea about the descriptions.'

'It occurred to me that with the large number of attacks on Salvation Army members – mostly, fortunately, not fatal – we should be able to get a good number of descriptions. And if, as the general suggests, it's the same people behind the attacks who killed Captain Merchant, we might be able to wrap this up.'

'That's going to keep you busy, talking to all the victims,' commented Daniel.

'We'll rope in some of Sergeant Whetstone's men from Whitechapel. That'll speed things up. What about you two?'

'As we said, we'll poke around at Josiah Grundy as a possible weak link. I think this so-called old pal of his, Charlie Smith, sounds interesting. If, as I suspect, he forced Grundy to return to London, he did it for a reason, which I think may well be connected with whatever plans someone's got for the Tower. So we need to find out who this man is and question him. And to do that, we need to talk to Grundy's sister in Loughton and get a description of him.'

'Did you make a note of his sister's address?' asked Feather.

'I did,' said Abigail.

'In that case, time to go our separate ways,' said Feather. 'By the way, as I'm now restricted to the murders of Eric James and Captain Merchant, the chief super's put Inspector Jarrett in charge of the murders of Paul James and Ellie Mercer.'

'Jim Jarrett? But he's a moron.'

'Armstrong likes him because he does things by the book.'

'At least we won't be exposed to him,' said Daniel. 'Our brief is the murder of Eric James, not the others.'

'Even though we think they could be connected,' cautioned Abigail.

'The other thing to warn you about concerning the Eric James murder is that the chief superintendent has got it into his head that Yeoman Purbright is the most likely suspect. He's told me to bring him in for questioning.'

'Purbright?' said Daniel and Abigail together, bewildered.

'On what grounds?' asked Daniel.

'On the fact that it was he who discovered the body.'

'I've spoken to Purbright, said Daniel. 'There was nothing in the man that suggested he was the murderer.'

'As far as Armstrong's concerned, he's a main suspect.'

'Good luck with that,' said Abigail sarcastically.

'Do you want us to take you back to Scotland Yard?' asked Feather.

'No, thank you,' said Abigail. 'We'll take the Underground and head home. We need to get our plans worked out for our trip to Loughton.'

It was as they were walking from the Underground station to their house on Primrose Hill that Abigail threw an idea at Daniel.

'I've been thinking,' she said. 'This description of the mystery man we hope to get from Josiah Grundy's sister may be all very well, but it will only be of value if we can share it with people who might recognise it. So my idea is that we find an artist to make a drawing of the man's face from the description we get from Grundy's sister, and we put it in the newspapers under a caption, something like "Do You Know This Man?"'

'That is a really good idea.' Daniel nodded thoughtfully. 'But how do we find an artist that might do that sort of thing? Artists aren't cheap.'

'I'm thinking of an old friend of mine, Agnes de Souza. She's a portrait artist, who's very good. She catches the image of the person. I wonder if she could produce sketches of the man from the Grundy's sister's description? As I remember, her rates were reasonable. And if it helps us find this mysterious man, it'll be worth it.'

'Yes, it will,' agreed Daniel. 'Shall we go and see her and ask?'

'Perhaps it might be better if I saw her first,' said Abigail. 'After all, it's been some years since I've seen her, so I need to make sure she's still the amenable person she used to be.'

'Yes,' said Daniel. 'Good thinking. And while you're talking to her, I'll check on the best way to get to Loughton.'

CHAPTER TWENTY-TWO

Agnes de Souza's studio, which was also her bedroom and living accommodation to Abigail's observant glances, was at the top of a tall house. Agnes beamed in obvious pleasure when she opened her door and beheld her old friend.

'Abigail!' she cried in delight.

The two women hugged one another warmly.

'It's been a long time,' said Agnes.

'Ten years,' admitted Abigail with a rueful smile of apology. 'Things just seemed to spiral out of control.'

'The Museum Detectives,' said Agnes, leading Abigail into her living-room-cum-studio. 'I read about you in the papers and admire the huge successes you've been having. And your recent expedition to Egypt, as *leader*!'

'That was very fortunate,' said Abigail. 'But what about you? How's it going in the world of art?'

'Slow,' groaned Agnes. 'I had such high hopes. I imagined my pictures on display in the Royal Academy, or the National

Gallery, but, alas, there's no sign of that.'

'Are you doing many portraits?'

'Not of adults,' sighed Agnes. 'Most people seem to prefer to have their photograph taken. It's quicker, and cheaper. Most of my work is of babies and toddlers, who don't sit still long enough for a photograph, or people's pets.'

'Their pets?'

'Usually small dogs, and occasionally cats. I did paint a horse not long ago. Not exactly George Stubbs, but it was money.' Her attitude changed as she said, 'But here I am talking about myself! What brings you here? A portrait?' she asked hopefully.

'Yes, but not of me,' said Abigail. 'In fact, it's going to be rather unusual, and it may not be what you want to do.'

'Is it worse than doing portraits of babies and little dogs?'

'Absolutely not,' Abigail assured her. 'I can imagine their parents or owners would be rather hard to satisfy. To all parents and pet owners, theirs is the most perfect and loveliest.'

'And no one can make them appear as beautiful as they are in their owner's eyes. Or a parent's eyes,' said Agnes ruefully.

'In that case, this is going to be a stretch of your imagination. Daniel and I are going to Loughton in Essex to talk to a witness. We're hoping she'll be able to give us a description of a man who called at her house recently. We wondered if you'd come with us and draw a portrait of the man from her description, and change it according to any comments she's got. Things like, "make his hair shorter", that sort of thing, until we get an accurate image of him.'

191

'Let me guess, this is one of your Museum Mystery cases?' asked Agnes.

'It is,' said Abigail.

'And this man is a criminal?'

'We're not sure yet. That's why we need a good image of him. We hope to put it in the newspapers. With a credit to you, of course. Illustration by Agnes de Souza. You never know, it could lead to commissions.'

'From other criminals?' Agnes laughed.

'Criminals have pets and children.' Abigail laughed back at her.

Abigail returned to the house accompanied by Agnes de Souza, who carried a large leather satchel containing a sketchpad, sticks of charcoal and different thicknesses of pencils. Abigail introduced her to Daniel, who told the two women that Loughton was accessible by the Great Eastern Railway from Liverpool Street. 'So we'll take the Underground to Liverpool Street, and then from there to Loughton.'

'Oh, I love the underground railway!' exclaimed Agnes delightedly. 'You get so many interesting faces on it!'

Much as Daniel enjoyed Abigail and Agnes's pleasure travelling through the tunnels of London's Underground, he was relieved when they changed at Liverpool Street for the above-ground train journey. For one thing, the loud noise of the train was reduced to less deafening levels, and he could enjoy the view. There was a cab waiting for passengers at Loughton station, and it didn't take long before they were deposited at a smallholding with a small two-storey cottage on it, along with some barns. Chickens and geese roamed the yard, with a fence to stop them going onto the two small fields where a variety of crops were growing. A wooden board by the path that led to the house had the word 'Hickworth' on it. Beneath it was a list of items for sale, including eggs, cabbages and potatoes. The place had a slightly run-down air about it. By the look of it, quite a bit of repair work needed to be done to the house, and to the fences, as well as the barns. The middle-aged woman in an apron scattering grain for the chickens looked up as Daniel, Abigail and Agnes approached, a wary expression on her face. Daniel and Abigail exchanged glances, reading one another's thoughts: the Hickworths weren't in the habit of being visited by people who looked like Daniel, Abigail and Agnes. Especially by women like Abigail and Agnes, who gave of an air of confidence and social superiority.

'Good day to you,' said Daniel, doffing his hat. 'Am I addressing Mrs Hickworth?'

'You are,' said the woman. 'But if you're looking for my husband, he's out getting supplies at the moment.'

'Actually, Mrs Hickworth, it's you we would like to talk to.'

'Oh? What about?'

'Your brother, Josiah Grundy.'

Her face took on a look of annoyance mingled with scorn. 'Not more trouble! What's he done now?'

'We understand that a man called to see him recently, and urged him to go to London.'

'He didn't so much urge him as took him. Good riddance, that's what I say. Josiah just turned up here after months of having nothing to do with us, without a please or by-your-leave, and says he needs to hide out here for a day or two. Me, I was all for sending him on his way, but Fred, who's as soft as anything, said, "But he's your brother. We can't turn him away." Well, I could, but Fred insisted.'

'Did he say why he needed to hide out?'

She shook her head. 'No. But he's done that sort of thing before. Got into trouble and come running to us. Never tells us what it's about, just that he's in trouble. Mind, I never wanted to know what sort of trouble it was. The least I know the better, then I'm not involved.'

'Did the man who arrived give his name?'

'No. He said he was a private investigator. Mind, the two blokes he had with him looked a right pair of hard cases. Ex-boxers, they looked like.'

'Did you get the impression that this man was an old friend of your brother?'

'No. I got the impression neither of them knew the other from Adam. This bloke – the private investigator – said he'd been hired to find Josiah by a debt collector.'

Daniel and Abigail exchanged a look, and each knew what the other was thinking, *So much for Josiah's old pal Charlie Smith.*

'Did your brother leave willingly with these men?' asked Abigail.

Barbara Hickworth gave them a look of amusement. 'The size of those two bruisers the bloke had with him, Josiah didn't have a lot of choice.'

'The thing is, Mrs Hickworth, we're keen to make contact with the man who took your brother away, but we don't know who he is or where he can be found.'

'Ask Josiah,' snapped Barbara.

'We have, but he claims not to know,' said Daniel.

'Ha!' snorted Barbara sarcastically. 'He's always been a liar.'

'So our hope is that you might be able to give us a description of this man.' Daniel gestured at Agnes. 'This lady here is an artist and what we'd like is for you to tell her what this man looked like, and she'll make sketches of him, and we'll see how close we can get to a lifelike image of him.'

'Also, if we can do the same with the two men who were with him,' added Abigail. 'The ex-boxers you spoke of.'

'Them I didn't see properly,' said Barbara. 'It seemed to me they kept back, almost hiding themselves. They both had hats on, which they wore low, almost down to their eyes, and they had their coat collars pulled up. But there was one strange thing: one of them had eyes two different colours, one brown, one blue. I'd never seen that before.'

'In that case we'll concentrate on the main man, the one you did see properly. Is that all right?' asked Daniel.

'Is there anything in it for us?' asked Barbara warily.

'Ten shillings,' said Daniel. He took a ten-shilling note from his wallet and waved it at her, then put it back in his wallet.

The woman nodded. 'Ten shillings it is,' she said. She held out her hand. 'I prefer to be paid before we start. I don't know you and you're likely to nip off without paying me after I've given you the words.'

'Do we look the sort of people who'd cheat you like that?' asked Abigail, slightly affronted.

'Trust me, it don't matter what you look like, everyone's a suspect as far as I'm concerned.'

Daniel smiled. 'You're absolutely right to be suspicious. As you say, you don't know us.' He opened his wallet, took out the ten-shilling note, and gave it to her. 'There.'

'Right,' she said. 'Let's go in the house.'

As they walked with her towards the house, she asked Agnes, intrigued, 'So, you're really an artist?'

'I am,' said Agnes.

Barbara looked at Daniel and Abigail. 'And are they artists, too?'

'No,' said Agnes. 'They're the famous Museum Detectives.'

Barbara stopped in her tracks and turned to look at Daniel and Abigail, puzzled.

'Who?' she asked.

'The Museum Detectives,' said Agnes. 'They investigate crimes in museums. Often murders.'

For their part, Daniel and Abigail forced weak, embarrassed smiles.

'Never heard of them,' said Barbara. She looked at Daniel and Abigail again and asked suspiciously, 'Are you saying Josiah's involved in a murder? Only I'm not helping you if it gets him hanged. No matter what he's done to us in the past.'

'No, no,' Abigail reassured her hastily. 'Josiah's not in trouble. It's the man who collected him we're looking for.'

'Is he a murderer?' demanded Barbara.

'No,' said Daniel. 'But he might be able to lead us to

someone who might be involved in something. Not a murder, though.'

Barbara thought it over, then nodded. 'All right, then. I'll do it.'

Josiah Grundy made his way up the flights of stairs to the top of the building and the offices of Fishcock and Purse. The same young man he'd dealt with when he'd handed back the lease, Steven Darcy, was in the office and he looked up enquiringly from his desk as Grundy entered.

'Well, well,' said Darcy. 'Mr Grundy.'

'Mr Darcy.' Grundy nodded. 'I've just been to my old shop. It looks like it's still available.'

'It is, but we've had quite a few enquiries about it.'

'But no one's taken it on as yet?'

'Not as yet.'

'In that case, I'd like to take it on for a short rent. Not the shop. I'm only interested in the flat above the shop.'

'I doubt if the landlord will agree to that,' said Darcy.

'The landlord doesn't have to know,' said Grundy. 'I was thinking of a private arrangement. Between you and me.'

'He'll find out about it,' said Darcy.

'Only if someone wants the shop and pays up the deposit,' said Grundy. 'And if that happens, I move out.'

'Say someone sees you and there's questions?' asked Darcy.

'You say you were worried about intruders, so you hired me to stay at the flat over the shop occasionally to keep an eye on it. Security.'

* * *

197

Daniel and Abigail watched as Agnes, sitting at the table in the kitchen, translated Barbara's descriptive words into the image of a man's face, with Barbara making comments and Agnes revising her pencil strokes, rubbing some out, replacing others until an image of a man's face appeared out of the jumble of lines on her sketchpad.

'That's him!' exclaimed Barbara excitedly. 'As I live and breathe, you've captured him!'

'I'll just make a final finished sketch in charcoal,' said Agnes, 'and we'll see if that works better.'

They watched as Agnes's nimble fingers manipulated the stick of charcoal, some thin, others thick, on a fresh sheet of her sketchpad, until the full-face image of a well-dressed man in his forties emerged: long-nosed, sharp cheekbones, malevolent eyes, dark hair curling back from his high forehead, long ears that almost came to a point at the top.

'That's perfect!' said Barbara in awe. 'You really are an artist. It's almost as if you were here looking at him.'

'Thank you, Mrs Hickworth, for your time, and your excellent description,' said Daniel, getting to his feet and holding out his hand to her.

'What are you going to do with it?' she asked, shaking his hand, then shaking those of Abigail and Agnes. 'Will it go in the papers?'

'Indeed it will,' said Daniel.

Barbara looked at the portrait thoughtfully. 'I hope you find him,' she said. 'But I hope it doesn't bring trouble to us because of Josiah.'

* * *

When they got back to London, they made for Scotland Yard. Inspector Feather and Sergeant Cribbens were just packing up to go home. Abigail introduced Agnes to Sergeant Feather and Sergeant Cribbens, and then showed them Agnes's portrait of the mystery man.

'This is the man who persuaded Josiah Grundy to come to London to tell you his story,' said Abigail. 'We'd like to put it in the newspapers. We'll pay for it as an advert, because we know how the chief superintendent dislikes paying money out. But we'd like the caption to ask anyone who knows who this man is to contact you here at Scotland Yard.'

'The main reason is, because of our promise to the Prince of Wales, we're doing our best to keep our names out of the papers,' added Daniel. 'If journalists see our names included in this, they'll start digging, and might end up finding out about the dead Beefeater. Also, it gives it an air of being official if it's got Scotland Yard attached to it.'

'It's very good indeed,' said Feather admiringly. He turned to Agnes. 'You did this, Miss de Souza?'

'I did,' said Agnes.

'She's a real artist,' Abigail added, 'so we have to make sure the item also says: "Illustration by Agnes de Souza, artist".'

'It's got me thinking,' said Feather. 'General Booth and his son are going to be letting me have that list of his Salvation Army people who were attacked, and Sergeant Cribbens here and some of Sergeant Whetstone's men will go out and get descriptions from them. There are going to be quite a few, but some of them will be the same. It struck me that if we've got some good witnesses, we select the best ones and Miss de Souza does the same thing with them as she did with this picture: do some sketches, then adjust them into proper pictures. Showing people pictures will be a lot quicker than walking around the East End showing people descriptions. Especially because a lot of the people we'll be talking to can't read, and many of them can't understand English. But they'll all recognise a picture.'

'I think that's brilliant!' said Abigail.

'If you can do pictures of these attackers that are as good as this, you'll be the one who's brilliant,' said Feather to Agnes.

CHAPTER TWENTY-THREE

Inspector Jim Jarrett looked up from his desk as the door to his office opened and the burly figure of Chief Superintendent Armstrong entered. Immediately, Jarrett rose sharply to his feet and stood to attention.

'Good morning, sir,' he said.

'You may sit, Inspector,' said Armstrong.

Jarrett sat down again and waited expectantly for the reason for the chief superintendent's unannounced arrival.

'What have you got on at the moment?' asked Armstrong.

'That series of robberies from jewellers. They're hard to prevent because they're smash-and-grab raids. A gang turn up, smash the window and grab a handful of the stuff on display. We've tried telling jewellers not to put real stuff in their windows, put the fake stuff on display, but they say customers can tell when it's fake.'

'Keep on with that,' said Armstrong, 'but there's something else I want you to take on.'

'Oh?'

'Murders. Two, to be exact, in the East End. A low-life thief called Paul James, and his girlfriend, a woman called Ellie Mercer. Inspector Feather's been dealing with them so far, but there's another couple of murders I want him to concentrate on as a priority. So I want you to collect the notes he's made on these two cases from him and look after them.'

'Right, sir. Which murders are the others? The one Inspector Feather's handling as a priority?'

Armstrong hesitated, then said, 'One's the murder of a Salvation Army captain. No one's supposed to know about the other one, on orders from the royal family.'

Jarrett's face lit up with interest. 'The royal family?' he said.

'They don't want any publicity about it, so we've been barred from talking about it. I want you to bear that in mind, Jarrett. If any word leaks out about it and it's found out that it came from us, there'll be hell to pay. Possibly even sackings and forced resignations.'

'You can trust me, sir,' said Jarrett firmly. 'I won't breathe a word.' Then he added thoughtfully, 'Not that I'd need to as I won't be working on it.'

'Well that's the thing, Inspector,' said Armstrong awkwardly. 'This particular murder that the royal family don't want mentioned took place at the Tower of London: one of the Beefeaters. But it turns out he's the brother of this Paul James, the thief, so there might be a connection between the two. The Beefeater's name was Eric James. The two were twins. So, as you investigate the murder of Paul James, if you come across anything that points to a connection with Eric James, you're to pass it on to Inspector Feather. Is that clear?'

'Yes, sir. Perfectly clear. You can depend on me.'

'I've informed Inspector Feather of the change, with you taking over those cases from him. One other thing, Inspector. The Wilsons have been hired by the Prince of Wales to look into the murder of this Beefeater at the Tower. I'm warning you about this in case their investigation leaks into yours, especially the one involving the Beefeater's dead brother. You know how tricky the Wilsons can be. You have been warned. Be on your guard.'

'I will, sir.'

A four-page list with the names and addresses of twenty Salvation Army members who'd been attacked in the Whitechapel area arrived at Scotland Yard for Inspector Feather's attention in the middle of the morning.

'The Booths have moved fast,' commented Sergeant Cribbens.

'My guess is they already had the basis of this list ready,' said Feather. 'Right, Sergeant, talk to these people. Get descriptions of their attackers.' He handed the pages to the sergeant. 'You can do some of them. Take the rest to Stanley Whetstone and get him to give them to some of his men to do the same thing. That should speed things up. Ask Stanley if we can have Barney Brick as one of them. This would be a good time to test him out, see if he'll shape up.'

'Right, sir,' said Cribbens.

As he left the office, Inspector Jarrett appeared. Jarrett let the sergeant out, then entered the office.

'Inspector Feather,' he said. 'The chief superintendent has informed me that I'm to take on two murder cases you have been working on.'

'Paul James and Ellie Mercer.' Feather nodded. He picked up two paper folders and handed them to Jarrett. 'These are the notes we've made on both cases. You'll see that both victims were stabbed and their tongues cut out, which is usually a warning to others to keep their mouths shut.'

'So their murders are connected.'

'That's how it looks to me,' said Feather. 'But I'll leave you to draw your own conclusions.' He pointed at the two brown paper files Jarrett was holding and leafing through the notes inside.

'There are some things that aren't in the files,' said Feather. 'One person of interest we haven't talked to yet is a bloke called Harry Pickwick. We have reason to believe he's a criminal. We also think he's tied in to a corrupt crew of police officers at Fenchurch Street police station.'

Jarrett stopped looking at the notes and looked at Feather, shocked. 'Corrupt?'

Feather nodded. 'The station sergeant, Wesley Sims, is definitely on the take, and I suspect so are the other officers there. We were about to make a move against them, but it's your case now, so it's down to you.'

'Does the chief superintendent know about this?' asked Jarrett, obviously worried.

'The corrupt police crew? No. I was waiting to tell him

after we'd got more evidence. Sergeant Stanley Whetstone at Whitechapel nick knows all about it.'

'How long's it been going on?' asked Jarrett.

'A few months, if the stories are true. Sergeant Whetstone is very unhappy with the situation, as you can imagine.' He hesitated and added, 'There's even a rumour that a sergeant at Fenchurch Street nick called Bob Grillis was going to blow the whistle on them, but he died in mysterious circumstances.'

'What circumstances?'

'He fell and hit his head on a kerb and died. Evidence of this alleged accident was provided by a constable who was with him at the time and observed it.'

Jarrett stared at him, open-mouthed in shock.

'I only learnt about it in the last few days,' Feather continued. 'Sergeant Cribbens and I have been gathering evidence that we could present in order to move in and take action, but as it's your case I'll leave that with you.'

When Inspector Jarrett got back to his office, he found his sergeant, Thomas Pick, had returned and was sharpening pencils.

'Stand by, Pick,' announced Jarrett. 'You're about to hear some astounding news.'

'Yes, sir?' said Pick.

'I've been given a special task by the chief superintendent. Two murders, definitely connected.' Jarrett smirked. 'I get the feeling there may well be promotions coming out of this. There's been talk for some time that the job of chief inspector may be up for grabs.' He tapped the two folders. 'This could be our ticket up the ladder, if we play it careful.'

'Our?' queried Pick.

'Yes, *our*. Yours and mine. A chief inspector still needs a sergeant. We're a good team, Pick.' He gave a broad grin. 'And when you have a read of these, you'll find something alarming. It seems there's a whole police station riddled with corruption and crookery.'

Pick looked at him, horrified. 'A police station?'

'A *whole* police station. Fenchurch Street nick. Full of coppers on the take and in the pay of criminals. There's even a suggestion that a police sergeant at that nick was murdered because he was about to report them all.'

Pick's expression became even more horrified. 'No! It can't be!'

'It is.'

'What are you going to do?'

'Well, the first question is: what was Inspector Feather going to do about it, if anything? Or is he involved?'

'No, I can't believe that,' said Pick. 'Inspector Feather's one of the most honest people I know.'

'Then how come he didn't mention it to the chief superintendent?'

'Perhaps he did.'

Jarrett shook his head. 'If he had, the chief super would have told me. What we have here, Sergeant, is a gross dereliction of duty.' He smirked. 'Which could well rule him out of the running if it's true about the chief inspector job coming up.'

'What are you going to do?' asked Pick again.

'I'm going to do what it's my duty to do,' said Jarrett. 'I shall see the chief superintendent and ask him if he was aware of the situation at Fenchurch Street. And if it turns out he hadn't been made aware of it, then I shall do my duty and tell him.'

CHAPTER TWENTY-FOUR

Josiah Grundy stood in his old flat looking down onto Poultry and the pedestrians and traffic passing along the busy thoroughfare. Of one thing he was sure, he had no intention of returning to Scotland Yard and letting them know where he was staying. For starters, returning to his old flat was very much a temporary situation. The very fact those three men had turned up at his sister's place meant people were after him. Why, he had no idea. For some reason they'd pressurised him into doing what he'd already done: told the police that Bob Grillis's death was an accident. Why didn't they believe him? He could tell from the attitudes of Inspector Feather and that couple who'd been at his interrogation, those Museum Detectives, that they thought there was something wrong about his story. All right, they'd nearly caught him out about his old pal Charlie Smith, but they couldn't prove anything. Just as they couldn't prove anything about the way Bob Grillis had died. There'd been no witnesses except him.

No evidence of anything being wrong.

He remembered it as if it was yesterday. Bob stopping to take his helmet off to wipe his brow because he was sweating. It had been too good an opportunity to miss. One sudden sharp and heavy blow with his truncheon and then Bob was lying in the road. He'd been groaning and had tried to push himself up, and Grundy had given him another whack in the same place, this one even harder than the first. Bob had fallen unconscious, his head right by the kerb. It had been the work of a moment to lift Bob's head and smash it against the sharp kerbstone, splattering it with blood, the proof – if it was needed – of 'the accident'.

Not that anyone would query his story. He'd talked it through with Sergeant Sims. Bob Grillis had to be stopped from talking or they'd all be in jail. He'd be handsomely paid for his work. And the police crew at Fenchurch Street would back him up. They'd come out to look at the kerb and at Bob's dead body and sign statements to back up Grundy's story of the accident. Bob taking a sudden tumble and hitting his head on the kerb.

The trouble was, Bob didn't die straight away. He was unconscious, but Grundy could hear his breath wheezing.

That was when he'd looked around to make sure no one was about, and then smashed his truncheon into the front of Bob's throat, crushing his windpipe and cutting off his air supply. It still took a few minutes of Bob gurgling and shaking before he went silent and still.

No one questioned him about it, or remarked on the injury to Bob's throat. Sergeant Sims had made sure that the undertaker took good care to make him look good in his coffin. The injuries from the blow with the truncheon were patched up. He was dressed in his best uniform, the high collar concealing any damage.

Grundy scowled. Bob was dead and buried. He should have been home free. But then he'd heard that people were looking for him. Dangerous people, hence him seeking refuge at his sister's place, certain that no one would find him there. But they had.

He still didn't know who'd sent those men for him. But he remembered the menace of them. The very real menace.

He looked around at the flat. It would do for a night, but then he'd have to move to somewhere safer. He was vulnerable here. Whoever was after him knew about this place.

Harry Pickwick. The name popped into his head. Good old Harry. They'd had a deal. He'd go and see Harry. Harry would look after him.

Inspector Jarrett strode along the corridor to the chief superintendent's office and knocked on the door. At the call of 'Enter,' he walked in. Armstrong looked at him enquiringly.

'I'm sorry to trouble you, sir,' said Jarrett, 'but I've just been looking through these reports, and I wondered if you were aware of the situation at Fenchurch Street nick.'

Armstrong frowned, puzzled. 'What situation?'

'The corruption.'

Armstrong stared at him and echoed, 'Corruption?' in tones of horror.

'The station sergeant and other senior offices there,

apparently in the pay of criminals.'

Armstrong rose from his chair and held out his open hand, asking, 'I didn't see anything about that in the files. Give them to me and show me.'

'Actually, sir, there's nothing in files about it. I was told this by Inspector Feather. He said he's been investigating, so I presume he hadn't had time to add about the corruption to his notes.'

'What sort of corruption?' demanded Armstrong.

'According to what Inspector Feather told me, it involves a local criminal called Harry Pickwick. There's even a suggestion that a sergeant at Fenchurch Street was killed by some of these corrupt officers to stop him grassing on them.'

Armstrong pointed a stubby finger at the brown paper folders in Jarrett's grasp. 'And there's nothing about that in those folders?'

'No, sir. Just about the actual murders.'

Armstrong sat in thought for a moment, then said grimly, 'Tell Inspector Feather I want to see him in my office. Now.'

'Yes, sir,' said Jarrett.

As he walked along the corridor towards Inspector Feather's office, he felt a warm glow of satisfaction. This was definitely going to scupper Feather's chances of the chief inspector's job. Then all he, Jarrett, had to do was solve these two murders. The victims were both low-life people so that shouldn't be too difficult. There'd be no press intruding on the investigation, as happened when the victim was someone from high society, or a public figure, like an entertainer. With people like this Paul James and his girlfriend, Ellie Mercer, he'd be able to get away with 'person or person unknown' as the culprits.

He knocked at Feather's door and opened it to find Inspector Feather and Sergeant Cribbens engaged in deep conversation. *Discussing the fact that Feather has had two murders taken away from him, I expect*, thought Jarrett.

'The chief superintendent wants to see you, Inspector,' said Jarrett.

'Did he say what it was about?' asked Feather.

'No,' said Jarrett airily. 'Just that he wanted to see you.'

'Thank you,' said Feather. He waited until the door had closed and Jarrett was gone before saying to his sergeant, 'I suspect Inspector Jarrett's been up to his tricks in some way. The chief super will hardly have gone to Jarrett's office to ask him to tell me that, he'd have come straight to me, so Jarrett must have been to see him about something. And that can only be about this Fenchurch Street business.'

'Why Fenchurch Street?' asked Cribbens.

'Because we didn't put anything about it in the files we gave him. It's all word of mouth. He'll be using that to drop me in it.' He stood up. 'Time to go and see if I'm right.'

Feather made his way to the chief superintendent's office, and the opening words from Armstrong told him his calculation was the correct one.

'Why didn't you tell me what was going on at Fenchurch Street?' Armstrong demanded angrily. 'The whole crew being rotten. This criminal, Harry Pickwick?'

'Because it was a case in progress, sir. We were digging for evidence. I felt we needed something stronger than just suspicions before I brought it to your attention.'

'Wrong, Inspector!' thundered Armstrong. 'Something as serious as this is like a bomb waiting to go off. If word gets out, it could destroy the reputation of the whole police force. Why was there nothing about it in your notes?'

'Precisely for the reason you said. Anyone could look at those notes, including the men at Fenchurch Street station. That's why we kept it under wraps until we had concrete evidence to move against them.'

'So what are you doing about gathering this evidence?'

'I've got a couple of detective constables in plain clothes watching Harry Pickwick's yard and seeing who goes in and out. I've arranged a couple of constables from Whitechapel to accompany them. They know the local villains and will mark their cards if any of them are crooked. My plan is to pick these crooks up and get them to grass up Harry Pickwick, then we can round them all up. I'm waiting until they put themselves at risk by taking stolen stuff to Pickwick's place, then we can grab them red-handed.'

Armstrong shook his head. 'It's not fast enough, Inspector. Also, it appears to be linked to the other murders if the rumour about the dead sergeant is true.'

'That's possible, sir.'

'And Inspector Jarrett has taken those over to give you room to get on with the murder of the Beefeater at the Tower, and the Salvation Army captain.' He scowled. 'And I'm annoyed that you chose to discuss this with a station sergeant – a uniformed officer – before you mentioned it to me!'

'Whitechapel is right next door to Fenchurch Street. They know what's been going on. We needed their inside information.'

'Is there anyone else you confided this to?' demanded Armstrong angrily.

'No, sir.' Then he stopped and said awkwardly, 'Although the Wilsons were involved.'

'The Wilsons!' thundered Armstrong, outraged.

'They'd already had their suspicions aroused,' defended Feather.

'How did they even get involved in the first place?'

'Because the case they're on, the murder of the Beefeater at the Tower, led them to look into the murder of his twin brother two days before that. And that was how it all became unravelled, the tie-up between the sergeant at Fenchurch Street and this alleged criminal, Harry Pickwick.'

'I'm going to have to take this to the commissioner,' said Armstrong grimly. 'We need to clear out this rats' nest of corruption *now*.'

'That's what we were planning, sir, Sergeant Whetstone and me, and replace them with honest men. But that's not an easy thing to carry out without awkward questions being asked.'

'Bugger awkward questions!' raged Armstrong. 'I'll go and see the commissioner and suggest he suspends everyone at Fenchurch Street with immediate effect and closes the station, and re-opens it with a staff drawn from Whitechapel.'

'That's what we were planning, sir!' Feather reminded him.

'But not fast enough! You should have come to me with

this as soon as you knew about it.'

'Yes, sir, but I thought—'

'That's your trouble, Feather. You think too much. That's the influence of the Wilsons. Less thought, more action, that's what should have happened here. I'm glad I found out about this now, before the situation got worse.'

'Yes, sir,' said Feather.

Armstrong wagged his finger at Feather as he continued to berate him: 'Purbright, Inspector. That's who I want you to concentrate on. Haul him in.'

Sergeant Cribbens sat in the kitchen of the Brent family house in Whitechapel, talking to Baldwin and Marie Brent, and their seventeen-year-old son, Howard, a cadet with the Salvation Army.

'They beat him,' Marie Brent told them in tones of outrage.

'He was lucky he was able to get away from them,' said her husband, 'otherwise who knows what might have happened.'

'They'd have killed him, that's what,' said Mrs Brent. 'Luckily for Howard he's a fast runner. He's always been good at sports.'

Cribbens nodded and turned his attention to the young man, who still bore the marks of his ordeal: a gash over one eye and a livid bruise on one cheek. 'Did you see the people who did this?'

Howard nodded. 'Only briefly, because at first I was struggling with them because they were trying to take my copies of *The War Cry* from me. But then one of them punched me in the face.' And he pointed to the bruise on his cheek. 'That's when I decided to let go of my War Cry papers and run. But I saw the one who hit me clear as I see you. He was tall with a sneery face. He had this big moustache with curling ends.'

'What colour moustache?' asked Cribbens.

'Dark brown, but the ends were light-coloured, which I thought was odd. And he had a twisted ear.'

'Which one?'

'His left one,' said Howard. 'It was twisted as if someone had grabbed hold of it and bent it over.'

'An unusual, distinctive moustache and a twisted ear,' repeated Cribbens as he wrote the words down.

'That should help you find him, shouldn't it?' said Marie Brent. 'People like him should be in jail.'

'He will be once we get him, ma'am,' Cribbens assured her. He looked at Howard. 'Is there any more you remember about him? Or the others who were with him?'

'No,' said Howard apologetically. 'After that I started running and I didn't look back.'

Cribbens thanked the Brents and left their house, and walked to where Barney Brick had been doing the same questioning a couple of streets away.

'How did you get on?' asked Cribbens.

'Not bad,' said Brick. 'I got two really good descriptions. The others were a bit vague. But the two who stood out were a bloke with a distinctive moustache and a twisted ear, and a bald bloke.'

'I got the one with the twisted ear and the moustache as well.' Cribbens nodded. 'Right, let's get back to Whitechapel nick and see how Stanley Whetstone's men did.' He smiled happily. 'I've got a good feeling about this. The fact that the same faces keep popping up, it's a pound to a penny they'll be the same ones who killed the Salvation Amy captain. I think we're going to get them, Constable.'

CHAPTER TWENTY-FIVE

Abigail opened the front door to a knock and found Inspector Feather and Sergeant Cribbens on the doorstep.

'I've brought the descriptions of the men who've been attacking Salvation Army people in Whitechapel,' said Feather, patting a leather satchel.

Abigail invited them in and they walked through to the kitchen, where Daniel sat at the kitchen table reading the newspaper.

'I heard what you said,' said Daniel. 'It sounds like progress has been made.' He gestured at the kettle on the gas stove. 'The kettle will be boiling at any moment, so join us in a cup of tea while we take a look at these descriptions.'

Daniel made the tea while Feather took the descriptions from his satchel and put them on the table. Daniel and Abigail took turns to read them.

'Some of these are very clear,' commented Abigail. 'Very good observations.'

'I suggest that your friend Agnes has a look at them and decides which of the witnesses she wants to talk to,' said Feather. 'I've put them into four separate bundles because there are four descriptions that keep recurring: one talks of a man with a twisted ear and a particular moustache; another man has a tattoo on his face; a third has a flattened nose; and the fourth is fat and bald with tufts of hair just above his ears.'

'Do you want us to bring Agnes to Scotland Yard?' asked Abigail.

Feather looked awkwardly at them. 'I was thinking it might be better if at this stage we all go to her studio to talk about things.'

'You haven't told the chief superintendent what we're doing, have you?' said Abigail with a smile.

'You know what he's like,' said Feather defensively. 'He's not keen on new ideas. Look at how long it took him to admit that the idea of fingerprints was effective. I'm sure he'll agree about the idea of using an artist; they already use them for wanted posters, but those are by police artists. Your Miss de Souza is a class above them, a real artist, and the chief superintendent is suspicious of real artists. But, if this works, it will persuade him of the value of using artists in the future. Just like the business with fingerprints. It just takes him time to get used to new things.'

Abigail looked at Daniel and asked, 'Is it all right if I leave you three to go and see Agnes? I promised Sophie and Alice I'd call and see how they were doing with the skeleton.'

'Skeleton?' asked Feather, alert. 'What skeleton?'

'Two young women who are doing an archaeological

dig at the Tower have uncovered a skeleton. It's raised a few questions.'

'How recent is it?' asked Feather.

'It's difficult to say at this stage,' said Abigail. 'It could be six hundred years old. Perhaps more.'

'Not recent, then?'

'No.'

'Thank heavens for that,' said Feather. 'We've already got enough dead bodies to look into. Do you want a lift to the Tower?'

'Thanks, but it's in a different direction to Agnes's studio and I think it's important for you to get Agnes to work.'

Daniel, Feather and Cribbens left Abigail to prepare for her visit to the Tower while they left the house and made for the police vehicle waiting for them outside. Daniel gave directions to the driver for Agnes's studio, then joined the inspector and his sergeant inside the carriage.

'By the way, I thought I'd alert you to Jim Jarrett's activities,' said Feather.

'What sort of activities?' asked Daniel.

'I told him about our suspicions over Fenchurch Street station, and Harry Pickwick. He's taken it to Armstrong, who says he's going to intervene. He wasn't happy I hadn't mentioned it to him before.'

'It sounds like Jarrett's doing his best to stir things up for you and put you in the bad books,' observed Daniel.

'Yes, that was my thought as well,' agreed Feather. 'The bottom line is that Armstrong says he's going to see the commissioner and shut down Fenchurch Street and have everyone there arrested. He also accused me of not doing anything to stop what was going on. I tried to tell him that I've got a team of plainclothes detectives along with some from Whitechapel watching Harry Pickwick's place to get the evidence we need to round everyone up, but he said it couldn't wait that long.' He sighed. 'At the moment I'm in the bad books.'

'Have you ever thought of doing what me and Fred Abberline did? Leaving the force and setting up as a private investigator?' asked Daniel.

Feather shook his head. 'With a family of four kids to support, I can't take the chance.'

They arrived at Agnes's studio and Daniel led them up to the top floor. Agnes was at work on a small oil painting of a cat.

'A cat?' queried Feather.

'It's a commission, and a commission means money,' said Agnes. 'I assume you've got those descriptions you talked about?'

Feather handed her the satchel. Agnes sat down and took the descriptions from the satchel. She read them, then selected four. 'These seem to show the best powers of observation, and each has got a description of a separate individual. I'd like to work with them, see if I can work their descriptions up into pictorial images that hopefully they'll agree are accurate.'

'Thank you,' said Feather. 'Sergeant Cribbens here will escort you to Whitechapel, where the witnesses live. He's already met most of them so it'll save you long explanations at each place. Daniel and I will walk to Scotland Yard; it'll do us good.' He looked at Daniel. 'Is that all right with you? We can swap information about Yeoman Purbright and see if we can't persuade the chief superintendent of his innocence.'

'I'm happy to do that,' said Daniel, 'but with a word of caution. We both think that Purbright isn't the killer, but the chief superintendent could be right and we could be wrong. I think we're both going to have to be very careful.'

When Abigail arrived at the site of the dig, she found a large tent had been erected next to the trench. Inside, Professor Clement, Sophie, Alice and Viscount Dillon were looking at two small skeletons that had been laid out on two trestle tables.

'You found two!' she said.

'We did,' said Clement. 'Or, rather, Sophie and Alice did. My other students just helped with uncovering them and bringing them in here.'

Abigail looked at the skeletons. 'Two skeletons. Young. About ten or eleven years old at the time of death, at a guess.' She looked at Clement quizzically.

'Yes, we're thinking the same. Could it be that the skeletons interred at Westminster Abbey were wrongly identified as those of the two princes?'

'It could cause a constitutional problem,' said Dillon unhappily. 'The skeletons at Westminster Abbey would have to be removed and replaced with these. We would need to be absolutely sure that these skeletons are of the princes before we could suggest that to His Highness the Prince and the authorities at the abbey.'

'The Prince of Wales?' asked Alice.

'Of course,' said Dillon. 'If that's who they are, they would be his royal ancestors.'

* * *

Sergeant Cribbens and Agnes de Souza sat in the kitchen of Ivy Maton, one of the Salvation Army's many women recruits. Mrs Maton was in her forties and still bore the mark of the attack on her, a black eye and a bruised cheek. Her husband, dressed in his Salvation Army uniform, sat apart from them, a look of disapproval clear on his face. Agnes had her sketchpad lying open on the table, her pencils and sticks of charcoal lined up next to it.

'You're sure you're all right about doing this, Mrs Maton?' asked Agnes. 'It'll stir up bad memories for you.'

'I already have bad memories of what happened,' said Mrs Maton firmly. 'I want these thugs brought to justice.'

'The Lord says we should turn the other cheek,' said Mr Maton, his tone showing his disapproval of this process.

'I did, and the men struck that one as well,' said Mrs Maton angrily. 'The Bible also talks of an eye for an eye, a tooth for a tooth. Exodus 21:23. Or would you prefer me to be killed the next time it happens, the same as they did with poor Captain Merchant?'

'No, of course not,' said Mr Maton.

'Well, that's what this is doing, preventing any more such murders of our people,' said Mrs Maton. She turned to Sergeant Cribbens. 'Isn't that right?'

'It is indeed, ma'am,' said Cribbens.

'Then let's get on with it,' said Mrs Maton.

'I'm planning to do two studies for each person,' said Agnes. 'One showing their facial features, the other showing their body features: height, thin or fat, tall or short, that sort of thing. I thought we'd start with the faces. You saw two of them?'

'I saw two of them clearly. The others were blurs because I was trying to protect myself from the blows they rained down on me.'

Agnes selected one of the descriptions. 'Let's do the man with the flattened nose.'

'The brute,' said Mrs Maton scornfully. 'He seemed to take pleasure in hitting a woman.'

'What sort of shape was his face? Flattish? Thin? Round?'

'Long,' said Mrs Maton. 'Thin.'

Agnes drew an elongated elliptical shape, and in the middle of it drew a flattened nose.'

'Flatter and wider than that,' said Mrs Maton. 'It looked as if it had been squashed against his face.'

'Like a boxer's nose,' said Agnes.

'Possibly,' said Mrs Maton with a sniff. 'I do not know any boxers. I disapprove of pugilism in any form. It is a violent act that demeans those who partake in it and those who watch it.'

'Amen to that,' said Mr Maton.

Agnes adjusted the nose, then looked enquiringly at Mrs Maton, who nodded approvingly. 'That's good.'

'What about his eyebrows?' asked Agnes. 'Thick? Thin? Did they join together above his nose? What colour were they?'

'They were joined together, like one thick long eyebrow,' said Mrs Maton. 'Although there were gaps in the eyebrow.'

'Definitely a boxer,' said Cribbens. 'Most of them suffer from patchy eyebrows because of the punches they get to the face.' As Mrs Maton gave him a look of strong disapproval, the sergeant added hastily, 'So I've been told. I don't follow boxing. Like you, I feel it's a violent sport that brings out the worst in people.'

Mr Maton looked at him suspiciously, but before she could ask any more, Agnes began to fill in the single eyebrow, with a few gaps in it.

'Eyes?' she asked. 'What sort of eyes did he have? Were they deep-set or popping out?'

It took over an hour, but at the end of the time Agnes had very lifelike images of two different men in her sketch, the one with the flattened nose and the bald man.

'That's brilliant!' said Cribbens in admiration. 'They look alive!'

'You have a talent, young lady,' said Mrs Maton, her tone rather grudging. 'A God-given talent like that needs to be used for the power of the Lord.'

'It is,' said Cribbens. 'We can use these pictures to arrest these men and stop them attacking you and your people.'

CHAPTER TWENTY-SIX

Harry Pickwick looked up from his account pages as the door of his office opened, and a look of combined puzzlement and alarm came into his face as he saw his visitor was Josiah Grundy.

'Grundy!' he burst out. 'What are you doing here? I thought you'd gone away to somewhere safe.'

'I did, but it turned out not to be as safe as I thought,' said Grundy. He sat himself down in one of the chairs. 'I'm here because I need help.'

'What sort of help?' asked Pickwick warily. 'I've given you money.'

'Money, yes, but it hasn't bought me safety,' said Grundy. 'A bloke turned up with a couple of heavies at my sister's and brought me back to London.'

'Why did you come back with them?'

'Because he told me if I didn't, he'd tell these two blokes to kill me. And they would have, I can tell.'

'Who was he?' asked Pickwick.

'He never told me his name, nor who he was working for and I didn't think it would be very clever to ask him.'

'What did he want?'

'He wanted me to go to Scotland Yard and tell them that Bob Grillis died as the result of a fall. That his death was an accident.'

Pickwick looked puzzled. 'But it was. That's what you told me.'

'Exactly.' Grundy nodded. 'But this bloke wanted me to tell that to Scotland Yard. So I did.'

'And what happened then?'

'The police let me go. The trouble is, I don't feel that's the end of it. Whoever's behind it is up to something and I'm part of it. What part exactly, I don't know, but I do know I'm being watched.'

'Who by? The police?'

Grundy shook his head. 'No, by whoever's behind the bloke who brought me back to London. The trouble is, I don't know what he's got in store for me, but something tells me it ain't good. So I need somewhere safe to stay. Somewhere I can be protected.'

'What about your old place? The flat over the tobacconist's?'

'No, that's not safe at all. I was thinking of somewhere here.'

'Here? In Fenchurch Street?'

'No, *here*. Your yard. With your muscle always hanging around, I'd be safe.'

'But where would you stay?'

'In one of your barns. I could be your night watchman.'

* * *

In the room above William Oakes's locksmith shop, Constable Reeves wrote down Josiah Grundy's name on his list of visitors to the yard.

'You sure that's who he is?' he asked Barney Brick.

'Oh yes,' replied Brick grimly. 'The bastard who killed a decent copper and got away with it.'

Mrs Paxton, the Duke of Cranbrook's housekeeper, looked up from the sideboard she was polishing at the young maid walking along studying the newspaper she'd just collected from the front doormat.

'What are you up to, Queenie?' she demanded sharply. 'That's His Grace's paper; it's not for you to read.'

Queenie showed her the page that had caught her attention: the lifelike drawing of a man under the headline *Have You Seen This Man?*

'I was just looking at this, Mrs Paxton,' said Queenie. 'That looks like His Grace's valet, Mr Perkins.'

'Nonsense,' said Mrs Paxton. 'Why would he be in the paper?' She looked at the picture and frowned. She took the newspaper from Queenie. 'You carry on with this polishing while I take it to His Grace.'

The Duke was in his library. Mrs Paxton walked in and presented him with the newspaper, saying, 'Today's *Times*, Your Grace. There's a very interesting item in it, with a picture of a man who looks just like Mr Perkins.'

The Duke took the paper and looked at it, then gave a frown.

'Thank you, Mrs Paxton, for bringing this to my attention.

Do you happen to know where Perkins is at this moment?'

'I believe he's in the garage, Your Grace, doing something to the motor car.'

The Duke got up. 'Thank you.'

As the Duke walked across the cobbled rear yard towards the garage, formerly a stable block, he pondered over the implication of this picture in the newspaper. It was an interruption to his plans, that was for sure, one that would necessitate some rethinking. But it was not insurmountable.

Perkins was in the garage polishing the brasswork on the car, a Panhard and Levassor two-seater, the Duke's pride and joy. Perkins stopped when the Duke appeared.

'You wanted me, Your Grace?'

'Have you seen the newspapers this morning, Perkins?' asked the Duke.

'No, sir. Is there anything of note in them?'

'There is indeed,' said the Duke, and he handed the paper to Perkins, opened at the image of the valet. Perkins gaped at it, then looked at the Duke, bewildered.

'This isn't good, Perkins,' said the Duke.

'No, Your Grace.'

'It's a good likeness. I wonder where they got it from?'

'Not from me, Your Grace, or any of mine.' He looked thoughtful. 'Grundy?'

The Duke frowned. 'I would have thought he'd have been too scared to go to the police and describe you to them in this much detail. You gave him to understand what would happen to him if he talked to the police? '

'I did, Your Grace, in very clear terms. But perhaps I ought to have another word with him, just to make sure.'

'I don't think that's a good idea. People will have seen this and someone is bound to recognise you. I think you need to disappear for a week or two, just until this blows over.'

'If you think that's best, Your Grace.'

'I do. It's a pity, because I was depending on you when we carry out the job. You were the best person for this. Now, I think you need to be out of the country.'

'Out of the country, sir?' asked Perkins unhappily.

'Officially,' said the Duke. 'If anyone asks me or the staff, the official line is that you've gone to France to examine some motor manufacturing there. In reality, you will be here but staying out of sight. There is an attic at the top of the house where I keep private documents.'

'Yes, sir. I know it. The cord across the stairs that lead up to it with a sign saying "Private. No entry".'

'I thought of using the attic some time ago, Perkins, so the usual offices have been installed there. Mrs Paxton will deliver meals to you.'

'Mrs Paxton has got enough on her plate with those two in the cellar. Can't Queenie do that?'

The Duke shook his head. 'Queenie is young and can't be trusted not to chatter about what goes on. Fortunately, she's not involved in what we're planning, whereas Mrs Paxton is.'

Daniel laid the copy of *The Times* on the table.

'Your friend Agnes has done a superb job,' he said. 'It's very lifelike. Someone must recognise him.'

'Hopefully,' said Abigail.

'You seem preoccupied,' commented Daniel. 'Something about this man?'

'No,' said Abigail. 'I feel we're not doing justice to the killing of Eric James. That's the case the Prince of Wales hired us to investigate, and we've allowed ourselves to be sidetracked by other things.' She looked shamefaced as she added, 'Including me spending too much time on the dig at the Tower.'

'That's understandable,' said Daniel.

'But not excusable,' said Abigail. 'I've had a thought. We both agree the murder of Eric James is connected to that of his brother, Paul?'

'Agreed,' said Daniel. 'Personally, I can't believe the two of them happening within two days of one another was just coincidental.'

'We need to look into Paul James, find out who his recent associates were.'

'I think John Feather's been doing that.'

'Yes, but now Paul James's murder has been given to Inspector Jarrett to look into, we're not going to get the same co-operation.'

Daniel nodded. 'So you think we should talk to John and see what he's found so far, if anything, and then do our own digging?'

'I do,' said Abigail. 'Before Inspector Jarrett starts doing his best to stop us.'

'Agreed,' said Daniel.

They made their way to Scotland Yard, but were told that Inspector Feather was busy with Superintendent Armstrong and that he'd then be out for the rest of the day.

'We'll come back first thing tomorrow,' said Daniel as he and Abigail left the building. 'Hopefully, we'll get hold of him before he gets too busy.'

Inspector Feather laid the four pictures Agnes had created on Chief Superintendent Armstrong's desk.

'I thought you'd be interested to see what we've been doing on the Salvation Army captain's murder. These are the four men we believe carried out the murder.'

The chief superintendent stared at them, stunned. 'Where did you get these from?' he asked.

'They're from the descriptions we've got from other Salvation Army people who've been attacked in that area. At the moment we only have these pictures of them, but the victims have said they're very accurate. I'm hoping that once these get shown around in Whitechapel, we'll find out who these men are.'

'Excellent. That's good work, Inspector.'

'To be fair, sir, I got the idea from the Wilsons after they got an artist to draw an image of a man they're looking for, from a description they'd got. It was very lifelike and I thought the same could be done with the men who attacked these Salvation Amy members.'

'An artist?'

'Yes, sir. An Agnes de Souza.'

'A foreigner?'

'British. Her grandfather came from Portugal. She's very good at drawing. Very lifelike images.'

Armstrong scowled. 'You didn't need the Wilsons for that. You'd have thought of doing that yourself, Inspector.'

'Yes, sir, but I didn't.'

'Well, *I* would have if you'd asked me. You should have spent more of your time reporting to me what you've found, instead of spending it with the Wilsons.' But he nodded in grudging approval. 'It's still good work, Inspector. Let's hope someone recognises them.'

'Yes, sir. I'm off to the printer's. I'm going to get enough copies printed so we can get some of Sergeant Whetstone's men to show them around – speed things along.'

Fourteen-year-old Jake Petty mounted the steps of Scotland Yard, walked into the large reception area and made for the reception desk.

'What do you want, sonny?' asked the duty sergeant, Callum McDougall.

Jake produced a copy of that day's newspaper with the image of Caleb Perkins and held it out to the sergeant. 'I know who this bloke is,' he said. 'I want to see Inspector Feather.'

'Inspector Feather's out at the moment,' said Sergeant McDougall. He took a piece of paper and a pencil. 'If you tell me the bloke's name, I'll pass that on.'

Jake shook his head. 'This inspector has got a sergeant of his own, hasn't he?' he asked. 'That's how it works.'

Sergeant McDougall studied the small boy. 'How come you know so much about it? You got family in the force, or you've been nicked before?'

'No, I haven't,' said Jake.

Sergeant McDougall nodded. 'All right. You wait over there on those benches. I'll send a note up to Sergeant Cribbens and tell him you're here.'

Jake went to the long benches by the far wall and sat down. Sergeant McDougall wrote a brief note, which he handed to a messenger, who took it upstairs. A short time later the messenger returned accompanied by the burly figure of Sergeant Cribbens, who went to speak to Sergeant McDougall at the reception desk. McDougall pointed at Jake sitting on the bench, and Sergeant Cribbens walked over to him.

'The sergeant tells me you know who the bloke in the paper is,' he said.

'I do,' said Jake.

'Who is he?'

'How much is it worth?' asked Jake.

'Nothing,' said Cribbens. 'It's your civic duty to tell the police what you know.'

'Civic duty ain't gonna put food on my table,' said Jake. 'You've paid other people for information. I know because my uncle got a reward for handing in his next-door neighbour. Burglary, that was. He got four shillings.'

Cribbens shook his head. 'That reward would only have been paid out once the criminal was tried and put away. That can't happen here unless we know the identity of this person and talk to them.' He gave Jake a hard look and said, 'Of course, we can always arrest you for withholding information from the police.'

'You can't do that!' protested Jake.

'I can,' said Cribbens. Then his expression softened as he added, 'Or we can do this in a friendly fashion. You give me the name and I give you sixpence.'

'Sixpence?' said Jake scornfully.

'On account,' said Cribbens. 'And if your information means the case comes to fruition and there's a conviction, then we can discuss a reward. So that's your choice: give me the name and get sixpence now and maybe something later, or I put you in a cell for refusing to give information.'

Jakes hesitated, not happy with any part of this offer. Then he said, 'Let's see the sixpence.'

Cribbens reached into his trouser pocket and took out a few coins. He selected a silver sixpence and held it out to Jake. Jake reached out to take it, but Cribbens pulled it back.

'Name first,' he said.

'Caleb Perkins,' said Jake. 'He's valet to this rich bloke in Belgravia, the Duke of Cranbrook.'

'What's the address in Belgravia?' asked Cribbens.

Jake told him, at which point Cribbens handed him the sixpenny piece. 'There,' he said. 'Thank you.'

'What about the rest of the reward?' asked Jake suspiciously.

'If that happens we'll get in touch with you,' said Cribbens. He pulled out his notebook and a pencil. 'So I'll need your name and address.'

'Jake Petty,' said the boy. '4 Selous Street, Camden Town. But don't use my name when you go to see this Duke bloke. My sister works there as a maid. It was her who saw the picture in the paper and told me who he was. If you say it was Jake Petty, they'll know it came from her, and she'll get in trouble.'

'Your name won't be used, I promise,' said Cribbens.

CHAPTER TWENTY-SEVEN

Inspector Feather was surprised to find Daniel and Abigail sitting in his office with Sergeant Cribbens when he arrived for work the next morning, Friday.

'You two are up and about early,' he said.

'We've decided to be more active about looking into the killing of Paul James,' said Abigail.

'It's not our case any more,' said Feather.

'So we understand. But the thing is it's unlikely that Inspector Jarrett will welcome us nosing around in it.'

'Why the change of tack?' asked Feather.

'Because we've allowed ourselves to be sidetracked by the other things that are going on,' said Abigail.

'The murder of the Salvation Army captain,' added Daniel, 'Josiah Grundy, the robbery we suspect is going to happen at the Tower, Harry Pickwick, all the other stuff that's pulled us away from our original investigation, the one the Prince of Wales has commissioned us to look into. So what we've come to ask you is if you've found out who Paul James's associates were, and if any of them are suspects.'

Feather shook his head ruefully. 'Everyone we've spoken to who we think might have had contact with Paul James, like the two old ladies at the house where he lived, have said they had no idea who he mixed with. It's the same story with Ellie Mercer. No one knows who she mixed with, except for Paul James. I think someone's put the frighteners on everyone on that topic.'

'Connected with Fenchurch Street and Harry Pickwick?'

'Possibly,' said Feather. 'One of the two old ladies at Muscovy Court did let slip that Paul used to sometimes drink at The Happy Onion in Whitechapel.'

'The Happy Onion?' said Daniel. 'That's the one where Big Billy Buffett used to be a regular.'

'He's a bit more than a regular now,' said Feather. 'He owns it. He already had a half share, but when Steamy Fred, who owned the other half, died, Big Billy bought his share from Fred's family.'

'So what does Big Billy say about Paul James?'

'He claims he never even met Paul James.'

'I think I'll go and have a word with him,' said Daniel.

Feather shook his head. 'It won't do you any good. Big Billy's keeping schtum, as they say in that part of the East End.'

'I think he might make an exception for me,' said Daniel.

'Why? What makes you so special?'

'Ten years ago I saved his life.'

Feather looked at him in disbelief. 'You think that's going to make a difference?'

'It's worth a try,' said Daniel.

'Well, good luck with that,' said Feather. 'Right now, Sergeant Cribbens and I are off to get the prints of Miss de Souza's images of the men who killed Captain Merchant.'

'Agnes is starting to sound like a vitally important addition to the team,' said Abigail.

'Thanks to you,' said Feather. 'I'll see you later.'

The four left Scotland Yard together, and while Feather and Cribbens headed for the printer's, Daniel and Abigail discussed their next move.

'This Big Billy Buffett,' said Abigail. 'You said you saved his life. How did you do it?'

'It was when I was on the force during the Ripper enquiries. Big Billy's name was being bandied about by some of the locals. He knew four of the women quite well. He was also known to carry a knife. Unfortunately, some people put two and two together and made five, and they were the radicals. There was a lot of radical activity in the area at that time, anti-establishment revolutionaries set on overthrowing all recognised authority. Passions were running high, as you can imagine. Anyway, I happened to be in The Happy Onion talking to Big Billy when this mob burst in intent on stringing him up.'

'What did you do?'

Daniel shrugged. 'I did my best to reason with them.'

'And it worked?'

'After a fashion. Big Billy and I are still alive today to tell the tale.'

'So now we go to see this Big Billy.'

'No,' said Daniel. '*I'll* go to see him. It's an ambiguous relationship he and I have, but if anyone else is there he's sure to clam up. Just as he obviously did with John Feather.'

'But you think he'll talk to you?'

'As I said, it's worth a try.'

Feather and Cribbens arrived at the printer's to collect the images of the suspects: twenty copies of each of the four pictures.

'Be careful,' the printer, Humble Fraser, warned the inspector. 'We worked through the night to cut the blocks because of you saying how urgent it was. We left them to dry but the ink's a bit damp on some of them.'

'I'll leave it another hour,' said Feather.

He and Sergeant Cribbens made for a coffee house and discussed the information the sergeant had received from Jake Petty the previous day.

'Caleb Perkins,' mused Feather.

'Never heard of him,' said Cribbens. 'Nor this Duke of Cranbrook.'

Feather took out his watch and looked at it.

'On reflection,' he said, 'it might be a good idea for me to go along to this Duke of Cranbrook's place now and leave you to wait till the prints are dry. Just in case this Caleb Perkins has seen the picture in the paper and is about to do a runner. You pick up the pictures, making sure they're dry, and take them to Whitechapel. Give them to Sergeant Whetstone and tell him to select some good men to take them round, showing them. Keep a couple of the pictures back for yourself and you do some showing them around, see what the reaction is.' He finished his coffee. 'I'll see you back at the Yard.'

Leaving his sergeant at the coffee shop, Feather made his way to the address in Belgravia. Once there, he introduced himself to the housekeeper who opened the door and asked to see the Duke of Cranbrook. When the housekeeper asked the purpose of his visit, Feather replied simply, 'Tell him it's a police matter.'

The housekeeper disappeared into the house, returning a few moments later to show the inspector into the study where the Duke of Cranbrook was studying some maps.

'I understand you wish to see me on a police matter,' said the Duke.

'That is so, Your Grace,' said Feather. 'I wonder if I could have a word with your valet, Caleb Perkins?'

'Might I ask why?'

Feather produced the newspaper with the drawing of Perkins on the front and handed it to Cranbrook. 'Because we've been advised that this man, who we wish to talk to, is your valet, Caleb Perkins.'

The Duke took the paper and studied the drawing. 'Really? It doesn't look much like him.'

'If we can see him, we'll be able to judge for ourselves.'

The Duke handed the newspaper back to Feather. 'Unfortunately, Perkins is out of the country at the moment.'

'Where is he?'

'France, if you must know.'

'And what is he doing there?'

'He's checking on a new automobile I'm interested in. Are

you interested in automobiles, Inspector?'

'Only as far as the potential problems they pose on the roads.'

'It's not the automobiles that pose the problems, inspector, nor their drivers. It's the law-makers that create problems. I speak as one who's been driving these vehicles since 1896. In fact, I was one of those who drove in the Emancipation Run that year. From London to Brighton. The police were involved, as I recall.'

'Not Scotland Yard detective division, sir.'

'Have you driven an automobile, Inspector?'

'No, sir. I can't say I have.'

'Have you seen one up close? Touched it?' As Feather shook his head, the Duke said, 'In that case, allow me to introduce you to one.'

The Duke rose to his feet, slipped on a jacket, and led Feather out of the house and across the rear courtyard to the former stable block, now a garage. The doors of the garage were open, the metal cover of the front of the car had been removed, and a man in overalls was at work on the engine.

'My mechanic, Edmund Spencer,' announced the Duke. 'Edmund, this is Detective Inspector Feather from Scotland Yard. I've brought him here to show him this magnificent machine.'

Spencer stepped back to allow the Duke and Feather closer access to the car. To Feather it looked like a two-seater carriage with two large wheels at the rear and two slightly smaller ones at the front. It had a large metal box at the front, which Feather guessed housed the engine.

'The Panhard and Levassor two-seater,' said the Duke proudly. 'Four horse-power. A magnificent machine. This is the vehicle I used for the Emancipation Run. You know, of course, why it was called the Emancipation Run?'

'To celebrate the passing of the Locomotives on Highways Act, which replaced the earlier Locomotive Acts of 1861, 1865 and 1878,' replied Feather.

'I am impressed, Inspector,' said the Duke. 'Many officers I am stopped by as I drive my vehicle don't seem to be aware of it.'

'I may not have seen one up close, but I do keep track of every new law passed in parliament. As I recall, the 1878 Act restricted the speed of any road vehicle to 4 miles per hour. The 1896 act increased that to 14 miles per hour. It was the 1865 act that required all such vehicles to have an escort walking ahead of the vehicle to carry a red flag. The need for the red flag was discontinued with the introduction of the 1878 act.'

The Duke looked at Feather admiringly. 'I wish that all police officers had your knowledge, Inspector. It would make journeys so much easier. I am constantly badgered by people, including police officers, telling me I'm breaking some ancient and now non-applicable speed limit.' He gestured at the gleaming car. 'Would you like to have a ride in this machine? This really is the future of transport.'

'Thank you, sir, but I'm afraid I have to get on. If you are in touch with Mr Perkins, perhaps you'd ask him to return to England. We really do need to talk to him.'

'If I hear from him, I will. At this moment I'm not sure

where he is in France; he's travelling from manufacturer to manufacturer, looking at various machines. One day Britain will have its own proper automobile manufacturers, but at the moment the only two countries manufacturing them in any quantity are France and America.'

Feather returned to Scotland Yard and found a despondent Sergeant Cribbens sitting in the office, looking ruefully at the printed images of the men.

'You look like the exercise has not been a success,' observed Feather.

'No,' admitted Cribbens. 'Not just for me; it was the same for all of us. To be honest, we'd hardly got started, but right from the word go everyone was afraid to say who these men were in case they incur their wrath. I'm sure people recognised them, but I'm guessing these are the sort of men who'd hand out retribution if they thought they'd been grassed up.'

'Yes,' admitted Feather ruefully. 'That was always going to be a problem we'd come up against.'

'How did you get on, sir? With Caleb Perkins?'

'Perkins wasn't at the house. The Duke says he's gone to France on business for him. The Duke is an enthusiast about cars and Perkins is apparently there doing some work for him on them.'

'Very convenient, in view of that picture just appearing in the papers.'

'Exactly, Sergeant. It may be true that Perkins is out of the country, but I'm fairly sure the Duke arranged it.'

'You think this Duke is involved in something odd?'

'I do. But what his role in it is, I haven't the faintest idea. Frankly, we don't even know what *it* is. Daniel seems to think a robbery's planned at the Tower of London. But what sort of robbery, and how they're planning to do it, is another mystery.'

'One interesting thing's happened,' said Cribbens. He handed Feather the note that Barney Brick had sent over. 'Josiah Grundy was seen going into Harry Pickwick's yard. According to this note from Barney Brick, he was in there for about an hour.'

'Well, well,' murmured Feather thoughtfully. 'We'd better let Inspector Jarrett know. After all, he's in charge of anything concerning Harry Pickwick and Fenchurch Street.'

Cribbens nodded, then suddenly he looked at the inspector as an idea obviously struck him. 'I've just had a thought, sir.'

'About Inspector Jarrett?'

'No, sir. About these drawings.' He pointed to the pictures of the four suspects on his desk. 'Why don't we spin a different story, sir?'

'What do you mean?' asked Feather.

'We tell people we're looking for these men because there's a reward for a good deed they did.'

'What sort of good deed?' asked Feather.

'A dog. It was rescued from the Thames after it had fallen into the river, and these men were spotted pulling it out. They saved its life, but when the owner went to thank them, they ran off. The owner's a rich businessman and he wants to pay them for what they did.'

Feather looked at him in admiration. 'Did you think of that yourself?' he asked.

Cribbens looked uncomfortable. 'Actually, it was in a story I read in one of the wife's magazines.'

'It doesn't matter where it came from,' said Feather. 'That's brilliant, Sergeant!'

The door opened and Chief Superintendent Armstrong looked in. 'Have you picked up Purbright yet, Inspector?' he demanded.

'No, sir. We've been looking into the murder of the Salvation Army captain, following up those pictures I showed you of the suspects.'

Armstrong's impatience subsided a little. 'Yes, all right, but don't forget Purbright.'

'I'll bring him in first thing in the morning, sir,' said Feather. He indicated the clock. 'It's a bit too late to bring him in now, unless we keep him in the cells overnight, which would upset Viscount Dillon.'

'All right then, but first thing. And sweat him once he's here.'

'Yes, sir.'

The chief superintendent turned to leave, then stopped. 'One more thing, Inspector.'

'Yes, sir?'

'Those drawings you had made of the people suspected of killing the Salvation Army captain.'

'Yes, sir?'

'Let me have one of each. As I'm going to see the commissioner, it would be good to give him some positive news about what we've been doing to solve that murder'.

'What *we've* been doing,' sighed Feather as the door closed and they heard the chief superintendent's heavy footsteps walking away along the corridor.

Cribbens looked at him sympathetically. 'So, it's the Tower first thing tomorrow, sir, to pick up Yeoman Warder Purbright?'

'That's for me to do,' said Feather. 'First thing tomorrow, *you* go to Whitechapel and tell Stanley Whetstone your idea about the rescued dog. Get him to pass it on to his men, and do some more yourself.'

It's a long time since I was last in here, thought Daniel as he walked into The Happy Onion. The pub hadn't changed since his last visit, some ten years previously. The furniture still looked to be the same. The pictures on the walls were the same: mostly photographs of famous people. The clientele looked the same, mainly men wearing workmen's clothes with some women dressed for whatever trade they could pick up. And there, sitting in his favourite chair at his favourite table in the corner farthest from the door, was the bulky figure of Big Billy Buffett. His hair was thinner and greying, but he looked healthy, his face lighting up as he saw Daniel and he waved him over to join him.

Daniel walked through the pub and reached out a hand towards Buffett, who shook it and gestured for him to sit.

'Sergeant Wilson, as I live and breathe!'

'Not sergeant any more, Billy. I haven't been for quite a few years now.'

'Yes, I keep seeing you in the paper with that archaeologist woman. The Museum Detectives, they call you.' He chuckled.

'What's it like working with a woman?'

'Very good, especially as that woman – as you call her – is now my wife.'

'Mrs Wilson? This calls for a drink! What are you having?'

'A pint, if you please.'

Buffett called towards the bar: 'Norman. Two pints of best.'

Daniel looked around at the rest of the clientele. His initial entrance had been greeted with wariness and suspicion. *They know I'm a copper*, he'd thought. *It must be the feet.* But the friendly greeting from Big Billy himself had negated those somewhat hostile looks. Now, the customers returned to their talk and their drinks. Two men played a game of draughts.

Their drinks arrived and Daniel and Buffett clinked their glasses in a toast. 'Cheers!'

Their initial conversation was typical of two men who were meeting after an absence of a decade, catching up on what each had been up to.

'I'm also married now,' said Buffett. 'Do you remember Elsie Duffield?'

'I do,' said Daniel. 'Bright girl. Worked in Joe Bright's draper's shop.'

'That's her.' Buffett nodded. 'Five years now. We got two nippers. Both girls. Luckily, they take after Elsie when it comes to looks.'

As he sipped at his beer, Daniel weighed up his companion. Buffett had made his money through illegal bookmaking, at first standing on street corners taking in cash bets, then acquiring a half share in The Happy Onion where he could ply his trade in all weathers and protected against the sudden appearance of a constable. The protection here at The Happy Onion was twofold: the physical nature of the pub, with various hideaway rooms; and also bribes paid to the local constables – frowned upon but mutually beneficial.

Buffett's dark suit was discreetly expensive-looking, the only sign of wealth being the gold rings on his chubby fingers and a diamond tie-pin.

'I never thanked you properly for what you did for me all them years ago,' said Buffett. 'When I was in the frame for the Ripper murders. There were a lot of angry people at that time who took it seriously.'

'I remember. I was here when the lynch mob came in. I recall it took me a time to calm them down with the right words.'

'And that truncheon of yours,' said Buffett. 'I recall you laying out a few before you got on that table and told them you had proof that I definitely wasn't the Ripper.' He shuddered. 'You saved my neck that day. I can still see that bloke with the noosed rope standing here. They were going to hang me from that lamp post outside. And you did it on your own!'

'The uniforms turned up shortly after.'

'Only after you'd quietened the mob down. Bunch of cowards, those coppers were.'

'Be fair, Billy, there was quite a mob in here that night.'

'Yeah, but you didn't hide outside, and you could have.'

'No, I couldn't. I'd taken an oath to keep the peace.'

'And you were a rare one who stuck to it. So, what brings you here?'

'Paul James. The bloke who was stabbed over at Muscovy Court. I heard he used to drink here now and then.' He grinned. 'I also heard from my old friend Inspector Feather that you said you'd never met him.'

Buffett chuckled. 'Well, what do you expect me to say when Scotland Yard came calling? You know how it is round here. If I started talking to the police, I'd soon have no customers.'

'Then it's lucky I'm no longer in the police,' said Daniel.

The smile faded from Buffett's face to be replaced by one of doubt. 'So is this payback time for you saving my life all those years ago?'

'No,' said Daniel. 'If you don't want to talk to me about Paul James, I won't hold it against you. But I was hoping you might be able to help me.'

'Who are you working for?' asked Buffett. 'Like you said, you're not with the police any more. You're a private investigator, usually at the top of the range from what I can gather. I bet those museums pay top money.'

'They're good enough,' admitted Daniel.

'So who with money would be interested in finding out who killed Paul James? The only one I could think of as caring that much about him would be Ellie Mercer. But she never had money, and she's dead.'

'You knew Ellie?'

Buffett nodded. 'She used to come in with him. They were no trouble. In fact, they were quite sweet together. They'd have too much to drink then stagger out. There's no one else I can think of who'd be interested in what happened to him. Or to her.' He frowned thoughtfully. 'Paul used to talk about his brother who was a Beefeater at the Tower. Is it him who's paying you?'

'Client confidentiality, I'm afraid, Billy.'

Buffett regarded Daniel warily. 'A Beefeater at the Tower wouldn't be in a position to pay your kind of fees. They don't get much more than food and lodging.'

'It's not always about the money. Sometimes it's about doing what's right. Yes, you're right, Paul James didn't have people with money who cared about what happened to him; but what happened to him wasn't right. Even though he's dead, he deserves someone to look into how and why he died.'

'You always did have a social conscience, Mr Wilson. And for that, and for what you did for me, I do owe you. So what I'll do is mark your card. Leave it alone. I'm guessing you want to know who Paul hung around with before he died.'

'Yes,' said Daniel. 'That would be what I'd like to know.'

'All I'll say is that there were two of them, but they only ever came in here with Paul. They've never come in without him, and I'm glad of that. We're talking two very dangerous characters. Very, very dangerous.'

'Too dangerous to whisper a name?'

'Far too dangerous. These blokes play nasty.'

'Like cutting out the tongues of people they suspect might be wagging them?'

Buffett nodded. 'Got it in one. And I value this old tongue of mine too much to risk it. Even for a bloke who saved my life. What I will tell you, so you'll know them if you run into them, is that one of 'em has got eyes two different colours: one blue, one brown. I've never seen that before.'

'No, nor have I,' said Daniel.

'And I pray you don't see it now.'

The two men chatted for a few more minutes as they finished their pints, then Daniel said he had to go. 'I promised Abigail I wouldn't be long.'

'I'm the same with Elsie,' said Buffett.

The two men shook hands and Daniel ambled out of the pub. He had been gone less than two minutes before two men entered. They walked to the table where Buffett was sitting and sat down, and the taller of the pair, a man with two different-coloured eyes, one brown and one blue, said, 'So, you've just been having a chat with Daniel Wilson.'

'Have I?' asked Buffett casually.

'You see, a certain person asked us to keep an eye on Wilson and what he was up to, so we decided to follow him. And, lo and behold, he came in here. Now we decided it wouldn't be clever to come in while he was here because we've been told to keep out of his way. But we peeked through the door and saw him sitting with you, chatting away very friendly like.'

'I'm a friendly bloke, and me and him have a history,' said Buffett. 'It's always good to see an old friend and talk over old times.'

'He's a copper,' said the man.

'An ex-copper,' Buffett corrected him.

'But he works with coppers.'

'So do lots of people. He saved my life, you know.'

'What did he want to know?'

'How I was keeping.'

'And what did you tell him?'

'I told him I was keeping well.'

'Did he ask about Paul James and Ellie Mercer?'

Buffett nodded. 'He did, now you come to mention it.'

'And what did you tell him?'

'That I didn't know anything. That's always been my motto. I don't know anything so I can't say anything to anyone about anything.'

The two men exchanged suspicious looks, then the one with different-coloured eyes said meaningfully, 'I'd hate to find out you wasn't telling the truth about that, because then we'd have to do something about it.'

Buffett returned their hard glares with an equally hard one of his own. Then, with his eyes fixed on the two men, he raised his hand and called out, 'Ooky! Andy! Pob!'

Three men got up from a nearby table and walked over to join Buffett. Buffett gestured at the two men sitting at his table and said to his three pals, 'You see these two, boys? Take a good hard look at them and commit them to memory.'

The three men studied the pair, then nodded.

'Got 'em, boss,' said Ooky.

'I've just told these men that I have never in my life grassed to anyone about anything, or anybody.'

'That's right, boss,' said Ooky.

'The trouble is, they don't seem to believe me. So I'm telling you blokes that if anything should happen to me, an accident, a stabbing, a shooting, anything at all, you find these blokes and kill 'em. And brutally, so they hurt a lot before they die.'

The two men looked at Buffett, indignant.

'That's not necessary,' complained the man with different-coloured eyes.

'I think it is,' said Buffett. 'You see, I've been around a long time, in a dodgy area of employment and in what some people think is a dangerous place to live. I intend to stay alive a lot longer. Now, I know most of the people who wish me harm, and they're either dead or gone. So that leaves you two. I don't think you're going to be moving away, so it'll have to be the other option. *If* anything happens to me. Just so we're clear.'

CHAPTER TWENTY-EIGHT

When Inspector Feather arrived at Scotland Yard the next morning, he was surprised to see Daniel and Abigail waiting in the reception area.

'Are you two thinking of taking up residence here?' he asked.

'We wanted to update you on my meeting yesterday with Big Billy Buffett,' said Daniel.

Feather was immediately interested and sat down on the long bench where Daniel and Abigail had been sitting. 'So you got something from him?'

'I did,' said Daniel. 'I told Abigail about it when I got home yesterday, and she thought it worth passing on to you.'

'Which is why we came in early, before you disappeared,' added Abigail.

'According to Billy — and I've got to stress that you don't know he told me — two men were involved with Paul James, and both are very dangerous. He wouldn't tell me their names, but one of them has got eyes of two different colours: one brown, one blue. When we met Josiah Grundy's sister, she told us the man who took her brother away—'

'Who we now believe to be a man called Caleb Perkins,' interrupted Feather. 'Sergeant Cribbens got the name yesterday from an informant. Perkins is the valet to the Duke of Cranbrook, who lives in a grand house in Belgravia. I called at the house yesterday, but the Duke informed me that his valet is out of the country, in France.'

'Very convenient,' said Abigail.

'Exactly,' agreed Feather. 'But I'm sorry, I interrupted you. You were talking about what Josiah Grundy's sister told you.'

'That the two men who accompanied this Caleb Perkins – if it is him – one of them had eyes of different colours: one brown, one blue,' said Daniel. 'Which sounds like the same two men Billy Buffett told us about who hung around with Paul James. Two very dangerous men. Those two different-coloured eyes sound quite distinctive. I wondered if it jogged any memories.'

Feather shook his head. 'No.' He looked around to make sure no one was near them, then leant towards them and whispered, 'But the chief superintendent is mounting a raid this morning on Fenchurch Street and Pickwick's yard. He's gone to see the commissioner to get approval. I'm going up to the office to see Sergeant Cribbens before I go to the Tower, so I'll get him to pass the word on to the raiding squads to check the men they pick up in case there's anyone answering that description.'

'You're not on the raid?' asked Daniel.

'No. Like I said, I'm on my way to the Tower. Armstrong

wants me to pick up Purbright this morning and question him. Or "sweat him", as he termed it. The chief superintendent's taking charge of the raid on Fenchurch Street himself, with Jim Jarrett detailed to do Harry Pickwick's yard. What are you two planning to do?'

'We're going to look for the man with the different-coloured eyes,' said Daniel. 'We're sure he was involved in the murder of Paul James and Ellie Mercer, and therefore, by association, with the killing of Eric James.'

'Good luck with that,' said Feather. He stood up. 'I'll see you later.'

'I can't believe Purbright's responsible for the murder of Eric James,' said Daniel.

'Nor can I,' said Feather. 'But orders are orders.'

Daniel and Abigail watched him head to the stairs that led up to the first floor and his office, then Abigail asked, 'What's our next move?'

'As we said, we look for this particular man. But we need to do it without letting people know where our information came from. If these men are as dangerous as Billy said, I don't want them going after him.'

Sir Henry Pomeroy stared at the chief superintendent, aghast.

'Corruption?' he stammered.

'From top to bottom I'm afraid, sir,' said Armstrong grimly. 'It seems that a local gangster has the whole of Fenchurch Street station in his pocket.'

'Are you sure of this?'

'Inspector Feather has been conducting an undercover

investigation. I'd like your permission to mount a raid on the station and bring them all in, along with this gangster, Harry Pickwick, and his accomplices.'

'Of course, but what about the publicity? This could adversely affect the reputation of the police.'

'I'm hoping we can accomplish this without the press getting wind of it. If they do, I suggest we fob them off with something like "This matter is currently under investigation. A full report will be issued shortly." But we don't name any names. My plan is to lock up the station and put a notice on the door referring all enquiries to Whitechapel station. The desk sergeant there, Stanley Whetstone, is a good man. He won't give anything away. I'll also have a word with Bob Downey; he's the superintendent at Whitechapel, another good man. I'm confident they can keep a lid on this.'

'Where are you going to put the arrested men? Not at Fenchurch Street, surely?'

'No, sir. That wouldn't be wise. We don't know how many locals are involved in the whole conspiracy who might interfere. We'll split them up. The senior suspects we'll bring to Scotland Yard. The others we'll spread around local stations and sweat the information out of them.'

Sergeant Major West was crossing the green close to the White Tower when he saw a man he recognised as the police detective who'd arrived at the Tower shortly after Eric James's body had been discovered, escorting Hector Purbright towards the main gate.

'Inspector Feather!' West shouted.

The two men stopped and turned to face him.

'What's going on?' demanded West. 'Where are you taking Yeoman Purbright?'

'I've come to ask him to help us with our enquiries into the death of Yeoman James,' replied Feather.

'But where are you taking him?' repeated West.

Feather hesitated, before answering, 'Scotland Yard.'

'Why?' demanded the sergeant major. 'Why can't you talk to him here?'

'That's what I asked, sir,' said Purbright. He looked unhappy and confused.

'I'm afraid regulations mean that sometimes further questions need to be conducted at Scotland Yard,' said Feather.

'Is Yeoman Purbright being accused of anything?' demanded West.

'No, sir,' said Feather. 'It's just standard procedure.'

'If Yeoman Purbright is being questioned at Scotland Yard in an official way then he should be accompanied by a legal representative,' said West firmly.

'It's not that sort of questioning,' said Feather. 'It's more of a chat.'

'You can chat to him here,' countered West.

'Without the possibility of interruptions,' explained Feather.

'That can be arranged here, Inspector.'

'I'm sorry, sir, I have orders to take Mr Purbright to Scotland Yard to talk to him.'

'Orders from who?'

'My superior officer, sir. I'm sure, as a military man, you agree that orders from senior officers are to be obeyed. I can assure you there is nothing sinister in this. It is just standard procedure.'

The sergeant major looked at Feather, suspicion writ large on his features. Then he said, 'Very well. But I expect Yeoman Purbright to be returned to us very shortly.'

'He will be, sir,' Feather assured him.

With that, the inspector escorted the unhappy Yeoman out through the main gate to the carriage waiting for them.

'I've been thinking about Harry Pickwick,' said Daniel as he and Abigail made their way home. 'He arrives in the Fenchurch Street area six months ago from Islington, where he had a reputation as a bully and a bandit. But there's no suggestion he was involved in killing people. He's got two thugs with him, and these thugs force the station sergeant and his deputy out and Pickwick replaces them with senior officers in his pay. He also forces out the superintendent. The first death that comes to light is that of Sergeant Bob Grillis, who was killed, or so it appears, by Josiah Grundy. Was it intentional or accidental? Whatever it was, Grundy takes a pay-off and leaves the force.

'The next thing to consider is the death of Paul James, just a day or so before his brother, Eric, is murdered. Assuming that Bob Grillis's death may have been accidental, this is the first murder since Pickwick took over six months before. Why no murders before then?'

'Where are you going with this?' asked Abigail.

'Sergeant Cribbens was told by his cousin in Islington that there was no suggestion that Pickwick killed, or ordered anyone to kill, anybody when he was in Islington. So what changes? Why suddenly these three murders: Eric and Paul James and Ellie Mercer?'

'Perhaps it's not Pickwick who was behind them?' said Abigail.

'Yes, that's what I'm pondering on,' said Daniel. 'It's one thing to use muscle and money to take over a small local police station and run the area, but these sort of murders are in another league. Nasty. Vicious.'

'But if it's not Pickwick, who is it? And why?'

'It's connected to whatever's planned for the Tower of London,' said Daniel thoughtfully. 'So far the criminality that Pickwick's been involved in has been quite ordinary: bank raids, burglaries, that sort of thing. The raid on the Tower is something bigger.'

'So someone is using Pickwick's reputation to get him blamed for whatever they're planning.'

Daniel nodded. 'That's my theory. How does that sound to you?'

'It makes sense,' said Abigail. 'The big question is: who?'

'This Duke of Cranbrook's valet, Caleb Perkins, was the man who forced Josiah Grundy to return to London. Perkins was accompanied by two men, the same two men who went to see Big Billy. That links them to the Duke of Cranbrook. And the Duke of Cranbrook sounds like the kind of man who'd have the money and clout necessary to organise a robbery at the Tower of London.'

'So the Duke is now the chief suspect?'

'He is in my book.'

'So how do we go about finding out who these two men are?' asked Abigail.

'When we saw her, Barbara Hickworth mentioned that the men looked like boxers. So I thought I'd go to Whitechapel and ask around at some of the gyms where boxers train, see if anyone knows a man with different-coloured eyes.'

'Would they tell you if they did? By all accounts, the people of Whitechapel are pretty close-mouthed when comes to giving information to strangers.'

'But I won't be a stranger.' Daniel smiled. 'I'll be someone who's setting up as a boxing promoter and looking for good fighters, and I've heard good things about this bloke.'

'I'm guessing it will cramp your style if I go to these gyms with you?' said Abigail.

'I'm afraid it might,' said Daniel. 'These places, and the men who go to them, aren't exactly women-friendly. Except for certain types of women.'

'And you don't think I could pass as one of those certain types of women?' challenged Abigail.

'For a few moments, maybe,' said Daniel. 'But once someone takes you at face value you'd be in a difficult situation.'

'Which I can deal with,' said Abigail defiantly.

'I'm sure you can, but it would rather blow our cover.'

'True,' agreed Abigail reluctantly. Then a look of concern appeared on her face. 'You don't think this idea of yours might be dangerous?'

'I can handle myself,' said Daniel confidently.

'I wasn't thinking of you,' said Abigail. 'I was thinking of your friend, Big Billy. These gyms you're talking about are in

Whitechapel. You called on Big Billy at his pub in Whitechapel, and now here you are asking in the same area about a man with different-coloured eyes. Anyone who may have been keeping their eyes and ears open might suspect you got that information from Big Billy.'

Daniel looked at her, deeply concerned. 'Thank God for you and your alert brain. That didn't occur to me. You're absolutely right. So what do we do?'

'I go and see this Duke of Cranbrook,' said Abigail. 'I nose around.'

'But on what pretext?' asked Daniel.

'On the pretext that I'm an eminent archaeologist thanking him for the archaeological dig at the Tower that he's funding. I'll do my best to worm my way into his confidence and see what I can find from him, or his staff.'

'It's a bit thin,' said Daniel doubtfully.

'Oh, I'll have another string to my bow.' Abigail smiled. 'The way through any person's defences is through their passion.'

'And you think archaeology is the Duke's passion?'

'As I've never heard him mentioned in that context before, I doubt it,' said Abigail. 'But remember what John Feather said: he has a passion for cars.'

CHAPTER TWENTY-NINE

In the interview room in the basement of Scotland Yard, Inspector Feather looked at Yeoman Purbright, who was sitting on the other side of the bare wooden table, and noticed how nervous the man was. *What's making him so edgy?* he wondered. *He's an old soldier, a veteran of Heaven knows how many wars and battles.* Was it the uniformed police constables standing silently behind him, or the bare room, which Feather knew was often intimidating to those who'd never been in such a situation before.

'I'm sorry to bring you in here, Mr Purbright,' he said, hoping to put the man at ease, despite the chief superintendent's orders to 'sweat him', 'but you were the person who found Mr James, so we're trying to get every last piece of information about that, no matter how small and insignificant.'

'Yes, sir,' said Purbright. 'As an old soldier, I understand the way things have to be.'

'You have been in the army for many years, I believe,' said Feather.

'Yes, sir. Thirty-six years. I joined as a boy soldier in 1863, when I was fourteen years old.'

'You saw action?'

'Oh yes, sir. Particularly in Afghanistan. The Battle of Kandahar.'

'Kandahar?' asked Feather.

'You don't recall it, sir?' asked Purbright, obviously disappointed.

'I'm afraid not. But I'd like to hear about it.'

Sweat him, the chief superintendent had ordered Feather. But sitting across the bare wooden table from the fifty-year-old army veteran, who gave off nothing other than military bearing and pride, Feather had no intention of treating the man with anything less than the respect he felt he merited. The problem was the chief superintendent would expect a report from him about the interview, which meant Feather couldn't cut it short as he would have liked to. He was sure that Purbright had told them everything he knew about discovering Eric James's body.

Unless I'm wrong, thought Feather. *Unless this man did kill Eric James and is a very clever actor Get him talking,* thought Feather. *Gain his confidence.* He knew that some old soldiers like to talk about their life in the army, especially the battles they'd taken part in. Not all, of course. Many of them wanted never to be reminded about that, but that wasn't usually the case with those who now served as Yeoman Warders at the Tower. For them, their life had been about military service, and they took pride in it. Hector Purbright was obviously one of those proud soldiers.

265

'You really would, sir? Like to hear about Kandahar?'

'Yes, Mr Purbright. I really would.'

This would stretch the time, thought Feather. And if the chief superintendent came back early from his raids and looked in, he'd see Purbright talking. That's what Armstrong wanted.

'It was the Second Afghan War,' said Purbright. 'From 1878 to 1880. Kandahar followed on from the Battle of Maiwand. There was a small British force at Maiwand, two thousand, seven hundred men, under the command of General Burrows, against twenty-five thousand Afghans led by Ayub Khan. Our men were overwhelmed. The enemy outnumbered them ten to one. Nearly a thousand British soldiers died at Maiwand. More would have died if it hadn't been for the bravery of the 66th Berkshire Regiment and the Royal Horse Artillery. They fought a last-ditch action to allow as many of the surviving British forces to retreat from Maiwand as they could and make for Kandahar. All of those who stayed to defend the line were killed. Brave men, every one.

'General Burrows and his surviving men trekked forty-five miles over mountain and desert, through hostile country, under attack the whole time and pursued by Ayub Khan's army, before those who were left reached the garrison at Kandahar, which was where Ayub Khan laid siege to them. Only a hundred and sixty of those soldiers survived the trek and reached Kandahar.

'I was in Kabul with General Sir Frederick Roberts and we were ordered to march to Kandahar to relieve the garrison. We covered three hundred and twenty miles in twenty days, across mountains and desert. Some days the temperature was 110 degrees, and then at night it would drop to freezing. But we made it. Luckily for us, a large part of our force was made up of Punjabis, Sikhs and Gurkhas, who were accustomed to those conditions. Our force was fourteen thousand men, including the regular force at the garrison, against the fifteen thousand of Ayub Khan. Ayub Khan had lost a vast number of his men at Maiwand, so now we were more equally matched.

'We won, sir. It was a fierce battle, but at the end Ayub Khan's army was defeated. Many of them ran away, intending to hide and fight again another day. Khan lost two thousand men and we lost two hundred and fifty. It was the battle that ended the Afghan War.

'I fought in other campaigns, sir. I was in Sudan in 1884 and 1885, but the one I'll always remember is Kandahar.'

'When did you become a Yeoman Warder at the Tower?' asked Feather.

'Six years ago. 1893. And I'm very grateful to the army for letting me see out my days of active service there. It's a wonderful place, and the company are excellent.'

'Did you know Eric James before you went to the Tower?'

'No, sir.'

'But you were about the same age? You would have been in the army at the same time.'

'There are hundreds of thousands of us at any one time in the army, sir. And scattered all over the world.'

'Yes, of course,' said Feather.

Purbright looked anxiously at Feather. 'How long will this take, sir? I only ask because, as the Ravenmaster, I need to be there to put the ravens in their cages at the end of the day.'

'We won't be much longer, I promise,' said Feather. 'Tell me about Eric James.'

'He was a bachelor, same as me,' said Purbright. 'Being a soldier doesn't fit well with marrying and having a family. You're away in foreign countries so often. And for long whiles. It's all right for senior officers, they can take their families with them, but for the ordinary soldier, it doesn't really work.'

Sergeant Sims sat in his small office at Fenchurch Street police station with his second in command, police constable Len Prescott, counting pound notes into two piles, while Prescott watched. When Sims had finished, he pushed one of the piles across the desk to Prescott.

'There you are, Len. That's your share for you to distribute among the men.'

Prescott looked at the notes doubtfully. 'It's not as big as it was last month,' he said.

'That's because, ever since Scotland Yard began to take an interest, Harry has had to keep a lower profile,' said Sims. 'We're going to have to learn to live with this until things ease off.'

There was the sound of raised voices from the reception area just outside the office, and Sims and Prescott exchanged looks of concern.

'What's going on?' asked Prescott.

The door of the office burst open and Constable Riggs, who'd been on duty at the desk, began, 'Sergeant—' before he was thrust to one side and a burly figure in an overcoat crashed into the room. Behind him they saw several uniformed officers.

'Chief Superintendent Armstrong from Scotland Yard,' announced the man in the overcoat, his voice harsh. Then he saw the two piles of banknotes on the desk and a note of triumph entered his voice. 'Well, well! The evidence!'

'This is money we confiscated!' bleated Sims.

'Like hell it is!' barked Armstrong. 'Get your hands off it. You're all under arrest and we're closing this station until further notice.' He turned to the uniformed officers behind him. 'Handcuff these two and put them in the van. Do the same with anyone else you find on the premises. Then seal the station and put this notice on the door.'

And he took a rolled-up piece of paper from his inside pocket and spread it out on the desk so others could read it, *This station is temporarily closed. All enquiries to Whitechapel police station.*

The woman in the grocer's shop in Whitechapel looked at the picture of the man that Sergeant Cribbens had given her, stunned.

'He rescued a dog?' she said. 'Archie Williams?'

'He did,' said Cribbens. 'Pulled it out of the Thames. And, like a true hero, he ran off before the dog's owner could thank him.'

'I didn't even know he could swim,' said the woman.

'Which makes what he did even braver.' Then, in case the woman got suspicious, he added, 'Although he may have only gone in the water up to his knees. It might have been one of the others who actually swam out and grabbed it. But they all were part of it and the owner wants to see them rewarded.'

He showed the woman the other three pictures again. She looked at them, then shook her head. 'I don't know them, but that's Archie Williams right enough. He comes in here for stuff. When he's got the money, that is, which ain't as often as he'd like. He'll be so pleased when he hears there's money coming to him.'

'Yes, well, I'd rather you didn't tell him if you see him,' said Cribbens. 'Or, rather, the owner of the dog has asked us that. He wants the money to go to the right men, and if word leaks out about it he'll have all sorts holding their hands out, pretending they were there. Where can I find Archie Williams?'

Harry Pickwick stood in one of the sheds in his yard and looked at the piles of old papers and cardboard stacked on one side, and the heaps of rags stored on the other side.

'We're gonna have to start shifting some of this stuff,' he said to his muscle, Nipper Sedgewick and Josh Kent. 'Before, it was a useful cover to show we had a legitimate business turning over money, but now, with real money falling off, we need to turn this stuff into cash.' He shook his head. 'I can't work out what went wrong. We had everything so sweet. It was them murders that's done this, bringing in Scotland Yard.'

'Harry Pickwick!' came a shout behind them.

The three men turned and saw that two men in plain clothes had appeared in the doorway of the shed. Behind them were half a dozen uniformed policemen.

'No,' said Pickwick. 'He's not here at the moment.'

'Good try,' said the man who was obviously in charge. He produced his warrant card and waved it in the air. 'Inspector Jarrett from Scotland Yard. You're under arrest. All three of you.'

'On what charge?' protested Kent.

'Corruption,' said Jarrett. 'Handcuff 'em and put 'em in the van.'

Abigail stood in her local newsagent's, studying the magazines on display.

'Is there anything special you're looking for, Mrs Wilson?' asked Ken Plum, the newsagent.

'Have you got any magazines about motor vehicles?' she asked.

'Cars? Yes, they're at the other end of the shelf.' He joined her and pointed at half a dozen magazines in a small pile. 'They're suddenly becoming very popular. Is Mr Wilson thinking of getting a car?'

Abigail was on the point of retorting, *No, Mrs Wilson is*, before stopping herself. She didn't want to risk upsetting Mr Plum; she might need him on her side.

'It's being considered,' she said. 'Which is the best? The one with the most practical knowledge?'

'Mr Wilson's thinking of doing his own mechanics, is he?' asked Plum.

Again, Abigail had to stop herself from retorting, *No, I am. I have had experience of mechanical appliances archaeological digs in Egypt and other countries. I am not afraid to get my hands dirty.* Instead, she said, 'What we're looking for is a magazine that has details of what's happening in the world of vehicle manufacturing today. Modern vehicles.'

'Ah, he'll want *The Popular Motorist*,' said Mr Plum. 'It's very up to date. At least, that's what Eric Pratt says, and he knows quite a bit about cars. Tell Mr Wilson it might be worth having a word with him. He's got the blacksmith's forge at Chalk Farm.'

CHAPTER THIRTY

Viscount Dillon was checking through the duty rotas when there was a tap at his door.

'Enter!' he called.

The door opened and Algernon Dewberry entered. 'Excuse me, Your Grace.'

'Yes? What is it, Dewberry?'

'I've just been informed by the divisional sergeant major that Yeoman Warder Purbright was taken to Scotland Yard this morning, apparently to be questioned.'

'About what?'

'The murder of Eric James.'

Dillon stared at Dewberry, stunned. 'They believe he was responsible?'

'They haven't said, sir. But they took him in at nine-thirty this morning, and it's now nearly noon.'

'Who took him in?'

'Detective Inspector Feather, sir. The divisional sergeant

major is concerned as to when they will be releasing him because of the ravens.' He hesitated, then added pointedly, 'That is, if they do release him.'

Dillon rose to his feet. 'Call my carriage, Dewberry.'

Inspector Feather looked at the clock on the wall behind Purbright. They'd been here in the interview room for over two hours, gone backwards and forwards through the Yeoman's statements, and there was no chink in the man. Purbright was as polite as ever. Instead of the length of time he was being kept in this room and questioned causing him to become more anxious and agitated, as often happened with people undergoing a long interrogation, Purbright had actually settled down from his initial nervousness and seemed quite happy to talk.

He didn't do it, thought Feather again. *Either he's a very clever actor, or he didn't kill Eric James.*

The door opened and a uniformed constable appeared holding a small, folded piece of paper, which he handed to the inspector. 'From the reception desk, sir.'

Feather unfolded it and read the note: *Viscount Dillon from the Tower of London in reception. Wishes to see you.*

Feather groaned inwardly. It had to happen. Feather had expected someone from the Tower to call and demand what was going on, but not the top man himself.

'Excuse me, Mr Purbright, but someone wants to see me.' He looked at the constable on duty behind the Yeoman. 'Perhaps you'd look after Mr Purbright while I'm out. Get him a cup of tea or coffee. Whatever he would like.'

Purbright looked at him, grateful. 'I'd love a cup of tea, please, sir. Two sugars.'

'Two sugars it is. Arrange that, Constable. I won't be long.'

Feather made his way up the stairs to the reception area, where he saw Viscount Dillon standing by the reception desk.

'Good day, Your Grace,' he said.

Dillon wasted no time with pleasantries. 'Where is Yeoman Warder Purbright?' he demanded, his tone showing that his politeness was a thin cover for the resentment he was feeling.

'He's in an interview room,' said Feather.

'Has he been here the whole time?'

'He has, sir—' began Feather, but he was cut off by an angry outburst.

'This is an outrage! A disgrace!'

His raised voice brought looks of concern to the faces of those in the reception area, in particular to that of Chief Superintendent Armstrong, who'd just arrived back at Scotland Yard. The chief superintendent hurried over to the two men.

'What's going on, Inspector?'

'Are you the senior officer here?' demanded Dillon.

'I am Chief Superintendent Armstrong.'

'I am Viscount Dillon, curator at the Tower of London, and I have come to complain about the appalling way that Yeoman Warder Purbright, one of my most respected Yeomen, has been treated.'

'Appalling?' repeated Armstrong uncertainly. He shot a look at Feather, who returned his look with a non-committal one of his own.

'He was taken in for questioning at nine-thirty this morning and he is still being held in custody,' continued the viscount angrily. 'The Prince of Wales shall be informed of this and I'm sure he will, in turn, mention the appalling way one of our most trusted servants at the Tower has been treated by you and your officers to the commissioner of police.'

Armstrong's expression changed to one of horror. 'Your Grace, I must protest!'

'Protest all you want but the fact remains that Yeoman Purbright—'

'Was due to be released some time ago,' said Armstrong quickly. 'And he would have been, except for some unusual circumstances here at Scotland Yard. A major investigation has been under way today, which has delayed normal business.' He looked at Feather. 'Isn't that the case, Inspector?'

'It is, sir, and I was just about to explain that to Viscount Dillon when you arrived.'

Dillon regarded the two men with suspicion, then asked, 'Then I assume I can take Yeoman Purbright with me? I have my carriage here.'

'Of course, Your Grace,' said Armstrong, and he nodded impatiently at Feather, who departed for the basement.

'And please accept our apologies for the bureaucratic problems that led to this delay. I will have severe words with the people responsible,' continued Armstrong.

'I am more concerned at the fact that Yeoman Purbright was brought here in full public gaze,' said Dillon sternly. 'You know the instructions from the Prince, that there should be no publicity of any sort concerning this case. I can imagine nothing more guaranteed to create interest from the press than the arrest of a Yeoman Warder.'

'He has not been arrested,' said Armstrong. 'It was merely to double-check the information he'd given us about his finding of the body.'

'And that took two hours?' said Dillon indignantly.

Just then, Inspector Feather appeared with Hector Purbright.

'How are you, Purbright?' asked the viscount.

'I'm fine, sir. Thank you for asking.'

'How have they treated you?'

The chief superintendent grimaced and gave an unhappy look towards Feather.

'They treated me well, sir. They gave me a cup of tea.'

Relief flooded through Armstrong at these words. The chief superintendent and Inspector Feather watched as Purbright and the viscount exited the reception area to the street, then Armstrong turned to Feather and demanded in an anguished voice, 'What on earth were you thinking of, Inspector? Two hours!'

'I was carrying out your orders, sir. "Bring him in for questioning and sweat him." Those were your exact words, sir.'

'Yes, but I didn't mean . . .' Armstrong stopped, then

said awkwardly, 'When I said "sweat him", I meant . . .' He faltered, then asked anxiously, 'What did you actually do to him?'

'Nothing of a physical nature, sir. I just questioned him. Intensely, but in a civilised manner.'

'Thank God for that!'

'How did you get on with the raids, sir?' asked Feather, eager to change the topic of conversation.

'We got 'em all. Those that were on site, that is. The ones who were off duty are being rounded up.' He gave a mirthless smile. 'We've rooted them out.'

With that, he made for the marble stairs and headed for his office.

Thank God that's over, thought Feather.

'Inspector!'

Feather turned and saw Sergeant Cribbens heading towards him, a broad grin on his face.

'You look very pleased, Sergeant,' said Feather.

'I am, sir. We've got the lot!'

'The lot?'

'The four men who attacked and killed Captain Merchant. Archie Williams, Joe Berman, George Stride and Louie Lobb. Stanley Whetstone's got them all at Whitechapel under lock and key.'

'You actually got them?'

Cribbens nodded. 'It was those pictures that did the business, along with that tale of the dog.' He chuckled. 'We had three of them but couldn't find the fourth, Louie Lobb. Then, lo and behold, he walks into Whitechapel nick while I was in there with Sergeant Whetstone and says: "I'm here to collect my reward."

'"What reward?" says Stanley.

'"For rescuing that dog," says Lobb. "My aunt says there's police constables walking around showing people a picture of me and saying I rescued a drowning dog and there's a reward due to me."

'"And did you rescue a drowning dog?" asked Stanley.

'"I did," says Lobb. "And I want my reward."' Cribbens broke off to give a huge laugh. 'He was furious when he found out what it was all about, that he was under arrest on a charge of murder. He tried to fight his way out of the station, but luckily there were enough constables there to calm him down.' He beamed happily. 'Anyway, it's all done and dusted.'

'Not so fast,' cautioned Feather. 'We've got to prove it was them first.'

'Oh, that's done,' said Cribbens. 'Archie Williams tried to get out of it by blaming the others. Once the others heard about this, they in turn put the blame on Archie Williams. In the end, they were all eager to blame each other, but in so doing they tripped themselves up. I left Stanley Whetstone getting their statements taken down. We've got 'em.'

'That is going to be music to the ears of the chief superintendent, the commissioner and General Booth and his son. And credit where credit is due, Sergeant. Your story about the drowning dog is what clinched this, and I shall make sure those people at the top know about it.'

* * *

Chief Superintendent Armstrong sat at his desk, drumming his fingers on the top in nervous agitation. By rights he should be feeling pleased: all those corrupt officers under lock and key, along with Harry Pickwick and his thugs. But his confrontation with Viscount Dillon had upset him, especially when Dillon had talked about complaining to the Prince of Wales about the way Purbright had been treated. That would be a disaster! There had to be a way to head that off, to stop Dillon from registering his complaint. He could try putting the blame on Inspector Feather, but he knew that wouldn't wash.

He was interrupted in his thoughts by a knock at his door, and then Inspector Feather entered with such a broad smile on his face that it made Armstrong wonder at what could have caused it after the recent hoo-hah with Viscount Dillon.

'We've got them, sir!' Feather beamed. 'Or, rather, Sergeant Cribbens has got them. He's the one who did the hard work and got the result.'

'Got who?' asked the chief superintendent, bewildered.

'The men who killed the Salvation Army captain, Captain Merchant. All four of them. They're currently being held at Whitechapel because there's no room here.'

Armstrong stared at Feather, his expression of doubt and unhappiness being replaced with one of rising delight.

'You're sure it's them?' he asked, still unsure that it was true.

Feather nodded. 'Sergeant Cribbens got confessions from all four of them. I believe he should get a commendation for his work on this case, sir.'

'And he will, by God!' burst out Armstrong. He rose to his feet. 'I'm off to deliver the news to the commissioner. I'm sure he'll want to be the one to inform General Booth and the home secretary. That's brilliant work, Inspector!'

CHAPTER THIRTY-ONE

Chief Superintendent Armstrong was halfway across the reception area of Scotland Yard to the main door when he stopped and looked back at the reception desk, where Sergeant McDougall was going through some paperwork. Or pretending to, thought Armstrong. McDougall was one of the old school who'd perfected the art of always looking busy. It was the telephone, the newfangled device beside the sergeant on the desk that caught his attention. Armstrong was suspicious of new procedures and especially of new inventions. To his mind, most of these new things took the gravitas away from proper policework, not to mention much-needed money. He didn't know how much it had cost to install this telephone, but he guessed it hadn't come cheap. A feeling of trepidation filled him as he approached the desk, but he did his best to repress it. This was a chance to get himself involved with this new technology, and at the same time show the commissioner his proficiency with it, and impress those listening, here at Scotland Yard and the operators who'd undoubtedly be listening in to his conversation.

Sergeant McDougall looked up as the chief superintendent approached.

'Yes, sir?' he asked. 'Can I be of assistance?'

Armstrong pointed at the telephone. 'Do you know how to use this device?'

'Yes, sir. You pick up the receiver, which is this speaker with the handle attached, and when the operator answers, you ask her to call a number. She then puts you through to the person you want to talk to.'

Armstrong nodded. 'Good. I want to talk to the commissioner of police, Sir Henry Pomeroy. Would you do that for me?'

'Yes, sir,' said McDougall. He looked at a list of names and numbers pinned to his wall. 'We have a list of all the important numbers we expect to be calling regularly,' he said. 'Sir Henry's is here.'

McDougall picked up the receiver and when the operator answered, gave her the number for Sir Henry Pomeroy. There were various clicks and buzzes, and then finally a man's voice said: 'This is Sir Henry Pomeroy's office and this is his secretary, Jason Ormerod, speaking.'

'This is Scotland Yard. I have Chief Superintendent Armstrong, who wishes to speak to the commissioner.'

'Is it urgent?' asked Ormerod.

'Yes, it is!' snapped Armstrong. 'Very urgent.'

'If you'll ask the chief superintendent to hold on, I'll arrange for the commissioner to pick up the telephone.'

Armstrong looked at McDougall quizzically.

'He has to walk through to the commissioner's office,' explained McDougall. 'They haven't installed an internal buzzer on his telephone yet. And – er – just to advise you, sir, everything you say will be heard by everyone at the other end, and the line between.'

There were more clicks, then Armstrong heard the voice of Sir Henry Pomeroy saying, 'Chief Superintendent, this is a surprise for you to be using this instrument.'

'It is, sir, but due to the enormity of what I have to tell you, I wanted to waste no time in travelling to your office, but to get you the news by the fastest means possible. We have arrested the four villains who killed Captain Merchant. They are in custody and will stand trial for his murder. I thought you'd like to be the one to inform General Booth and his son.'

There was a long silence at the other end of the line, and for a moment Armstrong thought they'd been disconnected, then Pomeroy's voice was heard, filled with emotion.

'Chief Superintendent, my warmest congratulations. Indeed, I will inform the general and his son of this success, and thank you for thinking of advising me of this great news using this new means of communication. We are being modern, Chief Superintendent. Modern!'

'We are, sir,' said Armstrong. 'And, as we approach the arrival shortly of the twentieth century, we at Scotland Yard are proud to be part of this modern technological revolution.'

He listened to a few more words of congratulations from Sir Henry Pomeroy, then there was a click to indicate the call had ended and he handed the receiver back to Sergeant McDougall.

'We are modern, Sergeant!' he announced proudly.

'Yes, sir,' said McDougall.

'If there is ever a telephone call for me, just send a messenger to my office and I will come down and take it. In the meantime, I will see if I can arrange for one of those machines to be installed in my office. It is the future, Sergeant. Speedier means of communications.'

'Yes, sir,' said McDougall again.

He watched the chief superintendent make for the stairs that would take him up to the first floor and his office. *A telephone in his office*, he thought ruefully. *Somehow, I can see this meaning more work for me.*

Daniel walked into the living room and found Abigail sitting in an armchair absorbed in a magazine. He assumed it was one of her archaeological magazines until he looked down at the open pages and saw pictures of motor vehicles and lists of figures comparing speeds and engine sizes.

'What's that?' he asked.

'A magazine about motor vehicles,' replied Abigail. 'According to Mr Plum at the newsagent's, it's the best one there is. I'm also intending to visit a Mr Eric Pratt, a blacksmith at Chalk Farm, who I'm told knows everything there is to know about these machines. I'm brushing up on everything to do with motor vehicles before I call on the Duke of Cranbrook.'

'Are you sure that's a wise move?' asked Daniel, concerned. 'Now we know what his two thugs are capable of, it shows how ruthless this Duke is. You could be putting yourself in danger.'

'I am an eminent archaeologist come to thank the Duke for sponsoring the dig at the Tower of London, which I am now part of. I will also enthuse over cars. There is nothing in either of those that will arouse his suspicions.'

'I wouldn't count on it,' said Daniel. 'The fact that he's got away with things so far suggests he's very careful. And, if he's some sort of elite criminal, he'll surely know about our work as the Museum Detectives.'

'Not necessarily,' said Abigail. 'And, if he does, I'm sure I'll be able to gloss over it. Incidentally, Mr Plum thinks that you wanted this magazine, so you'd better be prepared when you see him and he asks what sort of car you're thinking of getting.'

'I'll tell him we've changed our minds and will continue to use carriages and public transport,' said Daniel. 'I must admit, from the little I've seen of these things on the roads, I'm not impressed. They're noisy and belch out as much smoke as a railway engine.'

'They're very fast,' commented Abigail.

'Too fast,' said Daniel. 'If someone runs out in front of them, I don't believe they'll be able to stop in time.'

'It's the future,' said Abigail. 'That's what this magazine says, and I believe it. Engineering and technology are on the rise. Look at what we saw when we were in Manchester with the cotton mills. They led to Manchester becoming the fastest-developing city in the world.'

'That doesn't mean it's a good thing,' cautioned Daniel. 'Remember the other side of Manchester that we saw, the social deprivation that went with the new technology. It was machines at the expense of people.'

'That's been said about every technological innovation, right from the time fire was discovered and someone invented the wheel.' She put on a mock tone of outrage as she said, 'This will only lead to disaster!'

'I hate to sound like a prophet of doom, but these motor vehicles are going to have a drastic effect on so many aspects of our society,' said Daniel. 'For one thing, what will happen to all the horses that currently pull our buses, our wagons, if every vehicle that's currently drawn by a horse is replaced with one of these machines?'

'More horsemeat found in the butchers' shops, I expect,' said Abigail.

Chief Superintendent Armstrong looked at the list of prisoners the raids had netted. The key players – Harry Pickwick and his two pet thugs, Josh Kent and Nipper Sedgewick, Station Sergeant Sims and Josiah Grundy – were all safely locked up at Scotland Yard. What was needed were quick confessions from all of them to make sure they stayed locked up, but on remand in a proper prison, freeing up the cells at the Yard.

'I'll take Sims,' muttered Armstrong, putting a tick against his name. 'Jim Jarrett can take Pickwick, Kent and Sedgewick. Inspector Feather can handle Grundy; he's dealt with him before. Play 'em off against one another, that's the way to play it. Like Sergeant Cribbens did with those four thugs who killed the Salvation Army captain.'

At the thought of Sergeant Cribbens, Armstrong felt a twinge of conscience. He hadn't mentioned to the commissioner the role the sergeant had played in bringing the four killers to justice, despite his promise to Inspector Feather. The truth was he'd been so overawed at using the telephone – the modern technology – it had vanished from his mind.

I'll do it later, he promised himself. *Once we've got this lot banged up.*

The little maid, Queenie, walked into the kitchen carrying a feather duster.

'Mrs Paxton?' she said.

'Yes?' asked the housekeeper.

'I was doing the dusting in the passage near the back of the house and I heard this peculiar noise, like a little girl crying.'

'What were you doing there?' demanded Mrs Paxton angrily.

'Well, I hadn't dusted that part of the house for a while and I thought it must need it.'

'No, it doesn't,' said Mrs Paxton firmly. 'You keep away from there.'

'Right, Mrs Paxton. But what about the noise I heard?'

'Cats,' said Mrs Paxton. 'They get in some way and get trapped in the cellar.' She took off her apron and hung it on a hook, then picked up a broom. 'I'll deal with it.'

'How do they get in?' asked Queenie, following the housekeeper out of the kitchen.

'I don't know. I'll get someone to check the place and find out.'

'I've never been down the cellar,' said Queenie. 'Can I come with you?'

'No,' said Mrs Paxton. 'Now get about your work.'

Queenie hesitated, wondering if it was worth asking again, but one look at the expression of grim determination on Mrs

288

Paxton's face made her mind up for her and she headed for the living room to do her dusting.

Mrs Paxton waited until she was sure Queenie was gone, then she made for the back of the house. She reached a part of the passage where the walls had wooden panelling decorated with beading. She pressed at one particular piece of beading and a panel sprang open, revealing a flight of steps going down. She could hear the sound of a little girl crying clearly, despite the thick walls and the thick wooden door at the bottom of the stairs. She took a key from her pocket and unlocked the padlock that kept the door shut. She walked in and the woman and the little girl in the cellar shrank back from her. The woman was cuddling the little girl, who was sobbing and calling, 'I want my daddy!'

'Shut up!' barked Mrs Paxton. She brandished the broom at them. 'Or I'll beat you with this.'

'How long are we going to be kept here like this?' begged the woman.

'When they say you can go.'

'Why are we being kept prisoner?' asked the woman helplessly.

'Because those are my orders,' said Mrs Paxton. She glared at the little girl. 'I don't want to hear any more crying.' She strode forward and snatched the rag doll the little girl was holding from her. 'I'm taking this to make sure you stop that noise. If you're good and stop crying, I'll let you have it back. If not, I'll put it on the fire. Is that clear?'

The little girl looked as if she was about to burst out crying again at this threat to her beloved rag doll, but she did her best to stifle her tears and nodded.

'You will let me have Dolly back?' she begged. 'You won't put her on the fire? Please!'

'If you're good and I don't hear any more noise from you. Either of you,' said Mrs Paxton.

With that, she walked out of the cellar carrying her broom and the rag doll. She locked the padlock and went back up the steps, then through the open wooden panel, pushing it shut beside her.

She looked at the rag doll. What to do with it? If she left it lying around the house, Queenie would be sure to spot it and ask about it. But she wouldn't be coming to this part of the house again, not after Mrs Paxton had expressly forbidden her to. Mrs Paxton threw the doll on the passage floor and then headed back to the kitchen.

CHAPTER THIRTY-TWO

Chief Superintendent Armstrong faced Wesley Sims across the bare wooden table, the only furniture apart from the wooden chairs in the interview room in the basement of Scotland Yard. Two uniformed constables stood by the walls, ready to move in if the prisoner became truculent. However, there looked to be no risk of that. Sims was still wearing his uniform trousers, but he'd been stripped of his tunic and was now in shirtsleeves. Initially he'd done his best to look defiant and put on an air of outraged innocence, but the menacing looks he was receiving from the bulky figure of the chief superintendent had taken that defiance out of him.

'Right, Sims,' snapped Armstrong. 'I'm not going to address you as Sergeant, because you aren't any longer. Pretty soon you'll be prisoner number whatever, breaking rocks as hard labour.'

'On what charge?' demanded Sims. 'I'm innocent. All I've ever done is my job as a police officer.'

'You took bribes from Harry Pickwick to turn a blind eye to crimes his mob committed. That's not just corruption; that's aiding and abetting a criminal. There's also the matter of the death of Bob Grillis.'

'That was an accident,' said Sims sharply.

'Yes, so I keep being told. But recently the story seems to have changed. It now looks likely that Josiah Grundy killed Grillis and reported it as an accident. I got a look at the autopsy report and far from it being death from accidentally banging his head on the kerb, there's also the matter of the blow to the back of the head with what appears to have been a police truncheon, and the smashing of his windpipe with the same weapon.' Here, the chief superintendent fixed Sims with a hard and ferocious glare. 'On your orders, because Grillis was about to put in a complaint about what was going on at Fenchurch Street. The backhanders. The corruption.'

Sims shook his head vigorously. 'Nothing to do with me. I wasn't even there.'

'Like I said: on your orders. You were in charge at Fenchurch Street. It'll be interesting what Grundy says when he realises he's facing the gallows.'

'You can't believe anything Grundy says,' said Sims defensively. 'He'll say anything to save his skin.'

Inspector Jarrett walked into the interview room, a stack of papers in his hands, which he slammed down on the table before sitting down to glare at Harry Pickwick.

'Evidence,' said Jarrett, tapping the papers. 'Statements from various people, about you and your activities.'

'I'm just a businessman,' protested Pickwick. 'Rag-and-bone. Paper and cardboard.'

'Burglary,' said Jarrett. 'Aiding and abetting. Bribing former Sergeant Sims and the rest of that rotten mob at Fenchurch Street to turn a blind eye to thefts and robberies.' Again, he tapped the bundle of papers. 'Statements from your accomplices, naming you as the chief conspirator.'

'Who?' demanded Pickwick. 'Who's named me?'

Jarrett smirked at him. 'That's for you to find out at your trial. Now you can make it easier on yourself by naming names.'

'What names?'

'We can start with Nipper Sedgewick and Josh Kent. They work for you, right?'

'Yes,' said Pickwick. 'And legitimate.'

'Well, that depends on how you define legitimate,' said Jarrett. Once more he tapped a finger on the pile of papers. 'Using threats of violence against former police officers to persuade them to retire from the police force so you could take control of Fenchurch Street police station.'

'Who says?' demanded Pickwick indignantly.

'We have statements from four different officers to that effect, naming Mr Kent and Mr Sedgewick as those who uttered such threats against them and their families.'

'They're lying!'

'We also have statements from Mr Kent and Mr Sedgewick confirming those allegations.'

'What?' exploded Pickwick, and he began to rise from his chair, but a burly constable moved forward and pushed him back down on it.

'This is rubbish!' said Pickwick angrily. 'All lies. I never told them to do any such thing.'

'Do you deny that you ordered Kent and Sedgewick to threaten some police officers at Fenchurch Street in order to get them to resign or retire?'

'I do,' said Pickwick. Then, abruptly, his manner changed to pleading: 'It wasn't like that at all. Sergeant Sims, who was station sergeant at Fenchurch Street, asked me, as a favour to him, if I could help persuade some officers at the station to leave the force because they were either too old or not very good at their job, and he wanted to improve the quality of the officers at the station.'

'If he felt that, why didn't he just get rid of them himself?'

'He said it wasn't that easy to get rid of poor-quality police officers. It had to be done carefully. Offers of money, that kind of thing. But he couldn't do it himself.'

'But why you?'

'Because I'm a successful businessman, and he knew I had a social conscience. I wanted to improve things for the people in the area.'

'By bribing certain officers to leave the force.'

'No, not bribing,' Pickwick corrected him. 'Compensating them.'

'And when they wouldn't go, threatening them with physical violence.'

'No,' insisted Pickwick. 'If Josh and Nipper did that, it was them acting off their own bat. I never ordered them to do anything like that.'

'Just like, I suppose, you claim you never ordered Constable Grundy to kill Sergeant Grillis?'

'Never!' burst out Pickwick. 'It was an accident!'

'Not according to the autopsy report,' said Jarrett, and he began to read from the sheet of paper at the top of the pile.

In the third interview room, Inspector Feather was also reading aloud from the autopsy report on Bob Gillis.

'A blow to the back of the head with what appears to have been a police truncheon, and the smashing of his windpipe with the same weapon,' said Feather. He looked at Josiah Grundy, who was sitting across the table. 'What have you got to say to that?'

'It wasn't me,' said Grundy. 'Someone must have done those things after I'd gone to the station to report the accident of him falling down and banging his head on the kerb.'

'What, so someone was watching and waiting for you to go, and then they came out and killed him?'

'That must be what happened,' said Grundy.

'You said in your report he was dead when you left him to report to the station.'

Grundy nodded. 'Yes, that's right.'

'If he was dead, why would anyone want to bash his head in and then crush his windpipe?'

'Who knows why people do that sort of thing? They're a rough lot in that area.'

'Using a police truncheon,' pointed out Feather.

'They don't *know* it was a police truncheon,' countered Grundy. 'There are plenty of other things that do that sort of damage.'

'Where's your old truncheon?' asked Feather.

'I threw it away,' said Grundy. 'After I left the force.'

'Most officers keep theirs as a memento,' said Feather.

'Yeah, well, I didn't,' said Grundy.

'Where did you get the money to start up the tobacconist's shop?'

'It was an inheritance.'

'Who from?'

'An uncle of mine. He died and left me some money.'

Feather picked up a pencil. 'What's his name and where did he live? When did he die, and where?'

'Albert Smith,' said Grundy. 'I don't know where he lived. I just had a letter from this solicitor telling me he'd died and he'd left me some money.'

'Paid by cheque, I presume, so you'll have the details of it.'

Grundy shook his head. 'Cash,' he said.

'Name and address of this solicitor?'

'I can't remember,' said Grundy.

'You must have gone to his office to collect the money.'

'No. We arranged to meet in a pub.'

'Which pub?'

'The Four Feathers in Byward Street. He came in and gave me the money, and I signed a piece of paper. That was it. I can't remember his name or the address of his office. I never kept the letter.'

'Why were you staying at Harry Pickwick's yard?'

'I'm working for him. Night watchman.'

'So you saw what went on at the yard? The people bringing stuff in to him and paying him off.'

Grundy shook his head. 'No. I never saw anything like that. Strictly legit.'

'That's not what Nipper and Josh say,' said Feather genially.

'Who?'

'Nipper Sedgewick and Josh Kent. Harry Pickwick's muscle and your accomplices in crime.'

'They're nothing to do with me,' said Grundy.

'That's interesting, because they've been very informative about you and what happened to Bob Grillis, and how it was Harry Pickwick who gave you the money for your shop after Bob Grillis died.'

'They're lying!' snapped Grundy. 'They're a pair of villains. And they never liked me. If you ask me, it was them who did for Bob Grillis if he was done the way you said he was. Josh Kent always carried a cosh made of wood.'

CHAPTER THIRTY-THREE

Abigail rang the bell beside the door at the elegant and very expensive Belgravia house. The door was opened by a woman who Abigail assumed to be the housekeeper, who looked enquiringly at her.

'Good morning,' said Abigail. 'Would you ask His Grace, the Duke, if he has a few moments to see Mrs Abigail Wilson. Although he may know me better as Abigail Fenton.'

'One moment,' said the woman. 'I'll see if he's available.'

She closed the door and left Abigail waiting on the doorstep. *I hope he agrees to see me, otherwise I've wasted an awful lot of time memorising articles from a magazine about cars that is of little interest to me*, thought Abigail. She'd left the magazine at home in the belief that if the Duke saw she had it on her, he would dismiss any idea that her interest in these machines was real.

She didn't have to wait long before the door was opened

and the Duke himself was beaming at her. He was a tall, handsome man, dressed impeccably.

'This is an enormous pleasure, Mrs Wilson,' he said. 'To have one half of the famous Museum Detective duo calling on me. Please, do come in.'

Abigail followed him through the house to the library, filled with impeccably placed books and paintings, mostly – Abigail observed – of motor cars.

They seated themselves, Abigail on a comfortable sofa and the Duke in an armchair.

'So, what can I do for the famous Museum Detectives?' asked the Duke.

'Thank you, Your Grace, but it's in my capacity as an archaeologist I'm here. Professor Stafford and Viscount Dillon have very kindly invited me to work with them on the dig they are undertaking at the Tower of London, of which I understand you are the sponsor.'

'One of the sponsors, dear lady. I must admit that it's only recently that I have discovered archaeology as a pastime, and when I learnt that the Tower was considering such a dig at a site so close to hand, it seemed an opportune moment to explore things further. I understand there have been interesting discoveries made. Two skeletons, suspected of being those of the princes who went missing from the Tower during the time of Richard III.'

'Yes indeed. I really came to offer my personal thanks for subscribing so generously to the operation. It is only with people like yourself providing the finances that archaeology can continue making new discoveries.'

'You are very kind. Fortunately I am in a position to help, and I am a great believer in the philosophy that good fortune needs to be spread.' He smiled. 'It's not completely altruistic. I believe that money spent that way is also an investment. It introduces me to interesting, and often powerful, people, and opportunities to advance my own interests. People like yourself.'

Abigail smiled. 'I would hardly describe myself as powerful, Your Grace.'

'But you are. You feature in the newspapers and magazines as both a detective and an internationally renowned archaeologist. Important people listen to you and take heed of what you say.'

'Thank you, Your Grace, but that would surely apply here only if you were planning on developing archaeology further as one of your interests.'

'And I'm sure I will.' He smiled. 'At the moment, I must admit my prime interest is in the world of the motor car. I am considering manufacturing a prototype that will help to establish this country as a leading manufacturer.' He gave her an apologetic smile. 'Although I doubt if the subject would be of much interest to you, so it's lucky I stopped myself before I embarked on a long and rambling discourse on the topic.'

'Why? Because I am a woman?' asked Abigail. 'On the contrary, I have always been interested in the world of technology and sciences of all sorts. For example, I am aware that to date the majority of advances in car manufacture have taken place in France and America.'

'That is true, although there have been important automobile developments in Britain,' said the Duke.

'Ah yes, Richard Stephens.' Abigail nodded.

The Duke stared at her, awed. 'You've heard of Stephens?'

'I'm sure that anyone in Britain who's interested in motor cars must have heard of Richard Stephens. I believe he produced his first car in 1897, and it was notable because it was the first truly all-British car. As I understand it, George Lanchester's claim to have produced the first all-British motor car is somewhat tenuous. Although it was made in Britain, it included components from French and German manufacturers. Stephens, by contrast, made everything for his car at his works in Somerset. With the exception of the wheels, but he bought them from Starley in Coventry, so it is truly an all-British car.'

'My God!' exclaimed the Duke, the expression of awe still on his face. 'Mrs Wilson, if you weren't already taken, I'd ask you to marry me. I have never heard anyone talk with such knowledge on the subject of British cars.'

'If something interests me, I do my best to find out as much as I can about it. It was the same when I was excavating and exploring the pyramids in Egypt at various sites. Now it is with cars.'

'Mrs Wilson, would you care to see my own vehicle? It is in the garage, just a few steps across the rear yard.'

'I would be delighted,' said Abigail.

As they were rising to their feet, the housekeeper appeared.

'Would you and your guest like coffee, Your Grace?' she asked.

'Later, Mrs Paxton. First, I have to show Mrs Wilson my pride and joy, Esmerelda.' He smiled at Abigail. 'That's what I have named my motor car. Do follow me.'

He led the way through the house, then out of the door at the rear of the house into the courtyard and across it to what had once been a stable but had now been converted to a garage. The door of the garage was open and the Duke proudly gestured for Abigail to enter.

Inside, the two-seater vehicle with large wire wheels gleamed, polished to perfection.

'The Panhard and Levassor two-seater,' announced the Duke proudly, just as he had to Inspector Feather. 'Four horse-power. A magnificent machine. In my opinion, Émile Levassor can truly be called the real father of the modern motor car, although there are many who give Daimler, Benz and Peugeot the credit. It was Levassor who moved the engine from the rear to the front and cooled it by using a front-mounted water radiator. It was Levassor who introduced a crankshaft to link the engine with the gearing. He also installed a clutch pedal and a gearstick to operate the gearbox. Unfortunately for Levassor, and unfairly to him, because he was in partnership with Panhard and Panhard's name came first on the company name, most people called this new transmission system the Panhard. But for those who know, Émile Levassor is the true genius of modern automotive engineering. Have you done much travelling in cars, Mrs Wilson?'

'Alas, no. So far my experience has been theoretical, that of a very interested spectator.'

'Then allow me to give you a journey,' said the Duke.

'That's very kind of you,' said Abigail. 'But at this moment my current work at the Tower means I have to stay in London.'

'Then we shall do both.' The Duke beamed. 'I have been meaning to call at the Tower to see how the dig is progressing. Are you free tomorrow?'

'I'm sure I can be,' said Abigail.

'Then call here tomorrow at about eleven. That will give time for my mechanic to give the vehicle a once-over. We'll take a picnic hamper with us to the Tower. What do you say?'

Abigail smiled. 'I say a very grateful yes.'

Inspector Feather had sent Grundy back to his cell and now he had Nipper Sedgewick and Josh Kent facing him on the other side of the table. Feather had also brought in Sergeant Cribbens so the prisoners had two detectives to cope with.

'You're Harry Pickwick's muscle,' said Feather.

'No, we're his business associates,' growled Sedgewick.

'And what sort of equipment do you use?'

'What do you mean?' asked Sedgewick, puzzled.

'Well, if you were clerks you'd use pens and pencils and paper.'

Both men looked at him, uncertain.

'So, are you clerks, doing paperwork?' asked Feather.

'No,' said Sedgwick. 'We're more on the practical side.'

'That's right.' Kent nodded. 'We do practical stuff.'

'What sort of stuff?' asked Feather.

The two men looked at him, uncomfortable with the question.

'Whatever needs doing,' said Sedgewick.

'Like unloading wagons?'

'Now and then we do,' said Sedgewick.

'And what do you use your wooden cosh for, Mr Kent?' asked Feather politely.

'What wooden cosh?' asked Kent.

'The one we've been told you carry with you when you're out doing stuff for Mr Pickwick. We understand it's very similar to the one that was used to beat Bob Grillis to death. You remember Bob Grillis? He was a sergeant at Fenchurch Street station before he was murdered.'

'He wasn't murdered,' said Kent curtly. 'He had an accident. Fell over and banged his head on a kerb. Police Constable Grundy saw it happen. You can ask the local police. They've got it on record.'

'Ah yes, Constable Grundy.' Feather smiled. 'But that was before we looked into Grillis's death and got the autopsy report. As well as the blow to his forehead on the kerb, there was also a savage blow to the back of his head with the wooden cosh that I've mentioned – similar to the one you use, Mr Kent, and which was in your possession when you were taken into custody. According to the autopsy, this same weapon was used to smash the front of Bob Grillis's throat, crushing his windpipe and so stopping him breathing.'

Kent rose angrily to his feet, and immediately two constables hurried forward, grabbed him, and forced him down onto his chair.

'You can't pin that on me!' Kent shouted.

'Oh, I think we can,' said Feather. 'We've got the autopsy report and we've got your weapon, the wooden cosh.'

'I never did it! We wasn't even there when it happened!'

'That's not what Josiah Grundy says,' said Feather calmly. 'He suggests both of you were there at the time, and that you attacked Bob Grillis after he'd left to report the accident.'

'The lying bastard!' burst out Kent. 'It was him who did it.'

'Paid to do it by Harry Pickwick, I assume,' said Feather. When both men fell silent, their faces showing a refusal to answer, the inspector added, 'It's up to you. We know Pickwick paid for it to be done as a favour to Wesley Sims, who was sergeant at Fenchurch Street. At this moment, your friend Harry is weighing up whether to tell us who he paid to do it: you or Grundy.'

'Grundy!' shouted Kent.

'You know that for a fact?' asked Feather.

Kent nodded. 'We was there when Harry told Grundy what he wanted done. But he never said to kill him. He told Grundy to put him out of action, that's all.'

'And where does the Duke of Cranbrook come into it?' asked Feather.

It was the worried glance between the two men that gave them away. Sedgewick swallowed and asked, 'Who?'

Feather gave a little laugh. 'Nice try, but the look between you gave you away. So, I'll ask you again: where does the Duke of Cranbrook come into it?'

'We've never heard of him,' said Sedgewick.

Feather gave a sigh and smiled genially at them.

'Oh dear,' he said. 'It looks like we're going to be here a long time if you keep this up.' He looked towards the constables. 'Constable, take them back to their cells and lock them up. Sergeant Cribbens and I are going for a nice cup of tea, and after we're nice and relaxed we'll start again. Only next time we won't be so nice. And we'll be looking again at the idea that it was you two who killed Bob Grillis.'

'It was Grundy!' insisted Sedgewick.

'With or without the help of Caleb Perkins?' asked Feather.

'Who?' said Kent.

'You may know him as the valet to the Duke of Cranbrook. He was the man who brought Grundy back to London and delivered him to me. Why he did that, we're still not sure, but we're looking for Perkins and we're sure we'll find all the answers from him. Including what your relationship is with the Duke.'

'He asked us to keep an eye on what Harry was up to and report back to him,' said Sedgewick desperately. He looked apologetically at Kent, who was looking at him in outrage. 'It's no good, Josh. They know too much and if we don't come clean they're going to pin a killing on us that we didn't do. It's our necks at stake.'

'What is the Duke up to?' asked Feather. 'Why does he want to know what Harry Pickwick's up to?'

'No idea,' said Sedgewick. 'Honest, that's all we've got!'

* * *

The Duke waved Abigail goodbye, then made his way up the stairs to the top of the house. Caleb Perkins was in the attic, reading the day's newspaper, and he stood up when the Duke entered.

'Is everything all right, Your Grace?' he asked.

'I suspect it isn't,' replied the Duke, 'but I'll know more tomorrow.'

'What's happening tomorrow?' asked Perkins.

'I am taking Mrs Wilson for a ride in Esmerelda and we shall be having a picnic at the Tower.'

Perkins looked at his employer warily. 'Is this Mrs Wilson the same as those Museum Detective people?'

'She is indeed. However, today she came unaccompanied by her husband.'

'Why? What did she want?'

'She claimed she came to thank me for sponsoring the archaeological dig at the Tower. She's an archaeologist as well as being a detective. I checked up on her. She seems to have established an international reputation for her work in Egypt and various Roman sites.'

'But you don't believe that was really why she came to see you?'

'No, I don't. She spent a lot of time doing her best to impress me with her knowledge about motor cars.'

'Motor cars?'

'Not just the cars themselves but the different machinations of the industry. France versus America. She's also very well informed on the developments in the car industry here in Britain.' He frowned. '*Too* well informed. I suspect she's

307

trying to worm her way into my confidence.'

'Why?' asked Perkins.

'Because of the job we have ahead of us, of course!' snapped the Duke impatiently. 'I've already been told by our source that she and her husband are investigating the death of Yeoman James at the Tower. They're intelligent people, although in this case her intelligence has run away with her. She would have done better to just thank me for my sponsoring the dig and then gone on to talk about that, rather than showing off the knowledge she's picked up from somewhere about cars.'

'You think she knows what's planned?'

'Not the precise details. I suspect she knows that *something* is planned and she's trying to find out what. The fact that the Museum Detectives are digging means they feel that there's more to Yeoman James's death than a casual killing. It's something we have to nip in the bud.'

'Yes, Your Grace. Is there anything I can do?'

'Yes, Perkins, there is. Those two chaps you took to see our friend Josiah Grundy . . .'

'Yes, Your Grace?'

'I need them to carry out a task for me.'

'Yes, Your Grace. Do you wish me to make contact with them?'

'I do, but by letter. It's still not advisable for you to be seen in public. I'd like you to write a brief letter to them, making sure to put their names and address clearly on the envelope. I shall get a messenger to deliver it today.'

'Yes, sir. What do you wish me to say?'

'Tell them I have a job for them. They are to report here and ask for me.'

'Do you wish me to be with you when you see them?'

The Duke shook his head. 'We need to keep up the pretence that you are in France. I will deal with them.'

CHAPTER THIRTY-FOUR

Inspectors Feather and Jarrett sat around the desk in Chief Superintendent Armstrong's office, their reports of the interviews they'd conducted in front of them. It was time to compare notes.

'I'm confident we've got enough against Grundy to charge him with the murder of Bob Grillis,' said Feather. 'Harry Pickwick's muscle, Sedgewick and Kent, gave him up when they realised there was a chance they'd be charged with the murder.'

'What does Grundy say?' asked Armstrong. 'Has he admitted it?'

'No, but he lies all the time. He won't present well in court when he's questioned by a good prosecutor. The jury will see through him.'

'Good,' said Armstrong. He looked at Jarrett. 'What about Harry Pickwick?'

'He's a wrong 'un,' said Jarrett. 'He's also gutless. You can see that from the way he ran from the Pullman brothers.' He nodded towards Feather. 'It's all there in Inspector Feather's notes. We've rounded up some of his known criminal associates, the people who carried out burglaries and such and used Pickwick to fence the proceeds. One or two of them will cough up about their arrangement with Pickwick to try and do a deal, claiming they only did it because he forced them to.'

'Good,' said Armstrong again. 'And former Sergeant Sims is happy to stitch up Pickwick if he can pass the blame on to him.' He frowned. 'We've got enough here to put them all away on a variety of charges, but there's nothing that links any of them to the three outstanding murders: Paul James, Eric James, Ellie Mercer.'

'I think the Duke of Cranbrook might need looking into,' said Feather.

Jarrett and Armstrong looked at him, puzzled.

'Who?' asked Jarrett.

'The Duke of Cranbrook.'

'The one who's always going on about motor cars?' asked Armstrong. 'Always causing a fuss about the rights of motorists?'

'That's him,' said Feather.

'But what connection can he have with this load of roughs?' asked Armstrong. 'He's a peer of the realm. A gentleman.'

'He may be, but he's the one who sent his valet, Caleb Perkins, to bring Josiah Grundy back to London. He's also been paying Nipper Sedgewick and Josh Kent to report to him what Harry Pickwick is up to.'

'You think he's working hand in glove with Pickwick?' asked Armstrong.

'No,' admitted Feather. 'There's been no mention of the Duke and Pickwick having even met, but I've got a feeling that something's going on there. The Wilsons think that the Duke may well be behind something that's planned for the Tower. A robbery.'

'What robbery?' asked Armstrong.

'They're not sure,' said Feather.

Armstrong shook his head. 'They're just trying to stir things up to impress the Prince of Wales and his crowd. That's what the Wilsons do.'

'But why would the Duke be interested in what Harry Pickwick is up to?'

'Who says he is? You've only got the word of Sedgewick and Kent for that, and I wouldn't trust them as far as I can spit.'

'But we know that the Duke's valet was involved with Josiah Grundy.'

'Perkins may have been, but it doesn't mean the Duke was. Where is this Perkins? We could always bring him in.'

'He's in France, according to the Duke, checking on automobiles for him.'

Armstrong shook his head. 'We've got a load of criminals, including at least one murderer, bang to rights. I'm still not convinced that this Nipper Sedgewick and Josh Kent weren't involved in the killings. They're capable of it.' He turned to Jarrett. 'I think this is one for you, Inspector Jarrett. Sweat the pair of them. The murder of Paul James happened in Fenchurch

Street, and Ellie Mercer was his girlfriend, so somehow it's connected to all the rotten things that have been going on in that place.'

'And the murder of Eric James?' asked Feather.

'The same thing,' said Armstrong. 'The Tower of London is right next door to Fenchurch Street. They've got to be connected. Lean on Sedgewick and Kent, Inspector Jarrett. Sweat 'em hard enough and they'll cough up.'

'How did you get on with the Duke?' asked Daniel when Abigail returned home.

'Very well, thanks to my pretence of being an aficionado of the vehicles. However, I am still suspicious. His first reaction on meeting me was to describe me as one half of the Museum Detectives. There was no mention of my work as an archaeologist. Usually, when I meet people who know of my work, they ask questions about Flinders Petrie, or the pyramids. I'm not sure if His Grace had heard anything about my archaeological work, but he was very aware of our detective work.'

'You suspect he has an ulterior motive in sponsoring this dig at the Tower? Something not connected with archaeology?'

'I do,' said Abigail.

'We already know he's connected with Caleb Perkins, who has conveniently disappeared,' mused Daniel thoughtfully. 'And Perkins is linked to Grundy, and all the nefarious things going on at Fenchurch Street, which I'm sure include the murders of the James twins and Ellie Mercer.'

'The planned robbery?'

Daniel nodded. 'And this motoring machine would make an ideal getaway vehicle. I've been reading that magazine you left. They're fast.'

'So the Duke is the mastermind behind the murders and the robbery?' said Abigail.

'That's how it looks to me,' said Daniel.

'Well, hopefully I shall find out more tomorrow. The Duke has offered to drive me to the Tower to look at the dig, and partake of a picnic while we are there.'

'He's trying to woo you.' Daniel smiled.

'No, if he is the mastermind behind everything that's going on, his only ulterior motive is to find out what we know.'

'Just be careful,' warned Daniel. 'There have already been too many dead bodies in this case.'

'I'll be careful,' Abigail reassured him. She smiled. 'But it will be another new experience, travelling in a car.'

CHAPTER THIRTY-FIVE

The Duke of Cranbrook pulled the vehicle to a halt near enough to the trench in the Tower grounds for them to walk to it with case.

'There, what did you think?' he asked, putting on the brake so the car didn't roll.

'An incredible experience,' replied Abigail. 'The potential is enormous. I can see a day when the horse will be replaced by vehicles like this completely.'

'So can I, dear lady. Now, let's start with an exploration of this dig.'

Sophie and Alice were at work, continuing the slow and laborious task of scraping away the loose earth.

'Girls, I'd like to introduce the Duke of Cranbrook,' said Abigail. 'He's the one who's sponsoring the dig. Your Grace, these are Alice Potts-Weedon and Sophie Connor, archaeology students who have been assigned the exploration of the trench.'

The two young women smiled at the Duke and made

little bobbing curtseys, but decided against offering their soil-stained hands to shake.

'This is such a pleasure to meet you, Your Grace,' said Sophie. 'This dig is the most exciting event Alice and I have ever experienced.'

'I'm so glad.' The Duke smiled. 'I understand you have uncovered two interesting skeletons. Possibly the missing princes.'

'That's still debateable,' said Alice. 'At the moment, it's all circumstantial. We're hoping when Professor Clement arrives later today, he'll have more news for us.'

'Professor Clement?' asked the Duke.

'Stamford Clement, the noted archaeologist,' explained Abigail. 'He has the chair of archaeology at University College London.'

'Of course.' The Duke nodded. 'So many names to remember.' He turned to Abigail and said, 'I believe it is time for us to see what Mrs Paxton has prepared for us, if you are ready for an early lunch, Mrs Wilson?'

'Certainly,' said Abigail. To the two young women, she said, 'I'll see you later.'

She and the Duke returned to the car and the Duke took a large rug from behind the seats and spread it on the grass, then lifted a hamper from the car and put that on the rug.

'Please, make yourself comfortable,' he invited Abigail.

Abigail settled herself on the rug while the Duke opened the hamper. He produced plates and cutlery, as well as silver shakers containing salt and pepper, then set out the food that his housekeeper had prepared.

'Cold chicken, ham, cheese, potato salad, all sorts of pickles and chutneys,' he announced. 'I think you'll find Mrs Paxton has done us proud.'

'She certainly has,' enthused Abigail. 'Has she been with you long?'

'Five years,' said the Duke. 'She's a widow so having her live in suits her as well as me.'

'Does she have children?' asked Abigail.

The Duke looked at her, almost affronted. 'Children? Good heavens, no! I couldn't bear such upheaval as they'd cause. Why do you ask?'

'No reason,' said Abigail, and she picked up a leg of chicken and put it on her plate.

'I must confess to being curious,' said the Duke.

'About what?' asked Abigail.

'About why you are here? At The Tower?'

'I've told you, I've been invited to take part in the dig, in an advisory capacity.'

'Nothing to do with you and your husband being the Museum Detectives?'

'Absolutely not,' said Abigail.

'So, you're not investigating anything here? No mysteries that need to be examined?'

'At the moment, the only mystery here is the discovery of the two skeletons. Who were they? When were they buried? What happened to them? Were their deaths natural or accidental, or perhaps something sinister?'

'So, no present-day mystery for you to unravel?'

'I'm afraid not.'

'And your husband, Mr Wilson? I understand he has been here a lot recently.'

'He, too, is interested in archaeology. It's often the way with married couples; they each become interested in what occupies their partner. In the same way that I became interested in his detective work, he became intrigued by my archaeological activities.' She cut off a piece of cheese and popped it into her mouth.

'This cheddar is absolutely delicious,' she said. 'You must tell me where you buy it from.'

'I leave such things to Mrs Paxton,' said the Duke. 'But I shall certainly ask her and let you know.'

'I must ask you about how you came to sponsor the dig here at the Tower. Have you been involved in other archaeological undertakings?'

'No,' said the Duke. 'As I mentioned before, I have to admit for me it is a passing interest, but one I hope I will find attractive enough to want to pursue it further.'

'But at the moment the automobile is your big passion?' Abigail smiled.

'It is,' said the Duke.

'I'm curious as to why you chose the Tower for your first exploration,' mused Abigail.

'As I said before, it is close at hand.'

'Do you have much experience of the Tower? Its long history? The myths and stories about it? Like, if the ravens should ever leave, the Tower would fall, and so would the Empire. That's why the ravens have their wings clipped, to prevent them flying away.'

'Really?' said the Duke. 'How fascinating.'

'I suppose it's because security at the Tower is of paramount importance. Everything here is so precious and needs to be protected. Hence the ritual of the keys to the Tower, the locking of the main gate every evening. Have you ever seen the ritual of the keys?'

'I'm afraid not,' said the Duke. He gave a light laugh. 'To be honest, history has never really been my thing.'

'Despite the fact that you have a title? A dukedom, no less. The highest rank of peerage in the country. I'd have thought that the history of your family would at least have been considered a matter of interest.'

'I prefer to look ahead rather than backwards,' said the Duke with a smile. 'Hence my interest in mechanical inventions.' He pulled a watch from his waistcoat pocket and said, 'Good heavens, look at the time. I hadn't realised. I'd promised Mrs Paxton I'd deal with the household accounts today, otherwise the grocer in particular gets very worried. I think he's had some titled customers renege on him. Can I give you a lift to your home? It's at Primrose Hill, I believe.'

'It is, and thank you for the offer, but I think I need to catch up with the two young students who are conducting the dig. Viscount Dillon asked me to keep an eye on them.'

As the Duke drove away from the Tower, leaving Abigail talking to Alice and Sophie, he reflected on their conversation, and especially on Abigail's probing questions, so subtly delivered. His title and his family history, for example. Why had she raised that? Just how much did she know about his title? And why had she introduced the whole topic of security at the Tower?

Yes, there was definitely something going on with her and the Tower, and it was more than an archaeological dig. He felt a deep niggle of annoyance that his confidante inside the Tower hadn't been as informative as he should have been. He'd told the Duke that the Wilsons were investigating the murder of the Beefeater, but that their investigation was being kept secret by order of the Prince of Wales. The question was, how much had they uncovered? Abigail Wilson was clever, there was no doubting that. But just how much did she and her husband actually *know*?

When he arrived home, he left Spencer, his mechanic, to put the car into the garage while he went indoors, where he found Mrs Paxton waiting for him in a state of some agitation.

'Two men called for you while you were out, Your Grace,' she said. 'They said you'd invited them.'

'I did indeed, Mrs Paxton. Where are they?'

'In the office at the back of the house.'

The Duke strode through the house to his office, where two men were waiting for him. One was particularly noticeable because he had eyes of two different colours: one brown, one blue.

'Mr Shearing and Mr Albertson,' said the Duke. 'Good afternoon to you.'

'We got a letter from Caleb,' said the man with the different-coloured eyes, Butch Albertson.

'You did indeed,' said the Duke. 'You'll remember I asked you to keep an eye on Daniel Wilson?'

'And we did,' said Albertson. 'We told you about him going to see Big Billy Buffett.'

'As it turns out, his wife may be the more dangerous of the pair. I need you to take some action against her. Damage her a little.'

'Why only her?' asked Sam Shearing. 'Ain't he poking his nose in as well?'

'He is,' said the Duke. 'But he could be problematic. For one thing, he's an ex-Scotland Yard detective, quite a tough character, and it's possible he may be carrying a weapon. Some detectives do, I understand. Causing some harm to her will be enough to give him pause for thought. I believe they are very close, so he will be preoccupied with looking for the perpetrators rather than concentrating on my activities.'

'The perp what?' asked Albertson, looking puzzled.

'The people who carried out the attack,' the Duke clarified.

'Us,' said Shearing.

'Exactly,' said the Duke. 'So it's important you don't get caught.'

'Against a woman?' said Shearing scornfully.

'By others who may be in the area. So I advise you to attack swiftly, then get away equally quickly.'

'We know what to do,' said Shearing. 'How badly do you want her hurt?'

'Enough to hospitalise her for a few days. But don't kill her. That would create an outcry that could harm my plans. We'd have police swarming all over the Tower.' He handed them a page cut from an archaeological magazine, which had a photograph of Abigail prominently displayed. 'This is what she looks like. I've written her home address on the page. She also regularly visits an archaeological dig at the Tower of London. The site is near Tower Hill Underground station. I believe she may be there later today. Don't move in until you are sure she is on her own.' He produced a roll of banknotes from his desk drawer. 'Here you are, your payment.'

CHAPTER THIRTY-SIX

'He knows I'm not just there to look at the dig,' Abigail told Daniel when she got home and he'd made them a pot of tea.

'You're sure?'

'He keeps pressing on what aspect of detection I'm involved with at the Tower. And it's not just idle curiosity. He *knows*.'

'Someone at the Tower must have told him something,' said Daniel thoughtfully.

'Exactly. And as everyone there has been sworn to secrecy, it means there's some kind of conspiracy going on involving the Duke. He's getting information from inside. The question is: from who? Who's his informant?'

'Did you get any hint from him about if he's involved in anything untoward at the Tower?'

'No, and when I started to ask him questions about his title and its history, and started to ask him what he knew about security measures at the Tower, he called our time together short, saying he had important housekeeping accounts to settle at home.'

'Suspicious,' mused Daniel.

'Very. He wasn't even aware of who Professor Stamford Clement is, and he's the archaeologist in overall charge of the dig at the Tower. The very dig the Duke's sponsored. He has no interest in archaeology at all; it's all a front.' She put on her outdoor coat and picked up her bag.

'You're off out again?' asked Daniel.

'Yes. As my meeting with the Duke was truncated, I told Sophie and Alice I'd be coming back to the dig at the Tower. They said that Professor Clement would be calling later and I'd like to talk over with him what we're going to do about these skeletons, if anything.'

'Do you think they're those of the two princes?'

'I don't know,' admitted Abigail. 'It's a bit of a coincidence for two sets of skeletons to turn up at the same time, albeit many hundreds of years apart. But they certainly look as if they might be. Which raises the question about how accurate the detection was way back when the first two were found. As far as I can ascertain, they were just two skeletons that were automatically assumed to be those of the missing boy princes. For all we know they weren't the skeletons of boys at all, but a boy and a girl, or two girls. The study of anatomy was in its early stages in those far-off times.'

Sam Shearing and Butch Albertson stood by the archaeological dig site at the Tower of London, just two interested observers intrigued by the activity. Today there didn't seem to be a lot of activity. They saw their prey, Abigail Wilson, in the long trench with two young women and a large fleshy man with a beard. The man seemed to be in charge, pointing at various sections of the trench, whereupon the two young women moved to those places and began carefully scraping with their trowels.

'This is the best place,' said Shearing. 'No crowds around. We wait till she leaves and then do her. Then we nip off down Fenchurch Street.'

'Fenchurch Street.' Albertson chuckled. 'Safe territory.'

'Not any more. Haven't you heard? The police raided it the other day and arrested everyone.'

Albertson stared at him, shocked. 'Everyone?'

'Everyone,' confirmed Shearing. 'Sergeant Sims and every other police officer in the station. And there's talk they're rounding up the ones who were off duty at the time.'

'Does the Duke know?' asked Albertson, concerned.

'I don't know,' admitted Shearing.

'We ought to tell him after we've done the woman,' said Albertson.

'Yeah, I suppose so,' said Shearing reluctantly. 'I was only worried he might lose his temper when he hears about it. He looks like he's always controlled, but he can go a bit wild when he gets irate.' He looked towards the group working in the trench. 'Anyway, let's do this first. We do it quick and run. A couple of belts should be enough.'

In the trench, Abigail looked at where Sophie and Alice were working with great care and precision.

'It looks like everything is in order,' she said to Professor Clement. 'Is there any news on the skeletons?'

'I've got our medical people at UCL studying them, checking for nicks or cuts that might indicate how they died. I've also got some fossil-hunters examining them to try and date them. One's aged about twelve and the other about ten, so they could be those of the two princes.' He gave an unhappy sigh. 'I suppose the only way we'll know for sure is if we dig out the skeletons interred at Westminster Abbey and examine them. The problem is that I don't feel the authorities will feel happy about having the bones at Westminster Abbey disturbed.'

'No,' agreed Abigail. 'I suppose we need to talk to the Prince of Wales. It's his family we're talking about.'

'I'd rather not do that at this moment,' said Clement. 'I think I'd prefer to have these bones examined further, and if we've got anything more concrete to back up our suspicion then we can talk to him.'

'We?' queried Abigail.

'You know the Prince. You've talked to him. He'll listen to you.'

'Or he may not listen to anyone if he doesn't like the idea.'

'Exactly,' said Clement unhappily. He looked across at the Tower buildings. 'We might end up in the Bloody Tower.' He gave a wry shake of his head. 'As soon as I've got something to report, I'll let you know.'

'Thank you,' said Abigail.

She climbed the ladder out of the trench and began to make her way across the grass towards Tower Hill Underground station. She noticed that two burly, thickset men who had been standing watching the activity in the trench began to move away, also apparently making for the Underground station.

Although they appeared to be casual in their movements, strolling rather than striding, something about them made Abigail wary. She'd been attacked a few times before since she'd begun working with Daniel in their detective work, and she'd come to recognise the signs.

On an impulse, she stopped and retraced her steps to the trench but instead of climbing back down, she stood for a moment, apparently watching as Professor Clement gave further instructions to the two young women. Then she turned and headed once again towards Tower Hill station. The two men had stopped and seemed to be studying the entrance to the station from a distance.

Abigail made for the Underground station, quickening her pace, and as she did so the two men separated, the taller definitely barring her way, the shorter man moving so that he was behind her. Both men had put their hands in their pockets and now held weapons: the short one a knife, the taller one a cosh. With a shock, Abigail realised that the shorter man, the one with the knife, had eyes of different colours: one brown, one blue. These were the two men that Big Billy Buffett had described as very dangerous, the same two men who'd brought Josiah Grundy back to London.

The taller man moved menacingly towards her, the cosh swinging loosely from his hand. She imagined the man with the knife was advancing on her from the rear.

It was then she let out a loud cry of, 'Help! Murder!'

This seemed to take the tall man by surprise because he hesitated, but as Abigail shouted again he made a run towards her, the cosh raised. He swung the cosh down at her, and

Abigail dodged aside and then let fly with a kick into the man's groin.

The man screamed and fell to the grass, writhing in agony as he clutched his groin. Abigail now swung round to face the man with the knife, who had stopped at the sight of his pal lying in agony on the grass and screaming. There were shouts from the direction of the trench. The short man, who had a look of painful indecision on his face at this unexpected turn of events, now turned to see Professor Clement and the two young women running towards him. Hastily he stuffed his knife back in his pocket and fled.

Abigail turned her attention to the man on the grass, who was now just whimpering.

'I'll deal with him,' shouted Professor Clement, and he grabbed the man by the arm, rolled him over onto his front, then fell on him. 'There's rope back at the trench,' the professor shouted to Alice and Sophie. 'Fetch it and we'll tie this villain up.'

A uniformed police constable had appeared from the Underground station, his attention caught by Abigail's shouting and the man's screams, and he ran to join them.

'What's going on?' he asked.

'This man tried to kill me,' said Abigail. 'There were two of them, but the other man – who had a knife – ran away.'

The constable knelt down beside the fallen Sam Shearing, producing a pair of handcuffs from his belt, with which he imprisoned Shearing's wrists.

Alice and Sophie appeared running, holding a length of thick rope.

'It's all right,' Clement told them. 'We won't need that after all. The constable has handcuffed him.'

'Permit me to contradict you, Professor,' said Abigail. 'I've encountered situations like this before. He could still be troublesome. Tie his ankles together; that'll make sure he's no further danger.'

Inspector Feather had allowed Abigail to sit in on his questioning of Sam Shearing, while Sergeant Cribbens made notes.

'So who hired you and your companion to attack Mrs Wilson?' asked Feather.

'What companion?' growled Shearing.

'The short man with the knife,' said Abigail. 'The man with different-coloured eyes: one brown, one blue.'

Shearing shook his head. 'I never saw anyone else.'

'The witnesses who arrived did,' said Feather. 'They saw him running away.'

'Whoever he was, he was nothing to do with me.' Shearing shrugged.

'Let's get back to my original question,' said Feather. 'Who hired you to attack Mrs Wilson?'

'No one,' said Shearing.

'Why did you attack her?'

'More to the point, why did you try to kill me?' demanded Abigail.

Shearing shook his head. 'I didn't,' he said.

'One with a knife, one with a cosh,' said Feather. 'That sounds like attempted murder to me.'

'It was just a robbery, was all,' said Shearing. 'Me on my own. I saw this posh-looking woman and thought she might have some money on her, so I took a chance.' He scowled vengefully at Abigail as he added, 'I didn't expect her to be such a bitch.'

'Watch your language,' warned Feather.

'Well, how would you put it if she did to you what she did to me?' demanded Shearing. 'I'll never be able to have children now. I'm gonna sue her, that's what I'm going to do. It's not right. Women shouldn't do that sort of thing. Especially posh women.'

'Think of it as a lesson learnt,' said Feather. 'It might stop you committing the same mistake again. Not that you'll have much chance to. Attempted murder carries a long sentence. You're going to be behind bars for a lot of years. And hard labour, at that.' He paused. 'Unless you tell us who hired you. That might bring some leniency for you.'

'I've already said all I've got to say,' said Shearing defiantly.

Feather had Shearing returned to his remand cell, then he, Abigail and Sergeant Cribbens made their way up from the basement to the reception area at Scotland Yard, arriving there at the same time that Daniel entered from the street. He hurried to Abigail and took her in his arms.

'I just got the message,' he said.

'I sent an officer to let Daniel know what had happened, and that you were all right,' Feather told Abigail.

'A man with a cosh?' said Daniel, shocked.

'She dealt with him by means of a kick to the gonads,' said Feather. 'It could have been worse; the other man had a knife.'

'What happened to him? Was he caught?'

'No, he ran off,' said Abigail. 'Interestingly, he had different-coloured eyes, one blue, one brown, just like the man that Billy Buffett described to you. So they're definitely connected to Paul James.'

'What are you going to do with him?' asked Daniel.

'Sergeant Cribbens and I are going to take turns questioning him about Paul James and Ellie Mercer. Hopefully we'll wear him down.'

'He doesn't seem the kind of person it would be easy to wear down,' commented Abigail.

'That might change when we start pressing him on the murder of Paul James,' said Feather.

The Duke of Cranbrook was engrossed in a car magazine when Mrs Paxton knocked at the door of the library.

'One of those gentlemen who called the other day has returned, Your Grace,' she said. 'He seemed rather agitated. I have put him in the office.'

'Thank you, Mrs Paxton,' said Cranbrook, laying the magazine aside.

A short time later, he walked into his office to encounter a very agitated Butch Albertson.

'I assume something has gone wrong,' said the Duke coldly.

'She kicked Sam in the balls! Then she shouted for help and these people came running. We didn't expect that.'

'Where's Shearing now?'

'He got caught. Before he could get up, these people were all over him.'

'You didn't go to his help?' demanded the Duke, and Albertson could see the anger in him. 'You abandoned your friend?'

'I had to. If I'd stayed, I'd have been caught too, and then I wouldn't have been able to tell you what happened.'

The Duke made a visible effort to control his anger at this thought, then he nodded.

'Sam won't talk,' said Albertson. 'He's never grassed in his life. Anyway, the police will be too busy with everything else that's happened to spend a lot of time on Sam.'

'What do you mean?' asked the Duke.

'They've raided Fenchurch Street. Taken everyone at the nick into custody. The sergeant and everyone.'

'Why?' demanded the Duke.

Albertson shrugged. 'I don't know. They must have got wind of something not being right there.'

'What about Harry Pickwick?' asked the Duke. 'Has he been picked up?'

Albertson nodded. 'Sam was telling me about it. All of them rounded up. There's so many of them, with all the coppers who've been picked up, the cells at Scotland Yard are full. They've had to spread them round other nicks.'

The Duke looked thoughtful. 'You'd better stay here for the moment. Now they've got Shearing, plus the crew from Fenchurch Street and Harry Pickwick and his boys, they'll be looking for you.'

'They don't know about me,' protested Albertson.

'You can't be sure of that,' said the Duke curtly.

'How long have I got to stay here?'

'Hardly any time at all,' said the Duke. 'In view of what's happened, I'm going to have to bring the job forward. You can stay up in the attic with Perkins until it's over.'

He dismissed Albertson with orders for him to go to the attic at the top of the house and find Perkins, while he returned to his study in a disturbed mood.

Things were at risk. His plan had depended on suspicion falling on Harry Pickwick and his two pet thugs, along with the corrupt police at Fenchurch Street. False trails had been laid, which – after the job had been carried out – would have meant Pickwick and the Fenchurch Street crowd being considered automatic suspects. Now, with them all under lock and key, that no longer applied.

There were just two options: abandon the job, or bring it forward.

Abandon it? No. He'd spent too much time planning it. People and things were in place. The police would be nosing around, but more importantly, so would the Wilsons, and they were much more dangerous to his plans.

He'd have to bring it forward.

CHAPTER THIRTY-SEVEN

Next morning, Daniel went to their local newsagent's to collect their usual *Times*, and at the same time check on the front pages of the other papers.

'Your missus is on the front page of the *North London Echo*, Mr Wilson,' said Ken Plum, the newsagent, and he handed Daniel a copy.

Daniel smiled as he looked at the front page. Beneath the headline *Local Archaeologist Attacked* was a picture of Abigail standing in front of the Egyptian pyramids, and a police mugshot of Sam Shearing.

'I'll take that as well, thanks, Ken,' he said, handing over the money for the two papers.

He was still smiling as he gave the paper to Abigail.

'Local archaeologist?' she said, slightly put out.

'It is the *North London Echo*,' Daniel pointed out. 'I'm sure if it had appeared in *The Times* it would have said "internationally famous archaeologist attacked".'

'I'm not put out that the story hasn't appeared anywhere else; in fact, I'm pleased it hasn't, it's just this preoccupation the papers have with obsessing over a local connection. I remember once when there was an earthquake in Turkey that killed hundreds of people, and a local Bournemouth paper carried a story headlined: "Earthquake in Turkey: Bournemouth man injured".'

In Loughton, unknown to Daniel and Abigail, Barbara Hickworth was reading the same story in the *Essex Echo*, which also carried stories from its sister papers in adjacent areas.

'Look at this!' she exclaimed.

She thrust the paper at her husband, Fred. He looked at it blankly.

'What am I supposed to be looking at?' he asked.

'That's a picture of the woman who was here,' she said. 'The posh one, with her husband, asking about Josiah. They came with the artist woman.' Barbara tapped the photograph of Sam Shearing. 'I recognise him. He was one of the pair who came with that shifty bloke and took Josiah away. You got to send a telegram.'

Fred looked at her, shocked. 'A telegram?'

'To Mrs Wilson, telling her that bloke who attacked her was the one who took Josiah.'

'Why a telegram?' demanded Fred. 'Why not a letter?'

'Because she could be in danger. There were two other blokes, remember, and this story says that when she was attacked, one of them got away. He could still be after her.'

'Telegrams cost money,' he protested.

'Mr Wilson paid us ten shillings for the information. We can afford it out of that. Put in it, *he isn't the one with the eyes.*'

'The one with the eyes?' asked Fred, puzzled.

'They'll know what it means. Just go and send it!'

In the attic of the large house in Belgravia, the Duke was engaged in deep conversation with Albertson and Perkins.

'It's going to be too dangerous to allow you to go on the job, Albertson, especially if Mrs Wilson might be at the Tower. She's seen you; she knows who you are. So your task will be to take care of the woman and the girl.' He regarded Albertson sternly. 'I assume you have no qualms about it? After all, you dealt with that other woman, Ellie Mercer.'

'You want their tongues cut out as well?'

'No. It will be enough just to cut their throats. My only concern is that Mrs Paxton might get the jitters once she realises what you're going to do. She can be squeamish.'

'Do you want me to kill her as well?'

'That may be necessary, but only if you think she's about to raise the alarm. She's been a good and loyal housekeeper; I'd prefer to keep her alive. But don't do anything to the woman and her daughter until you think we'll be well away.'

'When will that be?'

'I would imagine any time after midnight, when most of the Beefeaters and the other residents of the Tower will be safely tucked up in bed. The best thing would be to arrange to take them somewhere else and dispose of them; that way, Mrs Paxton won't suspect what's going to happen to them.'

'What, in the car?' asked Albertson hopefully.

'No,' said the Duke firmly. 'The car will be in use. Arrange a carriage.'

He turned to Perkins. 'I'm going to have to take a chance with you, Perkins. I need you on the job. I'm leaving now for the Tower to take up residency. You'll come with me.'

'Say someone recognises me?' asked Perkins, concerned. 'People always take a good look when they see a car rolling along a road, it's such a rare sight.'

'Wear a deerstalker hat and goggles while we're travelling. Once we're inside the Tower, stay in the house we'll be occupying.'

'You're sure that bloke won't talk?' asked Perkins.

'Not while we have his wife and daughter and he thinks we'll let them go if he does what we want.'

Abigail opened the telegram that had just been delivered, then walked into the living room where Daniel was engrossed in reading the papers and handed it to him.

'So, the story wasn't just confined to the *North London Echo*,' he said.

'I wondered about that,' said Abigail. 'Local newspapers often swap stories because sometimes there's not enough good copy for the local area. There will always be plenty to report in London, but I imagine Essex is not fertile ground for exciting tales.'

'So, now we know that this Sam Shearing was one of the men who went with Caleb Perkins to bring Josiah Grundy back to London,' said Daniel. 'But we still don't know the name of the other man, the one with the different-coloured eyes.'

'But we're starting to get connections,' said Abigail. 'Sam Shearing and Caleb Perkins. Caleb Perkins and the Duke of Cranbrook.'

'I've got a feeling that things are building to a climax,' said Daniel thoughtfully.

'Intuition?' asked Abigail.

'More the evidence of what's been happening. Like you, I'm sure the Duke of Cranbrook is involved in what's going on. His valet, Perkins, has vanished, allegedly to France, although I have my doubts about that. The two men who went with Perkins to Loughton to pick up Grundy attacked you. That definitely links them with the Duke. The recent action by Armstrong, closing Fenchurch Street and arresting all the officers, I think will have stirred things up.'

'You think Fenchurch Street were connected to the robbery that's planned for the Tower of London?' asked Abigail.

'I do. Josiah Grundy was part of the corrupt squad at Fenchurch Street. We know he's tied in with Perkins and the Duke in some way, although how exactly is unclear. What I am sure of is that all these things, including the attack on you, mean the robbery at the Tower is imminent. I think we should talk to Viscount Dillon and make arrangements for us to stay for a couple of nights at the Tower.'

'Will he allow that?'

'We're employed by the Prince of Wales to protect the Tower. He'll allow it.'

Daniel and Abigail walked through the main gate at the Tower and headed for Viscount Dillon's office. Suddenly Abigail stopped. 'Look,' she said, alert. 'There, by the green. That's Cranbrook's car.'

'So he's here,' said Daniel. 'Perhaps he's visiting the dig.'

'I don't think so,' said Abigail. 'The dig's a cosmetic thing to allow him access to the Tower. He's not really interested in archaeology.'

'Another of his smokescreens,' mused Daniel.

'You think he's here for the robbery?' asked Abigail.

'I told you I had a feeling things were about to happen. This could be it.'

'He may be just here on a daytime visit.'

'There's one way to find out,' said Daniel.

Viscount Dillon was in his office and welcomed Daniel and Abigail.

'I trust you are recovered, Mrs Wilson?' he asked. 'That was a dreadful thing to happen. Do the police know why they attacked you?'

'According to the man who's been arrested, it was a robbery,' said Abigail. 'But we have our doubts about that. We think it's connected to the robbery that we believe is planned here at the Tower.'

'And, if we're right, the indications are that this robbery is imminent,' added Daniel. 'We believe it may happen tonight.'

Dillon looked at them, deeply shocked. 'We must take steps to tighten up security. I shall inform Sergeant Major West and Algernon Dewberry.'

'No,' said Daniel quickly. 'We need to catch them in the act. If security here is suddenly seen to be strengthened, that may put them off tonight. All that means is the robbery is delayed. We will have security tightened, but outside through the police. We shall inform Inspector Feather of our fears and ask for a guard outside the gate.'

'Why outside?'

'Because we believe any robbery is planned for night-time.'

'But they won't be able to get away. The gates will be locked.'

'Gates can be unlocked, and the person we think is behind it is very resourceful,' said Abigail.

'Who?' asked Dillon. 'Who is the person behind it?'

'At the moment we'd rather not say, in case we're wrong,' said Abigail.

'What we'd like to do is have your permission for us to stay here the night at the Tower and keep an eye on things inside, while the police keep watch outside.'

'Of course,' said Dillon. 'You can use Eric James's flat. We haven't replaced him yet, so his flat is empty.' He smiled. 'You'll not be the only visitors staying. The Duke of Cranbrook has requested staying here tonight. He's keen to look at the dig he's sponsoring before he goes to France for a week or so. Some motoring activity, I understand. He'll be staying with Algernon Dewberry, who's kindly offered to put him up for the night as his own family are away at the moment.'

'Away where?' asked Daniel.

'Dewberry's wife and daughter are staying with his wife's mother in Ealing for a week or two. I believe she is an invalid and needs their help.'

'It's good to hear of families looking after elderly relatives,' said Daniel. Then he added, 'Your Grace, at this moment we feel it would be better if our presence overnight wasn't passed on to anyone else here. The Duke of Cranbrook, for example.'

'You suspect the Duke of being involved in whatever's going on?'

'We do.'

The viscount looked shocked. 'But he's sponsoring the dig that's going on here! He's a peer of the realm. And wealthy. Why would he do something as rash as to rob the Tower?'

'As we say, it's only a suspicion, which is why we hadn't wanted to say anything before. But now we know he's staying here overnight, the possibility that he's involved has just become stronger.'

Dillon frowned. 'In that case I'd better warn Dewberry not to mention it to the Duke, as the Duke is lodging with Dewberry overnight.'

'We also think it best not to mention anything about this to Mr Dewberry,' said Daniel.

The viscount looked at Daniel, bewildered. 'But he's my deputy!'

'True, but it would prevent him inadvertently mentioning anything about our presence here to the Duke. An accidental slip of the tongue.'

'Very well,' said Dillon. He got to his feet and walked to a cabinet fixed to the wall, which he opened and took out a bunch of keys. 'The keys to Eric James's flat,' he said. 'I'll take you there and show you where things are.'

'If we should see anyone, we'd like to let them know that we're only here for a an hour or so, checking some things out.'

'Of course.' Dillon nodded.

The only people they saw as they walked with the viscount

to the flat were Hector Purbright and Sergeant Major West, who were engaged in conversation. They waved at the men but didn't stop to talk.

The flat was neat and tidy with one bedroom, a sitting room and a small kitchen and a bathroom.

'As you'll see, Yeoman James was immaculate when it came to keeping things orderly.' He handed them the keys. 'I will not be here myself tonight. As you know I'm a non-resident. But if you need assistance once the gates are shut then you can call on Mr Dewberry, Sergeant Major West, or – if necessary – the two most senior officers in residence: General Sir Frederick Stephenson and Major Sir George Bryan. Their houses are just across the green. And there's also Waterloo barracks.'

'Thank you,' said Abigail. 'But we promise not to trouble them unless absolutely necessary.'

Abigail waited until the viscount had left them before asking Daniel, 'Why are you suspicious of Mr Dewberry?'

'Because when I talked to him before and asked him about his family, he made no mention of the fact that his wife and daughter were away.'

'Why should he?'

'No reason,' Daniel admitted. 'But I think it could be the final piece of the jigsaw. You and I agreed that there seems to be information leaking to people outside from inside the Tower. Especially to the Duke of Cranbrook. Now we find that the Duke is staying overnight as a guest of Mr Dewberry. Who better than Mr Dewberry to be in possession of vital information about what's going on here? The fact that we've been hired to look into the murder of Eric James. That we believe there could be a robbery taking place here. It's only natural that the viscount would pass that information to Dewberry.'

'And Dewberry passes it on to the Duke? But why would he do that? Money?'

Daniel shook his head. 'No. He said something to me that I thought was strange at the time. He said that he would do anything to protect his wife and keep her safe. Now I think about it, I'm sure he was trying to send me a message, but I didn't pick up on it. I should have. It reminded me of a previous case when I was at Scotland Yard. A gang of thieves took the wife and family of a bank manager hostage and threatened to kill them unless he gave them the keys to the bank and the safe.'

'And did he?'

'He did.' His voice took on a sombre tone as he added, 'Sadly, the gang killed his family anyway to prevent them from identifying them. We caught them when they returned to the bank manager's house to kill him.'

'And you believe that Cranbrook is holding Dewberry's wife and daughter hostage?'

'I do,' said Daniel. 'And I fear that he'll kill them, just as those bank thieves did. We know from what happened to Ellie Mercer and the James brothers that he's absolutely ruthless.

'I suggest you go to Scotland Yard and tell John Feather what we believe is going to happen here tonight. See if he can mount a guard on the entrance to the Tower, stopping anyone who leaves. Including the Duke. The main gate will be locked tonight, but if the Duke is holding Dewberry's family hostage to force him to be part of this, Dewberry will be able to lay his hands on the key. He is the deputy curator, after all. He can order the gates to be opened using an excuse that the Duke has to leave urgently. I'll stay here and keep an eye on things, in case there's a sudden change.'

'It might be a good idea if you stay out of sight. If Cranbrook sees you, you'll be in danger,' said Abigail. 'There's too much at stake for him to keep you alive.'

'Yes, I was thinking the same. I'll stay here until the gates are shut, then prowl around after dark.'

CHAPTER THIRTY-EIGHT

Abigail elected to take the Underground from Tower Hill to Scotland Yard, making sure that she was seen to leave. If Cranbrook had spotted her when she and Daniel arrived and called on Viscount Dillon, she hoped this would reassure Cranbrook that they were no longer there.

Fortunately, Inspector Feather and Sergeant Cribbens were both in their office.

'Daniel thinks the robbery at the Tower of London is going to happen tonight,' she told them. 'He's convinced the Duke of Cranbrook is behind it. The Duke is staying tonight at the Tower with Algernon Dewberry, the deputy curator. He's got his car with him inside the Tower. Daniel is sure that Dewberry is being forced to be an accomplice to the robbery. He believes that Cranbrook has taken Dewberry's wife and daughter and is holding them hostage in order to force Dewberry to do what he says. He says he remembers a similar situation when he was here at the Yard. In that case it was a bank manager's family held hostage.'

'Yes, I remember that one,' said Feather grimly. 'The crooks killed the family.'

'Daniel is afraid the same may happen here,' said Abigail. 'If they are the same people who killed Eric and Paul James and Ellie Mercer, they've shown how ruthless they are, with little regard for human life.'

'Does Daniel think they're going to use the car to get away?'

'It's possible. After all, it's faster than a horse-driven carriage so it'll be difficult to catch. That's why Daniel suggests stopping anybody or any vehicle that tries to leave the Tower.'

Feather nodded, then turned to Sergeant Cribbens. 'That's a job for you, Sergeant. While Mrs Wilson and I go in search of Mrs Dewberry and her daughter, you take five or six other officers and mount a guard outside the gates of the Tower. Check everyone leaving during daytime. Once the gates are closed for the night, keep a close watch on them.'

'That's when Daniel expects it to happen, once the gates are shut,' added Abigail. 'I also advise arranging firearms for yourselves. These people are dangerous and we don't know what they might be armed with. Knives, definitely, but also possibly guns.' She looked at them earnestly and asked, 'Do you think we ought to let Chief Superintendent Armstrong know about this? I know we'll look foolish if it doesn't happen, but . . .'

'The chief superintendent's away at the moment,' said Feather. 'There's a conference of police bigwigs in St Albans and he's very proud to have been included, especially as he can boast about the recent mass arrest of all these crooks in Fenchurch Street.'

'Our first task is to find out is where the Duke is hiding Mrs Dewberry and her daughter. They could be anywhere,' said Abigail. 'I wondered if it's worth putting pressure on Sam Shearing. He must know.'

'I'm sure he would do, but so far he's been like a clam, refusing to answer questions. Sergeant Cribbens and I have been questioning him about Paul James and Ellie Mercer, taking turns to keep the pressure on him, but he refuses to talk.'

'He might if he realises there's a little girl at risk of being killed.'

Feather shook his head. 'So far there's been no sign of him having a conscience, just a steadfast refusal to say anything. But it's worth a try.'

Feather and Abigail went down to the basement interview rooms and had Shearing brought to them by two police constables. Shearing recoiled when he saw Abigail.

'Don't let her touch me,' he growled. 'I know what she's capable of.'

Feather gestured to the constables to sit Shearing down at the table.

'Right, where has the Duke of Cranbrook got Mrs Dewberry and her daughter hidden?'

'I've no idea what you're talking about,' sneered Shearing. 'I've never heard of the Duke of Cranbrook, nor this Mrs Newberry.'

'Dewberry,' Feather corrected him. 'The Duke of Cranbrook hired you and your partner with the two different-coloured eyes to go to Loughton with Caleb Perkins and pick up Josiah Grundy.'

'More names I've never heard of,' snorted Shearing derisively.

'Don't come the innocent with me,' said Feather. 'We know the Duke has got them stashed somewhere. Well, let me tell you, if anything happens to Mrs Dewberry or her little girl, you'll go to the gallows.'

'Me?!' protested Shearing, outraged. 'How can I be guilty of anything while I'm locked up here?'

'As an accomplice to murder, and that's a hanging offence. We're giving you the chance to save yourself from the gallows. Where are Mrs Dewberry and her daughter?'

'I've no idea what you're talking about,' retorted Shearing firmly.

'Maybe if you leave me alone with him for a few minutes, I can get him to talk,' said Abigail angrily, rising to her feet.

'Oh no you don't!' said Shearing. 'You can kick me all you want but I can't talk about things I don't know about. And I don't know about this Mrs Newberry and her kid.'

For another five minutes, Feather and Abigail fired more questions at Shearing, but he just sat resolutely silent. In the end, Feather ordered him to be taken back to his remand cell.

'As you said before, they could be anywhere,' groaned Feather in frustration.

'No!' said Abigail suddenly. 'I think I know where they are! When I visited the Duke at his house, I saw a rag doll lying on the floor in one of the passages. I assumed it belonged to his housekeeper's daughter and she'd dropped it. But there was no other sign of children in the house, and the Duke told me his housekeeper hasn't got any children. Mrs Dewberry and her daughter must be there, in the house.'

'Right,' said Feather, grimly determined. 'Then we'll take it apart.'

When Mrs Paxton opened the door to the bell and saw Abigail, Inspector Feather and three uniformed police officers on the doorstep, her manner became instantly hostile.

'What do you want?' she demanded.

Feather produced his search warrant. 'I have a warrant to search this property,' he told her.

'What for?'

'We are looking for a Mrs Dewberry and her young daughter. We have reason to suspect they are being kept prisoners here.'

'Well, they're not,' snapped Mrs Paxton. 'Now you can buzz off.'

She began to shut the door on them but it was stopped by Feather planting his boot firmly in the doorway. She looked shocked as Feather pushed the door open and Abigail and the uniformed officers walked in.

'You can't do this!' she raged.

'This warrant says I can.'

'The Duke will have something to say when he hears about this!' she threatened.

'Is the Duke in at this moment?' asked Feather, fully aware that the Duke was at the Tower.

'No,' she said.

'Where is he?' asked Feather.

'He's out.'

'When will he be back?'

She shook her head. 'I've no idea. He doesn't report his movements to me.'

'How many people are in the house at this moment?'

'Just me and Queenie, the live-in maid.'

'And where is Queenie?'

'She's in her room, upstairs, where she ought to be at this time.'

Feather turned to the police officers. 'Right, search the house. Start on the ground floor and work your way up.'

'You're not allowed in the attic,' said Mrs Paxton in firm tones. 'That's the Duke's private quarters.'

'Right, change of plan,' said Feather. 'Start upstairs and work your way down.'

'Not the Duke's quarters. They're marked private!' shouted Mrs Paxton.

'Start with the Duke's quarters,' ordered Feather, and the officers made for the stairs.

Upstairs, in the attic, Butch Albertson had been listening to the commotion from downstairs, and thanks to Mrs Paxton's raised and angry voice he knew that the police were on their way up to search it. He didn't know how many there were but it sounded like at least three or four. There was no way he could hide himself anywhere here, in a cupboard or the smallest room, because the police would simply break down the door and find him. He could try and fight his way out while wielding his knife, but he knew he'd be overpowered.

He looked at the window in the sloping ceiling. That was his only chance of escape. He hurried to the window and slid it up. He climbed out onto the tiles, then shut the window behind him. He worked his way along the narrow ledge, clinging to the tiles and the edge of the window. Then began to haul himself up the sloping roof until he was above the window. His hope now was that the police wouldn't bother with opening the window and looking up at the roof.

The house itself was very high, four storeys, and he had a view over London that was spectacular, but also dangerous. He clung on to the tiles by the tips of his fingers, pressing the toes of his boots into cracks in the tiles.

Below, from the attic, he heard the sound of the door opening and then the sounds of the police searching the rooms.

While the three uniformed officers went upstairs, Abigail and Feather had been through all the rooms on the ground floor, including the Duke's office, but found nothing. At first Mrs Paxton had trailed after them, keeping a venomous eye on what they were up to, until Feather finally tired of her muttered threats about complaining to the member of parliament, and ordered her into the living room, where he locked her in.

'They're not here,' said Abigail, exasperated.

'Maybe not in the house, but there are the outbuildings,' said Feather.

Suddenly Abigail remembered the last time she'd been to this house.

'This was where I saw the doll,' said Abigail. 'The Duke took me along this passage towards the rear of the house and the back door that led to his garage.'

'But where is the little girl?' asked Feather, helpless. 'There are no doors or cupboards along here.'

Suddenly a panel in the wall caught Abigail's attention.

'See those lengths of beading,' she said, pointing to a section of decorative rail. 'That piece looks out of kilter with the rest.'

She walked over to it and tugged at the rail, and a secret door swung open to reveal a flight of steps going down. They walked down the steps and came to a door with a heavy padlock on it. Abigail knocked at the door and called out, 'Mrs Dewberry! Are you there? We are the police.'

At first there was silence, then a woman's voice could be heard asking plaintively, 'The police?'

'I'm Inspector Feather from Scotland Yard,' said Feather. 'We've come to recue you and your daughter.'

'Thank God!' came the woman's voice.

'We're just going to find the key to this padlock,' called Abigail.

'That woman has it!' called Mrs Dewberry.

'I'll go and get it from her,' said Feather to Abigail. 'You stay here and keep talking to them, reassure them that it's going to be all right.'

He hurried up the stairs to the ground floor and met the three officers coming down from the upper part of the house.

'There's nothing upstairs, sir,' said one. 'The only room we haven't taken apart is the one where the young maid is fast asleep.'

'We've found them,' said Feather. He pointed at the opening to the cellar. 'You two stay there and guard it.' To the third, he said, 'You, come with me.'

Feather and the constable went to the living-room door, which Feather unlocked and charged into the room and glared at Mrs Paxton.

'We've found them,' he said. He held out his hand. 'Give me the key to that padlock.'

'I haven't got it,' said Mrs Paxton.

'Give it to me or I'll smash the padlock and break the door down.'

Mrs Paxton looked shocked at the thought of such damage to the house's furnishings.

'I'll get it,' she said. 'It's upstairs.'

'Go with her,' Feather ordered the constable.

Mrs Paxton reluctantly walked up the stairs to the attic. She opened the door and walked in, then dodged to one side as the burly figure of Butch Albertson appeared from within. He punched the constable and sent him tumbling back down the stairs.

'They've found the woman and her kid,' Mrs Paxton told Albertson. 'They want the key.'

She looked down and saw Feather and one of the constables hurrying up the stairs, brought by the sound of the constable crashing down the stairs. Albertson produced his knife and began to advance down the stairs towards the police officers. Suddenly a door opened beside him and Queenie, wearing a dressing gown, came out, worried.

'What's all that noise?' she demanded. 'What's going on?' Then she saw Albertson with his knife standing close to her and gave a squeal of alarm. 'Who are you?'

Albertson grabbed the small girl by her hair and pulled

her towards him, then placed the blade of the knife against Queenie's neck.

'Back off, coppers, or I cut her throat,' he warned.

Feather gestured for the constable to retreat partway down the stairs. 'You won't get away with this,' he said. 'Give yourself up.'

Albertson shook his head. 'No. You're going to let me walk out of here because I'll have this girl with me all the way out, with this knife at her throat. If you make a move towards me, I'll kill her.'

Queenie began to cry.

'Shut up or I'll knife you here and now!' snarled Albertson.

Immediately, Queenie stopped crying and instead began to make snuffling noises.

'Back off, coppers. Down those stairs and let me and the girl go.'

Feather hesitated, then gestured for the constable to join him in retreating slowly down the stairs. Albertson gave a smirk and began to move slowly down the stairs, one hand holding Queenie's hair tightly, the other keeping the knife pressed against her neck.

Suddenly there was a crash from just behind him; the next second Albertson was tumbling forwards towards Feather and the constable, the knife falling from his fingers, while Mrs Paxton pulled Queenie to safety.

The police officers grabbed Albertson as he crashed into them, the constable smashing his truncheon over Albertson's head, and the man crumpled into a heap on the stairs.

Feather looked up at Mrs Paxton, and now saw that she

was holding a heavy metal poker, which she must have picked up from inside the attic. With her other arm, she hugged the sobbing Queenie to her.

'He'd have killed her,' she said. 'I couldn't have that.'

Leaving Mrs Paxton in the care of the officers, Feather and Abigail hurried down to the cellar and the locked door. They opened the padlock, then the door, and peered in. The room was a cell, and in the gloom they saw a woman sitting on a bench, cuddling a little girl to her.

'You're really the police?' the woman asked, anxious and seeming unable to believe it.

'We are, Mrs Dewberry,' Feather assured. 'This is Mrs Wilson. You're safe, and the villains who've been holding you prisoner are in captivity. You can come out now and we'll take you somewhere you can recover.'

'How's my husband?' asked Mrs Dewberry. 'Is he safe?'

'He is,' said Abigail. 'We'll have you reunited very soon.'

CHAPTER THIRTY-NINE

At the Tower, Daniel left the Yeoman's flat and, keeping to the shadows, made his way towards the Wakefield Tower. As he neared it, he saw a four-wheeled trolley had been left outside it, with a man standing by it. As Daniel watched, a man appeared from the Tower and put a box on the trolley, then turned to go back into the Tower.

The man keeping guard by the trolley called to him, 'Here, Dog, can you hang about here for a moment? I really need to go and pee.'

Dog shook his head. 'The Duke's told me to get back quick. "Time is of the essence," he says, and it don't do to upset him.'

The man hurried up the steps and then disappeared into the Wakefield Tower.

The man by the trolley hopped uncomfortably around, obviously in distress as he clutched his groin. Then he took a decision. He ran to the corner of the Tower, and soon Daniel heard the sound of splashing.

Daniel darted out from his hiding place and hurried towards the steps that led up to the entrance to the Wakefield Tower. Once inside the tower, he stopped and listened. Above him he heard the sound of men's voices and the shuffle of boxes being moved around. So, the Crown Jewels were the target after all. The question was: how many men were up there, and were they armed? One thing was sure, there was no way he could tackle them on his own. The only answer was for him to go in search of assistance: Sergeant Major West and some Yeoman Warders. General Sir Frederick Stephenson and Major Sir George Bryan.

He was just about to descend the stairs to creep out, when he heard footsteps above him on the stairs, then the man called Dog appeared carrying a box.

'Oi!' called Dog. 'What you doing? Alf! Alf!'

Daniel ran down the stairs to the exit and ran out of the tower, just as the man by the trolley, Alf, came to answer the call from Dog. Alf ran towards Daniel, his long arms outstretched. Daniel let Alf rush at him, then stuck out a fist, catching Alf in the face. But Alf was obviously an experienced fighter, because Daniel's blow just glanced off Alf's head and the next second Alf's arms had wrapped themselves around Daniel, pinioning his arms to his sides. At that moment, Dog appeared in a rush and leapt on Daniel. Daniel tried to break free of their grip on him, but the sudden appearance of a knife in Dog's hand, which pressed against his neck, brought his struggles to a halt.

Daniel allowed himself to be manhandled into the tower and up the stairs. On the first floor he saw two Yeomen sitting on the floor, tied up and gagged. Dog and Alf hauled Daniel up the rest of the flights of stairs until they were in the Jewel Room, where the Duke of Cranbrook was supervising the removal of the Crown Jewels from the cages and placing them in wooden boxes. Algernon Dewberry was also there, though his shamefaced expression and unhappy body posture meant he did his best to avoid eye contact with Daniel. There were two other men engaged in taking the jewels out of the cages, including one who Daniel recognised as Caleb Perkins.

'Well, well, Mr Wilson!' said the Duke, forcing an angry smile. 'How irritating.'

'What do you want us to do with him? Kill him?' asked Dog.

'No, no. I assume his wife is somewhere around and she could be problematic. If she is, we threaten to kill him. That will hold her off.' He looked past Daniel. 'Where is the enterprising Mrs Wilson? I expected her to be accompanying you.'

'She is otherwise engaged,' said Daniel.

'With what?' demanded the Duke impatiently.

'Other matters.'

'Don't play with me, Wilson. What other matters? Where is she?'

'Want me to slice a bit off him, Your Grace?' asked Dog. 'That usually makes 'em talk.'

The Duke shook his head. 'No, we need to keep him looking intact for the moment.'

'You won't get away with this,' said Daniel.

'No?' said the Duke mockingly. 'And why not, pray? You

will have seen the Beefeaters downstairs, tied up. My men have orders to kill them if I give the word. And I promise you I will give the word, and the Beefeaters' comrades have been told that. Fortunately, Mr Dewberry, as the official assistant curator, has been enormously helpful in this undertaking. He has access to the keys to these cages, which has meant we have no need of strong-arm tactics to open them.'

Shamefaced, Dewberry looked away from Daniel.

'Someone will come and see what is happening and raise the alarm,' said Daniel.

'Really? Who, do you think?' asked the Duke with a mocking smile. 'As I said, the Beefeaters have been apprised of the very real danger to their comrades. General Sir Frederick Stephenson? Major Sir George Bryan? I have armed men outside the houses of both of these gentlemen. If either attempts to leave, he will be ordered back indoors. If he refuses, he will be told his family are at risk of death. That usually clarifies the mind of these military types. They are usually prepared to face death themselves, but reluctant for their families to suffer the same fate. All the doors of the Waterloo barracks have been locked, officially as a security measure, and I have armed guards there in case anyone attempts to break out.'

'So you have access to the keys to the whole Tower,' said Daniel, and he gave a caustic look to Dewberry, who turned his head away, unable to meet Daniel's gaze.

'Trust me, Mr Wilson, this undertaking has been a long time in the planning,' continued the Duke. 'I have thought of every possible obstacle to its success and dealt with it. Including your possible arrival. The fact that you are alone indicates to me that your wife is at Scotland Yard persuading the police to suddenly put in an appearance. Your silence on the matter merely confirms it.' He turned to Dog and Alf and said, 'Tie him to the cages, hand and foot, and gag him. Make sure the ropes are tight; he's tricky and perfectly capable of getting himself loose.'

'You don't want us to kill him?' asked Dog.

'No,' said the Duke. 'His humiliation will be sweeter for me in that he remains alive to experience it. The famous Museum Detective, outwitted and left in such an embarrassing situation.'

As Dog and Alf set to work to gag Daniel and tie him to the metal cages that had recently housed the Crown Jewels, the Duke gave orders for the last of the boxes to be taken to the waiting trolley.

'You will come with us,' the Duke said to Dewberry.

'What about my wife and daughter?' demanded Dewberry. 'You said you would release them.'

'And I will, once we are safely away. But until then, I can't take the chance of you reneging on our agreement.'

'Where are they?' pleaded Dewberry.

'They are safe,' said the Duke. 'As I promised.'

Daniel groaned as he watched the Duke and his people disappear down the stairs with the last of the boxes containing the Crown Jewels. They'd failed to stop the robbery. The only hope was that Abigail had managed to get Feather to mount a guard at the main gate and catch the crooks as they left the Tower.

* * *

Abigail and Inspector Feather climbed down from the carriage beside the closed gates of the Tower of London and Sergeant Cribbens hurried towards them.

'No sign of anyone yet, sir,' he said. 'Did you find Mrs Dewberry and her daughter?'

'We did,' said Feather. 'They've had a terrible experience but they are now at a hospital being checked and comforted. We've also arrested the Duke's housekeeper, and the other thug who attacked Mrs Wilson. Both are under lock and key at Scotland Yard.'

'Brilliant!' enthused Cribbens.

'We also took a young girl who was the maid at the Duke's house and sent her to the hospital,' added Abigail. 'Not because she was injured but so she could be in a safe place. She's had a terrible shock tonight.'

'She must be the sister of the boy who told us about Perkins,' said Cribbens.

'Sir!' shouted one of the constables, and pointed at the main gates, and they saw that they were opening. As they ran towards them, there was a roar and then a car burst through the open gates and raced away, belching smoke.

'After it!' shouted Feather.

Sergeant Cribbens ran to the police van, urging the watching uniformed officers to join him. They scrambled on board and then set off after the swiftly departing car.

'They'll never catch them!' groaned Feather.

'It's a diversion!' shouted Abigail.

'What?'

'I've seen the car up close. There's no room to hide jewels, or people, inside it. Beneath that housing, it's all engine.'

'So, they're still inside?' asked Feather.

'With Daniel.' Abigail nodded, and she ran to the open gates. A Yeoman Warder stood there looking bewildered.

'Mr Dewberry came and ordered us to open the gates,' he said.

'Where's Mr Dewberry now?' asked Feather.

'He went back inside. Towards the Wakefield Tower.'

'Have you seen Mr Wilson?' asked Abigail.

The warder shook his head.

Abigail broke into a run towards the Wakefield Tower, Feather and two of the other constables at her heels, while the others remained on guard at the main gate. They ran up the stairs, expecting to be attacked at any moment, but no one got in their way. On the first floor, they found the two Beefeaters tied and gagged. Feather ordered the constables to set them free, while he and Abigail continued upwards. They found Daniel, gagged and tied to the empty cages. Abigail undid the gag while Feather set to work on the ropes that bound Daniel.

'They got away!' said Daniel. 'I heard the car, that loud engine and the firing.'

'Another of the Duke's diversion,' said Abigail. 'There's no space to put anything in it.'

'So how did they get the jewels away?' asked Daniel. 'There's no other exit.'

'Yes there is! The wharf!' said Abigail. Daniel and Feather looked at her quizzically, and she explained. 'All the time I've been coming here to check on the dig, I've noticed that on the other side of the wall by Traitor's Gate there's a wharf on the Thames. There's an entrance from the wharf into the grounds of the Tower. It's known as Henry III's Watergate, although today there's no water there, just a door. The Duke of Wellington had the moat drained because the smell from the water in it was so bad.'

'Of course, the wharf!' exclaimed Feather. 'I bet they had a boat moored there ready.'

He saw that Daniel was already running for the stairs, Abigail following. They pounded down the stairs and out into the open, then Abigail led the way to the door in the outer wall that opened onto the wharf. The gate was unlocked. She, Daniel and Feather ran through and found a man in ragged clothes lying on the ground.

'Not another lot!' he grumbled as he got to his feet.

'Has a boat left here recently?' demanded Feather.

'Yeah, two of them. Steam launches, not three minutes ago,' said the man. 'One went upriver, the other down. This is where I sleep and normally it's as quiet as anything, dead peaceful, but tonight . . .'

Daniel ran to the wall where flares were stored for emergency use. He grabbed one and set it off, the plume of fire and orange smoke rising high into the air.

'What are you doing?' demanded the man, shocked. 'You'll have the police on us!'

'We are the police,' snapped Feather.

The man looked stunned. 'What? Even her?' he asked, pointing at Abigail.

A police launch must have been moored at nearby Tower Bridge because it wasn't many minutes before they became aware of the sound of a steam launch approaching, ploughing through the waters of the Thames; then the boat itself appeared, its oil lamps glowing eerily in the night. It pulled into the wharf and one of the officers leapt out onto the wharf with a length of rope, which he looped round a bollard. The commander began to demand, 'Who let off that flare . . .' then he stopped and said in relieved tones, 'Mr Wilson, sir! And Inspector Feather!'

'Donald Prentice!' shouted back Daniel. 'Thank God it's you. It saves a lot of explanations. There's been a robbery at the Tower. The criminals have fled using a launch.'

'What have they taken?'

'The Crown Jewels.'

'But we don't know which direction they've gone in,' said Feather. 'The criminals had two boats moored here. One's gone upriver, one downriver.'

'It's another of his diversion tactics,' said Daniel grimly.

'But which one do we go after? There are hiding places off the river in either direction.'

Daniel thought quickly, then said, 'East, towards the Estuary and the open sea. He's got more chance of getting a better price for the jewels on the continent. Amsterdam is the home of the international jewellery market.'

'Or he may have a buyer already here in this country,' pointed out Feather.

'No, I think Daniel's right,' said Abigail. 'East towards the sea.'

'In that case, climb aboard!' shouted Prentice, and Daniel, Feather and Abigail scrambled from the wharf into the launch.

As soon as they were on board, the rope was unwrapped from the bollard and brought back onto the boat.

'Full steam ahead!' shouted Prentice.

'Will you have the speed to catch them?' asked Feather.

'It depends on the size of their engine and the type of launch,' replied Prentice. 'What sort is it? Paddlewheels or propellers?'

'We don't know,' said Feather. 'It was gone before we got to the wharf.'

'Pile on the coal!' shouted Prentice.

As the stoker shovelled coal into the firebox, Prentice asked, 'What happened? Who did it? And how?'

While Feather and Abigail kept watch with the lookout at the bow, Daniel told Prentice what had happened: the robbery carried out while the crooks were in control of the Tower.

'You sure they're making for the sea?' asked Prentice. 'There are plenty of inlets and waterways running from the Thames, especially once you get past Tower Bridge. Between here and Silvertown there are all manner of docks and canals they could hide in.'

'I'm counting on the fact that they'll want to get away to the open sea while it's still dark. If they hide somewhere and wait till daylight, there'll be more chance of a patrol seeing them.'

'You could be wrong,' said Prentice doubtfully.

'I could,' admitted Daniel. 'But I'm trying to get inside the mind of the man who's behind it.'

'Who is that?'

'The Duke of Cranbrook.'

'The motoring duke?' asked Prentice, shocked.

'You know him?'

'I know of him. He's often featured in car magazines. I get them because they have articles about engines and I like to keep up to date with what's going on. This launch is the most up to date in the Thames fleet and I want to keep it that way.'

'Lights ahead!' called the lookout.

Daniel and Prentice joined the others at the bow. Yes, the glow of oil lamps could be seen in the distance.

'We're gaining on them, sir!' called the lookout.

'They'll be armed,' warned Daniel. 'Do you have weapons on board?'

'We do,' said Prentice grimly. 'With some of the people we encounter, smugglers and the like, we make sure we have the means to defend ourselves.' He shouted to one of the crew: 'Break out the rifles, Tunbridge. They'll be best from this distance.'

As the police launch drew nearer to the launch ahead, they could see on the deck the figures of the Duke, along with Algernon Dewberry, and the Duke's henchmen.

'Do you have a loudhailer?' Abigail asked Prentice.

In answer, Prentice lifted a horn-shaped device and handed it to her. 'Although I'm not sure if, even with this, your voice will carry to them, with their engine thumping away.'

Abigail took the loudhailer and moved to the very front of the launch.

'Mr Dewberry!' she shouted. 'Your wife and daughter are safe!' She then repeated the sentence, emphasising each word. As the police launch drew ever nearer to the other vessel, she kept up her shouting, and the others saw Dewberry turn towards them.

'He's heard you!' said Feather.

As they watched, Dewberry ran to the stern of the launch and the man at the tiller, where he grabbed hold of the handle of the tiller and tried to turn the boat so that it headed in the direction of the police launch. The Duke rushed at Dewberry, grabbed hold of him and pulled him away from the tiller, and the two men struggled, lurching from side to side across the deck. The Duke pushed Dewberry against the metal rail that ran along the side of the boat and began to punch the other man, forcing him over the rail.

'He's going to push him over the side!' shouted Feather in alarm.

'Get the lifebelts ready!' called Prentice.

'If he goes in, we won't be able to see him in the dark,' said Daniel.

'Get closer!' shouted Prentice urgently at his tillerman. 'More coal!'

As the police tillerman pushed against the handle, the launch turned and was now heading directly for the other boat, aimed at its midships.

'Aim for the bow!' shouted Prentice, and the tillerman adjusted the tiller so that it would glide into the other boat.

There was the sound of a shot and a flash from the deck of the other boat, then a clang as a bullet struck the police launch's smokestack.

Immediately, Prentice picked up the rifle, levelled it and fired. One of the men on the other boat collapsed, and the others scattered as best they could, searching for cover.

Meanwhile, Dewberry and the Duke were engaged in a desperate struggle, which it looked as if Dewberry was losing; he was now almost dangling over the rail as the Duke grabbed his legs and went to lift them to hurl Dewberry overboard. But as the Duke bent low, Dewberry reacted, grabbing the Duke and raising him up, then punching him in the face, knocking him almost over the rail. For a second, the Duke scrambled to recover his balance, but another hard blow from Dewberry sent him tumbling backwards, and then he disappeared over the rail and into the murky waters of the Thames.

CHAPTER FORTY

Inspector Feather sat in the interview room where he'd spent so much time lately. This time, the person facing him from the other side of the table was Caleb Perkins. They'd taken Caleb Perkins from the launch, along with a couple of heavies, Dennis Watts, known as Dog, and Alfred Parsons, who were in the boat with the jewels. Sam Shearing and Butch Albertson were already in custody, as were Mrs Paxton and Edmund Spencer, the Duke's mechanic, who'd been caught driving the Duke's car, as also were the owner and skipper of the launch, along with his two crewmen. The rest of the gang had disappeared in the other boat that had gone westward from Tower Wharf. That boat had been found in the early hours of the morning in a side-river off the Thames.

'We're not just talking the theft of the Crown Jewels, Mr Perkins,' said Feather. 'We're talking murder. Or, more specifically, *murders*. Paul James, Eric James, Ellie Mercer.'

'Nothing to do with me,' said Perkins sullenly.

'Oh, I think we can get a jury to find you guilty. All of those killings were related to the robbery at the Tower, the Crown Jewels, which you masterminded.'

'Me?!' exploded Perkins. 'I was just an unfortunate lackey forced into it by my master.'

'The Duke of Cranbrook?'

'That's him.'

'Who, it seems, died in the Thames. At least we assume so. We've dragged that part of the river but there's no sign of the body. So, with him gone our attention turns to his second-in-command: you. Because with him gone, that makes you the responsible one.'

'I was just following orders!'

'You threatened Josiah Grundy.'

'I never threatened him.'

'That's not what Sam Shearing and Butch Albertson say.'

'They were the ones who threatened him, not me.'

'They also say you were the one who killed Paul James. They admit they were there when it was done and saw you do it. And we've got other witnesses who put you and them at the place he was killed, when he was killed.'

'They're liars! Yes, we were there, but they were the ones who killed him.'

'On your orders'

'No! I'd been ordered to go and see Paul James and find out what he was up to.'

'He was part of your gang?'

'It wasn't *my* gang; it was the Duke's gang. He'd put it together. Some people he knew; some people he'd heard about through other people. Anyway, the Duke had heard that Paul had been seeing his brother, Eric, who was a Beefeater at the Tower, and going to Salvation Army meetings with him. The Duke was worried that Paul was getting religion and might squeal on us before we pulled the job, so he sent me and Sam and Butch to have a word with Paul, find out where he stood, and if he'd told his brother about what was planned. The trouble was Butch. He's too handy with that knife of his, and he started waving it at Paul to scare him. Paul got scared all right and he tried to take the knife off Butch, and that's when Butch stabbed him.'

'Why did he cut his tongue out?'

'That was Sam's idea. He thought it would send a message to anyone else who might be thinking of talking.'

'But Paul hadn't been about to talk about it to the police. I know that because Ellie Mercer told me.'

'Yeah, but because Paul hadn't said anything about what him and his brother had been talking about with the Salvation Army meetings – well, to be honest he didn't have much chance because Butch produced his knife almost as soon as we ran into Paul – we didn't know if Paul had talked to his brother about the robbery. So we were ordered to go and talk to Eric James at the Tower. Only this time I didn't go; I left it to Sam and Butch. Having seen Butch mess it up with Paul, I didn't want to be around if it happened again, and inside the Tower with all those Beefeaters about.'

'But they went in at night,' pointed out Feather.

'Yeah, well, I thought that was safest. I told them to arrange to meet Eric in the White Tower after dark. They were to go in during the day and find somewhere to hide, talk to Eric James that night, and then come out when the gates opened the following morning. But it went wrong.'

'Butch again?'

Perkins nodded. 'Sam told me about it. They met Eric in the White Tower by the Line of Kings, as arranged. He'd come because the message to him said someone had something to tell him about his brother's murder, but no one else had to be involved. No police, nothing.

'Eric asked them about his brother's murder, who did it, and why. They said they didn't know. Instead they wanted to know what Paul had told him about what he was up to. Eric said there was nothing, just that Paul had decided to get off the drink and had come to Eric for help.

'Well, Sam and Butch didn't believe him. They tried some force on him to get him to talk, but that didn't cut any ice with an old soldier like Eric. He took one of the swords and brandished it at them, said he was going to call the guard and have them arrested. That led to a struggle and Sam said that it was Butch who took the sword off him and ran him through.

'They then stuffed his body in a suit of armour. They didn't want to risk him being found before the gates opened and a hue and cry being raised. Then they went back to their hiding place and walked out with other visitors during the day.'

'And Ellie Mercer?'

'The Duke was told by one of his informants that she'd met you at that church, and she'd arranged to tell you what was going on. So Sam and Butch were told to deal with her.'

'They killed her and cut her tongue out?'

'Yeah. I wasn't there, but Sam told me about it afterwards. Like I said, I didn't kill anyone.'

* * *

Daniel and Abigail sat in the study with the Prince of Wales's secretary, Michael Shanks, who listened attentively as they related the events of the previous night.

'The men who murdered Eric James, the Beefeater at the Tower of London, have been apprehended. It was nothing to do with anti-royalist insurrection in any way; it was commonplace theft,' Daniel told him.

'When you say commonplace . . . ?' asked Shanks.

'Possibly "commonplace" is the wrong word,' said Abigail carefully. 'The thieves were after the Crown Jewels.'

'And I understand they got away with them.'

'They did,' said Daniel. 'But fortunately we were able to recover them.'

'And without the press discovering the fact,' added Abigail.

'Will the miscreants, the murderers, stand public trial?' asked Shanks.

'You'll need to ask the commissioner of police that,' said Daniel. 'At the moment, the men who committed the murders and the rest of the gang are all on remand. I expect the commissioner is waiting to be contacted by you as the Prince's representative. The Crown Jewels, after all, are royal possessions.'

'Yes.' Shanks nodded. 'There is another matter. I understand that two skeletons have been discovered during the archaeological dig at the Tower, and that there is speculation that these may be the skeletons of the two boys known as the Princes in the Tower.'

'There is that speculation.' Abigail nodded. 'But so far it is restricted to those involved in the work there.'

'Led by Professor Stanford Clement, I understand.'

'That is correct.'

Shanks paused, then he said, 'We shall be advising Professor Clement that we would prefer if the speculation over these two newly discovered skeletons was ended. After all, it could create terrible embarrassment over the two that were buried in Westminster Abbey all those years ago. It could undermine the history, both of the royal family and the abbey, if this rumour spread. And history is the root of the stability of the family, and of this country. I hope you understand?'

'We do, sir,' said Abigail. 'You can reassure the Prince that nothing of this incident will be heard from us. But might we suggest, sir, that it might help if His Highness were to meet with the two students who made the discovery and explain the importance of secrecy. It would have far more impact with them than if I or Professor Clement said that to them.'

Michael Shanks looked at them as he thought this suggestion over, then he nodded. 'That makes sense to me. I'm sure His Highness will make time in his diary.'

'Thank you,' said Abigail. 'There is one other matter we'd like to mention. One of the main reasons this case was solved and the attempted robbery at the Tower of London was prevented, along with the solving of other murders, was thanks to the work of an artist called Agnes de Souza. She created portraits of the main culprits from descriptions, and her images were so life-like it led to these villains being captured. I hope you won't think we're being too forward in suggesting to you that the next time the Prince is considering having his portrait painted, he look at the work of Miss de Souza. Her work is really superb; she seems to capture the soul of the sitter, not merely the physical appearance.'

Shanks sat, weighing up this suggestion, then nodded. 'I will be happy to suggest this to His Highness,' he said.

As Daniel and Abigail left the house, Daniel congratulated Abigail on her suggestion about Agnes. 'That was a brilliant idea,' he said. 'Let's hope that the Prince seriously considers it. Agnes certainly deserves the opportunity.'

'I get the impression that Mr Shanks is a fair and genuine person,' said Abigail. 'And that the Prince listens to his opinions. So we can but hope.' She smiled. 'In fact, I think we ought to take her to Scotland Yard so she can be in at the end of this case. After all, without her we wouldn't have succeeded.'

'That is a very good idea,' said Daniel.

As they made their way to Agnes's flat, Daniel said, 'The two girls are going to be dreadfully disappointed.'

'True, but their disappointment is going to be very much tempered by actually meeting with the Prince of Wales and hearing the reasons for the secrecy from himself.'

'Would you have been put off from talking about such a discovery if this had happened to you at their age?' asked Daniel.

'No,' said Abigail. 'But then I suppose I was always a bit of a rebel.'

Daniel and Abigail collected Agnes from her flat and told her they were taking her to Scotland Yard.

'Thanks to your work, everything has been solved,' Abigail told her. 'The murderers have been caught. A major robbery at the Tower of London has been averted. And the lives of a little girl and her mother have been saved.'

'Just because of my pictures?' said Agnes, stunned.

'And there may be more to come,' added Abigail. 'More work.'

'Pictures of professional criminals?'

Daniel laughed. 'Better than that,' he said.

'What?' asked Agnes.

'For the moment, we think it best to keep it under wraps until it actually happens,' said Abigail.

'No!' wailed Agnes. 'You can't start to tell me, then stop.'

Abigail and Daniel exchanged look, then Daniel nodded.

'We've proposed to the Prince of Wales's private secretary that the next time he has a portrait painted, he consider you,' said Abigail.

'Me?!' squealed Agnes. 'The Prince?!'

'It's only a suggestion,' cautioned Abigail.

'It doesn't matter,' said Agnes. 'The fact that I'm going to be considered is a dream.'

'Let's hope it's a dream that comes true,' said Abigail.

They made their way to Scotland Yard, where they found a very tired-looking Inspector Feather slumped over his desk. He perked up as he saw Daniel, Abigail and Agnes.

'Sergeant Cribbens and I have both been up most of the night interrogating Perkins, Shearing and Albertson,' he explained.

'Any confessions from any of them?'

'None from Shearing or Albertson, but Perkins has given evidence against them, so I think we have them for the three murders.' Then he gave a rueful look as he added, 'Depending on what interference we get from above. I've already been warned that as this involves royal property, it may never come to trial.'

'Still, at least all the murders have been solved, and the Crown

Jewels are safe,' said Daniel. 'So it can be counted a success.'

Feather stood up and held out his hand to Agnes. 'And it's all thanks to you, Miss de Souza. At least, a great part of it is.'

Agnes took his hand and shook it. 'Thank you, Inspector. And if you ever need my assistance again, don't hesitate to get in touch.'

Just then the door of the office opened and Sergeant Cribbens came in. Unlike the exhausted Inspector Feather, the sergeant looked exhilarated. With a broad smile on his face, he seemed unable to contain his excitement.

'What's happened, Sergeant?' asked Feather.

'This, sir,' said Cribbens, producing a large buff envelope, which he handed to Feather. 'The chief superintendent called me into his office and handed it to me. It's from the police commissioner.'

Intrigued, Feather opened the envelope and took out a sheet of elaborately designed paper bearing the crest of the police commissioner.

'There, sir! It's got my name on it. It's a commendation, in my name!'

'Congratulations, Sergeant,' said Abigail, and she held out her hand to shake the sergeant's. 'It's long overdue.'

'Absolutely,' said Daniel, and he also shook Cribbens's hand. 'Well done. Congratulations.'

Cribbens pushed the sheet of paper carefully back into the envelope. 'Can I have your permission to go home? I have to show this to my wife. She'd never believe it if she didn't see it with her own eyes.'

'Off you go, Sergeant,' said Feather. 'You deserved it.'

They waited until the happy sergeant had left, then Feather said, 'I must admit I owe the chief superintendent an apology. He said he'd arrange a commendation for Jeremiah, but I never thought he would. Usually, if there are any credits or commendations to be had, he prefers it if he gets them himself. But today . . .' He smiled. 'Miracles will never cease.'

ACKNOWLEDGEMENTS

I know I have used this section previously in my Museum Mysteries series to laud the team at Allison & Busby, but I hope you, dear reader, will permit me to repeat that again here in this, the ninth book in the series. As I've said before, writing a book is as much a team effort for me as it was during my forty years as a scriptwriter. In my scriptwriting days there would be input on my work from producers, directors, executive producers, actors, set and costume designers. Mostly these comments were supportive of what I'd written and created, but sometimes – especially when it was an international co-production – suggestions were made by the team that were the exact opposite of what I'd intended for the characters and story. Often the changes that were proposed were ego-driven on the part of someone at a high level in the production

My experience with Allison & Busby has been blissfully devoid of that. I have never worked with a less ego-driven team than at Allison and Busby, every suggestion or comment they make on my work has been them gently pointing out errors in my research, for example, or inconsistencies in my plotting. They are the guardians of quality in the books, and for that I am eternally grateful. They care for the work, and they have shown they care for me as a writer. So I use this section to offer my ever-grateful thanks to the team: Susie, my brilliant publishing director; Lesley, Fiona and Becca, my superb editors; Daniel, Libby and Christina, and everyone else at the company; and Jane, my agent who keeps me on the literary straight and narrow. Thank you all.

JIM ELDRIDGE was born in central London towards the end of World War II, and survived attacks by V2 rockets on the Kings Cross area where he lived. In 1971 he sold his first sitcom to the BBC and had his first book commissioned. Since then he has had more than one hundred books published, with sales of over three million copies. He lives in Kent with his wife.

jimeldridge.com

MURDER AT THE LOUVRE

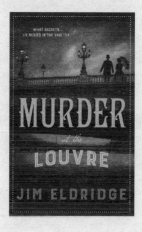

Paris, 1899. Abigail Wilson has received an invitation from Professor Alphonse Flamand, a prominent French Professor of Archaeology, to join him on a dig in Egypt. Overjoyed to be presented with such an opportunity, Abigail and her husband, Daniel, travel to Paris to meet the Professor at his office in the Louvre to discuss plans.

However, when Abigail goes to the appointment, she finds Flamand dead with a knife in his chest. In a whirl of confusion and despite her pleas of innocence, Abigail is arrested.

Determined to prove that she has been framed for Flamand's brutal murder, Daniel and Abigail, the Museum Detectives, will delve far into the shadowy corners of the City of Light for the truth.